Alford Khan

Demerara Adventures

novum pro

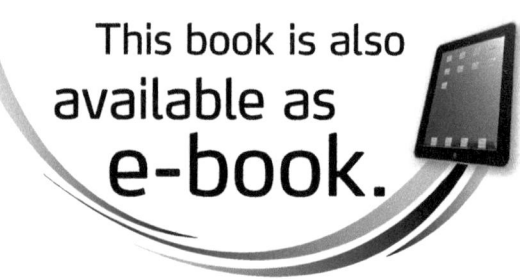

www.novum-publishing.co.uk

All rights of distribution, including via film, radio, and television, photomechanical reproduction, audio storage media, electronic data storage media, and the reprinting of portions of text, are reserved

Printed in the European Union on environmentally friendly, chlorine- and acid-free paper.

© 2016 novum publishing

ISBN 978-3-99048-562-0
Editing: Nicola Ratcliff, BA
Cover photo:
Kps1664, Bblood | Dreamstime.com
Cover design, layout & typesetting: novum publishing

www.novum-publishing.co.uk

This story is dedicated to my wife
Marja-Leena

ACKNOWLEGEMENTS

I wish to thank Ian Yardley for storing and editing this manuscript And to Reg Sandhu for his invaluable help to control my computer from a nervous breakdown and deleting my story at will To my friend Gerry Barran, a retired District Commissioner for his information of the duties of a Commissioner

CHAPTER 1
THE VISIT

I became interested in the life of a rare young British Guianese. His name is Peter D'Abrue. At twenty eight years of age he fought against all the odds to gain a degree in dentistry and in so doing, became one of the wealthiest men in the land. What was most extraordinary, he was also The Commissioner of the Hinterlands, an area of some fifty five thousand square miles of pristine forests. His job was the second most important in the land. Only the Governor held the most important post.

My name is Andrew Bowry; I was born in England of English parents. My father was a man of the cloth as they would describe him and he was sent to New Amsterdam to head the Mission Chapel Church in the aptly named, Chapel Street. I, being only six years old, was sent to school in the city of Georgetown. Later, I went to Queen's College, the best school in the colony. Had I stayed in New Amsterdam I would have been sent to the Berbice High School, which was the best in Berbice. There, I would have met Peter and his friends and undoubtedly we would have been friends.

An Englishman was considered a leper if he was seen socialising too closely with the other races. My father on the other hand, being a priest, was allowed this leeway and that also gave me the opportunity to delve into the other races' background. It was not enough for me to get a clear picture of their lives.

I was very excited when Peter agreed for me to come to Supenaam and interview him and the three others that made up the famous four. I was a journalist with the Chronicle and I had never done a biography of anyone.

Despite being a rainforest, it is also the home of many tribes who lived off the land, and at the same time protecting it from loggers, gold diggers and diamond seekers.

Peter's job was to see that the villagers and their villages were protected from these intruders. He had the authority to make his own laws and to punish anyone found violating them.

After he accepted my proposal to interview him, he also offered to fly me out in one of his planes. I declined the offer and set about making the journey exactly as he did, as a sixteen year old. I took a taxi to Sproston's wharf to board the river boat R.H. Carr to Mackenzie and then by locomotive to Ituni, there I went on board a truck that took me to the Demerara River and finally, by boat to Supenaam. It was the most arduous journey I have ever undertaken.

On arrival I was too tired to move so I watched the porters unloading their cargo. The owner of the boat was looking with great interest at the way they were handling the cargo. I could see he was annoyed, that the porters were treating his boat like a piece of junk. To be quite honest, his boat was no more than the bark of a giant greenheart tree, sturdily reinforced with tar and fibres from the numerous palm trees growing along the banks of the Demerara. His anger grew uncontrollable as he watched them drop an electrical generator that nearly went through the bottom of the boat.

He was a diminutive half Scot, half Amerindian with a Scottish name as long as the Demerara. Everyone that came to learn of his name ended up in hysterics. He was immune to their laughter, but he was proud to carry the name of his Scottish father. Duncan McGregor Stewart.

When the unloading was done, I followed him to the Commissioner's office where he had to report and have the papers signed for payment. As the Commissioner was signing the document, Duncan kept his eyes on the bottle of malt whisky on the desk. As he was handed his papers he asked. "Is that very good whisky?"

"The finest" The Commissioner's assistant replied.

"I want to taste it, if only to prove I still retain my sense of taste for the stuff" He said.

"You cannot have it you are a native. We are not allowed to give alcohol to the natives." The clerk pointed out.

"Would you be allowed to give a half native half a drink? I am also half Scottish, So how about it?" He argued.

"I would not be able to answer that question. It's up to the Commissioner." The clerk turned to the Commissioner and asked if it was allowed.

"Let him have the dammed drink and get him out of here before I lose my concentration" The Commissioner relented.

Then the Commissioner turned and looked at me and politely asked "Are you the journalist Andrew Bowry?"

"I am your Excellency." I replied.

"None of that Andrew; just call me Peter. We reserve that Excellency bit for the Governor," Peter informed him informally, "and I want it to stay that way". He then introduced me to Ben and told him that I would be sharing the smaller house. "Why don't you let Ben take you to your quarters where you can freshen up and relax until I finish here."

It is five years to the day since Peter D'Abrue took up his role as Commissioner of the Hinterlands. He was able to retain the respect and friendship of indigenous inhabitants, especially at Supenaam, his headquarters. The natives looked on him as a god and idolised him in the same manner as his predecessor.

Duncan went under a silk cotton tree to enjoy his drink and soon a number of Amerindian men came to watch him in the hope that he would offer them a sip. When they realized that a drop was not forthcoming, they sent their ladies to plead with him. Duncan was not having any of it. He stood up and protested and eventually declared, "My blood pressure always rises when ladies bother me. If it is not sexual, then it is always something aggravating. That is why they are called WOMEN. ...Woe to men. Now get out of here or I will call the Commissioner."

"You think you are clever Duncan McGregor Stewart because your drunken father is a Scotsman. You can keep your drink and go to hell." They told him before departing.

Duncan was happy when they left. He knew he could not offer them a drink or he would have been in serious trouble with the Commissioner.

Diego and his family arrived just as Duncan was about to leave. They exchanged a few words of welcome and on leaving, he gave Diego the rest of the whisky. Diego took a swig and handed the bottle back to him. Diego is also of a mixed race, half Spanish and half Amerindian. His wife, Bell came over and joined them in their conversation.

"What is so amusing?" She asked.

"Nothing very important." Diego replied.

"Stop messing around Diego. It must be of some importance for both of you to be laughing so heartily." She insisted.

"The truth is we were merely pointing out the fact that, with the exception of Matthew Longhorn and the Commissioner, we are all of mixed race. Duncan is half Scot, You are half English half Chinese, Ben is English and Black, and I am half Spanish, we can have our own club of mixed races. Is that not funny enough to cause laughter?" Diego explained.

"I don't think we should be laughing at who we are. You should be ashamed even to mention it" Bell told him, feeling a bit angry.

The Commissioner, being a dear friend of this band of mixed races soon joined them. Ben was not far away weaving his massive body from left to right, as he made his way through the bushes to join us. Eventually we all ambled down the river back to enjoy the cool breeze there. Ben had constructed some cosy seats for this very purpose. He told Peter that I looked sleepy and they thought it best to let me rest.

As they sat enjoying the coolness, the Commissioner told them there were some problems with the American pilot and the villagers, which needed his urgent attention. This was what had made him irritable. Now that Diego was there, perhaps he would be able to get some help in resolving the crisis.

The Commissioner was eager to hear what Diego had to offer.

"I think you should handle this matter personally Peter." Matthew intervened.

"Normally I would. This is a tricky situation and I think the American is trying to bully the chief. Personally, I think the chief is right. We cannot be relocating these reptiles forever. They have a right, like everyone else, to survive in whatever conditions nature throws at them. Let us not be the ones to give them a hard time. I think Diego is my best envoy to deal with this situation." Peter defended his decision.

"Since you put it that way, I must agree." Matthew conceded.

The problem was, that Sebastian, the American pilot, was landing his amphibious aircraft too near the colony of the caimans that were relocated there some five years ago and further relocation would have an adverse effect on the reptiles. The villagers insisted they remain where they were and that Sebastian land his craft at least two kilometers away. Sebastian wasn't going to be bullied where to land his plane. This impasse provoked a lot of hostility between the two parties.

Diego was only too pleased to help his friend. He suggested that Sebastian land his craft, as designated by the villagers and use one of the tractors or paddle boat to transport him to base. It took a lot of persuasion but eventually, Sebastian agreed. Diego had succeeded in averting a crisis.

They were joined by their old friend the vicar, to discuss the future of Margaret a confidant of Christine, the Commissioner's wife. She was restless and approaching her twenty first birthday, the opportunity of finding a husband in this wilderness was nonexistent. She wanted to return to the city to enjoy herself and find a suitable partner. It was not too much to ask, by any standard. The problem needed careful consideration. Margaret felt obliged to be loyal to the family that saved her father from ruin and disgrace, and also gave her a golden opportunity to rebuild her life. It remains to be seen what decision would emerge.

It had been a long time since aircrafts ended the arduous journey from Mackenzie to Supenaam; A journey that could take days in treacherous terrain. Now the planes have made life so much easier.

The tradition of the supply boat bringing vital supplies for the villagers still continued. It was not surprising to find the villagers swarming around the boat to collect their supplies.

Diego, as usual, helped them take it to the village in his tractor. In the centre of the village square, Sebastian was arguing with the chief and threatened him with his pistol.

Diego was so irritated by this that he jumped out of the tractor and stood between the two warring parties.

The tractor was still moving with no one at the controls it went crashing into Sebastian's newly built house. The villagers started laughing hysterically, which became infectious and even the chief forgot his worries temporarily and joined in the hysterics. It was inevitable that the contagion got to Sebastian. It ended what could have been an ugly affair.

Later that evening, they all gathered at Peter's residence to formally welcome me. I was thoroughly refreshed and ready for anything. The welcoming went in to the best part of the night, before it ended. At every introduction a drink was poured and when that ran out, they cheered Matthew, then Peter's wife Christine and their daughter Elizabeth. Then came the time when they started wishing happy birthdays months ahead. When all avenues were exhausted, they decided to call a halt to the celebrations and we all went completely exhausted, to bed.

The next morning I woke up with a vice around my head. It took the best part of the day to shake it off, eventually I went about my task talking to the natives and gathering as much information about Peter as I could. In my interviews, I found I was also writing a biography of Matthew Longhorn. Everyone loved him and his niece Christine. She apparently went back to the city to look after her daughter who had started her second year at the privately run Jewish school. Margaret, her confidant stayed behind to look after Peter and Matthew. She found her task boring, especially since she was not allowed to participate in any of the drinking sessions. It would not look right, an unmarried catholic maiden tossing back drinks in the company of virile men, in the heart of the wilderness. She was longing for the arms of someone who would love and care for her. At twenty one, she was desperate for the company of a young unmarried man. Here in the wilderness that was a forlorn hope. Despite her frustration she plodded on, grateful that Peter had rescued her from disgrace and ruin and had given her the chance to avert a life of a prostitute, if all else had failed. Such was her gratitude that she resolved to put her frustration aside and serve the family well.

Peter was aware of her dilemma and was working on a plan to make her happy. All this depended on Christine.

At dinner I began to question Matthew of the circumstances that brought great wealth to the fabulous four, as they were now known, the four being, Matthew, Peter, Ben and Diego. Matthew explained to me the reason why Peter got half of the diamonds and gold that they found. He told me that, because he became a believer in the Hindu philosophy, the Vedanta and mysticism, it had brought him the inner happiness he sought after years of fighting and killing. The happiness and peace of mind he found in his meditation forced him to give Peter all his share of the wealth. Matthew further explained that the main reason for doing so was because of Peter's obedience to his father and enduring the frustration and hardship of jungle life, without any complaint.

"You said you found complete happiness in your new way of life. Yet I see you drinking and having as much fun as anyone here. I also notice you have a very beautiful and young female companion."

"She is not my companion but my bonded wife." Matthew enlightened him.

"I don't understand. What is a bonded wife?" I asked.

"It is a system to give respectability to a woman who has formed a relationship with a man." Matthew told him.

I was busy with my pencil jotting down every detail. Then I asked Peter "There is one intriguing feature I do not fully understand. Margaret, you said, is grateful to you for saving her family from ruin. How did that come about?"

"I'd rather leave that bit out. This story is about me and not anyone else. I am not prepared to talk about any of my close friends because we are not just friends, more like brothers. There is one thing I can talk about and that is Margaret's dire position. In her earlier life, she was nearly forced to take a job as a hostess, in a night club. The scoundrel that owns the club expects the girls to be more than just hostesses. I am sure you understand my meaning. She remains untouched of any suspicion of immorality. That I can swear by."

Peter was very serious in his comments and I sensed it. I was now put on a new alert, stick to my task and keep well away from Peter and his close friends. I so much wanted to be a part of this group, I told myself it was early days and little by little I would work my way in and win their confidences. It was difficult to imagine four men and two women of different races, harmonised in such a strong bond of friendship.

This was the opening I was looking for. I always wanted to understand the deep feeling of racial division and what was the real cause of it. I was told that the British maintain their aloofness in order to show who is master of the colony. The Portuguese had their own circle, so did the East Indians and the Blacks. The people who fared worst were the Blacks. I could not see why. They were very sociable and would have embraced any social intercourse with any of the other races. The East Indians appears to guard against any pollution of their religion and especially their females. I also think, it was a bit of inferiority complex. Whatever the reason, they were determined to protect what they held dearly.

We, on the other hand, try desperately to disguise our own prejudices; the most unrealistic being classifying the Portuguese as non-white.

It was time for an evening sip on the river bank. The cool breeze was heaven on this very hot day. I could see the parrots flying past the wind charger with its dummy harpy eagle. The birds, apparently apprehensive of its presence showed their anger by screeching at it as they fly by. Even the monkeys showed their disgust, howling abuse at it without any results. I would have thought they would get used to its presence, after so many years. It was comical to a certain point, to a human but not to the creatures, it was a threat.

Sugar Bush, Matthew's bonded wife and Ben arrived with all the necessaries for a light drink. I couldn't help noticing Sugar

Bush eyeing me suspiciously. I'm not sure she accepts me. Getting along with this lot was proving more difficult than I expected, but I was determined to make it my crusade to win them over. The big question was how. Then I thought of the magic formula, maybe their interest in keeping the rain forest in its pristine state was the answer. I will show them that I too care about the future of the forest and the people that live in it. As a journalist and a biographer, I can do a lot, to make the outside world understand what is going on in this world of mystery and show them that the inhabitants are not the savages they think they are, but cultural people, who are happy to live off the land and face the hazards, as a way of life. I must try and learn their language, by doing so, I can win their confidence and trust, and who knows, I might winkle out a few of their innermost secrets. This part of my programme will take time, lots of time, and that I have in abundance.

As we sipped our malt slowly, Ben asked me if I could write a book about him. That gave me a new idea. Why not write a biography of the Fabulous Four.

I asked the others and they all agreed. Even Sugar Bush seemed less suspicious of me and pointing at herself she asked. "Me too?"

I nodded and she gave the most beautiful smile I have seen since coming up here. Matthew was a bit apprehensive at first, but with a little persuasion from his bonded wife, he agreed.

I began thinking. Should I make it one huge biography or should I do it individually. I must think carefully on this. I also needed Peter's permission, as he is the one whose biography I came up to do.

Peter hesitated for a minute and my heart sank briefly. Then he said. "What was the motto of the musketeers? All for one, and one for all. Andrew, it is a great idea, you have my permission to do it."

So finally, my task was to cut out and have a definite program to work on. I was beginning to enjoy the atmosphere and the lovely malt on hand.'

Half way through our sundowner, Peter asked how I proposed to let the outside world understand the inhabitants of this wonderful wilderness.

I told him that I would create a weekly article exposing life here and the people that have lived here for tens of thousands of years. I also said I would take photographs with him and Matthew, surrounded by the chiefs and their people.

"Not in his Commissioner's regalia. That will portray him in a different light." Matthew advised.

"As a slave owner, Matthew?" Peter asked.

"Precisely."

"And of course you will need to get the chiefs' permission to photograph them." Matthew advised.

"Of course, it goes without saying. I am aware of these people's pride and I promise I'll do everything with decorum. While we're on the subject of Native Amerindians, can you tell me why Sugar Bush decided to bond with you? I mean no disrespect, but you are considerably older."

"That will forever be my secret, and don't you forget it." Matthew replied.

"I think it is sheer charisma." Peter teased.

It was getting dark and Margaret came to tell us that supper was ready. It was all quiet now. I awaited the noise from the insects and thanked God for the netting that kept them away.

Then I asked Matthew "How do the villagers managed without netting? Are they immune to their bites?"

"No one is immune to their bites. They use the sap from the leaves of the silk cotton and rub themselves with it before retiring. I warn you though, it has the most repugnant smell. That should give you an idea why we don't use it." Matthew informed me.

I wanted to ask if Sugar Bush used it, I hoped not. Matthew looked at me and asked "Is there anything else you wanted to know before supper?"

I shook my head.

CHAPTER 2
THE CONFRONTATION

I was making my way to the village, accompanied by Ben and Sugar Bush. There was a lot of shouting in the village. Ben became agitated, so Sugar Bush ran ahead to investigate. It appeared that one of the men in the village had a problem with an outsider from the neighbouring village.

It turns out that the man from the other village is angry that a herd of cattle has grown too large and some of the space he'd intended to use for growing vegetables has been taken up by this increase.

It looked like a matter to be dealt with by Diego; he is the one who is responsible for their care and protection. Ben instructed Sugar Bush to tell the men that the problem would be put right as soon as Diego was informed. But, the stranger was not happy with this information and continued to harass the villager. The chief took an arrow dipped in curare and threatened to stab him with it, if he did not stop this harangue. I tried to stay calm and hoped that this episode would come to an end. I could see firsthand, the problems the chief had to face. Eventually, the stranger took his bow and arrows and slinked away.

I was in no mood to interview anyone at the moment. Instead, Ben suggested we took a tractor to visit Diego and his family. Sugar Bush insisted on coming along. No one was in authority to tell her she couldn't.

We arrived just in time for when the milking was over. I took a large glass and filled it with fresh milk and drank it. It has been several years since I last did that.

I was surprised at the complex arrangements on the cattle farm. I could see neat hedges around the corral, a superbly built lodge and neat little thatched houses for the young villagers and their families.

Diego invited us into his home and offered us some freshly brewed coffee. Bell asked us to stay for lunch, as she was preparing peccary and pigeon. It sounded great. I had no idea what peccary tasted like but I was willing to try.

Matthew and Peter must have heard of the crisis in the village, as they came racing down the dirt track on an old tractor.

Diego explained the situation and they were happy with it. They were invited to join us for lunch and with such a gathering, the inevitable malt was set before us. I wasn't a heavy drinker not like this lot anyway. But I was prepared to take my share as it came, and that went down well with the others.

Half way through lunch Diego started explaining. "We do have a problem on our hands and I think we are at fault. The herd is too large for such a small space and obviously they spilled out onto land that isn't really ours. We have two options, one is to get rid of half the herd by giving them to the neighboring village, or secondly, take them across the river in the open savanna. There is enough shade from the trees scattered about. The only problem is, they'll be open to attacks from roaming jaguars. It means we will have to dig trenches all around the corral and fence it. That will take a very long time.

Matthew suggested we used the draglines and tractors to dig the trenches and the villagers could put up the barricades. "For their hard work we could give them vegetables?" Matthew suggested, "And maybe even a bull, when there are too many of them, until a permanent relocation is found." He added.

"Would it not be risky relocating the animals on the same bank as the caimans?" I asked.

"It's a risky situation but we are prepared to chance it. That is why we are erecting the barricades. The trench around the perimeter is not enough to deter them from entering the area." Diego told them.

The final decision will depend on the outcome of the negotiation with the villagers next door. And that can be tricky.

While Diego and the others were planning a solution for the neighboring villagers, an uprising was taking place a hundred yards away. Obeyo, the chief from the next village was in a heated confrontation with Watachara, the resident chief. Men from both villages were armed with their poisoned arrows to do battle, if called upon. I wondered how many fights there were in this community. I had witnessed several and it always appeared to be something petty and as always, it was Diego to be the one to solve their differences.

So I was not surprised, when I heard Ben had taken initiative and summoned Diego; and asked him to bring the tractor. I volunteered to drive a second tractor if it would help. So the three of us raced down the embankment to meet the Commissioner. I was surprised and full of admiration when I saw both Peter and Matthew in full Commissioner's uniform. Their impressive plumed helmet looked daunting, especially when you saw their revolvers hanging from their belts. This really was the scene of cowboys and Indians, Guianese style. Diego, Ben and I were carrying loaded rifles. I'd never fired a gun in my life; but Ben was quick to show me how.

Peter and Matthew marched bravely in front of the tractors until we reached two parties in heated arguments. It was impossible to learn what it was all about.

Matthew shouted a command in their language and told them to be orderly. They ignored him, so again he shouted his command. They looked angry and turned their attention to us, menacingly.

Peter drew his pistol and shouted. "In the name of his Britannic Majesty King George IV, I command you to drop your weapons or I will be forced to shoot anyone that disobeys this order."

They remained as menacing as before and threatened us with their poisoned arrows. Matthew stepped six paces forward and pointed his revolver at Obeyo and told him to drop his arrows or he would be dead. Then, he calmly said. "I am an old man and have been your Commissioner for twenty five years. I have always been fair and kind to you. You may shoot me with your arrow Obeyo, but you will not live to enjoy the victory."

At this point Warachara stepped in and said. "If he shoots you, I will burn his body in his house and all his ancestors' bones in it."

Obeyo winced at the threat, as he knew Warachara did not make empty promises. He then commanded his tribe to drop their arrows and sit down for a peace talk.

The two chiefs and some of their advisors were invited to the long house which was erected in the center of the square, just outside the main village. Peter and Matthew, still dressed in their official uniforms, sat at the head of the long table. The two warring parties sat opposite each other. Diego, Ben and I sat at the other end. The two chiefs stood up placed their left hand under their chins and stretched forth their right hand. In unison they said "A wiki aye bala." Peter and Matthew replied, "A wiki aye nou." Then, the two chiefs answered with "Soo, awah." This was a submissive welcome to parley.

The ceremony completed, and Peter and Matthew took off their helmets and wiped their brows, as they outlined the proposals that were originally thought up by Diego and the others.

Obeyo rejected the idea of taking half the herd, preferring to accept fruits and vegetables from the farm instead, until such time as the area for the herd is ready. They all agreed to assist in digging the trenches around the corral where the cattle would be resting, during the night. It was also agreed by both parties that, on a rotational basis, a guard would be on hand all night to warn off any attacks, from the caimans or jaguars.

I have been a journalist for over a decade and witnessed many confrontations with workers and management in the sugar industry. I have even seen men shot and killed in a strike that threatened the sugar industry. This was so easily resolved, I wish the so called civilized people on the outside would take a leaf from these simple people's book.

Matthew asked them to send their advisors away and invited the two chiefs and the rest of us to the official residence. Contrary to official regulations, Matthew brought out a bottle of malt whisky and poured generous amounts in each glass. Then he announced. "Gentlemen, this is against official regulations, since I am no longer the Commissioner. I am taking advantage of that fact to perform this ceremony, and to show my friends that I am still their friend, in spite of the harsh exchanges we had earlier. Peter, my dear friend, who I sometimes look upon as the son I never had, is spared any reproach from anyone, least of all from me. I think it is time they be considered as a nation, to determine what's good for them and what is not." Matthew then went around clinking his glass with all of us and drank the lot in one gulp. The two chiefs followed, and presented their glasses for a second drink. Matthew obliged and Peter got a bit agitated. Matthew sensed this and announced that this was their last drink. He ended by saying "I was so overwhelmed by the events of today and the bravery shown by our Commissioner that I decided to do the extraordinary, by inviting my friends for this drink." The chiefs took their leave and disappeared into the forest. Warachara and Obeyo walked shoulder to shoulder, like brothers.

I was not only shocked by these events that I'd never anticipated, but also by the valour Peter and Matthew had exhibited. It was getting late and Diego and Ben had gone to bed. Peter had invited me to stay on with him and had said that when tiredness became overwhelming I could sleep in the next room. I was thankful that he'd asked. I'd always wanted to spend a night in this house with its luxury en-suite bedrooms, a luxury I'd never enjoyed before. In my city of Georgetown, there were grand colonial houses but I doubt any of them had an en-suite bedroom. I imagine it was Peter's idea, after returning from England. He wanted so much to make Christine happy during her visit to Supenaam, I think he has succeeded.

Margaret came in with her father, Joseph D'Costa, the resident engineer and pilot. He sat next to me enjoying a cold drink. "Would you not like me to pour you a whisky?" I asked. "No thank you." he replied. His reply was short. "A teetotaler?" I asked. "I was an alcoholic. I worked in a brewery and fell in love with their product" he replied, with a wink. He became friendlier and told me. "My daughter and I are now working for the man who helped us. It's a kindness I can never repay."

"What is it you cannot repay Joseph?" Peter asked, as he came in to join us. "I was merely mentioning the reason why I do not drink alcohol anymore."

"You should bury that thought and look to the future. When you mention the past, do you realise you are humiliating Margaret? It was not her fault that disaster came to you. Promise me you will never mention it again, not even to your priest?" Peter was looking at him in the eyes and with a seriousness that said he meant business.

I think Joseph understood his meaning and went off to his lodgings. Margaret came and placed an arm on Peter and thanked him for telling her father to forget the past.

"I am willing to forget and look forward to a new life, but father keeps reminding me, and I am, as you say, always embarrassed." She kissed Peter on the cheek. Peter looked surprised, but smiled eventually. In my Colonial circle it is a foregone conclusion that when a young woman, and one as beautiful as Margaret, kisses a man, whether on his cheek or on his lips, it is considered an invitation for romantic exchanges. I am not sure Margaret is conscious of this. Whether Peter realises this or not, is a matter of conjecture. I began taking a closer look at events that followed, if only to prove I was wrong. After all, she is an extremely beautiful young lady and proportionately endowed. She walked slowly towards the drinks cabinet and poured herself a large brandy. As she sipped it slowly, I saw her looking at Peter from behind her glass. Peter seemed oblivious to her attention. She only looked away when she saw I was observing her. I finished my drink and said goodnight. I thought it was the decent thing to do, if they wanted to carry on. My bedroom was separated from the living area by a single wall and it was not difficult to hear what someone was saying. I heard movements and glasses clinking; and then I knew I was right, she had given him the signal for something more than just gratitude.

It was quiet for a long time and I was desperate to know what was going on. I couldn't pretend I wanted to go to the toilet, as my room had everything. Then, I heard his bedroom door shut and I waited for the second sound of her door to close. No such sound came and then I heard whispering and the sound of someone falling heavily on a bed. I knew I had the evidence of a romance, but I could not be sure. I focused my hearing to its full intensity. I heard muffled mutterings and then silence. After a while there was heavy breathing. I was in no doubt that Peter had committed adultery. The sensual breathing continued for some time, then I heard the door open and close. I knew she'd got what she wanted. I felt happy for her, but at the same time I wondered if her beauty was not casting a spell over me.

In the morning I found that Peter had already gone to his office without breakfast. Margaret and Sugar bush were still preparing it. Half an hour later Peter came in, followed by Diego. They were going through some papers together while breakfast was laid on the table. There was an enormous struggle within me to contain what I knew had happened. I could hardly consume my breakfast. After some deliberation with myself, I asked to be excused and went and sat on the verandah. Peter sensed something was bothering me, so he came out to enquire. At first, I tried to conceal the fact that I knew something happened between the two of them during the night. "Come on man spit it out before it chokes you. What is it that is bothering you?" He asked authoritatively.

Unable to contain my curiosity I told him what I suspected. Peter became enraged and his face reddened with anger as he denied the accusation. Margaret must have heard him and came out to say that breakfast was ready. Peter took her by the hand and told her what I had disclosed.

She instantly slapped me so hard my head went half way round my shoulder. "I swear in the name of The Holy Mother Mary that I am still the virgin I was from birth." And she burst into tears.

I felt like a right moron and thought my presence had become untenable. After breakfast, Peter told me to complete my work as soon as possible. This request, he insisted, had nothing to do with what was said this morning. I'd gone down to the office early this morning to take a phone call from my father. He wants me in Berbice as soon as I can make it. I am to take my family, who are in the city at the moment. Matthew and the others will want to come.

After he left for the office, I managed to get hold of Margaret alone and went down on my knees and apologised most vehemently. I told her it must have been the drinks and my own imagination that must have conjured up such a sad tale. She smiled and held my hand in gesture to stand up. Then she opened her heart to me. "I love Peter secretly from the moment I set eyes on him. I am his wife's confidant and I will never allow myself to betray her or the family. I forgive you, because you may have seen the tenderness I have for him in my eyes. I knew you were observing me when I was having my brandy. I am unhappy here as, as you can see, there are no eligible bachelors around. I have lived in more hopelessness than this, so I can take it. Peter himself, has endured six years of hopelessness in this place and he survived, so shall I, as intact as I came." Her smile was one of forgiveness and I thanked my lucky stars that this awful episode had come to a peaceful end.

Ben and Diego asked me to join them on a fishing trip. Matthew must have heard, as he came out and asked. "Where do you think you musketeers are going without me? Diego, you know how much I love fishing, yet you fail to invite me."

"You were not around. I thought you are still resting." Diego defended his decision.

"I know exactly what you are up to, not fishing but visiting that village of Obeyo, I too noticed those lovely beauties that followed him. I am still a man and up to anything you can take" Matthew told them.

"You know me Matthew, Bell will chop my head off if she knew I was up to no good. It is Andrew who wanted to get to know the young ladies. He is seriously thinking of marrying one of them". Diego told him.

The four of us set off to the village of the young ladies, nervousness crept up in me and I became a bit apprehensive. I do not normally drink but right now a glass of whisky would do no harm. We arrived at the village and Obeyo came and greeted us. He spoke in his dialect and three young ladies brought drinks for us, it was their local brew. I'd never tasted it before but it was beyond vile. It was the most horrible drink I had ever tasted. Protocol forbade anyone from refusing a chief's hospitality. He looked at me, curious to know what I thought of his drink. I smiled and lied "Good, very good." He looked pleased and poured me another. I could not believe I'd invited another drink by my comment.

Matthew decided to let him know why we were there. The chief looked pleased and invited another young lady to come forward. She was not the oil painting I was looking for. There were incisors missing from both her upper and lower jaw and she giggled like an imbecile. I became agitated and looked away. "Say something, man." Matthew shouted at me. "What can I say; it is not I who is looking for a bride. Tell the chief I was looking for my brother. I will write and tell him to come and see for himself. I said nervously."

"You no want to bond with my sister?" The chief asked. "My brother will bond with her, I will find a suitable young lady to bond with after he has chosen." I replied, still shaking within.

"Then have some more drink." he said, and without warning, poured me a very large drink. I would have rather drank all he had, than chosen the woman that was before me. Matthew looked at me with great concern and I was getting legless with the poison that had been given to me.

Diego, who is more knowledgeable with tribal custom, explained that I would come again and choose one of his ladies, but only after I'd had the opportunity to speak with her.

Without warning Obeyo said. "You go speak now. Go… go… go he urged me. I was terribly embarrassed. I didn't know what to do. Again, Diego came to the rescue and defended me. He told the chief that I was ignorant of tribal customs and that, perhaps, when I learnt a bit more, I would come for a visit, with good intentions. This appeared to satisfy Obeyo. We left and I felt a complete moron for a second time!

The others were needling me all the way back to base. I was worried about the foul taste in my mouth.

As soon as I reached my lodgings, I took a big swig of whisky and normality was restored. Bell was smiling at me and asked if I had selected a bride. I simply shook my head and went indoors.

Sebastian came and asked us to help him restore his house. I was in no mood for that kind of work. I told him of the nasty experiences I'd had and would only come to give moral support.

The rest of the day was spent rebuilding the house. Afterwards, we all went down the river to cool ourselves. Ben, Sebastian and Diego went in the river for a swim. I am no great friend of the piranha, so I stayed on the bank with Matthew and watched them playing like little boys, having a great time. Matthew then told me that piranha have a notorious reputation for stripping a man or animal to the bone, in a matter of minutes. "Are they not afraid they may be attacked?" I asked. "Diego knows when it is safe to swim and if he says it is safe, then you can believe him. It is safe." Matthew told me.

They were dressed just in time, as Margaret and her father joined us. Not long afterwards Peter strolled along.

Sebastian suggested we take the sea plane and go up river. He wanted to visit the village on the other side, to negotiate with the villagers about helping to dig the trenches where the cattle will be rehoused.

"Everyone seemed to forget we have a gigantic task ahead and I am prepared to get started." We all agreed and we were off. It was my first flight in an aircraft and I was surprised how delightful it was.

The villagers were very welcoming. The first thing they asked. "Where is doctor man?" Matthew told them he was resting and would come and see them when time permitted."

"Very busy doctor man. Wife come with him next time?" the chief asked.

"Wife and daughter in city." Matthew enlightened them.

"Clever doctor man, keep far from wife and have a happy life" The chief replied, with a roguish smile.

Sebastian then negotiated with them of coming to the farm to help dig the trenches. They suggested that he come in his plane and fetch them, all they wanted in return was enough to feed the villagers, while the work was going on. It looked like a good bargain and it was agreed. We flew back to base.

Peter was delighted that we'd accomplished something useful. "Looking for brides and swimming in the river was getting you nowhere." Peter told me. Matthew agreed.

I had been here a week and not one word had been written for the actual work I'd come to do. I was too busy getting to know what life in Supenaam was really like, from an outsider's point of view. I thought the best way forward was to interview Ben and the others, one by one. In that way, I can relate their personality and blend it into a coordinated biographical round up, with Peter and Matthew at the forefront.

This, I must try to do in earnest and not be diverted by anything or anyone. Perhaps it easier said than done, here in this wilderness where events can dictate what and when to do certain things.

My only wish was, never to visit that village again, or take another sip of that vile drink. No sooner had I contented myself with that promise, when Obeyo arrived with his sister to discuss bonding.

I was getting absolutely fed up with this bonding business. I told him, that in our culture the eldest must bond first and only then can I think of bonding. He was shaking his head as I spoke. I wondered if he really understood what I was saying. I was only too happy when he took her hand and marched off looking a bit angry. I do not want any confrontation with people I can hardly understand. I must ask Diego to send home that message to him and the sooner the better. I can never tell when he may shoot me with a poisoned arrow.

The other thing on my mind was this drinking. I think they are taking advantage of the fact that since there are no other means of leisure, drinking was the only substitute. I could think of many other things they could do to relax and pass the time.

I decided I would try and please my editor and by sending him some pictures of the community and the villagers, and to expose life in the wilderness. I was sure that would please him no end and increase sales. Then, I thought of Obeyo's daughter. If only I could persuade Diego to take me to his village and persuade the chief to let me photograph his daughter, under the pretext that my non-existent brother could see her picture and maybe want to be bonded with her. I was ashamed of myself for this dubious activity. It would serve a good purpose in the end. I was happy I'd found some justification for my actions.

Diego was not happy in the least, of my proposal. He suggested I tell the truth and tell the chief my real reason for wanting the photograph. In this way, I would not be deceiving anyone, more so myself.

Much to my surprise the chief was overwhelmed with what Diego told him and he went and adorned himself in his chieftain attire and stood as rigid as a post next to his daughter.

CHAPTER 3

CHRISTINE'S SUDDEN ARRIVAL

We heard the sea plane landing two miles away and Diego scrambled on his tractor to investigate. We all clambered aboard and headed for the landing site. It was Christine and Elizabeth in company with Isabel, her maid. We put them in a paddle boat and took them to Peter. He was as much surprised as were we, at their arrival.

It had been several months since she last visited Supenaam and Peter was overjoyed that she had come.

I discovered later, that it was not a pleasant visit. Peter knew that she was pregnant and wanted to return to England, until the baby was born. He was not at all happy with her decision. He was insisting she remained in the city and have the baby. She was adamant and they failed to reach an agreement on the issue. She would prefer it if he agreed to let her return to England and have the baby there. The outcome of this decision was a secret.

In the morning I could see Peter's face all drawn, with anger written all over it. I knew it would be some time before I could approach him for his life story. All was not lost, I had the others I could interview.

I would start with Ben. He has a colourful life. I was content to wait though, as I had my first story and photograph to send in.

I could see Matthew and Diego chatting with Mrs. D'Abrue and she was laughing and joking with them. It seemed all her problems were behind her. I would be the happiest man if it all goes well.

After lunch I asked Ben to walk down the river, where we could sit and chat about his life. He was overwhelmed with enthusiasm.

I started out by asking him to tell me all he could remember from the first time he met Peter.

"Let me tell you first my origin. My great grandmother was a slave, working for an Irish overseer at the sugar plantation. He made her pregnant and after the child was born, she brought her up with love and care, without any help from the father. I was told she was a beautiful girl who grew up into a more beautiful young lady. She in turn, was made pregnant by an English man, and they had a beautiful daughter. That daughter was my mother. She was extremely beautiful and at the age of fifteen, married an English man and that child is me"

Ben stopped and asked. "Are you writing this down? I am not wasting my time telling you secrets of my life in vain. Or am I?"

"No Ben, it is all in my head, I promise." I told him.

Then he continued. "As you can see, I come from a line of bastards. I am bigger than most men. I measure twenty four inches at the shoulder and weigh over two hundred and fifty pounds. Because of my enormous size, I could not find suitable work and also, the fact I did not have a secondary education, so I found a European family that needed a handy man. All I wanted was a room and my meals and I'd do all they asked. It turned out to be a good deal. All the families I worked for treated me with respect. I did sometimes get into trouble with the ladies. I remember one lady in particular. She was a bit of a sex machine and her husband was not up to her sexual demands. She turned to me for satisfaction"

I interrupted, by pointing out that, since his mother was married, he was not a bastard. He told me he knew that, but that people still referred to him as 'that bastard'. He continued "I let it remain that way. If people can be that ignorant, who am I to tell them the truth?" Then he continued in the same breath.

"At first, I was very scared. I did not want my head blown off by an enraged husband. But it turned out that he did not mind her having an extra marital affair, providing it was discreet. I soon got fed up with her demands and left. I can tell you, that woman was so enraged, she followed me to my temporary lodgings and demanded my services. I told her, in no uncertain terms, that I was leaving and I had no desire to see her again. She wept convulsively for a long time before leaving. I never saw her again."

"On another occasion I was in the service of another European family. Her husband loved fishing and hunting and I went with him everywhere, we had a great time. But, she became jealous of the friendship that had developed between us and insisted that she came along or I would have to stay and protect her, while he went deep sea fishing. In order to keep his freedom, he agreed. It turned out, she really liked me and would often measure my biceps and press her body against mine". Ben stopped for a while and then asked me. "How much of this temptation do you think a man can take before he loses control?"

"I am waiting for you to tell me Ben." I said. Then he continued. "Well, I am not one of those men with scruples where sex is concerned. It turned out she was another sex machine. Now I knew why her husband would leave her days on end to go fishing or hunting. The husband never did find out. I nevertheless, became nervous with the situation. Her husband had some serious guns and he had a temper. Eventually, I decided to skip town and head for Mackenzie. It was on that journey that I met Doctor Joseph D'Abrue and his sixteen year old son, Peter. For eight years, I protected him, while he struggled to come to terms with life in the wilderness. I even knew when he picked his first cherry and many after that, until he met the lovely Christine."

I interrupted and asked. "Does he like cherries that much? Tell me how they met."

"My god man, you are ignorant. It is not the fruit you get from a tree. You must know what I mean. I would like you to answer my questions truthfully. Was it right here in Supenaam he picked his first cherry?" He started out. "I cannot tell you more, it is too private and it will be up to Peter to say what he wants." Ben ended his story.

In the meantime, Christine was still negotiating with her husband of returning to England. She even sought the help of her uncle Matthew. He appeared reluctant to intervene and with good reasons. She was his niece and Peter had become the son he never had. He was immensely attached to both of them. Hence, his reluctance to mediate.

My mind was still reflecting on what Ben had told me. I found his life rather strange and complicated. I trusted that when I interviewed Diego, it would be more straightforward.

In the morning, after breakfast, it was Diego's turn. Bell wanted to be present when I did the interview, so I agreed. His ancestral lineage was less complicated than Ben's. What intrigued me most, was the fact that all the descendants of the conquistadors did not inter marry with the natives. He was not sure of the reasons, but from what I gathered, they looked down on the native Amerindians as inferior. They were therefore, able to retain their distinct Spanish features. Bell on the other hand, was the only off spring of a brief liaison between an Englishman and his Chinese housekeeper. Diego, had a colourful life as an assistant engineer, in the bauxite ship that lies between Mackenzie and Canada. He learnt a lot of arctic conditions, when stranded in Canada, where he got the knowledge of building his timbered lodge, the only one of its kind in the country. He and Bell got married after a short romance and have lived in Supenaam ever since. He is one of the famous four.

I think I have had enough material to write about for now. I shall take Matthew's advice and relax as often as possible. At the same time, I would try to deter them from their regular sipping, as they called it.

It was bad news for Diego, an Amerindian had come running to tell him that a young bull had been taken by a jaguar. It was the third bull in a month and Diego was a bit concerned. He told Matthew that he would not shoot it. He must track it down and see for sure, it was a jaguar and not some marauding Brazilian bandit. These men are notorious for stealing anything they fancy. They have been known to capture young ladies and rape them, before fleeing in the forest. Two months ago, Matthew told me they shot dead one of these bandits, as he attempted to capture Sugar Bush. It was the feisty resistance of the young woman and her call for help that alerted Matthew and Diego. He was trying to strangle the young woman when Matthew shot him in the head. I asked him what happened to Matthew after that. "Did the authorities have anything to say?

"Yes, they read the report Peter sent and that was the end of the matter" Diego told me.

"Was there not any investigation?" I asked.

"No". He responded. "The Commissioner's report was the official document needed to be recorded for future reference."

I was too excited about tracking down a wild animal and a jaguar at that, that I momentarily forgot why I was here. Matthew announced that he had checked all the antivenin, even that of the infamous bush master. He was not taking any more chances. He had been bitten by one before and he would not survive a second bite. I felt safer from his announcements. In the meantime, plans were afoot for a three day trek, at least. Some of the younger villagers were keen to go and Diego was only too pleased, as they had a better knowledge of tracking than he. Matthew on the other hand, was not so sure; he felt, if there was too many people around, the chances of tracking this animal down would be almost nil. A jaguar, I was told, could smell a man from about two miles or more. It all came down to the trackers, to keep down wind to the creature. It was eventually decided, to take two of the villagers. Diego, Matthew, Ben and myself would make up the rest of the party. The sun was too high in the sky for the journey to begin. So we started very early in the morning.

We were already about two miles in the forest the next morning and so far, we could not hear or see any sign of the jaguar. The two trackers told us that jaguars usually hunt at night and that early morning was the best time to see if they were successful or not. If they were successful then we had a good chance of finding the culprit. Slowly, they crept forward and signaled us to follow, some distance behind. I was getting nervous and turned around to look at every sound behind me. I felt safer when I noticed Ben was right behind me. In an instant, the trackers signaled us to a halt. We could hear an animal feeding on something. I could hear bones cracking. We kept very low and the trackers tipped their arrows in an intoxicating mild poison and were ready for any eventuality. The poison would not kill the animal but immobilise it for an hour or so. Movements in the undergrowth signaled caution. Then suddenly, I saw it licking its paws and crouched near to whatever it was eating. A closer observation, indicated that it was the young bull he had before him. It was a great distance from where he killed it. Then it dawned on me, the enormous strength of this beast.

Diego told the trackers not to shoot it, as it would be difficult to carry him all the way back, to be relocated. The wind began to change course and that put us all at risk. The trackers began making a lot of noise, hitting the trunk of a tree with a dead branch. This had the desired effect we wanted, as the animal went racing in the other direction in the forest.

We returned to base, to find Peter. Christine and another woman were waiting for us. We told them we'd found the culprit, but was unable to do anything, as it was too far. Diego told Peter that he had a plan and if all went well, he hoped to relocate it a hundred miles from here.

"That cat will not stop taking our bulls. He finds it too easy."

"How do you plan to relocate it?" I asked. "First I will have to get a peccary and use it as bait. The rest will unfold itself. We have to wait for a while until he has eaten that bull and started to get hungry again, then I will make my move" Diego informed me.

The young woman with Christine looked intriguing. It was time I introduced myself. As she was walking towards the river, I seized the opportunity and hailed to her, she turned around and stopped. "I am Andrew Bowry, The biographer." I said, and stretched my hand out. She looked at me, puzzled, and then blurted out "Biographer? What is that?" She asked. "I write people's life story." I told her. Her eyes beamed with surprise. "Are you going to write about me?" She asked. "I was not prepared for it but if you want to tell me, I may write about if I found it interesting." I told her

Then she started out. "My name is Isabel. I am the maid to the Commissioner's wife I have been a maid for his mother for many years. Now I am here." She stopped short and looked at me inquiringly. Then she continued. "When you say you write about people's life, does that mean everything?"

"Yes Isabel, everything that you want the public to know." I told her. She hesitated for a minute and asked.

"Everything?"

"Yes, everything you want people to know." I again informed her.

She shook her head vehemently and said. "No, oh no, I can't tell you my life story. It is too bad to write about. People will think I am a whore. I am not; I just like men, lots of men and the men like me very much. That is why I cannot tell you my life story. I do not do it for money, just for the fun of it. I like sex, it's the only thing that makes me happy."

"When you are not making, love what else do you do for your happiness?" I asked getting interested.

"I tease the other men about it. They call me a whore. I don't care, it is my happiness." She then asked. "Do you think I am bad My mother said I am bad. What do you think?"

"I cannot make a moral judgment on such issues. You say you do not do it for money, then you are not a prostitute. If you did it for money then I would say you are a bad woman."

She held me and gave me a sweet kiss on the lips and then she thanked me for saying what I said.

Ben saw us and came and joined in. She held Ben and gave him the same type of kiss I received. I imagined Ben was probably one of her lovers. I dared not ask.

The rest of the team joined us. I managed to dissuade them from their regular sippy, all except Ben. He reminded me that sipping by the river was a regular thing with them and I should not interfere. It was not long before Diego, Bell and Diego junior ambled along. They sensed something was not right when they saw Ben alone drinking. I left them and joined D'Costa at the other end and tried to interview him. He was not in a good frame of mind for this exercise. He'd stopped drinking since working for the Commissioner, and I was not a lover of spirits so was happy to be in his company. He realised this and made casual conversation, without revealing much about himself, or Margaret.

He eventually decided to take me across the river, as he wanted to make a survey of the land where the cattle would be relocated. I counted four draglines, four wheeled diesel tractors and three bulldozers. I thought for a minute, that's a lot of machinery for the wilderness they wanted to keep pristine, they do not need the villagers up river to dig the trenches. There is enough machinery to do that in two days.

Joseph D'Costa told me that the draglines would dig the trenches and heap the earth on the inner side, as a protection from the caiman and any other predators. The villager's job was to tidy up and make some strong fences all along the perimeter. When this was done, the water from the river would be let in and create the trenches. A clever idea, whoever thought about it?

In the meantime, I was waiting for a more propitious moment to speak to Christine. I knew she was a bluestocking and wouldn't suffer fools. She would not tolerate anyone trying to pry into her life without good reasons. I guess I will have to wait until such time as the Commissioner sees fit for me to interview them.

I was looking forward to seeing the capture of this jaguar. I just hoped some other jaguar steals his meal.

The villagers were busy building a cage and strengthened it with palm fibers. They were actually building it on the trailer and securing it down on the base. I could see the purpose of this and eagerly awaited the moment of truth.

Several days later, the truth arrived. Diego and one of the young men from his village came back with a peccary. The trailer was driven to the edge of the corral and the peccary tied inside the cage. It was screaming nonstop, as if it knew it was destined for the jaguar's jaw. Diego gave it some nut and that stopped it for a while.

At about four in the morning, we heard some very loud screaming and then it suddenly stopped. We knew the jaguar was in the cage; but we were too cautious to go and look. It was best to wait for daylight. Jaguars are cunning animals and could be waiting for us in the dark.

As daylight broke, there it was, large as life and eating his kill in captivity. As soon as he saw we were approaching, he stood up and growled at us fiercely. Its head was bent at an angle and all his teeth were on show, as if to tell us to leave it alone. One of the young men dipped his arrow in the sleeping poison and fired it into his leg. The animal went mad and tried to escape from his confines. The cage was built to withstand this battering. As the drug began to take effect, it became subdued until it lay on its side well sedated.

We hurriedly took it to the river and loaded it in the plane and flew for about an hour, until we came to a very large lake. By this time, the animal was showing signs of waking up. Hurriedly, as soon as we landed, the door was opened and we waited until it was fully conscious. It stood up, still dazed and then the cage door was opened. It looked at the water for a full minute and without warning, plunged into the lake and like the adept swimmer he is, disappeared into the jungle.

The men clapped and wished the animal well. I was heartened by this exercise. The time, energy and not to mention, the expensive plane journey was something that will live in my memory for a very long time. If a jaguar was seen in the city, I am positive that rather than try to capture it alive, the town mayor would have sent for a marksman and shot it dead. Then, they would have skinned it and tried to sell the hide to the highest bidder. I have seen this happen before. On that occasion it was a puma.

I now await my next adventure and that is, fishing for arapaima and piranha with my bare hands. I shudder to think about it. If they can do it, I do not see why I cannot.

Trouble was brewing in the home of the Commissioner. It appears that his wife was adamant about leaving for England and the Commissioner was just as adamant that she stay in the city until the child is born. Matthew was caught in the middle. He was definitely disturbed by all the stubbornness shown by both parties.

It appeared that Diego was probably the only one to end this impasse. Ben and I took the tractor to fetch him. Unfortunately, he had taken his young son fishing and would not be back for some time. So Ben left a message with Bell, asking him to come down to see the Commissioner, as soon as possible.

Bell wanted to know what was so urgent. We were reluctant to explain. This deepened the mystery for this urgent visit and Bell seemed perplexed at our hesitance to explain. Nonetheless, she accepted our silence and promised to inform him.

When we got back to our home, we saw a gathering of the chief Warachara and a dozen of his people, milling around a young lady. We thought a tragedy had occurred during our absence. It turned out this young lady had come from a great distance to look for her father, whom she never saw. Her mother told her who the father was and she had travelled all alone for days to get here.

We were still trying to find the name of her father. Her dialect was unknown, even to Warachara, only Diego would know. He was familiar with many of the dialects in the region. It was a blessing to hear his tractor approaching. On board, was Bell and young Diego. Bell took the youngster indoors while Diego came to investigate. It was several minutes before he was toying with his chin in contemplation.

He looked worried. He ignored our urges to explain. Diego was unmoved. He dispatched Warachara and his followers. He took the young lady by the hand and led her into the Commissioner's home.

Matthew invited us. As Ben and I entered the house, I could see they were all seated with the young lady at the far end.

Diego started to explain. "What this young woman is saying, is that her father is the Commissioner and she is here to claim his protection. Her mother was killed and her step father threw her out of the family lodgings and told her to find her real father. She has a picture of him in full regalia but does not know his name.

Christine hearing this, came out full of anger. Anger, brought about by her husband's refusal to let her have her way. She seized this opportunity to extinguish her anger by screaming at him saying. "You told me you did not indulge with the women here!

I can see that you are nothing more than the average man. I hate you Peter D'Àbrue. You hear me, I hate you and I never want to see you again"

"Steady on young lady." Matthew told her. "We must satisfy ourselves with the truth before you start hurling accusations at Peter. I know you are looking for an excuse to return to England, but not this way. I will get to the bottom of this affair." He beckoned to Diego to ask the questions he will put forward. "First how old is this young lady." She replied by saying she is two hundred and sixteen moons old. Diego told us that, two hundred and sixteen moons old means she is 18 years old.

"Well, you see Matthew; I could not be the father if she is eighteen years. It makes it impossible for me to be her father. I came to Supenaam in 1938." Peter pointed out.

"There is one certain way to know for sure who the father is." Diego told us. "She said she has a picture of the Commissioner. I will show it to you." Matthew suspected it was him all the time. The young lady was a spitting image of him and he knew it and the photo proved it.

"I did not know someone had taken this picture." Matthew blurted out. "It must have been that vicar. He is the only one with a camera in this settlement. All my life I wished for a son, now I have a real daughter." He threw his arms around her and gave her a warm embrace.

"Diego!" he ordered "You will have to teach her to speak English. The king's English! You hear me?" "Yes father, I hear you." Diego teased.

"Now, I need to know her name." Matthew demanded. "Her name is Amelia." Diego responded.

Christine started sobbing and went and hugged Peter, asking for forgiveness. Peter did not have to say anything, his cuddles and kisses were enough testament that all was forgiven. Then turning to Matthew, he asked. "Am I still the son you never had?"

"It goes without saying. Come and let me hug my son and daughter in one embrace."

It was great to see Matthew in such a happy state. I do not think I will ever understand what all this means until I get all my stories together.

The thought of going fishing for piranha with my bare hands, sent a shudder through me. What will I do if one of them decides to feast on my hand or any part of my anatomy that is vital? What then?

It was the usual scenario. The malt whisky came out. Margaret and Isabel were in attendance. I was surprised when Margaret sat next to Christine, and they joined us in an afternoon drinking session. One drink is my limit, but I was not allowed to get away with it this time. Matthew said to me after I finished my first drink and declined a second. "Now listen to me young man. Can you walk on one leg?" "No, sir, no one can walk on one leg." I replied. "Then behave yourself and have another, you are among men, not those damn sissies in the city." I realised this wasn't just a request, this was an order, and orders are made to be obeyed.

Sebastian soon joined us, accompanied by Margaret's father, Joseph. They had between them, a guitar and a harmonica. After Sebastian had a couple of glasses of malt, he started strumming on his guitar and then he started singing a sad song about a Spaniard on his retreat in war. He sang of his love for his sweetheart and wishing she would still love him, even though he might not survive capture. Then he livened it up with songs from Red river and all the favourite western songs, currently heard on Roy Rogers films.

I was beginning to see Margaret in a new light. She looked angelic against the dim lights and I felt my romanticism, suddenly awakened. She and Isabel went on the verandah for some fresh air. I followed them and asked Isabel to excuse us. She gave me a rude stare and left. "Why did you ask her to leave?" Margaret asked. "I wanted to be alone with you for a minute. I do not know how to begin, but I can reasonably say that I think I am falling in love with you." I told her, rather sheepishly.

"And what are you going to do about it?" It was Isabel, saying as she crept back to hear what was happening.

Margaret dispatched her and turned to me and asked. "So, what are you going to do about it?"

I told her I didn't know what to do. The only thing I could see, was to ask her to marry me. I took some courage from the drinks I'd had and said. "Margaret, if I asked you to marry me. What would your answer be?"

"If you do it in the right way, I may say yes." She replied, causally. Then I asked. "What is the right way?"

"Here," Sebastian said and produced a wild flower, "go inside and on one knee and ask her to marry you."

I was lost for words, it all happened so quickly. I kept thinking it must be a dream. Her father looked perplexed, as I pulled him aside and told him I was going to propose to his daughter and would he have any objections. His reply was that if she agrees then that's the end of it.

I struggled to get on one knee and put the flower between my teeth, then I discovered that I could not propose with the flower in my mouth.

So I took it in both hands and nervously said, "Margaret, in the presence of everyone here, I am asking you to marry me." She took the flower from me and said, "I've been waiting a long time for this. There is only one answer and that is YES!" She took my hands and clasped them, and then we kissed, much to the appreciation of those present.

I was curious as to the magic in a couple of whiskies. I would never have had the nerve to ask for her hand, without them.

Christine was so delighted, she even gave me a kiss on the cheek. Matthew was in a hurry to plan for our wedding. I was not having that. I appreciated his help, but this was one event so important that I had to think clearly, with a clear head, and plan it with Margaret.

It must have occurred in Christine's mind that when Margaret is married she will be left without a companion. She suddenly asked. "Do you have a house of your own Andrew?"

"No mam "I replied. "I am currently living with my parents"

"In that case you can have an apartment at our house in Georgetown, It will serve two purposes. One, Margaret will continue to be my companion and I will increase her salary; and two, she will not be alone when you go on your trips for your newspaper. Is that agreed?" she finally asked.

"Yes Maam. That arrangement will suit me fine. If you are going to give us an apartment, then we should pay something for it." I told her.

Peter interrupted. "That will be our wedding gift, you can stay as long as you like. I will feel more comfortable here, knowing Christine and Elizabeth are always with someone around."

There were more whiskies to be drunk. Margaret's father for the first time, since I met him took a glass and poured himself a large drink. Everyone was amazed by this act. Then he said. "Ladies and gentlemen, I made a vow not to touch this stuff again. I trust my maker will forgive me. I am so happy for my daughter that I must ask you all, to drink a toast to her future happiness. There are volumes to be said. I think those who know the circumstance that brought me here, will appreciate that I do not mention it, but I thank all of you for your kindness and support and to you Mrs. D'Abrue for your gracious support. Thank you all."

Sebastian started playing his guitar and it was so rhythmical, it drew nearly everyone to the floor. I say nearly everyone, because I never actually learned to dance and Margaret was prepared to put that right. I then discovered that I was not the only one needing dancing lessons. In the far corner, there was young Diego, trying to teach Amelia to dance and they were doing better than I was, even with the help of Margaret.

Everyone had gone to bed, leaving us in the living room with our privacy. I kissed her lightly on her lips. She held me tightly and responded energetically. I thought, I could go further and tried to be intimate with her, but she wasn't having any of it, she gently pushed me away and said, "I must not let you do this. Not before marriage. I cannot go to confession and say that I have done this outside of marriage. The priest will never forgive me." She stroked my cheeks as she spoke. I said goodnight and went to bed.

CHAPTER 4
THE FISHING EXPERIENCE

The day finally arrived, for us to go fishing for piranha with our bare hands. The thought was too terrible to consider. Nevertheless, Diego comforted me by telling me it was not as risky as I thought it was. The ladies agreed to come and watch. My only concern was that I did not show myself up as a coward.

Two paddle boats were at the ready. The young men doing the paddling looked amused at our silly venture. The ladies went in the bigger boat and we settled in the smaller one. It was a long way to go. Five miles upstream, we noticed the caimans on the other side of the river, looking at us with open jaws. One went in the water and made an abortive bid to get at the boat. One of the paddlers hit the paddle on the water and that made it changed its course. The ladies were thrilled to see them at close range.

Eventually, the two boats were abreast and it seemed a race was about to take place. Margaret splashed some water at me and me at her. Both of us started laughing. I saw Christine look at Peter and they both smiled. From what I had gleaned from Ben, that was exactly how their romance had started.

It took us another two hours to get to the spot, suitable for this adventure. When we finally reached, I saw some women with bundles of young branches. They took them down by the water's edge and were pounding and washing them in the river. I didn't know what they were making, but it seemed nonsensical to me. However, when we got out of the boat, Diego told us to be very still. He rolled up his trousers and we followed. The ladies tucked their dresses in the hems of their knickers. The young paddlers began laughing.

Diego told us to go calmly into the water and immerse our hands up to our elbows, quietly and pointed to a shoal of piranha. He said the exercise was to get our hands under the fish and heave it out of the water, onto the embankment. The shoal appeared dazed and it was easy to flick them out. Some other women were there, preparing them for cooking. They kept all the discarded bit on a heap and the rest of the fish were thrown in a bucket. They were singing a song in their own dialect and Diego and Matthew joined in. It was a sad song from the melody and I wondered if they were lamenting the death of the fish.

The women who were washing the branches up the river, went in the ladies' boat and the others who were cutting the fish, came in ours. They took the discarded bits and threw it in the river.

The water began bubbling and we could see the piranha snapping away at the pieces. All was devoured in a matter of minutes. I looked at Diego and asked. "Why did they not attack us when we were in the water?" Then he told me the secret. "Those ladies upstream were actually releasing a toxic sap from the branches that makes the fish immobile and unable to attack. Only an idiot would dare fish like that without the toxin." The others who knew the secret started laughing. Matthew told me it was something they do, only to special guests, as a way of creating some fear. He then told me how Rabbi Solomon nearly collapsed with fear when he saw the frenzied eating habits of those fish and would not for all the gold in the cold stream go into the water.

Ben as usual brought out the malt and handed glasses to all of us including the ladies and we had a drink to celebrate. The native ladies looked and hoped they will be offered some. They waited in vain.

Christine started singing some old romantic English songs Matthew and Peter joined in with us singing the chorus.

At the end of the journey, after we had disembarked, Matthew gave the paddlers a large drink. I asked if that was not contrary to the laws of the land. "Now listen young man, here in the wilderness you observe and listen. If something you see does not concern you, stay quiet. I have Peter's blessing to do anything I see fit." He told me in an authoritative voice. I looked at Peter, and he nodded.

At the landing, I felt the whisky taking a hold of me. I became romantic and lifted Margaret up, in my arms and started walking towards the house singing the chorus from the song in the boat. Margaret pleaded with me to put her down. It was a plea that fell on deaf ears. It was Ben that came to her rescue. He took her from me and set her down, then he lifted me and carried me home.

In the morning, I was surprised my head was as clear as crystal. We sat on the long benches in the square and Joseph wanted to discuss the plans for the wedding. I was not even thinking of wedding preparations. They all insisted, that as a small community, we would have to decide where it was going to happen and what form it was going to take. "What form are you talking about Matthew?" I asked.

"Is it not up to us to decide what sort of wedding we will have?" I pointed out.

"Now listen, Andrew Bowry," Matthew intervened sternly, "here in Supenaam, we do things differently. The reason being, we lived among the natives .Whenever they celebrate an occasion, we are always invited. It would seem unfair to leave them out if we have a wedding here."

"How will it be different?" I asked.

"If we have it here and they are invited, then it is only courteous to let them do a bit of their own ceremony; that will please them tremendously" Diego joined in.

"I suggest we have it in the city where my family and most of my friends are located. I do not want to be the odd ball, but this is my only daughter and she is a Catholic, and as such, I want her to have a white wedding, in a proper church, with all the families and friends around." Joseph suggested and everyone agreed.

Peter suggested Ben be the best man and Amelia, the bridesmaid. Ben protested. He told us that he do not know how to be a best man. Eventually he was told how simple it is and he agreed.

The finer details were left to the ladies to sort out, while we went down the river to continue our own discussion and there were no sipping of fine malt. I discovered I was getting the others to be more moderate. Tucking away great quantities of the stuff and not getting drunk was, to Ben at least, proof that you are a man. Joseph told me quietly that if I want to get on in life and make his daughter happy I must control my intake. I agreed with him and made a promise to continue this trend.

Warachara and Obeyo joined us by the river and complained that they were not given any of the fish. Matthew told them that the ladies took all of it and could not account for him not to have any.

He told Matthew that he'd been Commissioner for a lifetime and he should have known that it was a bad day to give fish to women. They think men only shoot monkeys and peccaries and not eat fish.

Matthew promised to give him some from his own. Satisfied, they left.

"It is these little things that can flare up into something nasty." Diego told me.

I then asked Mathew about the gold in the cold stream that he spoke about, earlier. He told me all I wanted to know and also to be present when we divide it up, which would be soon. He also said he was waiting for Sebastian to return from the city, as he wanted to go there and sell the gold. I was intrigued by all this mystery and could not wait for Sebastian's return.

It was several days later when he arrived. He had a huge order for vegetables and beef from the wholesalers in Georgetown.

"It will take more than one load to fill this order." he told Matthew

Matthew looked at it and suggested that he take us to the city, while the natives were gathering the vegetables and the young men could slaughter the bull, intended for the market, when we came back. Also, he said it was best to take Joseph as he could bring the other plane down, when the meat was ready to be flown out.

First though, I had to see the division of the nuggets. This will be interesting, I thought, and wondered how it was done. Are they going to take nugget after nugget until it is all gone, or are they going to weigh it and split it equally. In the morning, prior to our departure, a bag of gold was laid on the table. Diego, Matthew, Ben and Peter watched, as it was spread out and estimated to be about three and a half pounds. Sebastian, who was watching, said it was more than four and a half pounds.

"It does not matter how much it is. The fact remains, that we have enough to be divided". Matthew told him. Then, he started to explain one of the most astounding stories of generosity I'd ever heard. He began "Now friends, as you know, ally share usually goes to Peter. It was my desire then and would still have been now, but circumstance has prevailed on me to change this. If Peter objects then I will withdraw. I now have a daughter and I wish my share that would have gone to Peter, be given to Amelia. I wi..." He was stopped in mid-sentence. Peter told him, it was in his mind to suggest exactly the same and thanked him again for his generosity in the past. The two then hugged and clapped shoulders. I then asked a silly question, "How are you going to divide the gold?"

"Simple, city gent, we sell the gold and divide the money." Ben told him.

Diego and Sebastian finally got Warachara and his men organised the gathering of the vegetables and told them when to start. Warachara was to instruct the young men in Diego's village for the slaughter.

We all bundled in the plane and went on our way, to Georgetown. The ladies stood on the bank and waved to us, as the plane lifted off.

That evening, we were invited to the home of Rabbi Solomon. I have never been to the home of a Jew and I wondered what it would be like. At first, I imagined it would be a very solemn state of affairs, with prayers and blessings and things that normally make me bored. On the contrary, it was quite pleasant and entertaining. I had not enjoyed myself, so much, in a stranger's home for a very long time. The last time I could remember, was when I was invited to the home of the President of the bauxite company, for an interview. This was different. I was made very welcome and offered some of the finest malt, then a lovely meal of baked fish. I felt so full, I could not take a message, as they say in British Guiana.

We then settled in a very large room that was separated from the living room The Rabbi called Peter aside and spoke to him. Peter looked at us and nodded. Whatever was said or asked, I never knew then. Later, Peter explained that the Rabbi wanted to know if some confidential matters could be discussed in our presence. I assumed, I was the stranger and for whatever reason, Peter had given his consent.

The Rabbi began by saying. "First, allow me to make one thing clear and that is, I am not an orthodox, but belong to the more liberal side of my faith and so what I am going to say, is without prejudice I know this may hurt my friend, Diego, but from past experience and exchanges with him, he will understand. I am sure he will want to bring about a peaceful solution. It has been brought to my attention that Christine is not too keen for any deep friendship between your son Young Diego and Elizabeth. She felt children can be very impressionable in their early years and feelings developed during those years, can be deep and lasting. I know Christine very well, she has a good relationship with my wife and I know she is not a racist. I can understand her concern, yet at the same time, no one should present obstacles in the path of nature. Is it not true then that a mother's welfare for her daughter is natural? How then, do we observe nature's path and at the same time, prevent it from happening? It is a dilemma, only the two parties concerned, can resolve. That is why I chose to speak to the fathers and friends, whom I am sure, will relieve me of this heavy burden.

It was Matthew who took up the argument by saying. "Christine, as you know is my niece and she is married to a young man, I always regarded as a son. So, I think as the eldest member of this party, I have a right to say something. We cannot separate our children from their friends, no matter what our own thoughts are. These are innocent children and if we are to start explaining why they must not be friends, then I think we would be treading on very dangerous grounds. The repercussions can be devastating.

Most important of all, is that when those children are grown up and think about it, and if they think it has affected their happiness then I am sorry to say, they are going to hate you for it. So I say to you both, as a friend and father figure, think carefully before making a decision.

Diego's comments were that he can understand why Christine is objecting to any lasting relationship. He then said with a touch of emotion. "The truth is I agree with her. There are too many mixed races already. I will want my son to marry someone from his own tribe. We are a proud people and proud of our ancestry, even though it was bastardised by the Conquistadores. It was only a few days ago I sat with Ben and Bell and discussed this very problem. We even jokingly suggested we could have our own club of mixed races. I will speak with Bell and I can assure all my friends, this is not going to escalate." Looking at Peter and Matthew he continued. "I will never allow this to come between our friendship. There are too many things we've gone through together, to allow this to happen and Bell will say the same."

I could see Peter's eyes were welling up, he resisted the tear and spoke with a broken voice. "It is true, what all of you, my friends, said. I never knew there was a problem. This has come as a shock and I really appreciate that this will not sever our bond of friendship. It will remain as intact, as it always was. It was very decent of you Rabbi Solomon to initiate this meeting. I am very grateful. If you all will excuse me gentlemen I need a drink" As he got up, the Rabbi took him by the hand and led him into the living room, where he was given a large drink. The matter rested on our minds all evening. I knew it wasn't the end of it. I awaited its progress.

Matthew suggested we go to his club and forget this matter, at least for the time being. It was to be a low key affair. On our arrival, we saw Aubrey and Marina with another couple who we didn't recognise. It has been a couple of years since we last saw each other. Aubrey jumped to his feet and hugged us all. He then turned to his friends and pointing to Ben, said "This is the big man I saved from the gallows. In one breath he introduced his friends as, Michael and Louise Donovan. Michael is a psychologist and Louise is an obstetrician. I could see Peter's face light up, at the mention of obstetrician and I knew straight away what was on his mind. After the conclusion of formalities, we settled down to some serious drinking. The problem at the Rabbi's home became a distant memory.

Peter explained to Louise, the situation with Christine and she laughed and said, I can put your mind at rest, she will be fine in my care.

As the night progressed, the crowd swelled to capacity. It was not surprising to meet old friends, as this was where everyone who was someone, meets for their evening relaxing. Matthew, being President of this club, was shown into the dining room to make way for the ever increasing crowd. This suited us perfectly. Here we could talk quietly, without having to shout and everyone hearing what we were saying. I looked in the bar and recognised quite a few friends I hadn't seen for a long time. I did not want to greet them at this point. When I was noticed, I waved enthusiastically.

Louise wanted to go to Supenaam to see Christine and maybe put her mind at rest. Christine felt there were not any obstetricians qualified enough to meet her needs. It turned out Louise was awarded by the General Medical Council for her work. It was getting late and time to get to our homes. I was eagerly to meet my parents and tell them the good news about my proposal to Margaret. I knew they would be overjoyed. They always felt my work would prevent me from meeting the right girl, and as the years, like the tide, do not stand still for any man, I must also remember that it has been two months since I went to Supenaam to interview the famous four and only half my work was done. I do have a time limit and unless I get started pretty fast and get on with what I set out to do, I will end up losing the contract.

With that thought heavy on my mind, I was a bit less enthusiastic in greeting my parents. But their warmth and love soon dispelled all thoughts of failure. They couldn't wait to see my marvelous young lady. My father jokingly remarked that I had to leave the city and go in the jungle, to find my princess. Much to my mother's annoyance, he added that had he known the jungle was full of beautiful women, he might have gone there before deciding whom to marry. He apologised when my mother stuck her fingers in his chest.

When we returned to Supenaam, I was all set to discuss our marriage plans with Margaret and my friends. I was told that Christine sent her and Isabel to help. Bell was having some pregnancy problems and would return late in the evening. I wanted to take the tractor and bring her here. Pregnancy problems are out of my deptth. I simply had to wait.

When they arrived late that evening I was so delighted and went to kiss her. She turned her face away and told me she was too tired and wanted to go to bed. I was completely bewildered by her action and put it down to women's unexplained behavior.

In the morning, instead of taking a shower in the house, Ben and I decided to go for a dip in the river. It was still a bit dark and we knew the caimans would not stir until the sun was high in the sky and the piranha would be active a couple of miles upriver. They normally scavenged the leftovers from the caiman's kill. The water was as refreshing as the morning dew, much more exhilarating than the shower.

I was wondering what reception I would receive from Margaret, now that she had rested and perhaps in a more receptive mood. I was beginning to suspect it was that time of month, when all women behave peculiar to their nature. I am only a novice in this field and can only surmise.

At breakfast, she was quiet and only spoke a few words to Isabel and the two of them went away, quietly down the river. I thought of following them but Ben held me back. I was completely devastated by her behaviour. I thought of all the nice things I'd told my parents about her. What would they think of her More to the point, what would they think of me? Ben told me to leave her alone for a while and only to approach her when she appeared receptive. "How will I know when she is receptive?" I asked.

"You will know. Trust me." He replied confidently.

Peter's dental assistant, Manny came up and asked if we would like to see a miracle. Ben looked at me surprisingly and asked. "Do you want to see a miracle?" "I've never seen a miracle but it would be interesting to see one." I told him.

Manny tried to explain, but it sounded too confusing, so we decided to go and see for ourselves.

As we entered the surgery, I saw Obeyo's sister, the ugly one without any incisors on both her maxilla and mandible. Manny sat her down on the dental chair and placed some wool under both her lips, she really looked like a gargoyle. Then I noticed he was mixing some dental cement and carefully putting it in the crowns that were to hold her missing teeth. With great dexterity, he pushed the appliance into her mouth and held it for a minute, then he carefully removed the excess from the gingival, a quick polish with the wool and then repeated the same on the lower. He then asked her to make an occlusion, which she did smiling. Pleased with himself, he asked her to turn around and look at us. It was a miracle. She had instantly turned from an ugly hag into one of the most beautiful women in the village. Ben was open mouthed. "I don't believe it… I just don't believe it." he kept on saying. The young lady looked in the mirror and feeling totally satisfied, turned and looked at us, in scorn. Manny was full of praise for the work he did. I didn;t know this fellow existed. I've never seen him around. Ben told me he was a loner and didn't drink anymore. Like Joseph, he kept away from alcohol to save his job.

"What is that young lady's name?" I asked Manny. "She is called Susheila. You like her?" he asked.

"Not for the reason you think" I told him.

"I can arrange for you to meet her, if you want. No one will ever know." he insisted.

"I do not want to meet her for any reason. You will get me in trouble with Margaret. Just forget I ever asked her name."

Manny was getting on my nerves and he sensed it. Immediately, he apologised and told me he did not know there were anything between Margaret and I. I instantly told him to forget the entire matter, before leaving. The thought of Margaret's peculiar behaviour returned to me. I must know exactly what it is. After all, I proposed and it was accepted, surely it gave me some grounds for wanting to know her problem. Ben noticed my silence and said. "If you are still thinking of Margaret's peculiar attitude and if it is worrying you, then I think you have the right to know the reason."

"Exactly what I was thinking, I can see we are thinking alike. Thank you Ben"

By the time we arrived home, I'd lost my nerve. I felt too nervous to go and ask of her problem. Instead, I went to Matthew and poured my heart out. He was at a loss for words and could not give me any advice on the matter. Instead he told me to ask Christine. I was too embarrassed to ask such delicate matters. It did not seem right to me. Yet the urge to get to the bottom of it, is propelling me forward.

Eventually, I took courage and confronted Christine. She told me she did not know there were any problems with us. She said she would definitely quiz her about it and let me know. She also made me promise to be patient.

I was beginning to regret the day I came to Supenaam. I had hardly accomplished the task I came for and would end up an alcoholic.

My story to my parents and all the glossiness that I'd attached to it was in tatters. I knew I had the strength to overcome disappointments. This was a more fragile situation and it needed a man with a lot of grit and experience. Grit I have. Experience, none.

CHAPTER 5
RELOCATION AND CONFRONTATION

It was a nice sunny day and there was not a speck of cloud in the sky and the wild life was enjoying it as much as we were. I saw a flock of parrots fly past and come and take fruits from the palm trees that lined the river bank. Clever, these birds. The palm is lined with sharp needles, but they wind their way through the needles to get at the fruit. The squirrel monkeys noticing them, came down to the ground, hoping for some of the fruits to reach them. They did not have to wait long. One of the parrots tugged at a nut and broke a segment from the main bunch, too heavy for it to hold, it let it drop, much to the monkeys' delight.

My thoughts were now focused on the men building the bridge, across a narrow part of the river. They were using the boulders that were in the centre to support their construction. It took nearly a day to complete. Diego drove a tractor across it to prove its structural strength. Everyone cheered, as the tractor crossed the bridge.

The cows could have been easily sent in the river, to make the crossing but the odds of all surviving the crossing, were not good. Caimans and piranha were too plentiful at that time of year and the men were not taking any chances. Now for the big drive.

The young men from Diego's village had already brought the cows to the embankment and they were driven towards the bridge. The tractor was parked in such a way, as to prevent them from going past. An hour later, they were relocated. The men were busy putting up barricades at the entrance when we left.

Diego raced back to his lodge and surveyed the empty space and then he announced that he would be rearing chickens there. Some special housing would have to be erected and he would purchase an incubator and some fine cockerels and leghorn hens and only raised chickens of good breeding. "This will be for my son." he said, as he expanded his chest and gave a mighty heave, exhaling a lung full of air.

He then turned his attention to Bell and shaking his head, he told us that she was not having a good pregnancy. He remembered meeting Dr. Louise Donovan in Georgetown and they'd expressed a desire to visit Supenaam. Ideally, they needed to go soon and give Bell a thorough check up. He invited us to see her and she did look a bit down. She was also concerned that Margaret was very upset from what she'd seen and promised never to have any children. "I tried to dissuade her from making any rash promises but she appeared to be determined in her resolve". Bell told us.

I was beginning to wonder if that was why she was so aloof when she came back. If only we could talk this through. Perhaps when she met Dr Louise Donovan she might have a new perspective on pregnancy.

Peter sent for us to attend a meeting in his office. It was a strange request, since neither of us had any business with the affairs of the hinterland. Nonetheless, I was surprised to see Amelia and Chief Warachara seated next to him. Normally, it would have been Matthew's place to sit next to Peter. We were all in the dark as to why this meeting had been called. After a brief silence, Peter spoke.

"Friends I have a problem. In Georgetown, I promised the two doctors accommodation and hospitality, whenever they decided to visit. I received a message this morning that they would like to come up as soon as the seminar is finished. That gives me three weeks to prepare. As you all know, it would have been possible, if Christine and the two ladies were not here. I cannot ask my wife to take her companions and return to the city while I accommodate strangers. I am in a dilemma and I need ideas from all of you to circumvent this headache."

I was not a full member of the community and therefore I felt it was out of my jurisdiction to comment. Both Diego and Matthew were seen to be engrossed in a deep discussion. Peter was getting impatient and urged one or the other to speak up. As usual, it was Matthew, who came up with a suggestion that he and Diego thought would solve the problem.

"Diego and I thought about this problem, some time ago, especially when the Rabbi and his friends came here and decided to stop over for a couple of days. I am sure you can remember. I gave up my part of the house to accommodate them. Then there was the other time, when the Governor wanted his visitors from London to spend a few days here and you pointed out the fact of inadequate accommodation. These two doctors are going to be here for a considerable time. Now Peter, we are always having important people coming here and wanting to stay over. Supenaam is becoming an interesting focal point for the preservation of our heritage. Before, we used to have the occasional visitor. Recently, we have more than we bargained for. With the army of workers at our disposal, we could build you a beautiful residence fit for any dignitary." Matthew told him convincingly.

"Are you sure three weeks is enough time?" Peter asked, not feeling so sure.

"A house large enough to house an army, of course I am exaggerating. It can be done if Chief Warachara and the other young men assist. Diego told me Sebastian is good at this sort of thing. He and Christine can design it and we will do the rest. We will not only build the dam house but have it painted as well. Chief Warachara is here so let's ask him" Diego suggested

Before Peter could say a word, the chief got up and spoke. "I heard all and I say Matthew my friend, will get all the help from my people for house making, I, chief of my people, promise this".

Sebastian also promised, with the help of Joseph, to do the electrical wiring and plumbing. Ben told us he would get a crew to paint the house and the ladies could see to the furnishings. All he needed was the material to start.

"That's not a problem." Peter told us, then he explained that four of the paddle boats could be fitted with outboard engines and go to Ituni, where there is a saw mill and bring as much material for starters. "I know it will take two days at least for the return journey, If we have enough to start, I am sure the boats can bring more materials before we actually need it." Everyone was nodding approval.

The boats were immediately dispatched and workers were preparing the ground for the foundation to be laid. Within hours, the area looked like an industrial site. Sebastian was keeping a close eye on the design of the building, before laying the foundations. Eventually, they were laid just in time. The boats arrived with all that was necessary, for work to begin. It was turning out to be an enormous two storied house with towers on both ends, with elevation that makes it look like a mock Tudor.

I was useless at this sort of thing and soon got bored. I drifted off towards the river with my own personal thoughts on my mind.

Two weeks later, the house was nearing completion. Christine and Margaret went to the city for the furnishings, while Sebastian was doing the electricity and plumbing. I could watch him work all day and never get bored. It was fascinating watching Ben on his back, waiting for instructions. He was doing very well, for an enormous man.

Finally an army of men were busy painting the outside. Ben had his own army inside doing the same. They finished with two days to spare. It was time for the ladies to do their bit and they did not need us around. Occasionally, they would send for Ben to help with something or the other. This exercise was done with military planning and it was Matthew, who oversaw it all. It turned out to be the biggest house in the compound.

Christine had a name for it, but she decided to keep it a secret, until it was ready to be occupied.

The priest arrived for his Sunday sermon and was completely taken aback by this huge new building. Matthew explained it all to him. Then his eyes opened wider than usual and he said. "This edifice will have to be blessed. It will be my contribution."

Chief Warachara objected. He told the priest. "This is my land, I will bless this house, our people's way. You bless after." Oliver could not deny the chief his wish.

Sebastian had gone to collect the guests and we were waiting patiently for their arrival. It was getting dark. Peter suggested we go inside and celebrate.

This was a community where there are no cinemas or night clubs, not a proper bar, as you would find in the city. The only way to pass the time and enjoy yourself, was chatting, making jokes and sipping malt whisky. Matthew had a record player, but his style of music was classical. He loved his Mozart, Sibelius's Finlandia, which I heard, for the first time, and agreed, when he told me the pleasure it always brought him, when he was alone here or Brahms Hungarian dances was another of his favourites. Popular music was out of his league.

We were having breakfast when we heard the plane landing. We rushed down in time to see Warachara and his men bringing our visitors ashore. They effectively formed two lines, as the doctors walked between, Louise told her husband. "They are treating us like royalties, simply smile and for God's sake do not wave."

Lunch will be served in the Great House, as it became temporarily known. Christine's taste for fine furnishings was immaculate. The hand carved dining chairs stood out as a centre piece for comment. Its beauty did not go unnoticed. She then unveiled the name for the house, written in black and white calligraphy the name "TUDOR GRANGE." Isabel went and fetched a magnum of champagne and gave it to Ben to uncork before lunch was served.

The two doctors were very surprised, the priest did not offer to say grace before meals. Doctor Louise asked his reason. He merely replied that not all of us were Christians and sometimes it can be offensive to those who are not.

After lunch, we sat on the veranda, taking in the cool air from the river. Matthew told the visitors that he had those two towers built for two reasons; first, to keep the insects away during the rainy season, secondly and more importantly, was the constant flow of cool air from the river. "It is nature's air conditioning."

"And where am I sleeping Matt?" Doctor Louise asked. "Right at the top my dear." he replied.

The doctors were busy with their work for the next few days and Margaret was asked to assist Dr. Louise. This was a ploy by Christine to extinguish her fear of pregnancy. She paid special attention when Bell was examined and still had that expression of fear on her face. It was time for me to confront her about our future. This uncertainty simply could not go on. Only then would I be sure whether it was real or a figment of my intoxicated imagination

Susheila came to the house to ask the doctor to come to the village and examine one of the ladies. The doctor told her she would be there soon. As she walked away, the doctor told Matthew that the young lady would not have problems with the birth of her children.

"Why is that Louise? How can you tell without examining her?" He asked.

"Look at her hips, they are rather wide. It is a known fact that women with wide hips have trouble free births." She told him.

At this point Margaret started crying and held on to Louise for comfort.

"What is the matter, dear? Why are you so distressed?" Louise asked.

Sobbingly she said "I do not have wide hips." Her sobbing became more intense. I decided to take the opportunity and question her about our future. Matthew intervened and told me not to. I had a great respect for the man, so I decided not to pursue the matter for now. It always appeared that whenever I wanted to sort out my personal life, someone or the other, steps in and stops me. This was getting more irritating each time.

In the morning, I followed some of the men who were going to the corral. They told me that a caiman had broken through the fences and had taken one of the calves.

This was disturbing news for Diego. He was speeding down the track on his tractor with a pronounced look of worry on his face. I hitched a ride and we went off. Ben was running to catch up but Diego was in no mood to wait for him.

In the river, we saw the calf's legs in the air and the caiman was nowhere to be seen. Diego lassoed it and dragged it on the embankment. He then tied the carcass to a palm tree and waited. We sat there for hours; eventually the reptile came out of the water and headed for its meal. Diego aimed the rifle at its head and paused for a few minutes.

I knew he did not want to kill it and waited to see what his next action would be. Ben told him to hold his fire. He waited for the caiman to start twisting a chunk of meat from the calf and while it was swallowing it, Ben jumped on its back and an almighty struggle began.

Ben shouted to Diego to throw him a rope and wrapped it around the reptile's snout. I helped Diego and Ben to lift it up onto the trailer and took it five miles upriver and set it free. I was beginning to feel like a zoo keeper.

"Will that stop it from coming again?" I asked

"It may not stop it but it will certainly have a second thought. He looked rather distressed when we set it free." Diego told me. "We will have to reinforce the fences and put a guard around the clock for a week or so. Any attempt for a similar incursion will be met with a severe punishment."

The excitement brought the ladies down the river. They were extremely disappointed at missing the wrestling match with Ben and the caiman. It was refreshing to learn from Michael the psychologist, that animals contrary to our thinking, can reason within themselves and also understand what can threaten their survival. He also assured Diego that it would be a foolhardy caiman to return for a similar treatment. I must see for myself what happens in the next week or so I thought to myself, before I was convinced that a reptile has the capacity to reason.

The ladies' disappointment from missing the wrestling match was soon rewarded with the arrival of the chiefs, Warachara and Obeyo. They and their followers were congregating by the river bank to perform a ceremony dedicated to the spirits of the forest. It was a colourful display of dancing and mock sacrifices.

One very young man was tied by his hands and feet, with a rope and thrown in the river. He was then dragged very slowly, his body submerged for a long time. I was fearful he would drown. Matthew assured me he would be fine after the ordeal. He also informed me that he never understood the reason for this type of ritual and the chiefs never told him.

Then came a tricky bit, Matthew was not happy when they stripped Amelia to her waist and garlanded her with many necklaces of flowers covering her breasts. Then they danced erotically around her, for quite a few minutes. Matthew was getting red in the face and only Diego prevented him from stopping the ceremony.

When it was finished, she put her top on and ran towards Matthew, who then cuddled her. She did not look as terrified as I thought she would. Then it was Susheila's turn. This turned it to be even more erotic. They undressed her completely, placed garlands around her waist and neck. This was deliberately done, to conceal her femaleness. Then tied her hands and pulled her up a tree.

She looked down smiling at the men below, then one by one, they spun her round and tried to kiss the bottom of her feet. She probably felt tickled by this and kicked and giggled.

The two chiefs then knelt under her, uttering chants in their language. The rest of the men started singing a haunting song and then prostrate themselves before the chiefs. When it was over, they brought her down and she danced with the same eroticism, in which the ceremony seemed to be following.

She was then ceremoniously dressed as a tribal Princess and allowed to choose the man she wanted to be bonded with. There was a bit of outcry from some of the other men. It seemed that there were more suitors who wished to be bonded with her and since she did not give the others a chance to lay their claim, they felt cheated.

The chiefs intervened. She was then led into the forest, holding the hand of her chosen one with the rest of the men following.

Matthew told me that the twenty five years he had been Commissioner he had never seen anything like it and wondered when it all started. It was Diego who told him that such a ceremony only happens every four years and as far as he remembered, it always occurred in the forest. Why they did it on the river bank was a mystery to him. The ladies were very pleased with the display and cheered with rapture.

I said to Matthew. "You always accuse me of saying these people are primitive. Do you honestly think that was a civilized display of a solemn ritual?"

It was the priest who chose to answer that question. "I can say from their point of view, it was a civilized performance. I remember in the early days when I first visited Supenaam. Matthew had only recently been appointed Commissioner and I tried to introduce Christianity. Everything went well, until I was preparing for mass. When it was over, they stormed out of the church and ran to their villages. The following Sunday no one turned up, so Matthew and I went to investigate. It turned out that they felt the wafer and wine I administered was actually the body and blood of Christ.

Now in their minds they would call us cannibals and that is exactly the word the chief used. It took weeks of explaining that it was not actually the body or blood of Christ but a symbol of it. Reluctantly, they started drifting in. There is another reason they came back, it was not for my sermon. I doubt whether they understood what I was saying. It was for the goodies I gave them after the service. I hope that explains it all."

"I am not convinced totally of what you said. I think you and Matthew are protecting these people. From what, and for what reason, I am not sure." I replied.

Matthew was definitely upset with my reply. He looked red in the face and turning to me, in a bit of anger then said with a bit of seriousness, "I know you chaps from the city are so embroiled with your so called civilized way of life. You ought to see the Berbicians demonstrating civilized behaviour, a people with real humanity and culture. It is a pity I am not in a position to invite you there. You would see what living is really about."

Peter stepped in and told me that Matthew does have the privilege to invite whom he chooses. He knows my parents will always welcome him and any of his friends. He beckoned the rest and as they assembled around him he told us.

"Matthew wanted to host a Berbician hospitality for the benefit of our guests, especially to prove a point to our biographer. I think it is a wonderful idea. Not only will it serve to prove how hospitable Berbicians claim to be but it also gives an insight of life in the ancient county. It is not possible to take all of you to Berbice, so I suggest since we cannot get all of you there, how about bringing Berbice to Supenaam."

"You are not serious Peter, bringing Berbice to Supenaam?" Matthew exclaimed.

"Not the entire county. I mean bringing our life style here. It will also give the chiefs and their people something to talk about, for generations." Peter informed him.

"What a jolly good idea. You are a genius." Diego joined in and shook Peter's hand enthusiastically. "I suppose you are going to tell us how you would do this."

It was Christine's turn to join in. "I will ask Peter's mother to bring Beda, her new maid, and some of the men and women from the village to help with the cooking, and also to bring their music with them. We will have a party as we never had before."

I never attended any of their Berbice parties but I can imagine it. I heard a bit of the wild Berbicians and to see it first hand is something worth waiting for.

As usual it was Ben who asked. "Can I help the men with the cooking?"

"Absolutely, I know your reason" Matthew added.

"So it is settled then?" Peter concluded.

"When are you proposing to have this grand occasion Peter?" I asked. I told him I was planning to go further inland to meet some of the other tribes to find out more about them and their way of life.

"It will be next weekend. Would that fit in your itinerary?"
"Sure."

"Who will take you further inland sonny boy?" Matthew inquired.

"The priest" I told him.

"The priest!" he exclaimed in horror. "The priest could not find his way to a cold stream. Taking you to Kakaburi is no easy trek. Ben and I will take you there, when you are ready."

Everyone appeared very excited with Peter and his grand banquet. Especially Matthew and Ben. All except me.

The crowd started milling back to the Great House. I decided to linger by the river to compose and comfort myself. I noticed Amelia standing all alone, not far from where I was and was looking in my direction. I wondered how her English had progressed. The best way to find out is to have a conversation. I hailed her name and she came running. It was if she was waiting for an invitation.

She said "Hello" and I replied by asking. "You can speak English now." She nodded and asked what is my name in jerky English, but understandable enough. Then she pressed her index finger on my chest and asked. "You like me?" "Yes I like you. Do you like me?" She nodded vehemently and smiling. Then she asked "You go to big party" I told her I would and would be happy to see her dance. "Me know not to dance. Me not invited. Big Peter not say to Amelia you come to big party."

"Of course you are invited. You did not see him go to everyone and say you are welcome to my party, did you?" She shook her head and smiled. Then said "Me come to party and you teach me to dance…?"

"Yes I will teach you to dance." She then ran away leaving me standing all alone. I was happy with this meeting. It made my trouble vanished temporarily. I needed to join the others and take some of that lovely malt. It was then, that I thought if Margaret did not want to meet my parents, I could introduce Amelia instead. It may appear dishonest. I did not want my parents to be disappointed. I would have to think of a decent way of doing it without embarrassing anyone.

When I arrived there, Ben was standing with an empty glass in his hand and held it out to me.

"Are you not drinking?" I asked.

"Of course I am drinking. This glass is for you. I saw you chatting up that young lass and I thought you would need a drink. What were you telling her?" he asked, curious to know all that was happening.

As the crowd thinned out, I saw Margaret with Isabel, standing under the silk cotton tree. For the second time in a week, I had to dismiss Isabel from Margaret's company and for the second time, she looked rudely at me and as she turned, lifted the back of her skirt and sucked at her teeth. It is a definite sign of discourtesy and the ultimate insult.

"You ought to teach that servant girl to be more respectful. Or, I may have to let Christine know about it." I told her.

She told me she would sort out her manners and promised me it would never happen again. Then she asked, "What is it you want of me?" I told her how I felt towards her and also that I was confused about her attitude of pregnancy. She placed her finger on my lips and told me that she would never marry anyone, because she never wanted to be pregnant. I told her she need not get pregnant, as there are ways of stopping it. She looked at me horrified and asked.

"Are you saying I use those funny stuff to prevent myself getting pregnant? What will my priest say about that? What will God say about that? How can I go to confession and tell my priest that I have sinned by preventing any pregnancy? I am sorry Andrew, I have made up my mind."

It was my turn to place my finger on her lips and tell her. "Margaret, why not allow Doctor Louise to examine you and see if you are capable of having children. Not all women can have children. I am not saying something is wrong with you. All I am asking, is for you to put yourself to be examined. If you are not alright, then I will accept what you have decided and not to hold it against you and we can still be friends. Is that too much to ask?"

"I don't think so. Yet I am concerned about the examination. Are you sure it will not interfere with my anatomy?"

"I am positive of it. The Doctor will tell you the same"

She agreed to have the examination. Before she left, I reminded her about Isabel's rude behavior and made her promise me that Christine would be told. This, she promised and kissed my cheeks.

Ben must have seen us talking for a while and the inquisitive character he is, came to ask what it was all about. I simply told him it was confidential. He did not look too happy as he went his way.

That evening, we sat in Tudor Grange and Peter outlined his plans for the great party. He told Sebastian to collect Andrew McIntosh and Isme from Skeldon and then collect my parents and any other guest, they may want to bring. It all seemed a lot of preparations for a party. Then I must remember Peter's word. It was to be a party like no other.

My mind was at ease and I deserved it. Margaret's promise to have the examination had a lot to do with it and I was grateful.

My parents were be coming for the party and I had promised to show them my bride to be when they got there. I was worried what would happen if she was not capable of producing children without any problem? Who would I show to my parents, as my bride to save me from disgrace? The thought of presenting Amelia was ludicrous. I had to dismiss it completely from my mind. What sanity came over me to think of it in the first place is beyond explanation. I simply had to face up to the truth and I was sure my parents would understand.

The big party is a week away and anything could happen in that time. I decided not to have any drink for the rest of the evening. I would not allow it to be my mode of escape. I sat there, watching them sipping away and each hour that passed, their voices became more and more slurred and the nonsense that came out was unbelievable. I thought to myself, I must be like that when I was intoxicated. I remembered I was only a casual drinker before I came here and eventually got caught up with their style of sipping malt at every occasion. This would have to stop, I told myself.

CHAPTER 6

MURDER AND BROKEN HEARTS

I was awakened in the middle of the night by a lot of shouting. I could hear Peter and Matthew enquiring of the noise. I rushed out to see Ben, carrying one of the rangers in his arms, towards the square and laid him down on the long table. He was bleeding profusely, with a deep wound across his chest.

Doctor Louise was asked to come and take a look. She appeared with her emergency kit and began cleaning the wound. It revealed a deep incision on the left side. We were assured it was not a life threatening wound. She patched him up and as he sat up, he revealed what had happened.

"I was invited by one of Peter's subordinates, to come and help him investigate illegal logging in the Camaroo region. I had seen this part of the forest before and knew exactly who was responsible. He told me. He sent Ben to look for Jango, who was their most senior ranger. We together, went to look and found his crew cutting a greenheart. Jango immediately challenged them for their illegal activities. They fired a shot and the subordinate fell dead in front of us. The men looked startled, when they discovered they had killed a ranger. They then tried to shoot us, so I ran with my machete in hand, to counter attack. Then, one of the men tried to slash me across the chest. Jango hit him very hard on the head and he fell, the other men became afraid and started running. Jango shot one of them in the leg with an arrow. As he fell the others stopped and lifted their arms in surrender thinking their friend was shot with a poisoned arrow."

Ben interrupted him and asked. "Was the arrow poisoned?"

"No sir, we never use poisoned arrows in self defence. Retired Commissioner Matthew told us that."

"Quite right, it is illegal. Where has Jango gone?"

"He told me to stay here and he would be back as quickly as he could. I think some other rangers are helping him arrest the loggers."

Back at base, I made the ranger as comfortable as I could, while I waited for first aid to arrive.

The ranger then asked. "Can I lie down for a minute sir? I am feeling a bit faint."

I told him to rest and asked Ben to bring him some brandy. It is the kind of favour Ben likes to do. He came back with two glasses of brandy. The other one was of course for him. "Here's to your quick recovery." Ben said to him as he downed his drink

We heard talking in the dark. It soon became clear, that Jango and two of the other rangers were bringing in the rest of the loggers, their hands tied behind their backs.

Matthew jumped to his feet and exclaimed. "I know this bastard. I had to punish him a few years ago for his illegal activities. So you are back to your old tricks again Mr. Franklin? This time, you are not going with just a fine and confiscation of your equipment. You are going to be tried for murder and attempted murder." He then turned to Peter, his face as red as a lobster, "Well say something Peter. You are the Commissioner."

"I was waiting for you to finish. I think we ought to lock them up in the tool shed until the morning. I have been asking for a secured building for this kind of eventuality, but the Governor insisted we improvised. That tool shed is not very strong. I will have to put a guard on duty."

"I will provide him with a shotgun in case they try to escape." Matthew said, then added. "Murder is a very serious offence. That Franklin is a ruthless son of a bitch. He knows I mean business when it comes to deforestation."

"I did not kill your ranger. Neither did these two men you are holding illegally."

"The law will determine who did what." Peter told him in no uncertain tone of voice. "Lock him up."

We all retired leaving the sentry with his task. In the morning, it was like a dream until I saw the sentry standing guard and shivering with cold. I could not imagine me running in the jungle, with a machete in my hand to attack loggers. I must have been mesmerised by events. I called Peter who immediately relieved the guard.

Whatever happened next would depend on the Commissioner. He would conduct an interim investigation to ascertain if there were any charges to be filed, against the three in custody. It would be interesting to see what happened next.

Peter asked Diego and Matthew to assist him, in dealing with the three men. Diego suggested that Jango send for the rangers involved in the incident, and that they discuss what really happened.

It sounded fair to me. After all, no one knew who exactly shot the ranger and they did surrender in the end, albeit only when they thought they would be shot with poisoned arrows.

Peter suggested to Matthew and Diego that it was best to send the matter to the Crown Prosecutor's Office for consideration. It was a very serious offence for them to deal with. They both agreed. The three men would have to stay confined until such time.

We all joined in and constructed a more secure accommodation, for the prisoners with a bucket and temporary shower included.

That evening, Peter sat in council with his rangers to make arrangements for the funeral and for compensation to be paid to the widow. She was sitting next to Jango and looked intently at Peter, as he spoke. As soon as she heard the word compensation, her face lit up. It appeared to me that these people take life as they get it. I suppose they feel it is the way of the gods they worshipped, the same way as they felt about their forest and its animals.

The meeting ended with the woman getting forty dollars compensation and Jango was to go to Georgetown and make a report, something he had done many times in the past.

It was a very short meeting. After which, we all went about our usual tasks. I was still trying to find the appropriate time to get both Peter and Matthew together, for a joint interview. One or the other always seemed to be engaged, when the other was free. I was sure

I would find the opportune time for my interview. My editor in Georgetown was getting anxious that I had spent nearly a month, without forwarding anything for him to read. I kept making excuses, which he accepted for now, but I was going to be in serious trouble if something was not sent soon and I meant, very soon.

One afternoon I saw Margaret down by the river, in company with Louise. I guess she was in consultation with what I'd proposed. She saw me and waved. I thought this must be a good sign. I promised that I would allow her to come to me, when it was all sorted. So far, I had kept my promise. I trusted she would keep her side of the bargain. We kissed and I was certain she has good news for me, but would not divulge anything. She told me to wait for another day, as she wanted to be certain in her mind that, whatever she tells me, will be the truth. I had no other choice but to adhere to her wishes.

One morning I was having a lonely stroll by the river. It is interesting what animals and birds can be seen drinking. I was never a nature lover but this place had a magic like no other. This brief encounter with nature was interrupted when Ben decided to join me. He was beaming with delight. Of what, I could not tell. I knew him well enough to know when he was thinking of something exciting.

"What's up Ben?" I asked, as he put his arm on my shoulder. "I was thinking of throwing these dull days away and do something really exciting." he replied. Then, he started to explain. "You don't know this, but when I was in Berbice, on my last trip that is, the villagers took me to a bush cook." He was beaming just thinking about it.

"Who is a bush cook?" I asked.

"It is something you do in the bush. Cooking a nice meal in a pot, under a blazing fire and getting almost everything you need from your surroundings."

"Diego will tell you it's great fun. But we need a lot of people to really enjoy it."

"Well, we could invite the doctors; there was Matthew and Peter, Diego, Bell and her son, Sebastian, and Joseph. And of course, the ladies, if they want to join us." I suggested.

"We will do this as a prelude to the big party Peter is planning. I was thinking of inviting Susheila she would be a good companion for Amelia." Ben told me.

"Why do we need Susheila, Amelia can find her own feet among us. She speaks good English. Is there an ulterior motive behind this suggestion Ben?"

"Not exactly" he replied sheepishly.

Ben left me alone and he hurriedly ran off to tell the good news to the others. I felt someone hug me from behind. I noticed the hands and knew immediately it was Margaret; I turned around as she released her grip.

Ben realized that it was time to leave us alone.

It was still misty over the river. I looked right in her eyes and she was smiling. She said she could not sleep and saw me walking so she decided to join me. I pressed my lips on her and she responded immediately and with an intensity I did not expect.

I responded and my hands went walk about, she did not mind and I thought I might as well try my luck at the ultimate goal. With the mist as a shield, I was ever so surprised when she allowed me to partly undress her and laid her on the embankment. I could hear her heavy breathing matching mine. The ground was ever so damp. We did not seem to mind.

When it was over, I noticed how profusely, she was perspiring and panting. I cuddled her and we lay unashamed, not caring if someone came up and saw us. Then, she told me the most extraordinary story, a young woman was able to diverge. She started by asking. "Can you tell if I was a virgin or not?"

To be quite honest, I was not thinking of anything at that moment. I told her I could not honestly say, as I'd never had any encounter of this nature, with any woman.

"I must let you know that I love you and wish to marry you. But first, you must know the truth. I do not want any accusations hurled at me later."

I was puzzled by this remark. It seemed a mystery to me. I asked her to continue. She then told me that, after meeting Doctor Louise and her secret was exposed, she felt it only fair to tell me the whole truth. I was getting impatient and urged her to tell me all of it, without any interruptions. Then, she continued hanging her head and toying with her fingers.

"There is a certain married man who fell in love with me. I harbour no such feelings for him. He keeps pestering me to run away with him to Barbados. I wanted to tell him that he is asking the impossible. I am a catholic and my father will die of shame if I should do such a thing. It would be futile. The respect I have for him is rapidly evaporating. I assume that as time went by, this love became stronger, especially when he sees me chatting with his wife. I made a vow that no man would have my virginity before marriage. Two weeks ago, when I accompanied Peter and Christine to the city, I was left alone in the house. Christine went to see the Rabbi about Elizabeth. The man in question was no stranger to the house. I was alone. I looked nervously at him. I was never alone with him before. He sat on the verandah facing the sea and asked me to join him. I told him I had things to do, so I went in the bedroom, he followed me and locked the door. I was too terrified to scream. The next thing I knew he was kissing me. The next thing I knew, we both fell on the bed and he had his way. He calmly took a drink before leaving. I've never felt so dirty in my life; I started blaming myself for my foolish behavior. I should have never gone in that bedroom I asked myself several questions; did I unconsciously do that to encourage him? Did my frustration force me to do what I did? Or was it sheer ignorance or naiveness. To this day, I cannot find the real answer. One thing's for sure, I did not want any man to have my virginity, other than the man I will one day marry. I was still crying, when Both Peter and Christine came home. I told them what had happened and Peter promised to kill him, if he caught him. Then, he had a thought "I will get him arrested for rape: that should teach him a lesson he will never forget." I told him I would be very angry with him if he was to do that. He looked at me in amazement.

I said to Peter, "I know you mean well, Peter. Think of the shame I will face. I can never walk with my head held high and everyone will point a finger and say she is no virgin. I knew Doctor Louise will know the truth. I am thankful he did not make me pregnant. I guess Jesus heard my prayer. I am telling you this because I wanted you to know the truth. I was deeply embarrassed to speak about it. I was no virgin as I claimed and I did not want it to come from her and expose me as a liar. I do love you and I am willing to marry you if you still want me. I realise in hind sight, I may have caused you a lot of heart ache. I could not help myself. This feeling inside of me was like the fire of hell and doing what I did was the only way to extinguish it not to hurt you. Turn away from me and I would not blame you."

I was, as expected, shattered. She did not shed any tears, as I expected. In my heart, I felt pity. I wished I knew who this man was so I could slap him in the face and demand satisfaction, as gentlemen did in the days of chivalry. Those days are long gone and I am left with a dilemma. I needed time to think and to reflect on these events. I told her quite gently that she must allow me time to discuss this with my conscience and argue the pros and cons in great lengths. I would then stick to the winning side of this debate.

She nodded, got dressed and left. I did not know what to think. Must I respect her honesty? If she had not tell me I would not have known any difference. Was it her honesty or her conscience? Fortunately for me, I met Doctor Louise and asked her what her findings were when she examined Margaret. Doctor Louise looked at me in horror and almost shouted. "You expect me to tell you my findings of a woman I examined in confidence! Andrew, you may be a journalist, but you are naïve. You do not have any idea of the confidentiality that exists between a patient and her doctor. I am downright appalled by your behaviour."

She was so angry, I thought she would hit me. Instead, I apologised vehemently, until she calmed down and in the most gentle voice she said. "I know how much you love her and these things must be discussed. Whatever she told you, must be the truth and if you really love her, you will love her with all her faults. We are not all blameless in our lives. Some have sinister secrets and when I say that, believe me, I know what I am saying."

I was grateful for her advice, perhaps it would help me decide my future. Oh God! How I wished it would come right for me. Another man has picked my cherry and I must live with that.

I thought of Ben and the crazy advice he sometimes gave. Yet, despite his boyish thinking, I must admire him for some of the home spun philosophy and advice he has on hand.

I thought of his bush cooking and it sounded a great idea to me. At that moment, anything to distract me from my woes would have been welcomed.

I had to dash and see what progress he was making. At the same time, I did not want to see Margaret right now. It was best we are left alone and discover what our deliberations have left us. I was beginning to feel a bit sad for her. I knew then, there were possibilities for forgiveness. I must also think of my pride. I kept thinking, if we were married when the man who has deprived me, see us together, he may well have thoughts of how stupid I was, to marry a used vessel. But these things are in my imagination. I must for the sake of sanity, think clearly and constructively.

Although I was a European, living in the colony, since childhood, I was thinking like the locals. My parents would not care a farthing that she was not the wholesome woman I thought she was. So I must stop thinking like a bloody colonial and think positively. Lucky for me, I caught up with Ben. He was smiling as soon as he saw me and stretched his hand in friendship and told me all is set for the big cook up.

It was a sunny Saturday morning. I had a feeling the birds and squirrel monkeys suspected something was afoot. The birds were hovering and chirping in excitement. The monkeys were chasing each other up and down the trees and making a nuisance with their bickering. Ben threw a stick in mock aggression, at them, careful not to hurt any of them. They looked at him for a while and dashed up the tree, screeching at his intervention. One brave enough, came down and stood on its hind legs and looked at Ben in defiance. Ben went to pick it up, but it soon raced up the tree.

At this point, everyone interested in this cook up were congregated by the embankment. Bell had a basket of something and Diego was carrying a gun, while his son had a fishing rod. I also noticed Sebastian, with what I suspected to be a box of wines and malt. After all, there wouldn't be much fun in just cooking what you got from the forest.

Margaret was with Doctor Louise, Amelia and Susheila. Matthew, as expected, was in a small group consisting of Peter, Joseph, Christine and Elizabeth. We went on board the plane and soon it was airborne. An hour's flight brought us to a lake; it must be the same one from where we released the jaguar, not so long ago. I wondered if it was anywhere nearby. I would have loved to see it stalking. Instead, all we saw was a few peccaries. As soon as they heard us, they scampered in the forest, leaving a trail of dust behind.

Some of the men were busy collecting dead tree trunks and Susheila and Amelia were clearing an area, where the cooking would be done.

Diego asked whether we preferred fish or meat and said the fish would cook much quicker and if we were really hungry, we should go for the fish. Everyone agreed on the fish.

He and his son went about that task. I noticed they tied a piece of foil around the hooks and did not use any other bait. They skimmed the hooks, just below the surface. They were at it for some time and I thought we would have to settle for meat. But, in an instant, Young Diego shouted and a very large fish was on the hook. His father came to assist removing it and chopped its head to prevent it jumping back in the water.

It was a very large fish indeed, weighing about nine or ten pounds. After they caught

about a dozen, they called a halt and the ladies went about cooking them. It was a fish the locals called, hymara, A bit like halibut, only a bit more tender.

Then the master chef, Ben, took the pieces and cooked them over a slow fire. He had earlier tied the wine with palm fibers and sunk it in the lake to be cooled. In the meantime, we were sipping our malt, no ice this time.

I watched as Ben cooked the fish and placed them on a banana leaf. He changed into his swimming gear and went in the cold water for a dip. They all followed. I was told that it was not very safe to swim in these lakes, as they are connected with some of the larger rivers and arapaima could prove a threat. I ignored that caution, went head first in the lake, in my underpants. The ladies cheered as I caught up with Margaret and chased her to the other end of the lake. We came ashore and kissed for everyone to see. There was more cheering.

Then I heard someone say, "Go on take her in the bush and have some fun." We laughed and ignored the suggestion. We looked in each other's eyes and knew straight away that everything was going to be alright. We swam back to join the others and I toasted our future with a very large glass of wine. I was in a buoyant mood and all my troubles seemed to have vanished.

I turned to Ben and accused him of lying. "What?" he growled and approached me menacingly. I raised my hand and explained that he told me this bush cook was to be from everything you can get from the forest. It's not a bush cook but a cock up.

The only thing I saw we collected from the forest was the fish and herbs. Not even the coconut, which we could have had from those trees not far away. They would have made a contribution to our collection.

"Well," replied Ben with nonchalance "who would risk climbing a coconut tree? Those things are as tall as mountains."

The meal was excellent. The fish was superbly cooked. I had never had anything like it, in my life and would not mind having it again.

I must remember to thank Ben for his bush cook. It served so many purposes; Camaraderie, appeasement and a delicious meal.

On our way back, we noticed Warachara and his men, scattered from the embankment and into the forest. Peter became concerned. As soon as we landed, words were sent to Warachara to come immediately to see the Commissioner.

He came with three of his men and told Peter that the men escaped, while they were away and had taken Diego's chickens and headed East. He also said he was only aware, when they abducted two young girls from the village. Their screaming was heard, but it was too late to prevent them running away. Fortunately, we found the girls unharmed, not very far away. He also said they were heading towards cold stream.

"That could be unfortunate for us." Matthew said and then added, "If they discovered that there is gold there, it will mean endless problems for us. We must find these bastards pretty soon."

"I could not agree with you more." Peter added and he suggested that they take the aircraft and search the area thoroughly.

"I don't see how that will help." Ben told them. "They can hear the plane coming from a mile away and hide from our view."

"That may be so, but we can see the tracks they made and the direction they are going. If it is possible to land the plane at cold stream, then we have a chance of catching them. I think I can land the plane at cold stream but it will be tight." Sebastian assured us.

"We did see fresh tracks, but I don't know in what direction cold stream lies. It was only when Matthew said that they were heading there that I knew. As Sebastian said, it will be a tight landing." Ben continued.

The rangers dispersed in the forest and we waited anxiously by the stream. I looked in the water but couldn't see any gold. I asked Ben where the gold was. He was rude in his reply.

"It's none of your darn business. This is a secret place and it will stay that way, even if I have to kill the murderers with my bare hands." He then gave me one of his boyish smiles, winked, and asked. "You want to see gold?"

"Yes" I replied, eagerly awaiting his next words. "Get in the water and feel at the bottom, you will find gold alright." I jumped in the stream and immediately let out an ear piercing scream. Everyone turned around and looked at me and shook their heads. It turned out that it was Ben's regular habit of shocking visitors, when they tried to claim a nugget.

Hesitantly, I went in again, gritting my teeth and feverishly searching the bottom, every handful I brought up were pebbles. I tried over and over again, without success. The cold water was getting me blue.

Ben saw this and pulled me out and rubbed me violently to activate circulation. Then he calmly went in and produced a couple of nuggets and showed them to me. I was flabbergasted. I heard them speak of it, but always thought it was bush men's talk. Now I had seen it for the first time, I was convinced. I then asked Ben who else knew of it. He told me most visitors were brought here and given a nugget before they leave.

"Do the rangers know of it?" I asked.

"Of course they do. We can trust them. They have pledged allegiance to the Commissioner and respect Matthew like a god. They will never betray us. They would rather die." Ben told me, with reverence in his voice.

While we were talking, we heard voices. Harsh words were being exchanged and then we saw them, the rangers with the prisoners. Matthew pointed his rifle at them and swore that any attempt to escape and they would be dead. Their hands and feet were tied and they were carried aboard the plane.

We stopped off at Supenaam to allow the rangers to go about their work. Peter went in his office and made a phone call. He came back and assured us that a police escort would be waiting for them, at his residence. I was only too happy to leave this place, albeit briefly and to see my beloved Georgetown from the air.

On our arrival a police escort was waiting, which surprised me. The police are normally very lax in their duties. I suppose they have to be more alert, when dealing with the Commissioner.

While formalities were taking place, Ben went in the cabinet and found an opened bottle of malt. He called Sebastian and invited him for a drink. Sebastian appeared concerned for a minute and said to Ben, "You cannot go in the Commissioner's cabinet and take his drink without asking."

Ben poked his finger in Sebastian's chest and said, "Look here friend, in this house I can do anything. If I want a drink, I take it. If I want to sleep, I know where to go." There was a cocky look about him, as he spoke.

"What gives you such privilege?" I asked.

"It's a long story and you would not be interested. Now, do you want to have a drink or not?" he asked.

I would be very interested to know what gave him such privileges in the Commissioner's residence. I guessed I would have to wait when I interview them back in Supenaam.

The chief of police arrived with two of his juniors and took statements from each of us. "I know you." he said to me. "You are that journalist with the Chronicle. What are you doing in the jungle?"

I told him the purpose of being there. He then tried to sell me some tickets for the Officers' Ball. I declined and told him I would give a donation when I returned, as I did not have any money on me right then. He looked pleased. They were then offered a drink before departing.

I wanted to visit my parents, just to see how they were coping, in my absence. Matthew told me that time was not on my side. They must return to Supenaam because Peter was behind with his report and the Governor would not be too pleased. Peter may be the second most important official in the colony, but that does not excuse him from any tardiness.

His comments gave me an idea. When Peter comes to town I could accompany him and take time to see my parents. My father is a retired minister with the Mission Chapel Church. He decided to remain in British Guiana because of the climate and as he always said that a minister's job was never done. The Governor, in order to supplement his small pension, made him a Justice of the Peace, which carried a stipend.

CHAPTER 7
POLITICS ARRIVED IN SUPENAAM

Matthew came in the office and interrupted an interview I was having with Peter. He asked to be excused and told me that he needed to speak urgently with Peter. He then reminded Peter of the scholarship, the four of them gave to the sons of the villagers. Peter nodded in agreement "I think we have sown the seeds of trouble and I mean big trouble. Three of them Sattar, Narine and Ali have asked the Governor's permission to come up here and promote their idea for a free British Guiana. They are thinking of creating a constituent and to give the right to vote to the people of the interior."

"Is it such a bad idea? Remember the thing we call democracy? Is it not their right to be given the freedom to vote for the person they see as fit and proper to represent them in the Legislative Assembly?"

"I am not saying they should not have the right to vote. What I am trying to say is, that they have no idea of politics, no idea whatsoever. Democracy can be dangerous to those that don't understand its full meaning. These people are best left alone, to live as they have lived for thousands of years. I ask you do not pollute their honest and sincere way of life with the dirtiness of politics. I mean it Peter."

"Why don't we call a meeting of the chiefs and ask their opinion." I suggested.

"You keep out of this. You are an outsider." Matthew said to me. I felt humbled by this remark. Peter came to my rescue by telling him "You will not be denied your god like stature you enjoy here. The people will still love you and they will love you all the more, if you were to explain to them, what is involved. This way, you will be giving them the opportunity to decide for themselves and not be dictated to, by you or me."

"I guess you are right." Matthew conceded. He then went on to say "Some people live a better life when they are governed with a firm hand. Politics has a habit of corrupting people with false hopes and promises. When they fail dismally to fulfill their end of the bargain, they blame others. I do not want to see this happen, not while I am alive."

"It is better you see what's happening when you are alive and to try and fix it if things were to go askew. You will always have my respect and love. It is because of you I became the richest man in the colony, not that it matters. You were like a father to me for most of my teenage life and well into maturity. You supported me in every way that saw me clear all the obstacles in life and to make myself the man I am today. I have not forgotten your insistence on your friend, the former Governor, to instate me as Commissioner. You must come to terms with the modern world and reality, I must tell you this Matthew, I took this post not only to satisfy you, but it gives me the prestige I always wanted. Surely you must remember the days when I was stranded in this wilderness with no sight of a way out. I hung on while all my friends became professionals and professors. I persevered because you helped me in a spiritual way and Ben in the worldly way. I let you override my decisions because I could see it was right. I go so far as to let you run this place, as if you are still the Commissioner, because I still love you as a son." Peter told him, in the most sympathetic and kind way. It was a moving sight when he placed his hand on Matthew's shoulder and added "Wake up to a new beginning and be a part of it. Let us do this together and bring this new beginning in the open."

"I guess you may be right. I spent too many long years in India and going native. But that's my life, the happiness I sought, I found. As you said, I must take part in this new beginning." Matthew looked at Peter in the eyes and in no uncertain terms, told him. "You must let me speak to the chiefs first and I want Diego to be there also." Then he asked "How are these three ingrates coming here and when?"

Peter replied "Very soon I heard they are using the government's amphibian to fly out here."

"Good! I will not tolerate them using our plane for their wild goose chase. What about accommodation? Are we to provide accommodation for them?" Matthew responded.

"Only the odd meal, I don't think they will be here for more than a day." Peter said, trying to sound persuausive.

A couple of days later Matthew, Peter, Diego and myself met the chiefs in the long house. I was invited so I could write of the outcome of this meeting. The chiefs were surrounded by the Paramount Warachara. They took up most of the space around the table. There was just enough for us. Matthew rearranged their seating order, so that he could be at the top end, accompanied by Peter.

Matthew tapped gently on the table and spoke at great length; he was honest in saying that it was possible, they would be used for the benefit of those who wanted their votes. He also advised them that they should consult either Peter, Diego and of course, himself, if something was not clear. He warned them not to be rowdy, or interrupt the speakers, as this could have a beneficial effect for the speakers. He told them that their way of life must be seen as paramount in their eyes, and that changes can only come, if they are prepared to compromise.

He also said that one of the most important aspects, was that they must insist on naming their own candidate for the Legislative Council; and only then, would they support their party. At this point, Peter asked if their party had a name. Diego told him it was called the Freedom Movement. The chiefs repeated the name several times and nodded when Matthew was finished.

Paramount Chief Warachara stood up and in halting English, expressed thanks on behalf of his subordinates and praised Matthew for his honest address. He then said that he wanted to say something more. He started. "It may not please you to hear what I have in my mind, but that is not important. What is important, is the fact that I, Paramount Chief Warachara, is told how to govern my people. These faceless men, from across the great waters, they do not know us, they have not even seen us, or the way we live. They have rights to tell us how to live?

"This is our land, we were here long before King ever heard of this land. The priest told us this and I believe priests do not lie." He was getting agitated and a bit angry.

Matthew asked him to calm down and try to be more articulate. "I know not the meaning of articulate, but if you mean to swallow my anger, then I will listen to you and swallow my anger." He then asked "Who will be that representative?" Matthew told him that would have to be decided, but that he had a candidate in mind and would reveal it when the time is right. They all nodded in agreement.

Then, it was Peter's turn to address the congregation. He praised Matthew for his honest views and for not trying to make the chiefs see that they must not do anything without his permission. He also stressed the point that they do not have to participate, as members of this movement. They have the choice to be independent from any party, but will support the right party in the Legislative Council, be it the Freedom Movement or the People's party. Again, they were thankful for the advice.

Diego asked why he was invited, since he was not able to participate in anything that was said. Matthew told him it was for the benefit of him knowing what was happening and perhaps, later he may understand why.

After the chiefs and their followers left, Diego turned to me and said "I can understand why you were invited and yet I did not see you writing anything down. I am still puzzled why I was invited." He looked at me puzzled and went on his way.

It was very early in the morning when we heard the amphibian come in to land. There were men on the embankment waiting to bring the visitors ashore. Peter, Matthew, Diego, Ben and I were there to greet them.

They came ashore and immediately embraced the famous four. I was introduced and for the first time, I was able to see the faces behind the slogans that were posted everywhere. They were invited indoors and given hot coffee, while the four reminisced of times not so long ago.

By noon, the square was filled with villagers from everywhere. The one they called Narine, stood on the veranda of the Great House and addressed them as brothers. He told them that it was time they had a representative in the Legislative Council. Then he went into his political tirade "I want to tell you that this country is bled of its natural resources. The labourers in the sugar industry are exploited and all the profits find their way into the pockets of the landlords, in the UK. The revenues from the timber and gold and diamond, are all in the UK. If we were to be an independent nation we can use those revenues to build infra structures. Create small industries to manufacture shoes; Glass and jute bags for the sugar and rice industries. This country can emerge stronger with your help. New towns can be erected to accommodate the growing population. Here in Supenaam we can build you nice schools and shops to buy all the things the people in the city have."

At this point, there were some murmurings and, as it grew louder, Matthew went on the veranda and asked that they be quiet until the speaker had finished. This plea was noted and all went quiet again. Matthew then told them that at the end of his address, they would be asked to put forward questions, one at a time.

Chief Obeyo asked where they would build these towns and on whose land. Narine told him that it would be built in Supenaam. The protests from all the tribes, were instantaneous.

Again, Matthew intervened and told them that it would be built, only if they approved its construction. They appeared satisfied with that explanation, and became subdued.

Ali took his turn on the veranda and as Narine did address them as brothers, he told them they must join his movement, to get access to the Council. They must consult the party leader before putting any questions to the Council.

What I found important in his address, is the fact that he told them that. Should the colony become independent under their flag, they would seek closer ties with the other South American countries, rather than an alliance with the West Indies.

He further disclosed, that he visited Trinidad and Barbados, and he could not see anything they had to offer, for striding towards a more cultural society. They appeared to be embroiled with this calypso music. It is quite disgustingly vulgar, some of them.

He told them he would like to see the colony developed, a culture like he saw in Venezuela or Brazil. There are theatres where they enact daily life of love and tragedy, also that he visited a theatre where they sang such beautiful songs and danced with such elegance. It made his heart pound with pride. This is what I would introduce to the westernised British Guianese.

I think I received the message that the people here, would not like change in any dramatic way. Not least with the world he was talking about. I was sure, with the help of our mentors, we could come to an arrangement that would give them the power to live as they pleased.

It's men like Matthew Longhorn, who helped to preserve these people from exploitation and their very beloved Commissioner, who continued in his footsteps and that he looked forward to a harmonious cooperation with them and his policies. He bowed courteously to them and walked back to his seat.

At first, they did not like what Narine told them and threatened to leave. It was Peter who went on the veranda and told them to listen, and then when they finished speaking they could debate all the propositions they put forward, and come to some agreement. "We will get nowhere if there are interruptions." he finally told them.

This was a very low key political rally, if I can call it that. As with Ali, they were calm as lambs and listened intently, most of the time. Matthew was observing the difference they showed with Ali's oration especially when they tapped their bows on the ground, as a sign of approval.

It was time for a break; Matthew thought it was the best time to play his ace of trump. During this interlude, he told us he would propose that Diego, be the representative of these people. Diego was stunned; never in his wildest imagination did he think he would be a representative of the indigenous nation. His protest was mild and Matthew soon took the situation by the horns and told him he had no say in the matter, "It is written that you should represent this nation."

"But I have no experience in politics or how to address an assembly; and why do they refer to them as the indigenous nation?"

"All in good time my boy, All in good time." Matthew assured him. I guess he accepted what he was told, because it came from Matthew. The outcome of this complicated political bomb shell would no doubt unfold itself at a later time.

Arrangements were made for further meetings in Georgetown very soon in the future, with Matthew at the fore front of negotiations.

We waved them goodbye as they boarded their craft, homeward bound. It was malt time and no one objected, not even the ladies, who surprisingly sat quietly and listened. It was at sipping time, when the malt seemed to have loosened their tongues that Christine told Peter.

"I have been your wife for nearly five years and it is the first I heard, that you are the richest man in the colony. If that is so, why are you killing yourself in this God forsaken land?"

"Matthew is responsible for my commitment to these people. Not only am I Commissioner, I am also their dentist. Furthermore, I do not want to hear any more of this richest man business. It is irrelevant and embarrassing. I do not want it spreading around. The note in his voice was sincere.

I was gathering materials for the biography of these two, without even an interview. It is the best way forward. I realise it is not an easy task, to get the two together but I am making headway."

Sebastian must have heard that we were partying. He and Joseph came with their musical instruments and sat next to the ladies. After a drink or two, they started playing. Matthew was the first to go on the floor in company with Margaret. She turned out to be a superb dancer, her hips swaying as I have never seen them sway before. I was getting a bit jealous, so I took Bell by the hand and did my little shuffle. Soon, everyone was on the floor, even Amelia, was doing better than I ever imagined. Everyone was having a great time and our local musicians raised the tempo of our indulgence.

The rain was falling heavily with the occasional flashes of lightening and low murmuring of thunder, in the distance. All of a sudden, there was an almighty explosion and all the electricity went dead. We all fell flat on the floor, with shock and waited for some time. Peter called out to Christine and asked if she was alright. We all followed and called out to our loved ones. It was pitch dark and I managed to get near to Margret. I assumed the others got hold of their loved ones also.

I was the first to stand up, having given assurance to Margaret, she felt confident to stand up. I could hear the others moving and Matthew calling on Ben to get the hurricane lamps from the store room. How he managed to get there, is a miracle to me. The lights brought comfort. Joseph told us that he would not be able to do anything, with the electrical system, until the morning. This was understandable. We all decided to retire and assess the damage at dawn.

We were all awake at first light. Matthew and Ben went outside and I followed. The sight outside was not pleasant, it looked like there was a war on. The wonderful silk cotton tree, under which we spent some wonderful days, was burnt, its trunk bearing the scars of a fiery onslaught.

The wind charger was flat on the ground and the old rest house was scorched all along the front. It was nature showing us some of it powers. If it had struck the villagers' huts, it would have burnt the entire village to the ground. Diego arrived with his family and surveyed the damage, before checking his herd and coming back to tell us they are safe.

Isabel came and told Peter that the fridge was not working. Matthew asked her if she did not hear what happened last night. I do not think she paid any attention to what Matthew was saying. Instead she surveyed the wreck outside, with open mouth and asked. "What in the name of Jesus Christ happened here?" "Stop your blasphemy and go and prepare breakfast and make sure you prepare for Diego and his family." "I am going. Sir, Can someone tell me what happened here?" I told her all I knew and she ran inside, taking Elizabeth with her.

Young Diego came and sat next to me, holding a piece of paper in his hand. I enquired what it was and he told me that he was writing a poem of the cows in the fields. "You write poems?" I asked, "No, I just want to write about the cows. They are so funny sometimes."

"Do you like animals?"

"Yes. I love all the animals in the forests. I love the peccaries best not because they taste nice but they are so funny. Father told me he enjoys watching them escape from the jaguars. It's funnier to look at the jaguar when he is out running after a peccary and if he misses, he goes to the nearest tree and sharpens its claws and hopes he won't be out run, the next time. I wish we had a dog, a big one like uncle Matthew used to have. He was so fluffy and kind and very smart too. When Uncle Matthew gave him food he would not eat it until he is told to do so."

"You want to read to me what you've written." I suggested. "It is not finished yet but I will read it to you later." "You can read what you have written so far, then I will be able to tell you what I think."

He began.

Under the shade of my branches they sat
Chewing their cuds and getting real fat
And when its noon, the closer they'd come
Rushing and butting and tumbling down
So I swayed my branches to and fro
To keep them cool and their eyes will glow
I wish the insects chewing my leaves
Will go away like runaway thieves

At dusk when the sun went to sleep
I fold my branches and give a peep
To see if my friends are settled below
And then I'll go to sleep like the willow

"Not bad at all, young Diego." I told him and his face lit up. He then asked if I would write it in my paper. I told him it would be a good idea. Perhaps together, we can have a children's column and invite young poets, like himself to submit their little efforts. The more I thought about it, the more excited I got and all because of Young Diego.

I heard Ben calling for us to have breakfast. Without hesitation, we hurried in to join the others.

While we were eating I asked Diego if he knew his son was going to be a poet. "I always see him writing little bits here and there. He never allows me or his mother to see what it is." he told us

"Well he has written a nice little poem and I shall publish it in next Sunday's Chronicle and at the same time, create a children's column. I will give him a nice fat puppy for his reward." He looked at me and smiled. It was enough to know it was a 'thank you'.

Ben, always eager to have something going, he asked looking at Peter. "When are we going to bring Berbice here?"

Peter looked at him, a bit quizzical and said. "For God's sake man, we only recently had one of your bloody bush cook up and already you want another party? Allow your body to rest and take in the wonderful time you had. I should advise you, that drinking too much of the malt will one day come back to remind you of its deadly after effects."

"My body can take anything malt whisky can throw at me, I am twice your size, Peter, and I only drink as much as you do."

"Sure." Peter replied. "The difference is, you drink twice as many times as I do and that, my long serving friend, is the difference."

Matthew joined in the scolding. "I agree with Peter. The problem with you is you get bored too easily. Go for a long walk along the embankment. Go wrestle with the caimans. You seem to be able to control them with your strong muscles and heavy body."

"What is this, Sermon time, from my best friends? You are right. I drink too much. Perhaps I will get a bonded wife to nag me instead." he conceded.

"Ha! Ha!" Bell mocked. "You bond with one of the girls! I want to see that day when it happens."

"You are too free spirited to be bogged down with family life."

"I didn't say I wanted a family. I only wanted someone to attract my attention from boredom." he told her.

We were sitting under the fire, torn silk cotton and expressing regrets that such a huge wonderful tree was struck and will probably die. Diego told us that it would not die, if the heart of the tree is untouched. "These trees can survive droughts and floods, a little bit of lightning will not harm it too much." he said.

"I hope you are right, Diego. I love this tree, it was no taller than me when I came here and watched it grow to the giant it is." Matthew lamented, and then asked Diego, "What's the programme for today?"

"First, we will have to erect the wind charger on a new tripod, but first it is better if Joseph checks it out, to see if it will still operate. One of the propellers is broken, but that can be replaced. We can use the Delco plant for only a limited time, as the noise will disturb the wild life after dark and chief Warachara has pointed that out to me."

Joseph, with the help of a few young villagers was already at the scene. He told us that the wind charger was fine and he would replace the propellers, with the one in the store room. The main task was to get it on its feet.

It took several hours and nearly a dozen men to get it on its footing. Everyone was pleased. Ben suggested that it was time for a bit of malty. Young Diego took his hand and shook it and when he looked down at the lad, he saw a frown and a shaking head, indicating that it was not time for malty.

We all smiled and agreed with the youngster's advice. Then, Ben suggested we all go for a walk down in the forest and see what we could find, that would interest us. It sounds a good idea. Young Diego said he knows the forests better than most people.

This was encouraging news for Ben. So, after lunch, we filled our travelling bags with emergency first aid packs, including anti venin, for all kinds of poisonous snakes including the notorious bush master.

Young Diego and Ben led the way. I was a bit apprehensive at first, but soon got over it. The forest was indeed a beautiful place, the trees were like sentinels guarding every square yard of forest and the little rivulets dazzled in the sunlight. After an hour's walking, we rested under a huge greenheart tree and watched the parrots above socialising and preening themselves. I had no idea whether they had noticed us or not. They seemed oblivious to everything around them and I took the pleasure of admiring their lovely colours.

A troupe of monkeys came on the scene and the silence was broken. Ben shouted at them to be quiet. They looked at him in apprehension for a few minutes and went about their noisy business.

It was time to move on, a couple of hours later, we came to a small lake. The tannin coloured water looked inviting. Since there were no females around we decided to take a dive in our birthday suits which was great fun.

Later, after an hour's more walking, we saw a jaguar. It was resting its head on paws. It looked quite regal. Young Diego told us we were safe, as we were down wind and must walk very quietly so not to disturb it. Ben emitted an ear smashing sneeze and the jaguar lifted its head and stared in our direction. I could see it, smelling the air and starting to walk towards us, all the time looking towards us. He must have seen us and wanted to investigate.

Young Diego told us not to panic, as he could see I was shaking a little. If we stood quietly for a few minutes it would lose interest, I was told. I found it incredible that an eight year old knew so much about forest animals. We did as he asked and for sure, the animal did lose interest and dashed off in another direction. I was too nervous to continue, so I sat under a tree, where some dried leaves looked inviting. Suddenly, there was a movement under my rear, I jumped up and there it was, a snake about a hundred feet long, wriggling calmly and slowly away.

"Did you say a hundred feet long, Andrew?" Ben asked.

"Longer I think, you should have seen It.!"

"I saw the snake, it was a boa constrictor, only about twenty feet. The large lump you saw in its belly is probably a capybara or a peccary. You are fortunate it has had a meal not too long ago or you would have been in there instead." Ben told me, wearing a wicked smile.

We decided to return home. I asked Young Diego which way was home. "East" he pointed and told us to follow him. He must have taken a wrong turn, as we found ourselves at cold stream which was a good two hour walk, to our homes.

At least Ben told us, with confidence, that he knew the way well from here, as he had done this journey several times. I was still not convinced and did not regret bringing Matthew's pistol with me. I was not too sure of these intrepid forest dwellers, knowing everything.

I was so relieved when we reached our final destination. Margaret came running towards me to ask why we hadn't invite her. I told her how that I nearly got swallowed up by a huge boa constrictor. She shuddered and hugged me tight, for a good minute.

"You forgot to tell her how you chased away the jaguar and saved us all form being killed." Ben told me, with his wicked boyish grin, spread across his face. Margaret looked at me and I gave her a lingering kiss, lifted her in my arms and went indoors.

CHAPTER 8
REMINISCES IN BERBICE

One morning, without warning, the Commissioner told me if I wanted to get as many facts about his life as I wanted, I should accompany him to Berbice and meet his parents. He insisted that it would give me an insight into his early life. It would reveal much more than he could possibly relate to me. It sounded a reasonable suggestion, so I decided to go.

That morning, boarding the plane was a great surprise. There was Diego and his son accompanying them, and Bell, Ben, Joseph, Margaret, Amelia, Christine and Elizabeth with Matthew and Isabel bringing up the rear. I was flabbergasted. Margaret had kept it a secret from me all the time and Peter, hoping to give me a good surprise. It was a good surprise indeed. I might have been bored, most of the time stuck with the Commissioner. Then, when I thought that the entire community in Supenaam was onboard, Sugar Bush came running in, screaming Matthew's name. Without being invited she clambered aboard.

I helped the other ladies board the plane. There was a feeling of elation in me all the way to Berbice. I wondered what was going to be like. I had never been there. The furthest I'd been, East of Demerara was a place called Buxton, a predominantly black community. There was a wedding of a local dignitary and I was asked, by my editor, to cover the wedding for the Chronicle. A lively community, of the friendliest people I ever met.

If Berbice was like that, then I thought I was in for a treat. We landed in the Berbice River and a fleet of fishermen came and took us ashore. Two motor cars were waiting for us at the office of the manager of Transport and Harbours. Our first stop, was at the police station, to inform the chief of police that the

Commissioner was in town and for the guards to be posted. It all looked quite official and important.

We arrived in time to see his mother coming home from church, in company with an East Indian woman. The journey was not that tiring and we had enough energy to assist the ladies with their shopping. The first thing Ben did was to get some glasses and ask the East Indian woman to fetch some ice. Isabel instantly insisted that she got the ice. "I was the first maid here and I am senior to all others." She proudly declared. The East Indian woman was only too pleased to let her have her way. It turned out her name was Beda. It suited her, she may not have been as pretty as Isabel, but pretty enough to demand a second glance.

Peter's parents came to greet us and immediately told us to sort our sleeping arrangements. She spoke authoritatively to Ben saying "You are no stranger in this house, you and that usurper Matthew...Trying to steal my son indeed... Do remember your way around, so please help yourselves. Then she went and gave Matthew an endearing hug and kissed him several times on the cheeks.

After a hearty meal, Matthew accompanied us to the town proper. We were sitting in the Aster bar having a drink and Peter was chatting and introducing me to some of his friends when suddenly he exclaimed loud enough to awaken the dead. "It is my dear friend, Toolan. He rushed up and they embraced each other and I could see tears running from their eyes. "It has been a long time." Peter said. "Yes, too long for old friends to be parted." He introduced his friend to us saying "We are old school chums. Toolan is a moniker, only a few people would recognise. He left when I was still struggling in Supenaam, with my loneliness and frustration. We corresponded for a while and drifted apart. I know our friendship was still as strong as the first day I visited his home in Ferry Street and met his lovely family. He has been a frequent visitor in our house, as if he lived there." Turning to his friend he said, "My parents will be very pleased to see you again."

"I know. How are they? I have only arrived yesterday and thought of resting after that long flight from Washington and the bumpy ride to Rosignol. You know what the road is like." he explained. "I don't come by road anymore." Peter told him adding "Forgive my bad manners. This here is Matthew, the former Commissioner and this is my biographer, Andrew Bowry. Matthew is more than a friend, as a matter, he sometimes thinks I am his son."

"Whatever your mother will say to that!"

"She called him a usurper only a few minutes ago. Now Toolan when can we meet? I have quite a few friends home, will you be able to join us later?"

"Before he answered that question, he asked. "You do not travel by road, from Georgetown anymore? How do you get here?"

"By amphibian aircraft, surely you do not think I would risk driving on that potato field, they call a road". He then turned to me and said quite emphatically and pointing to his friend. "This is the only man I know that can take a dozen men together and run this country with the efficiency of a well-tuned engine."

"Come on Peter, you are more equipped to run this country. I am only a university lecturer. Politics is too dirty a game for my liking. I will come and see you tonight at about eight, is that alright?"

"Eight is fine and you will have dinner. How are you getting home. Don't tell me you will walk home?"

"No. I will take a taxi." he replied

Peter was having none of that "I will let my driver take you home and I will send him to pick you up for eight o'clock."

Again they hugged before his friend's departure. After this meeting with his friend, everything else appeared an anti-climax. Peter was not prepared to let that happen. Instead, he asked the manager at the bar to put a dozen magnum of his finest champagne in the car. Matthew's face suddenly brightened up and patted Peter on the back.

I was beginning to appreciate the Berbicians for their kindness and hospitality. I never dreamt that we could all find accommodation in his parents' house. It was an extremely large house, when I thought about it, and felt very lucky to have found these people.

We had just returned to his home and the first thing he said "Mother, who do you think I met at the Aster Bar?"

"I have no idea son. Are you going to tell me? Or do I have to keep guessing?" she urged.

"Toolan, he is in New Amsterdam. I invited him for dinner. You are not displeased? I know I have brought a lot of friends, one more will not hurt." he pleaded.

His mother replied, "Toolan eh, my God I can't remember the last time I saw him. Now I remember. He came and said good-bye just before he left for the States. Now he's coming to dinner. I'll have to rearrange the menu." Then, she shouted "Isabel! Get Bacchus to kill four ducks and have them prepared for cooking."

Isabel ran off and then she summoned the other maid and asked her if she could cook duck curry. The maid answered, so as to confirm that she could and also boasted that she cooked the best duck curry in town. Miriam looked at her, with a crossed eye and said. "I've been cooking duck curry, since I was a little girl and everyone praised my cooking. So you watch your tongue and don't praise yourself. Let others do it."

After the maid left she told us quietly "She can cook a better duck curry. Only, I can't let her know that."

The table was elegantly laid out. The silver shone as if they were in a competition. Napkins, immaculately folded and her Royal Albert set in a straight line as straight as soldiers. She inspected all before her and as we waited for Toolan's arrival we sat silent for a while, until Ben and Beda brought us a drink. Miriam frowned and then said in her matriarchal voice. "I don't see why only the men can drink my malt. Joseph, go and get us a drink. Margaret's father got up to do as she asked and everyone started laughing. It turned out that both Peter's and Margaret's fathers' first names were Joseph

In order not to cause confusion, she suggested that Margaret's father be addressed as Joe. Then, she said "I would not ask a guest to fetch a drink. What sort of woman would do such a thing?"

Joseph was about to go and get the drink, when Toolan arrived. After many introductions and hugs and kisses, we uncorked a couple of magnum and drank a welcome to Toolan. Several glasses later, we were invited into the dining room.

Miriam asked everyone to sit as they saw fit, as it was an informal dinner. She turned to Toolan and told him. "You know this house, so make yourself comfortable and enjoy your meal. Make sure you sit next to me."

"I can smell the duck. Am I right mum?"

"I know how you like it, so I changed my menu when I heard you were coming." she told him, with a maternal smile. He responded, by getting up and went and kissed her for her consideration.

"You know Matthew likes it as much as you." she told him

Beda brought the first course in and Toolan looked at her and asked "This is a new maid. What happened to the one you had before?"

"She's right behind you." Miriam pointed out.

Toolan turned around and in surprise exclaimed "This is not the same talkative flat chested young girl I used to tease? I can't believe it."

Miriam told him it was and added "She is very much the talkative, but not flat chested. As you can see, she has more of her share of feminine developments."

Toolan then asked. "Are you married?"

"No, Master Toolan I am not married. Do you want to marry me?" was her answer.

Miriam was a bit angry with her. "You are a rude young lady. Go in the kitchen and help Beda and you can curb her manners, while you are there. Toolan is too good a gentleman to marry you. Mind you, she has no end of suitors. All the unmarried young men are vying for her and some married men also. The truth is I am not certain how many she entertains. I keep a decent and strict home and would not tolerate any irregularities and she knows it."

"Oh Mistress D'Abrue" Isabel exclaimed in horror. "You make these people think I am a woman of the street."

"One of these good days, I'll extract all her teeth" Joseph added.

"Why would you do that Master?" she asked in surprise.

"So you would be ashamed to open your mouth to speak nonsense." He replied.

Miriam told her to stop her intervention at the dinner table and ordered her to go and prepare the dishes for the ice cream and to ask Beda not to touch the dishes with her butter fingers.

After dinner, we assembled on the veranda, nursing a brandy. Miriam asked Toolan if he would stay over, as the boys were planning to go swimming in the Canje River early in the morning. He told her he would love to stay over but he must phone his parents to tell them. They then started reminiscing of the times they had cooled off in the river, when the sun got very hot.

It was Toolan who said "Peter can you remember at end of term, we would traditionally go down by the ferry bridge and climb up to the highest part of the bridge and dive in the water. All the girls from fifth form would come on their bicycles to watch and we would perform some dare devil stunts to impress them."

"I remember it only too well." Peter replied. Then he went on to say "It was pretty dangerous. We never appreciated the danger then. There were a lot of things floating down the river, pieces of timber and rotten vegetation. I remember once, I dived from the highest point and before I surfaced, something struck my throat. I was alright, so I never mentioned it.

"Then, there was the time when the ferry bridge got stuck and could not close properly. Only pedestrians could get over and we used to see who could jump across the widest point of the gap. That was pretty hair raising. The cars used to drop off their passengers at the town's end and the passengers would walk over to the other side and get another car, to take them to their destinations."

"Are you taking notes Mr. Biographer?" Ben asked.

"It's all in my memory and it will stay there, until I need it" I told him.

"Have you seen Aubrey since you came back?" Peter asked his friend.

"Yes, I have always been in contact with him, more often than with you. Your problem was, I did not know where you were or would be at any time. …I used to send him books on American civil wars. As a matter of fact he and Marina came to greet me at the airport and drove me down to Rosignal. I am sure if they knew you were in Berbice, they would have crossed with the ferry and popped in. We talked about you, all the way down to the wharf. He told me he saved one of your men from being hanged. Is that true?"

"Not quite" Peter told him. "It is that giant sitting next to you? We were having lunch at Mr. Choo's luncheon rooms, when this Mrs. Ali got a chicken bone stuck in her throat… You remember Mrs. Ali, you used to visit them in Church Street and she used to cook you duck curry. Come to think about it, I always wondered if it was her duck you were after or that pretty daughter, I see you chatting with on many occasions."

"You still stretch your stories longer than is needed, Peter. Get to the point, what happened to Mrs. Ali?"

"This bone got stuck in her throat and she was suffocating. Ben tried to assist but she died in his arms. He was accused of murder and locked up for several days. It was Aubrey who defended him and our own Persotum was the Judge. It was discovered that no post mortem was done and the judge ordered one which revealed that she died from suffocation and not strangulation, as the prosecution was claiming. We must visit Mr. Choo's luncheon rooms and play the naughty boys tricks." Peter ended.

Toolan remarked on Peter's vivid memory of those times and shook his head in disbelief. that those care free days of young men learning of life are gone into history. He also expressed disbelief that Mrs. Ali was dead. He also disclosed what Peter suspected long ago, that he had strong feelings for her daughter. He then asked what became of her. Peter was unable to give him an answer.

It was Peter who took up the conversation. "You are coming to Supenaam when we return. I will not accept any excuses, do all your business as soon as possible. We leave in a week's time. I have to fly to Oreala to sort out some territorial disputes.

The chief is having serious problems with those Juckas from Surinam. It appears that they are claiming that a very large island in the river belongs to them and not to the British. I discussed this with the Governor and he asked me to sort it out. I am taking Matthew with me as a consultant. He is the former Commissioner, stationed in Supenaam. If you want to come aboard you are welcome."

"I'd love to go but as you say I must sort out my business if I am coming to Supenaam. Thank you."

After a couple more brandies, we were ready for bed. I must admit, I slept like a new born child and had to be awakened for our early morning swim. I was keen to see this bridge they spoke so much about. I did not know Berbice had a swing bridge. It was, as they said, a bridge that rotated to allow ocean going vessels to pass, to collect the sugar from the factory, four miles upriver.

At breakfast, Peter was sorting out those going to Oreala. The ladies wanted to go and Peter objected saying he will not take his family on this trip with the sea plane. Sebastian explained that the Corentyne River was dangerous, as it was exposed to the squalls coming in from the Atlantic. It could be sudden and without warning, huge waves that went with it, could make landing almost impossible.

Since all the ladies wanted an outing, Peter suggested that he phone Andrew McIntosh in Skeldon and asked to use his super motor boat, to take them there. He also quite rightly said that it was too risky for his entire family to travel together and that the boat was quite safe and luxurious.

After phoning McIntosh he told the ladies to get prepared and Sebastian would take them to Skeldon and come back for us. This would give them a couple of hours' start and we would all arrive, nearly the same time.

I could see Toolan was indeed, a man who knew his way around the house. He was helping sort out the travelling packs. More important to Ben especially, was the case full of malt. Why so much was anyone's guess.

Finally, Peter announced that he would not be having a party, only a barbeque up the Canje River and a very low key one. He was doing it for my benefit. He reminded us that he planned to take Berbice to Supenaam and now that his dear friend was here, he was even more determined to do it.

CHAPTER 9

THE GOVENOR IN SUPENAAM

Oreala was not quite the same as Supenaam. The houses were randomly erected and there was no long house, for meeting with the chief. Instead, the bar which only sold soft drinks, was used as a meeting place. An office for visiting officials was nearby.

Peter was shown some of the spears they retrieved from the intruders and also, three of his men dead and about a dozen seriously wounded.

"The Governor ought to send soldiers from Britain to secure the borders." the chief remarked, and looked very distressed, as he continued "I heard you are having the same problem in your area. I heard the Brazilians are raiding the forest in the South and the Venezuelans are doing the same from the West. Our three borders are not secured. Too much country and not enough people." he ended.

Peter replied by saying "The king will not send soldiers, unless the Governor requests them. I have a feeling the Governor wants the UK government to think that all is well and that he is doing a fine job."

"You can make him send for soldiers. Exaggerate the situation. It is called politics. You don't know to play political games. I can teach you." The chief told him in no uncertain terms.

"I am not going to go political, with the Governor. He has his spies. What will happen if he discovers I was lying to him? No I am sorry; I have to do this my way. You must be patient".

The chief hung his head and nodded. Then he came alive again, "You have Jango as your head ranger I heard. Jango is cleverer than you think. Why not discuss this with him and hear what he comes up with. Do I make any sense?"

"You make a lot of sense my friend. If I am to seek advice from my rangers, I will look inadequate in my job. I am sorry my friend, I must do this my way." Peter reluctantly told him.

"Okay! Okay! Don't talk to Jango. You have Matthew Longhorn at your side. Ask him to help." He then turned to Matthew and asked "You will not help your successor?"

Matthew's reply was "I will help him, only if he asks."

"Then why not ask the Commissioner?" The chief appears to be pleading. "I will not intervene." Matthew replied. I can see Peter's point of view. Also, I understand the chief's dilemma with his dead and wounded men. He is prepared to apply pressure, to get some sort of justice.

Their meeting went on for hours and I decided to join Ben and the others, in some drinking. After all, there was no other outlet to entertain themselves. Ben was up to his usual tricks. He offered a young man a shot of whisky which was forbidden to the Amerindians.

Thinking no one was watching, I kept quiet, to see his next move and as expected, a young lady was introduced. Sebastian soon intervened and stopped him making any contact with the young lady. He was not at all pleased.

I turned to him and said. "I understand, you were Peter's protector from his mid-teens, until he went to England. I also understand that you are his confidante and friend." He nodded as I was speaking. Then I said, perhaps out of context "Then why the hell are you jeopardizing his standing in this strange outpost?"

"I am bored to death. I only came to help Peter if he gets in difficulties. I mean no harm. Look! I am truly sorry. I know now how bad it looks. I am a single man and I love women."

"I am single too and I too love women. I don't go about procuring them with bribes and of all the places right under the nose of the man you professed to love."

"Okay professor! Stop the lecturing. I know I done wrong and I am sorry. If you want me to jump in that river where there are hundreds of piranha waiting, think again." He poked a finger in my chest to bring home his point.

Not long after, Peter and Matthew emerged from the tiny office. They looked haggard. Matthew snatched the whisky from Ben and for the first time, I saw him drink from the bottle. Peter did the same. This led me to believe that something important was discussed in there. Whatever it was was still a mystery to us outsiders.

Our return to New Amsterdam was like emerging from a nightmare; although I enjoyed the journey, I was a bit disappointed not to be able to see some of the Juckas at the meeting. I thought it would have been more productive, if some of them were there to assert some creditability as to why they fought. Arguments were solved when both disputing parties were present, to parley and put forward suggestions. That was my belief anyway. Perhaps these border disputes were something else beyond my comprehension, I thought to myself.

Now that Toolan had arrived, we were all set for Supenaam. On our way, Peter said we would stop in at Georgetown, as he wanted to go and see the Governor. This was fine by me and the others.

Peter left us to do as we pleased and he drove to the Governor's residence, in his new Jaguar which was kept covered in his garage. It truly was a beautiful vehicle. I had not seen another like it in town.

Toolan suggested that we go to Matthew's club as he would buy us lunch. This trip was getting better all the time. I always wanted to visit the Civil Servants' Club. It would be prestigious for me when I told my editor I'd lunched there.

As I always thought, the club was reminiscent of the English upper class. The service was beyond my imagination, immaculately dressed in black trousers and white tunic with a bow tie. Their manners were almost effeminate to my ears. Ben was having a lot of fun, asking many questions of their menu. I wondered how much he knew of English cuisine. Perhaps he was doing it to impress Toolan. Little does he know that Toolan was a much more sophisticated person than he could hope to be.

At this stage, Toolan's friend, Aubrey and his wife joined us. A few minutes later, their other friend, Persotum, came in with his German wife. I listened, as they reminisced and paid little attention, as I had heard it all before. I would not say it was boring, only a bit repetitive. I assumed that's what old friends did when they'd not seen each other for years.

Peter's arrival introduced a new mood. He was not at all pleased with his meeting and showed concern that the future of Supenaam, was not as secured as he would like it to be.

We left his two friends and their wives and went about our own pressing business. It was a long walk from his house to the ocean where the aircraft was moored. Eventually, we were able to take off and within an hour, we were in Supenaam.

The other plane was left in Berbice, to transport the food and his East Indian helpers, when the time was ready.

We were all set for the occasion, when Berbice would come to Supenaam. Joseph was informed by telephone and the villagers were already preparing the long house for the occasion. Diego and Peter looked over the arrangements with approval. Even Chief Warachara nodded in approval. Our party from Berbice was expected very early the next morning.

Oliver the priest, arrived late that afternoon and was pleasantly surprised to see the decorations. He thought it was the special church service he would be having the next Sunday.

He was mildly disappointed, when Peter told him what the decorations meant. He was, nevertheless, keen to join in.

"I don't see the point of bringing Berbice to Supenaam." he told Peter.

"I am doing this in honour of my friend and for the people of Supenaam, to see how we can really enjoy ourselves."

At about four in the morning, they arrived with four lambs and two dozen chickens. The East Indian men took charge and went about preparing the animals and birds for cooking. I have never seen such a huge preparation and it fascinated me, to watch the dexterity exhibited by these skinny men and women.

A few hours later, Peter received a telephone call from the Governor's office, informing him that the Governor and two of his aides were on their way.

"This is really an inconvenient time for an official visit." he told us. "However, he is the Governor and I must do whatever it takes to accommodate him."

The Governor's arrival was met with a ceremonious welcome from the chiefs and their men. Peter guided him to the great house and offered him some refreshments.

He went outside and looked at Tudor. He came back in and asked Peter when that edifice was erected and who was responsible for its amelioration. Without waiting for an answer, he suggested that it must be Christine, bringing a bit of the old country to the wilderness; Peter agreed and told him the purpose of it.

I was eventually introduced and he immediately recognised my name, saying that he had read some of my articles which was completely out of context with the truth.

"Your Excellency, newspapers must sell their products to thrive and if the basic truth is printed, it would make very boring reading. We do tell the true story but in a livelier light to amuse our readers." I told him in an apologetic way.

"In future, governmental news must be printed as they are. There are legalities involved and unless it is portrayed as it is, it can be damning for the government." His scolding was met with a humble apology.

"Now Commissioner, you thought I came here to discuss politics. You under estimated my intentions. I remember you telling me that as soon as you finished this party you planned several weeks ago, you and I will consult with Matthew, the long term security of the hinterlands. Now my friend, I have heard of your elaborate parties. My aide, who you know, has told me so much about it. I can understand why you did not invite me. I take no offence. So I hope you do not mind that I am here for this soiree". he ended, looking for a response.

"Your Excellency, this is more than an honour. If I had the slightest notion, that you enjoyed this sort of thing, my invitation would have been enthusiastically extended." Peter told him, with sincere honesty.

"Where is the old fox Matthew? Tell him to fetch me a drink."

"I heard that Sir Charles. I will get Ben to fix you one. He's good at that sort of thing."

Ben stood before the Governor, his mighty hands shaking. The Governor looked at him in disbelief and exclaimed "Good God, where did he come from?" Peter told him all that there was to tell, about Ben and the Governor added "No wonder you were able to live through your unhappy life in this God forsaken country.

During the course of the day, the Governor was having a jolly good time. He chatted with the men and women, doing the cooking and even found time to joke with them. He told them of his experiences in India and some of the friends he left behind. "I was there the same time as your former Commissioner, only we were stationed in different parts of the country. I am quite familiar with all this enormous cooking. When I heard about it, I could not resist coming.

By mid-afternoon, we were having lunch and later, we went down the river to cool off. His two aides went on the rocks, in the middle of the river, and as before, took off most of their clothing and lay on the rocks, looking cool and relaxed. The ladies were tempted to join in, but I think modesty was a better part of their judgment. Instead, they threw pebbles at us, some of it really hurt, No one seemed to mind.

An hour later, we joined the workers who had just finished eating and were warming their drums by the fire. The ladies went in one of the villager's huts and dressed themselves in ornate costume.

The silence was broken with the sudden burst of drum beats. The rhythm was so contagious that Ben immediately started swaying his hips, holding a glass of malt in one hand and twirling the other.

Matthew took Amelia and joined him. In a few minutes, the ground was filled with dancers.

Warachara and his men made a circle around us and swayed to the rhythm, circling us slowly at first and then increasing the spin with each completed circle. The Governor and his aides looked on, with admiration. It was Christine who went up to him and persuaded him to join in; his aides quickly took the cue and found themselves partners. Toolan was enjoying himself quietly with Bell, while Diego watched.

The music suddenly stopped and the head of the East Indian group announced that they would give us a demonstration of Indian dances and we cleared the area. It was a magnificent show and the ladies appeared to have elasticated hips! It was rather sensuous, but very entertaining, so much so, that I overheard the Governor telling Peter that he knew there was decent accommodation in the big house and he would like to stay overnight and have a meeting in the morning, with the chiefs. Peter told him that it would be an honour. At this point, the Governor appeared relaxed. He and Matthew were seen drinking and chatting, like old friends. I was never able to hear what was said. The dancing continued, until late in the evening.

In the morning, I discovered that most of the men were swimming in the river. Ben was standing, keeping guard that no caiman would make a sudden attack. I do not know exactly how he did it. but he appeared to know when they were about to move. The refreshed swimmers then took their clothes and went indoors.

I watched Peter, Matthew and the Governor strolling towards me, and Diego soon joined us. We were off to meet Warachara and the other chiefs in the long house. When we got there, we found they were already waiting for us. A lengthy ceremonious greeting followed and eventually, we were all seated.

The Governor repeated what Peter told him about the insecurity of the borders and the killing of some of the men. The chief listened intently and occasionally nodded to confirm all that was said was true.

Matthew was asked to give his views. He began "Sir Charles, with due respect I am of the opinion that the Colonial office is not very interested in what happened here. It is my feeling and with justification, that this is too unimportant a territory for vast sums to be paid for soldiers to patrol our borders. It may be too expensive, but if they are really interested in securing the borders, then at least have the nerve to do something about it.

I have a plan I discussed with the Commissioner prior to your unexpected visit. I propose that you create a training commander to train the young Amerindians in warfare and how to handle a rifle with accuracy. The pay for these brave men will be minimal, in comparison to the trained soldier."

"That sounds like a good idea. The only problem is to find this trainer."

"I can volunteer for that job. I trained men before and I can do it for a stipend that would entitle me to certain privileges and the authority to do the right thing, unhindered."

"Are you putting conditions under which you will undertake this job Matthew? I know you too well. You love to do things your way.

I remember too well, that incident with that bandit Ahmed Khan. You deliberately allowed him to make us look foolish in his eyes." The Governor told him.

"I did not do any such thing. It was your dare devil brother-in-law that was responsible. He was my superior at the time and that cowardly Commanding Officer, allowed him to get away with it.

If you read the official transcript, you would have read, that it was I, who saved the day, by pretending that the Army would send in heavy artillery to flatten their mountain and rid the country of his marauding activities." an angry Matthew told him. Then continuing in the same vein, he added "I know the mentality of the Colonial Office. If things were to go askew, they would deny all responsibilities and I may find myself facing sedition charges. The title and the stipend would give me official recognition to do what was necessary."

"When you say if things were to go wrong, what exactly are you referring to?"

"He means if there were to be an international incident with either The Brazilians or the Venezuelans and they feel their sovereignty is threatened. It could lead to border clashes that can develop into full scale war. I am not saying it would happen. He must look at all the possibilities and our roles in all of it." Diego told him, feeling justified, entering the argument.

"You are protecting yourselves. I did not know Diego would be involved. What do you think Peter?"

"I think Matthew knows these people better than I ever hoped and besides, he has all the military expertise to do the job and with Diego to assist, it's a pittance against a full military deployment. It's the best idea he is putting forward to you." Peter told him with conviction.

"Do I suspect a conspiracy here?"

"If it is a conspiracy, then I must say, it's a damn good one." Matthew replied, with a broad smile on his crinkled face. Then added "The Colonial Office will think you are a genius. I am sure when you put in your report, you will say it is the best solution you can think of"

"Okay. I will put this proposal forward to the Colonial Office and await their reply. You realise I have no mandate to ratify such an undertaking."

"One thing to remember when putting this proposal forward, is to remind them that the British Empire has a small footing on the South American continent and if that was to be lost to either the Venezuelans or the Brazilians, or even the Dutch for that matter, it would be a vital piece of territory, lost forever.

Moreover, they should be reminded that a war was fought for this piece of territory and that the Dutch has not forgotten that Britain stole their property and drove them out. Their army seemed to be peaceful, against our volunteers, but they are causing a lot of trouble in the East.

Their runaway African slaves still live a primitive life in the bush and they are being encouraged to cause problems in the Oreala area. If we were to take drastic action against those that killed four of Chiano's young men, the Surinam government will take that as an act of aggression against their people and I don't have to spell out what could happen. The sooner this plan of mine is put in force the better." Matthew added.

The rest of the group sensed that the meeting was over and came over and invited us for some refreshments.

"One final question Matthew." The Governor said, then asked "Where do you expect to train these men?"

"I am glad you brought that up. I will need some money up front to build a barrack and enough land to turn into a parade and training ground."

"You are asking a lot. I know of your little gold mine. I am not sure if I should levy a tax on that gold you found." the Governor informed him.

Peter said that if such a tax were to be introduced, then the government would find it difficult to sustain a Commissioner and all the expenses that go with it. Then, he explained "The aircraft you see we are using, to take us from place to place, is being financed by the gold we found. You know how much kerosene has gone up since after the war. It more than tripled. The cost of flying from here to Oreala is more than the salary you pay to one of your supervisors. The stipend Matthew is asking for, is a mere ten dollars a year, not enough to buy him a bottle of malt."

"Gentlemen, let's not keep the ladies waiting. I must get back to Georgetown post haste."

With the Governor's departure, Matthew and the others were able to sit down and work out their plans. Matthew knew the Governor would insist on the Colonial Office to sanction the plan.

He was overjoyed with this prospect. "I have been here, floating around with nothing in particular to do. No official standing. That is all in the past." He put an arm around Diego and told him that they had an important job in hand.

It was Ben, who interrupted, by asking "What will I do? I am not a babysitter anymore, to a fully grown man. I am joining you two and going to find myself a job." They both placed an arm around his broad shoulders and had a good laugh.

In the meantime, I was contemplating returning to Georgetown and taking Margaret with me, to introduce her to my parents. It was a pity that I did not invite them to the big soiree we had. My father is not a big drinker. He occasionally has a brandy with warm milk during the rainy season. He would have enjoyed it, especially the dancing.

He is only fifty five years old and was forced into mandatory retirement, as was the law, in the colony; he can barely survive with the pension he receives from the church, without a subsidy from me. He will not get his state pension from the UK until he is sixty five. That was the main reason he was still here

I knew it would cheer him up, to see I was getting married; I was looking forward to seeing him smile again. My mother, on the other, hand likes her malt, not excessive but can carry herself at a party. This is what partly sustains him, watching her enjoy herself.

CHAPTER 10
GOOD NEWS FROM LONDON

Peter was in company with Matthew and Diego at the river. I hailed Ben and asked him if he wanted to join us. Rarely, did you find them apart. I guess, it being such a small community, a bond so strong, has knitted them together. I was not jealous. I only wanted to be a part of their activities. Being their friend was not enough not for me, anyway. The trio was not surprised to see us and explained in detail what they were planning. Peter looked at me and asked, "How long have you been here malingering."

"If it appears that I am malingering, it is only because the two of you are like slippery eels. I could never pin you both together for a coordinated interview. That is why I am still here for nearly three months!" I replied, a bit rattled.

"Peter stretched his hand out and said "Welcome to our community."

It appeared that Matthew wanted to take up a square mile of land next to the cattle and build a temporary barrack and have the ground leveled for his training and parades. He pointed out that it would be fine in the dry season, but almost impossible when the rain arrived.

Peter pointed out to him, that he could begin his training, while the sun shined and prepare for his military exercises during the rainy season.

"What happens if the Colonial Office rejects the plan?" Matthew asked.

"Can you see them doing that?" Peter asked in reply.

"It will be a fool hardy and expensive decision if they do. I am sure Sir Charles will impress upon them, the importance and cost effectiveness of the entire scheme." Matthew assured him.

I interrupted when there was a gap in their conversation and asked "Commissioner, the next time, when the plane is going to Georgetown, can I and Margaret get a ride? I need to introduce her to my parents. I also intend to have an engagement party with some close friends while I am there. I cannot afford a large party like you have."

Matthew looked at me and said "Come to my office… sorry, I mean the Commissioner's office and you also." He was looking at Diego and Ben, as he spoke. The five of us went and sat and waited. Peter and Matthew were having a private conversation.

Eventually, Matthew told me "You have been tolerant with us, ever since you came up here, nearly three months ago and we have constantly dodged the issue of an interview. Now listen to me young man, we have all agreed to give you this diamond for an engagement ring. Also, there is a nugget to go with it. Furthermore, you will take this letter to Mr. Humphries, in the Water Street and it will explain everything. Go and prepare yourself for the engagement, but under no circumstance, are you to arrange a party before consulting with us. This is not a request. It is an order from an old fox, who means well."

"You did not ask Diego and me if we would agree with your suggestion." Ben told him, with a slight sign of indignation.

"I don't need to ask a small favour. Now be quiet."

Ben stood to attention and replied "Very well Commander."

It was a funny sight, watching Ben trying to stand to attention, like a pregnant woman which brought smiles all around.

I thanked them all for their generosity, and plans were made for me to travel on the next flight. Matthew had one more thing to add. "I will ask my daughter Amelia to accompany Margaret, to assist her in buying some new clothes. Men are bloody useless in this department. They will also stay at Peter's house and you are not to be present there later than ten o'clock.

I was speechless. I have never met such kind people in all my life, not one, but four of them, all in the same place.

When we arrived in Georgetown, my first port of call was to Mr. Abdool's department store, in Lombard Street. It was a family concern and I had always bought my clothing there. He was surprised to see me. "Hello Mr. Bowry. I heard you were in the jungle, chasing crocodiles."

"I am on a mission that will probably last another month. There are no crocodiles in this country. What we have are caimans." I told him, then he asked "What can I do for you? You appear to be an expert on our wildlife."

"I met a beautiful young lady there and we are going to be married. First I want a nice suit length for my engagement." I told him.

He called out to his wife, "Mamma, see the best material we have for a suit and measure three and a quarter yards and bring it here". His wife obeyed and I examined the cloth. It was indeed, the finest material I could buy. I then asked how much. He looked at me in horror and said "What kind of person do you think I am? You are more than a customer. You are my friend, and you ask how much. You are getting married and you expect me to ask you for money for your suit? Andrew! Andrew! Dear boy. This is my gift for your happy event. Now take it and go see Mr. Asro and let him sew it for you." He signaled me to go. I turned to him and said. "This is the second time today I've been overwhelmed by people's generosity. Perhaps one day I will be able to return that kindness to someone in need."

"You may be a Catholic Christian, Andrew, but you have a Muslim heart." he replied.

I went to see Mr. Asro, a fine and excellent tailor. He expressed surprise to see me. Then he asked "What's that you have in your hand?" "It's a suit length and I want you to make me a suit for my engagement. I will of course be wearing it for my wedding. He looked at the material and nodded vigorously. "Mmmm, the finest, now when do you want it?"

I told him as soon as possible. I would plan my engagement party when it was finished.

"So you are going to have a party and you want me to hurry up and make you the best suit I will ever make as soon as possible? I will ask God to make the days go by really slowly." he said, smiling.

"Now Mr. Asro, do I give you some money up front, or do I pay you when it is finished?"

"Money, Money! It is all I hear. I don't want to hear money from you. Your father is the kindest person I've ever met. He is liked by everyone. Even the Muslims and Hindus paid him respect. His son does not have respect. He asks Asro how much. If you are going to pay me, then I ask you take your suit to be made by someone else". He looked apologetically at me and said "I always wanted to do something for you or your family. You have given that opportunity and then you want to steal it from me."

Come back next week for a trial and your suit will be finished in another three days' time. Is that satisfactory to you?" Then he shouted to a lad in the back room "Oswald! Come and go to Pestano's and get me some thread and buttons to match this cloth. I want eight small ones and four large ones for the jacket." He then cut a small piece and gave it to the lad. I looked at him and said "I did not know you could afford an apprentice."

"I can't" he replied and then explained "When the lad finished school he came and asked me to teach him my trade. I told him I could not afford an apprentice. He replied by saying that he didn't want any payment, just the opportunity to be a tailor like me. How could I refuse such an offer? So here he is, learning the trade. Mind you, I give him a shilling every Friday, so he can socialise with his friends, on weekends."

The ladies had gone ahead of me, so I decided that I must pay Mr. Humphries a visit and present the letter from Matthew. Mr. Humphries looked at the diamond from under a magnifying glass and nodded. He looked at the nugget and told me that he could not make a diamond ring from pure gold, he must add some alloy to give it strength to hold the stone securely. "You leave it to me. I will need to see the young lady for her finger measurement. How soon can you arrange that?"

"Very early in the morning." I replied. He told me that he would not be in the shop before ten o'clock.

I left his workshop with a feeling of hopelessness. Hopeless, in the sense that there was no way I could repay these people for their overwhelming generosity. Three kindnesses in one day. That must surely be a world record. On second thoughts, I had great doubts if I was alive. Was it possible that I was actually dead and in a world of good people? I pinched myself so hard it hurt. I was alive alright.

When I returned to Peter's home I found the ladies had gone shopping. The gardener opened the locked door and let me in. I went on the veranda, with a malt and some ice, to refresh myself with the cool Atlantic breeze. I realised that I had picked up a very bad habit, something I'd never done, before I went to Supenaam. I was always having a drink when there was nothing else to do. I had to stop this behaviour before it became a bad habit.

It was several days before the plane came in to land and the famous four and Sebastian, strolled towards the house. I went half way down to meet them. Matthew told me that news from London had arrived and both Peter and he are required to meet at government house, before three o'clock.

Ben and Diego joined me on the veranda and we waited. The ladies told us they were going shopping and expected Ben to assist Isabel with preparing dinner. Ben was over himself with joy. I wonder what he conjures up when alone with Isabel. There were slight rumours that they had a relationship in Berbice.

It was late that evening when the pair returned from the meeting with the Governor. Matthew was beaming like a school boy. Peter was the one to speak. He told us the Colonial Office was only too happy with the arrangements and that Matthew will receive a salary of five hundred pounds per month. It was also to pay for one hundred volunteer trainees and to include all expenses for military clothing. Guns will be loaned and any damage or loss will have to be paid for in full.

"That's wonderful news." Matthew told us "I am not too keen on having to pay for rifles lost or damaged. They are a bit mean in that respect. But I was not expecting nearly four thousand dollars. I can expand my program. Never mind chaps. I have the mandate and I will use it to sort out those interlopers." a jubilant Matthew replied. Then he turned to me and asked "Have you made any arrangements?" I told him I had and also of the extraordinary reaction of generosity from everyone.

Christine and Elizabeth were happy to return to Tudor Grange and to return for the party Matthew would be arranging for my engagement, at his club, including all the catering.

On our way to Supenaam, Matthew told me in his most authoritative tone "You must not arrange anything. What we are doing, is our present to both of you, and be quiet about it."

More generosity. Will there be an end to all this? I am beginning to feel embarrassed by it. I could not make out, what all the fuss was about. I planned a small quiet dinner with my parents and a couple of my friends, to celebrate the occasion. It was taken completely out of my hands by people I only met a couples of months ago.

However I am not ungrateful and shall remember these kindnesses, for the rest of my life. My Editor! My God! I forgot to telephone him, as to the progress I was making. Perhaps when he hears the good news, he would forgive me for my tardiness for not sending him anything new. I thought the best way forward was to invite him to the party. Matthew told me that I could invite as many friends as I liked. I was sure my editor would be very happy. I often heard him say that if only he could get one of the members to introduce him to become a member. Matthew is the President of the club. It was going to be the most prestigious introduction. I had more good news for him. I thought the best way to appease my editor, should he reject my invitation, was to send him news of Matthew's appointment, as training Commander for the new force, to deal with the borders security. I know this will be headline news and relieve the pressure he has placed on me.

Matthew's response to introduce my editor was swift. I heard also, that Jonathan, Christine's father was made a peer and would soon be making his presence felt in the House of Lords.

I managed to get their attention without any fuss, after Christine joined us. She sat at the far end, listening. Looking at her, I began "First, I would like to congratulate you on your father's ennoblement. I am sure all of you must be proud."

"I am not sure Jonathan is that proud." Matthew told him. "It is a political ennoblement to boost the government's majority in the House of Lords."

"Well I am proud of my father and so is the rest of the family. Unlike you Uncle Matt, Dad is a realist." Christine replied.

"Why do you say that Christine?" I asked.

"Uncle Matt risked his life to save some of his men captured by Ahmed Khan and was to be given the Victoria Cross. He declined it. Could you imagine that? He declined the VC." was Christine's somewhat irritated reply,

"Mr. Commissioner," I started "I understand that life was really bleak for you initially. As a sixteen year old, how did you pass the time? Did you have a girlfriend among the local people here?"

"Go on Peter, tell him how you honed your sexual skills with the locals. I'd rather hear it firsthand than to read about it in your biography." Christine exploded, still irritated by Matthew's remarks about her father.

Peter's response to Christine's outburst, was simple. "This is the second time you are talking of sexual activities. Yes I did have some relationships with the local girls. What else was there to do in this God forsaken wilderness. I am not ashamed of it. I would like to point out that I did not have any amorous activities with any of them, after I met you. I fell in love with you the moment I set eyes on you. Coming ashore in your shimmering pink dress and hat to match you looked like an angel."

"I too fell in love with you the instant I saw you. Your long dark hair and green eyes. I thought you were the god of the forest. I am sorry darling. Would you forgive me?"

Peter turned to me and said in no uncertain terms that if I were to publish what was said a few minutes ago, I would have created an eternal enemy. I promised to print only the relevant facts."

I then said. "I must ask you this Peter "Your two friends Toolan and Persotum. Toolan is a mulatto and Persotum in an East Indian. How did they get in your inner circle?"

"I take everyone by their character. Toolan is energetic, philosophical and clever and my mother loves him. Persotum is a bit more aloof. I am not sure if he suffers from an inferiority complex, but we became firm friends eventually. Do I note a tone of racialism here? Are you not making a racial issue out of this? If you are, this interview will cease forthwith." Again Peter was as firm as ever.

"I was only trying to understand his relationships with two different races. Something I was unable to do. It was not by choice but the strictures imposed on me. There were brief moments under pretext of doing some favour for my father that I was able to have other races around me. The reason I asked, is the fact that we, and when I say we, I mean us British, do not classify you as European and by any stretch of the imagination, anyone can see you are Caucasian. Another reason I asked, is that you are the only Portuguese I know that have mixed friends. I admire you for that. It is not a criticism, only an observation. Can I print your remarks?" Peter nodded.

I tried to cover some very sensitive ground by asking "I note from our previous chat, that you met Christine in 1938 and that you were married in 1942. Elizabeth is ten years old. It does not take a mathematician to work out some discrepancies in all this."

Christine became agitated and told me. "Yes we did make love on the second evening of my trip here. Elizabeth is not a bastard. We swore our love before God and in our hearts. We were married the same as they do here in Supenaam. I think they call it bonding. What is the difference? People make their laws and create their Gods and become a slave to their own creation. If that is true then we have created our own doctrine and still live in its belief. Furthermore I do not wish that to be published."

"I seemed to be getting answers that are not to be published. I do not want to offend the beautiful lady, but would your friends not know the truth?"

"See Peter, he's flirting in order to escape my criticism. You very seldom tell me I am pretty." Christine teased.

"It is only because the word is not adequate enough to describe you. In my eyes you are and will remain, the most beautiful woman in the world." Peter replied with a roguish smile.

"Matthew, Christine said earlier, that you declined the Victoria Cross while you were stationed in India. Can you explain? Was my next question."

He offered an explanation with confidence "While I was there, I was introduced to the Vedanta, a strict Hindu philosophy and it was then, I discovered my inner self.

I scrutinised the Hindu religion and found it did not have much to offer, except in the Vedanta and then Buddhism. Buddha discovered that the Brahmins dominated the cultural and religious systems and created the caste system. It is no different than what we are doing today, as you pointed out earlier. So I turned to the mystics and found happiness beyond belief. That was the time I went native, because on the banks of the Ganges, I met the famous poet Rabindranaut Tagore and also a self-educated physicist. He was working on a theory that there was a particle smaller than an atom. He told me that it was the physicist, Brian Josephson who wrote that the Vedanta and the Sankhaya hold the key to the laws of the mind and thought processes, which are co-related in the quantum field… The operation and distribution of particle at atom and molecular levels."

I was forced to intervene "So this Indian you spoke about was not looking for this particle of his own accord, but was influenced by what Josephson wrote? To be quite honest I do not have the slightest idea of what you are saying. It is interesting."

"What he told me is at the moment the particle he was looking for has no name. He told me he intends to send his findings to the eminent Albert Einstein. Now I ask the question. These great people gathered there to listen to the teachings of the mystics sent a profound message to me. I became convinced that here in the sub-continent lies the secret for real harmony with yourself. It is the kind of happiness that not all the gold in cold stream can buy. If you have heard me saying that before, then I am not ashamed to say it again.

The army was embarrassed with my behaviour, especially when I referred to the Ganges as Ganga Ma the same as the Indians do. I was eventually pensioned off and sent home. I love this place. I can express myself with nature and see before me the vibrancy and beauty of her handy works. Here I am still happy and enjoying life.

If I had stayed in Somerset, helping my brother look after the estate I would have died of boredom. There are three phases in a man's life. The first is growing up. The second is to get the experience necessary for survival and the last, is to put that experience into practice.

This is what I am doing now. I am not ready to die. When I am ninety years old I shall start thinking of coming to terms with that force, I am convinced is responsible for my presence on earth. Not every man born, is given a mission in life. Those that are blessed with that mission must execute that duty of his own accord.

My friends, I am saying this for the first time, simply because I know there are wandering doubts in my friends' minds, about my reluctance to leave this place. Some of them think I am still here because I cannot stop being Commissioner. No, this is my heaven and here I will die. Peter is young and he will look after me until the time comes for me to return to my source."

Peter interrupted by saying. "I have to believe what Matthew said about his beliefs. It is what he is, that has made me one of the richest men in the country. His love and tolerance that caused him to impose on his dear friend, the former Governor to let me succeed him on retirement. There was no other way I could have been given the second most important post in the land. That is not all of his story. He has given his brother, Christine's father, his half of the inheritance. I can assure you, it is a massive fortune. I have seen the estate and only believed he did it for the happiness he craved."

"Can we continue this interview some other time?" Matthew interrupted. "I have to see what progress my lads are making, across the river. I am tired of repeating myself."

"I need to ask another question before…" I interrupted "You said you met this Indian physicist on the Ganges. Do you have his name?"

"I do not. I was too engrossed with a conversation with the great poet. I only had a glimpse of him chatting to one of the gurus. It was the great man himself that told me that the person he is pointing out will one day proved to be someone of great significance. At the time, I was too awe struck in his presence, to pay attention to anyone else." he confided.

"Then how did you recognise the poet?" I asked.

"Simply from pictures I saw of him in the newspapers. Remember, he was world famous." Matthew replied. There was a countenance of disbelief on his face as he spoke.

At this point, I agreed with the postponement. It was a bumpy interview, but interesting how people can manipulate events to suit their needs. Most interesting, was Matthew Longhorn's extraordinary life and the conviction in him, to live a long healthy life. Such thoughts are beyond the limits of my ambitions.

Before I could have cornered Peter, to ask him some personal questions. He disappeared in his office. On my way to see what the workers were doing with Matthew's project, I met Isabel. She looked at me and said "I can tell you a lot of stories you will never hear from anyone else. But you must promise not to tell who told you." I was intrigued by her remark and argued with my conscious, whether I should allow this. Curiosity got the better of me. As a journalist, I have the right to know the facts.

As a friend of Peter and his family, I do not have the right to publish anything controversial. It was with mixed feelings, I allowed Isabel to divulge all she knew. When she finished, I was in a daze. I knew I could not rely entirely on what a kitchen maid had to say. I also, must accept that not all of it could be fiction, not when the family who cared for her, since she was a child is concerned.

When I arrived at the site where Matthew hoped to build his barracks I saw Sebastian talking to him. Matthew was poking his finger at his chest and Sebastian was backing away from him, I confronted the two to find out what the argument was about.

Matthew told me Sebastian said that a dozen of Americans would secure our borders and all this nonsense of building a barracks and training savages are a waste of time. Matthew apparently became angry because Sebastian was referring to the Amerindians as savages. And his boastfulness that a handful of Americans could do what it would take an army to do. This argument was out of my league.

Their arguments became more intense when Sebastian, trying to defend himself, told Matthew that it was an inexperienced American army, who defeated the British, in the war for Independence. Matthew defended the defeat, saying that it was the actions of sympathetic British soldiers that let them win that war. I found this argument too infantile and left. I felt a man of Matthew's stature should not indulge in this school boy debate, with an American who appeared not to have much love for us.

Later that day, I watched the two of them chatting quite amicably and downing their malt. I went up and asked who won the argument.

"That was no argument." Matthew lamented. "We always teased each other about who is superior and I always win. This place creates the atmosphere for silly talks"

"Okay," Sebastian started "then tell me if this is silly talk. If we did not enter the war, who do you think would be occupying Buckingham Palace? Your king or Herr Hitler?"

"Come on chaps, the war is over. We and the Americans were victorious. So what, who has the better army." I told them, still embarrassed by this ludicrous conversation.

The trouble with drinking is it can bring out the most mundane banter. I told him I admit that should they not have fought alongside us, we may not have been victorious. Perhaps with the Russian on our side, who knows, we might have succeeded.

Then, something occurred in my mind. I never thought about it before. I must put it to him and see the reaction.

"Sebastian." I began. "I heard you boasting so much about the American Army. Can you tell me where you were engaged in Europe, during the conflict?

"I don't get you." he replied vaguely.

"Let me make it quite clear. What part of Europe did you engage the enemy?" I repeated

"I think it was in Italy. Yes, somewhere in Italy. I cannot remember the name of the town. What is this leading up to?" he asked, looking a bit sheepish.

"Then surely, you can remember the unit under which you served?" I began to press him.

"The Infantry. Yes the Infantry, under General Patton." he responded, with a vague look on his face.

"I have a friend in Washington who served under General Patton. I shall ask him to investigate your role in the war and precisely under whose command you served and the exact name of your unit." He saw I had him cornered. He raised his hand and told me the most extraordinary story.

"I am a Mormon and I could not, for the life of me, go and kill my fellow men. So when we were shipped to the Virgin Islands, I stole a plane and came here. My intention was to go to Venezuela. Instead I landed the plane at Atkinson air field and walked out of the area. Those that saw me in American uniform thought I was here on some under cover mission. A friend took me to Essequibo, where I met some other Americans. I told them I was doing some undercover work for my unit. And they believed me. That is how I was able to meet you people.

After the war, my fellow Americans returned home and left the planes we have now, to do what I like with it. They thought it was not worth shipping home."

"So, why did you come to the auction?" Did you think someone might recognize you?" I quizzed.

"Not really. All my countrymen returned to their families. I could not, for fear of being arrested, as a deserter and stealing one of the US aircrafts." he explained.

"Where is that plane now?" I again asked.

"Right where I left it. Unless your government recognised it as stolen property and confiscated it. I am not ashamed of my actions, but I will not surrender myself to people who think they have the right to kill their fellow men, with impunity. Can I ask you a question, Andrew? I know you are a journalist and have a sharp mind. What made you dream up the investigation?"

"I thought, if you are the person you claimed to be, why on earth did you not return home? You must have family and friends waiting for you. I then started to ask myself the question. Why would an American, accustomed to a lavish lifestyle, spend his life in the wilderness, flying an old plane for a pittance?

"You are more clever than I ever thought you would be. So what are you going to do about it? I will not surrender to the authority for what I believe to be my right, not to kill my fellow men."

"It is not for me to make a decision. I will have to consult with Matthew and the Commissioner and for the sake of all concerned, discuss it with the entire community. They will be your judge and jurors." he held both my shoulders and thanked me for this small consideration.

Later that evening, I called a meeting of the famous four and the six of us discussed the matter at length. Peter told us that as Commissioner, he could not participate in this discussion, or he would be forced to inform the Governor. Matthew suggested that he listened and if he feels it is a matter to be reported then so be it. "You are his employer and you have a duty for his welfare."

Sebastian welcomed the decision of the Commissioner and the rest of us. The matter must be reported and they promised that they would plead that he remains in the colony, providing he gives up his US citizenship and remain here, as a British Guianese. They will point out the important work he did, and is continuing to do, for the colony's indigenous inhabitants. They assured him that the Governor would listen to their plea.

"There is a slight hope that the Governor might succeed, simply by the fact that the Americans are seeking permission from Whitehall to drill for oil. It is suspected that the bulk of oil supplying Venezuela and Trinidad might be running across the Guiana Atlantic coast. This, will be a big step forward for the Guiana economy. Britain will benefit enormously, from its revenue. So you see, there is hope." Peter told him and it brought a glimmer of hope for all concerned.

There was one final question I needed to ask Sebastian, why did he go to the auction? I knew he told me that he felt free to attend, because he was aware that all his countrymen had returned home. I was not too happy with that. There must be a more important reason. He told me that whoever bought the plane or planes would need someone to fly them. It turned out to be exactly as he predicted.

I was sitting under the silk cotton pondering over events and of Sebastian's confession. I wanted to write something to my editor. I felt it would be a betrayal to those that trusted me. I was still engrossed with my thoughts, when Matthew and Diego joined me. I was surprised Ben was not with them.

Matthew asked "Andrew, can you do me a favour? I would like you to write to your editor and ask him to publish my role as training commander, for a new force to be deployed on the Brazilian and Venezuelan borders, a force of one thousand trained Wakaburu warriors. The Brazilians knew these men as fierce warriors and have a great respect for them. It would help our cause, if this news should reach them."

"But it is not a thousand men, you are authorised to train one hundred." I pointed out.

"Yes you and I know that, but the enemy does not. You get my point? Anyway, papers have a way of exaggerating. It will not be difficult to continue doing what you people have been doing all the time."

"It is no wonder the Governor calls you an old fox. I will do it .Thank you I was racking my brain to find something important to get to my editor's desk and relieve me of the pressure, he always places on me."

"It will make it more interesting if you were to tell him it was information you got from secret meetings with the commander and his friends, or words to that effect. Use your conniving skills." he ended.

I was thankful for his suggestion. I remembered, I promised young Diego to publish his poem and to create a children's column. I would see to that right now.

CHAPTER 11
TROUBLE FOR THE COMMISSIONER

Several weeks later, after I submitted my article, Matthew asked to be printed, I was watching the final stage of construction; he would not allow anyone near it, until completion. I would have been very happy to see what that monstrosity would look like inside.

Eventually, the day came, when we were all invited to see his creation. As I said, it was a monstrosity. There were bunks for about forty persons at a time and communal showers at both ends of the building. The bunks were in triple tiers and cleverly, he had the roof opened at both ends, where the showers were. This was to allow the cool air from the river to circulate for comfort, from the searing heat.

As usual, there were lots of drinks flowing and Ben, as usual, was busy with bottle in hand, pouring for everyone. Matthew was accepting congratulations for his imaginative work. Christine told him that she knew he was clever, but not as an architect. Celebrations were well on their way, when we heard, beyond belief, gun shots, firing in succession. Matthew ordered everyone to stay calm and sent two of the rangers to investigate. Hours later, when they failed to report, Matthew asked Ben to accompany him to investigate. I was extremely fearful for Margaret's safety. A long time passed, when the duo appeared, with the two rangers.

There were dozens of Brazilians in company with men, from the Monato tribe, old enemies of Paramount Chief Warachara. Apparently, they must have read of Matthew's ambition, of securing the borders and conspired, with members of the Monato, to stage this pre-emptive attack. More seriously, is that, they have Chiefs Warachara and Obeyo and also Susheila, as captives.

An envoy under the white flag of truce, came forward and demanded our surrender and that Matthew must accompany him to meet their leader.

Peter told him that he was the Commissioner and that any negotiations they wanted to discuss would be through him. He looked scornfully at Peter and left.

For the first time, I saw Ben throw away his drink and creep up to Matthew, for consultation of his next step.

"I will have to hear what the bastards have to offer. I will not allow Peter to compromise any of my plans. These people need to be taught a lesson once and for all. I think now they have forced my hand, I have a plan, that I think may work and perhaps teach them a lesson on warfare. He then called on Peter, Diego and Ben and Sebastian. I could not hear what they were planning. I could only think that his suggestions were met with approval.

He soon joined the rest of us and ordered Ben to take a rifle and stay with the ladies and protect them with his life. This, Ben promised to do.

It was several hours later, when their envoy arrived and told Matthew that the Commissioner would be allowed to negotiate.

He signaled to Diego and Sebastian and asked me to follow. It was Peter, Matthew and I in the forefront of this dangerous mission. I prayed Matthew knew what he was doing. My father would never forgive me, if I got myself killed over a bit of land. It was getting a bit dark and in an hour, it would be totally dark and I wondered what dangers that in itself, would present.

Eventually, we came to a large clearing and a blazing bon fire, brightened the surrounding area. Peter tied his white handkerchief on a stick and walked forward. He told the leader, whose name was revealed as Perez, that I was a journalist, and not a fighting man. Furthermore, he told him that I would write of this event in my newspaper. He looked at me querulously and made me stand aside. I was out of firing line and for that, I was grateful.

Pimento wanted to be taken to where the gold was. He said he was told that there was gold in a river they called, cold stream, also, that Peter and Matthew must accompany them to it.

Peter told him he is unaware of gold and a cold stream and the only gold he has is for his dental work. He raised his hand to strike Peter. Matthew reminded him that we were under the flag of truce. He hesitated, and then he played his ace.

"I have your chiefs and one of your women as hostage. I will not hesitate to shoot them, if I do not get my wish." he told us, showing the way they were held.

Matthew, pretending he was angry shouted on top of his voice "YOU WANT US TO TAKE YOU TO COLD STREAM THEN SO BE IT, BUT NOT BEFORE SUNLIGHT." Then he lowered his voice and told Perez he must allow them to return to their homes and would come back early in the morning. He agreed and told us that four of his men would accompany us and escort us back there. "I don't want you to get up to monkey tricks. I heard a lot about you. The one they call the 'Fox'. I am cleverer than any fox in the forest. You remember that, Senor Longhorn."

I then realised these men were not Brazilians, but Venezuelans. Only the Spaniards refer to men as senor. I conveyed this information to Peter. He nodded and told me he knew that immediately they mentioned that word.

The four men stayed outside when we went indoors, to be greeted by weeping women. Matthew told them that this crisis would be over in the morning. He then explained why he shouted that he would take them at dawn. It was Diego and Sebastian to hear and put his plan into action. Pimento has a son among his men. I heard him addressing him and telling him to observe his father's cunning and pretty soon, they would return home with bags of gold. He also told us that, for his plan to work, he would have to find a way for Diego to identify the son. He relieved all of us, when he said that he thought he had found a way to do it.

Morning came and I do not think any one of us slept. Isabel was summoned and given some instructions before we left.

Some of Monato's men stayed behind to guard the three hostages, while we proceeded towards cold stream.

Instead of going to where I thought would be cold stream, we were instead heading North East. I did not have a clue where this direction would lead us. Pimento and his men were getting agitated and stopped to ask Peter where he was going. Peter told him another hour and they would be there. It was more than an hour that we came to a small stream.

"There, Matthew shouted as loud as he could, pretending he was angry. Pimento must have heard a lot of this gold bearing stream. The first thing he did was to place his hand in the water and he immediately withdrew it. He told one of his men to go in and get the gold.

Matthew informed him that the gold is not always there, only when it rains and the river brings it at this junction. They ignored what Matthew was saying and continued to scoop up handfuls of pebbles. Pimento was getting impatient and pointed at Matthew's head and threatened to shoot him, if no gold is found.

Matthew shrugged his shoulders and told him, that if he had listened, he would have heard him saying that gold is not always found when you want it, but only when it rains for a few days. Fortunately for him, they did find a few small nuggets. He sent in more men to scoop up the pebbles. They were getting blue from the cold water and refused to dig any further. A few more men took turns and produced a small amount of very tiny nuggets.

It was at this point, we heard his son shout that he had been taken prisoner by Diego and Sebastian. Diego put his pistol in the son's ear and demanded that they dropped their weapons. Perez was not adhering to the demand. It was only when Sebastian shouted "Senor, I am Americano. And I would shoot your mother f… head clean off your shoulders. Drop your weapons and I don't mean tomorrow or next week. I mean NOW. See Diego has a gun in your son's ear and he will do the same to him."

Reluctantly they dropped their weapons, except one mean looking thug. He raised his gun to shoot Sebastian, in an instant he fell dead on the ground. Isabel came from behind the trees shouting and asking for Peter who went and consoled her, the bandits were quickly tied up and marched off to Supenaam.

When we arrived, there was more weeping from Christine, Margaret and Bell. Eventually, Matthew let us in on the reason why he shouted that he would take Perez to cold stream. It was for Diego to hear and also Matthew instructed Isabel to tell him where to go. It was a risky situation. I guess that is why Matthew was known as the fox. They were taken to the new barracks and locked up, until communications were relayed to the Governor, of what happened.

We sat down celebrating our lucky escape. Everyone was telling the girls of Diego and Sebastian's brave effort. Matthew reminded them that it was his plan that saved the day. He also told Sebastian that the Governor would be given a glowing report of his bravery, which ought to go well with his plea to be considered for a new citizenship.

Then they remembered that the chiefs and Susheila were still held captive. Ben, wanting to get some of the action, said he would go with Sebastian and rescue them. There was a tendency to laugh at his suggestion.

Eventually, the duo set out on their mission. They had only gone for a minute, when Diego asked me to follow him. We kept well out of their reach until they arrived.

The four men pointed their guns at them and demanded to know what happened to their leader and his son. They reminded Sebastian that they were to kill all the hostages and anyone trying to rescue them. At this point, Diego fired a shot in the air and told them to drop their guns or they would all be dead.

They tried to peer through the vegetation, to see who and how many were there. Diego fired a second shot and reminded them that the next shots would be in their heads. Confused, they dropped their guns and walked away from the hostages. They were, in turn, bound and joined their countrymen, in the barracks.

This would be sensational news for my editor. I intended on glossing it up considerably, to portray Sebastian as one of the major players in this episode.

Sebastian, still concerned about his future, was listening to Peter's conversation to the Governor, on the telephone. The line was apparently not very good. He was getting impatient with the repetitiveness of their conversation. It turned out, that the Governor's wish was for Peter and Matthew to visit him and discuss the matter urgently. This promise was given and it was decided that they go to Georgetown the next day.

Sebastian wanted to go but Matthew told him it would be wiser that his plea be discussed in his absence. He also said that the prisoners would go on that flight and be placed in custody, with the authorities in the capital.

I insisted on going, since I would not be able to interview either of them and then I would have the opportunity to see my editor and give him a vivid account of events and the creation of the children's column.

It was all settled. Ben sulked, because he had to stay behind to look after the ladies. Whether that was a sulk of pretence, is hard to follow. I know for a fact, from what Isabel confided, that they did have a relationship. I could not say for sure, whether it was still an ongoing situation.

The Jaguar was waiting in the driveway and the prisoners were handed over to the police. I was told that I would be taken to my office first and the two of them would drive to Main Street to see the Governor.

This would give me time to see Mr. Humphries about the ring and Mr. Asro for my suit. The engagement party was soon and it was time to get myself ready for it.

Back at the house, Matthew asked if I could take him to see the tailor that was making my suit. I told him, I only saw him an hour ago but I was willing to take him there. He explained that he wished to place a contract for him to make two hundred khaki drill uniforms for his trained rangers. He emphasised the importance of it, under the circumstance.

I asked if there was any decision, concerning Sebastian. He told me it looked good and a decision within the next week or so was expected.

The troubles in the last few days was taking a toll on our reserves. Matthew, being the eldest, suggested that we have a real rest for a few days. He told us that his friend, Andrew McIntosh, in the sugar plantation in Skeldon, knew somewhere not far from where he was, of a nice resort where we could relax and rejuvenate.

He told us that if we take the plane to Berbice, then motor up the Corentyne to number sixty three village, he would meet us there and take us to the resort. He also mentioned the fact that this resort was not like the one we found in the Bahamas or the Mediterranean. The water is a bit muddy, but safe enough to have a swim and relax on its golden sands. It was exactly as described. The more I saw of Berbice, the more fascinating it got.

The ladies were enjoying themselves splashing about, which drew a lot of spectators who probably thought they were mad splashing around in their skinny swimsuits. It must be remembered, Europeans usually do not do this sort of thing in public. The crowd was enjoying themselves and shouting encouragements to Margaret, who was a bit shy.

Ben, without saying anything, was pouring out the drinks and handing them to us. The sun was really hot and I suppose, I could not blame the ladies for their somewhat unashamed behaviour. Isme, the sugar plantation manager gave support when she joined the happy lot. I must say, for a middle aged lady, she kept a good figure and Andrew was proud of it.

It was not long before Narine and Ali came on the scene. This was surprising. We knew there was a political meeting somewhere on the coast.

It was inevitable that some political discussions came into play and Matthew, always ready to defend the land of his birth, took the challenge.

Ali insisted that a free general election would put either the People's Party, or the Freedom Movement in power. Whichever won the election, would be the same, a free British Guiana. He went on with the same old criticism of the British, forcing men and women onto boats and bringing them here as indentured labourers, when in essence, they were more or less paid slaves.

Matthew interrupted, having a redder complexion than what the sun gave him. "Now you listen to me and listen carefully. I would not believe that we would force people to come to a strange land and treat them like slaves. You have never visited the land of your fathers. I lived here for eighteen years. I know Calcutta as I know Supenaam. I know of the poverty that existed there. You have not seen real poverty. It is only when you see it, that you would realise what a good life you have here. Sure, the sugar plantation owners may have treated you a bit harshly and you have dreamt of a brighter life, as any thinking man would. But I would like to defend my country, by telling you Narine and Ali, Britain has a responsibility to be a great empire. It is a monumental task.

Sometimes, little things, like what you are fighting for, are overlooked, not deliberately. This monumental task I spoke of, concerns all humanity within the frame work of the empire. You are intelligent enough to know that it is the overall picture that matters and sometimes it does not show what you may have considered important.

British Guiana is not ready for your dream. The people are not ready. The economy is not ready and more importantly, of all you are not ready to take on the mantle of premiership. Not you, nor that flamboyant leader of the People's Movement. You know me as being fair to all men. I would not even mention what the four of us did. Surely you must know in your heart that this is a futile mission? I will leave you to your dreams. Remember my words and I will always be there if you need me. I would be pretending if I say I wish you good luck. What I can say, is that you think things over seriously, consult with the elders of your village and you will receive good counselling."

They replied that Britain is was supporting the owners of the sugar industry and if that trend continued, it would make it impossible to seek any other course, but to take hold of their destiny. If it all goes askew then they only have themselves to blame. It was not a positive answer and Matthew realised this.

Of course the two young men were really fired up with their dreams and no matter what Matthew told them, it would fall on deaf ears.

This interruption made the ladies want to go back to New Amsterdam. Andrew McIntosh was not accepting that. Instead, he offered to put them up at the guest house. We all accepted the invitation.

That evening, we had a marvellous time, socialising with the rest of his most senior staff. Again, I must admit I am baffled by these Berbicians and their hospitality.

In the morning, the factory workers filed past, looking at us and perhaps thinking we were the new members of the manager's staff. What surprised me most, was that they took their hats or caps off when passing the manager. Those without head gear would tip their forehead, signifying a mark of respect. McIntosh stood rigid, as they filed past and only smiled at us when the last one went through the gate. I asked McIntosh. "Is that a rule of the management?" He told me it certainly was not. They themselves adopted this mode of respect. I had a feeling it was passed down the generation. I returned their respect by acknowledging it, if only to please them.

It was time to go. Isme brought the ladies in her car and we were soon speeding towards New Amsterdam and on to our plane, bound for Supenaam.

I thought of the many parties we had in the last month and felt that I should really have a low keyed affair, with my parents and two other friends for the engagement. The ring was ready, so was the suit.

Matthew would not tolerate my suggestion. He told me he had already booked the evening at his club. The caterers were given their instructions and there was no turning back now. It was with great reluctance, I agreed.

As it turned out, the party was not as stressful as I imagined. The pleasure from the praises Margaret received from everyone, pleased my parents so much so, that my father, who is not a drinker, by any stretch of the imagination, was taking the champagne like everyone else. Matthew, as usual, stole the show, with his glittering praise of everyone concerned, for bringing about a happy conclusion to a very romantic evening.

CHAPTER 12
THE EXODUS

Peter was having an argument with Christine on the veranda. I heard Doctor Louise telling him that it was no fault of hers that Christine wanted to return to England. Doctor Louise further said "I assured her that I would be able to see her through her pregnancy safely, despite the lack of suitable facilities here, or in Georgetown."

"I cannot imagine why she would want to leave. Especially since Elizabeth is settling down in her new school. The Rabbi will be upset, moving children can have a devastating effect on their long term ability to settle down and take their studies seriously." he told the doctor.

"I am sorry Peter; you ought to speak to her again. Why not let Matthew talk to her?" she asked.

"This is my problem. I must deal with it as I see fit." he told her.

Matthew came, just as he finished his statement. "What do you want me to talk about?" he asked.

It was inevitable that Matthew got involved with this domestic disagreement. I think it is because Christine was his niece and being far away from home, he felt obliged to make sure she is happy.

Christine insisted on going. She decided that it would be during the school summer break. That somehow, seemed to have satisfied Peter. He became agitated, when he heard that Diego and Bell would be travelling with her "This is a conspiracy!" he yelled.

"It's not a conspiracy. It was I who told Bell of my intentions and she proposed that it would be a good idea if she comes along." Diego told her he would not permit it unless he accompanied her, was her defense.

"Ben agreed to look after him until they return." she replied.

"So Ben has conspired to do his babysitting without consulting me?" an angry Peter asked.

Christine used the old feminine touch to soften him. She caressed him and whispered words in his ear. That appeared to calm him down, before he remarked "You said one month. You will return after one month."

"I promise you darling, I'll be back in a month's time. Besides, I haven't seen my parents for a whole year. Papa will be ever so pleased their beautiful granddaughter is coming to celebrate her tenth birthday with them."

I was ever so delighted to see them hug and kiss, like two newly met lovers, much to the embarrassment of both Matthew and myself. Ben arrived just as we were leaving and I could hear Peter scolding him about conspiring against him. Ben defended his decision by telling Peter that he was no longer his body guard. It was only brotherly friendship that had anchored him with them. I knew Peter never meant to offend him. It was his way of consoling himself and Ben knew it.

Later that day, in a unique stroke of luck, I managed to get both Peter and Matthew together for this long awaited interview. Their lives were certainly interesting and intriguing. I had to be careful, not to over emphasise Matthew's involvement in Peter's life and vice versa. I did managed to get a couple hours of their time and all I had to do was wait until Christine leaves and I know I will be able to return to 'civilisation' and a happy editor.

Christine and Bell decided to fly to Georgetown, to inform the Rabbi of her decision and then fly to Berbice, to spend a few days with Peter's parents. This pleased Peter and he was happy to see them off; Diego Junior and Ben looked on, with blank expressions on their faces.

I strolled back to the house, taking a good look at the silk cotton and the devastation it suffered at the hands of nature. Ben reminded me that in a year's time, that tree will look like nothing happened to it. The branches would have new foliage and it would be as vibrant as it used to be.

"So why don't we comfort it by having our usual sip under it?" Ben suggested.

"Good idea" I replied. I was beginning to miss Diego and the others and they had only been gone a few minutes.

Ben did not need any reminding. He was off like a shot to get the malt and we sat and drank our hearts out. I was celebrating my victory in getting those two eels together and Ben was drowning his sorrows.

With the ladies gone, it was up to Margaret to run the affairs of the home and with Isabel in her argumentative mood, I could see she had her hands full.

Warachara and Obeyo came and asked me to write their story. For a minute, I did not know what to say. It then occurred to me that the outside world had no idea of how these people lived, or even how they existed. The chiefs had given a real opening and enough to forward to my Editor.

It turned out, that Warachara became chief when his father died. He became Paramount Chief after a fierce battle with the Monato tribe. They wanted their leader to be Paramount Chief. Obeyo and the other chiefs wanted Warachara. There were conflicts that eventually escalated in a full scale tribal war. It went on for a few years. It was Matthew who put an end to it and a shaky truce saw them living in near harmony.

"How did Matthew stopped the war?" I asked.

Warachara explained "Matthew not want to get involved. He thought war end quickly. No end in sight. So he must do something, Matthew strong man with jaguar heart. We listened and he forced Monata people to sit at table in long house and make peace. To make peace strong I marry their chief's sister. Not a very pretty woman, I said to myself, when alone in my bed with her, she can be any woman I want. So as you from city say 'What the hell.' I been in hell many times she no like me to smile at other women. So I send her back to her people. Not because she was ugly but she give me no children. Now with new woman I have eight strong young men to fight if war comes again."

He turned to Obeyo and nudged him, saying "Now you tell storyteller your life, but not mentioned time you and I fight for same woman."

"What's this about two friends fighting for the same woman?" I asked, as a feeling of excitement gripped me of this intriguing bit of news.

"No tell." Obeyo interrupted, as Warachara tried to speak. In unison, they both spoke at the same time. "We made a promise not to tell, Must keep promise."

I was beginning to have quite a good insight into the lives of these extraordinary people. With Matthew and Diego absent, the chief thought they'd try their luck, by asking for some whisky. I told them that if I were to do that, then Commissioner would be very angry and send me away. They both drew their breaths and shook their heads. Then tilting their heads from me and squinting their eyes. They asked again. "No whisky?"

One look from me was enough to tell them my answer. Disappointed, they then tried to make me their friends again. Warachara asked me if I ever went to THE Great Waterfalls. He told me it is where he fought Monato's people and the site where many died and were buried. "It is now a sacred place. You will see strange structures built by people of long ago." "It sounds very interesting. Maybe I will uncover some prehistoric monuments and gain a better knowledge of these people." I replied. Then he offered to take me there. I must consider Diego junior and ask permission from Peter, to travel inland. It was a prerequisite for all non-residents, when not accompanied by the commissioner to have a pass. This would not be a problem. The only problem was to see Diego's son is in good hands, in our absence. Also, I would not venture further, in the interior without Ben by my side. This, I discussed with the chiefs before making preparations.

Margaret and Isobel were happy to care for Junior. This is what I would call him in future. Ben was a bit apprehensive at first claiming that he never ventured inland without Diego. It took several days for the chiefs to make the necessary preparations. I left all our preparations to Ben.

When the time came, we loaded all the chiefs' and our equipment on the trailer. The two chiefs and some of their people clambered aboard. Ben decided to drive while I sat next to him on an improvised seat. The going was smooth for the first two days, then it became bumpy and at times, we thought the tractor would get stuck in some muddy areas. Our good luck held until after the eighth day, we arrived at our destination. We were now about two hundred miles west of the Demerara. This, according to my calculations, would put us in the middle of the county of Essequibo.

It was an incredible sight. I must have been dreaming, the buildings were of Dutch Gothic architecture in complete ruins. I could still make out its beauty. Whoever constructed this magnificent place and for what purpose was a complete mystery to me. I took my camera and photographed every square inch of it. This would be a real sensation when it hit the press.

The chiefs were impressed with my reactions and started telling me what they knew of the place.

It went without saying, having to remind myself that this was built by the Dutch. History had revealed that they built a fort at the junction, where the Mazaruni. Cayuni and Essequibo rivers meet. Also, along the Atlantic coast. No record of them settling anywhere else in the interior of the country.

I could not see the purpose for constructing these massive buildings. It was not built like a fortress, as there was nothing in sight to protect. The waterfalls were about four hundred yards away. There was a huge mound where the bones of the fallen were buried. I was told it was tribal custom to allow the animals to eat the bodies and then the bones were gathered and buried in a ritualistic manner.

I began examining in detail, what was left of the buildings. Inside one of the less deteriorated structures, I found what looked like, official papers. I could see the stamp marks clearly on some of them and the language was definitely Dutch. There was a huge iron safe corroded on the outside with the inner casing still intact. I shouted to Ben and asked him to take it outside for further examination. As he tried to lift the safe off the ground, the whole thing just collapsed, revealing more documents and some Dutch guilders. There was also a very large amount of stones in one compartment.

From what I learned from Matthew and the others, they were probably uncut diamonds. I wondered who it belonged to, now it was found. This site would have to be reported and I imagine, an army of experts would have to determine its future. I began to calculate the distance from where they originally built their fort and found it was reasonable to assume that they could have chosen thus place, as a safe haven for housing their officials. It was never clear historically, why they built Fort Kyke overall, in the first place.

The chiefs told me not to remove anything, until Matthew Longhorn and the Commissioner were informed. I told them that I needed to take one stone, to show the man concerned to assess what it is. They all agreed and insisted it was not to be kept as a souvenir. This was understandable

Ben was rummaging through some other rooms and found rusting swords and muskets, lots of them; there were a few that survived the ravishes of time and remained intact. I was not prepared to test them to see if they still worked. I am terrified of guns. As usual, I took as many pictures, as my camera allowed.

We camped there for a few more days, exploring the surrounding areas for clues, to this mysterious place. So far, we could find nothing. I decided to question Warachara. He started to explain "Only tribal people come here. No Matthew Longhorn. No Commissioner. No Diego. You first white man see this place."

"But why did you not tell the Commissioners who protected you all these years?" I queried.

"This here sacred ground for long, long time. Father of my father and many more fathers say sacred ground only tribal people visit." he told me.

"Chief Obeyo. Why did you bring me here?" I asked.

"You write story of chiefs so you must see history of tribal people. You go inside big house not so good for you. We must ask spirit of fathers not to harm you and me and Warachara will clean your body." he told me, looking very solemn.

They then set about, scrubbing my nude body with leaves from a greenheart tree and other bushes, found in the surrounding area. I felt and smelled like an alchemist in his experimenting laboratory. I felt good, not because I was given a good massage and washing, but because I felt I was free from harm, by the spirit of their ancestors not that I believed in such nonsense, but it was better to be safe than sorry.

We were having roasted wild boar for supper and it was a very bright moonlit evening. Ben decided to stroll around, making sure he stayed within earshot of us. We heard a crash, as if someone was ripping apart the undergrowth and an ear splitting scream. We looked in the direction from whence it came and could see neither Ben nor whatever terrified him. Then, there was this loud shouting for help. We could not see him, only hear his groaning.

Obeyo went forward and he also disappeared. He called out to Watachara and explained where he was. I could not understand a word of what he was saying. Instead I followed the chief and found him looking down a great deep hole which was covered with undergrowth. He took his machete and cleared away most of it. I could see Ben's head towering above that of Obeyo. Warachara made a rope from the vines and tied it to a tree, then he dropped the length of it down. It took what seemed like ages before Ben was able to push Obeyo up and he, in turn, dragged himself up. He was covered in vegetation but refused to wash until the sun came up. We finished our supper and went to sleep.

In the morning, we discovered that it was a mine, going down hundreds of feet away from the falls. The chiefs sent some of their men down, to clear the pit which was supported with greenheart timbers. Greenheart is a wood that can survive any conditions for centuries, even longer when sunken in salt water for building harbours. So it was not surprising to see it could still hold up the roof of this mine.

We made a cursory examination, but was none the wiser, as to the reason it was dug. Was it words came through that the

British was nearby and it was dug hurriedly to bury their valuables? Or was there another reason. Digging for gold or diamonds. This part of South America was renowned for tales of the golden city of El dorado. It's a known fact that this part of the colony, is rich in gold and diamonds. It was still a mystery why that fort was built.

Historians never gave any reason. Perhaps, they knew all along and kept it a secret. My own theory was that they found huge quantities of gold, diamonds and other precious stones and that fort was to protect their find. I was only hoping that when Matthew returned, the mystery would be solved. The chiefs did not know anything about it and I was not going to question them. It was only logical that they would see its importance and shroud it in more mystery.

We decided to pack our things and leave this place to its secrets for now. Before we departed, the chiefs and their men went to the pit and performed a ceremony. They then covered the entrance with undergrowth before joining us.

Ben and I discussed the presence of mine for some time. He pointed out that, although Peter was the Commissioner, he would be unable to do anything until Matthew arrived. Peter was Commissioner for only a couple of years, that is why Matthew remained to instruct him on some of the laws of the hinterland. Peter, was of course, only too happy to have him around.

On our arrival, Ben took the initiative to enlighten Peter of the latest events. Peter was as baffled as we were and he also suggested that we go no further, until Matthew returned.

They had been gone for only a week and already it seemed like a year. Peter was not the regular happy man he used to be. It is only the saucy Isabel that occasionally brings out a smile. Ben also, has been a bit melancholy. Perhaps it was because I wouldn't join him, in his daily sipping. Joseph would not have been any help either. It was good he was in Berbice, helping Peter's father, in his daily rounds at the surgery, in the hospitals.

One morning, I was waiting for Peter at his office, when the telephone rang. The clerk picked up the instrument and smiled. He then shouted to Peter "It's for you Sir. It's your friend, Toolan."

Peter rushed out in his robe and took the call. I heard him chuckle and say "Don't waste a minute. Get up here as soon as you can. My pilot is in Berbice. I will give you a number to ring and tell him to bring you here. Tell him to ring me if there is a problem. Christine and the others have gone to the UK and I am here almost alone."

CHAPTER 13

THE LONG WAIT

I was walking down to Peter's office and I saw him standing with Ben. They were speaking out of earshot. I finally heard Peter saying a bit loud, "God will not be pleased."

"What will God not be pleased about?" I asked.

Peter explained "Ben was thinking of going and playing with the caiman that has a nest on the incline across the river. He calls it 'Catch me if you can'. This overgrown man wants to play, with an expectant mother. Can you believe it, Andy?"

"What harm is there if he wants his leg bitten off.? It will certainly slow him down a bit." I responded, without really meaning what I said. Then continuing, I asked "What's this game about?"

"Let's walk down the river and he will demonstrate." Peter suggested.

While walking down the river, I could understand why Ben was drumming up some activities If only to keep boredom locked away. The absence of Matthew, Diego and the ladies had left a vacuous atmosphere in Supenaam. However, since I had never seen this death defying action before, I was only too keen to entertain myself, albeit on Ben's life.

Whenever we strolled down the river, the original inhabitants would try to see what we were after. On this occasion, it was more than a handful of them. By the way, I decided to refer to the indigenous population, as the original inhabitants. It gives them a more dignified standing.

They all lined the upper reaches of the incline. The three of us went down the river's bank and waited for Ben to start his act. First, he stepped on the rocks, across the river, until he reached the other side, then stealthily, he crept up to the nest and threw a twig at it. There was a rustling noise from the undergrowth and then it stopped. Ben took a long branch and started to imitate an intruder at the nest. The caiman rushed at great speed towards Ben, who immediately withdrew and clambered up a tree. The caiman gave an upward glance before returning to its resting place.

Ben came down the tree and repeated his previous actions. This time, the caiman was more alert and rushed like a steam train, towards Ben. He was unable to reach the tree, so instead, he stood his ground; and as the caiman came inches to him, he threw his entire weight on top of the reptile. The reptile rolled and Ben rolled with it. The original inhabitants were cheering and some were shouting 'Naga noma… Naga noma' Others were shouting 'Noma… noma' I turned to Peter and asked what they were saying. He told me Naga noma meant don't kill and Noma meant kill.

Obviously there was Warachara's people wanting to save the reptile, while the Monatoes wanted to see Ben kill it. The Chief Warachara came down the incline and shot an arrow in the air. It went passed the Monatoes and there was silence. Warachara raised his bow and uttered 'Naga noma… Naga noma. In an instant and in unison, they all shouted Naga noma… Naga noma. They kept repeating it, while Ben was struggling with the reptile.

Eventually, he was able to get the better of the creature and as it lay on its stomach, Ben straddled it, as a rider would a horse, pressing his hand heavily on the caiman's head. It started trashing with its tail. At this point, another caiman appeared on the scene. Ben had a look of horror on his face. He hastily pulled one of the front legs to its back, gave it a quick slap on the head and ran up the tree. The two caimans rushed after him, but they were too late.

They tried to climb the tree and as everyone knows, caimans cannot climb trees. They hurled their bodies as far as their hind legs would carry them and looked at Ben like an hungry man looks at a delicious dinner, he's unable to have. When they realised their waiting was futile, they went back to the river, occasionally turning back, looking towards the nest.

The original inhabitants cheered and strummed the strings on their bows, which made a beautiful rhythmical sound. They kept it up until Ben was safely on our side of the river.

After they departed, satisfied with the day's entertainment, Peter turned to Ben and said "You are truly a very strong man. I guess that caiman was far heavier than you. Now that you have entertained us, I want you to tell Margaret and Isabel to prepare to travel to Georgetown when her father returns with the plane."

"I thought your friend Toolan was coming up." I reminded him. It was then, he told me that he must go to Georgetown for the all faith service at Saint Paul's Cathedral on Sunday. "Because of that, I asked Toolan to wait for me and he could come along as well. It was then he reminded me that it was Empire's Day celebration. All the children would march past the Governor, flanked by the Commissioner and his chief of police. I was asked to wear my plumed helmet and uniform. I really don't like wearing it in the city. Here in Supenaam it's different it is a show of authority. There in Georgetown I will be seen as a Colonial Master,"

"But you are a Colonial Master." I joked.

The next couple of days were spent getting ready for this big day. Peter gave strict instructions to Isabel, to iron his uniform, as she had never done before and to give his trousers a sharp crease. Plumes cleaned and helmet whitened.

We were all set to leave, but no plane arrived, so Peter telephoned to find out what was causing the hold up. He was told that Joseph was on his way. A few seconds later he did land and we all boarded, after some cursory examinations of the craft.

Saturday afternoon in the city was always a busy time. Everyone waited for the last minute, to do their shopping and the nearer it gets to closing time the busier it gets. The two ladies were given some time off, to do their last minute shopping, while we sorted ourselves out. I decided to leave Peter and Ben by themselves and went and visited my parents. They were ever so pleased that I remembered Empire Day and asked if I would be attending the service. Giving an affirmative answer, pleased them even more.

Sunday morning, the streets were deserted, even the sea wall, a place of recreational activities was empty. I assumed everyone was getting ready for the big event. I did not want to sound unpatriotic but it only reminds the colonist of their duty to pay homage to a queen long dead and an Empire that never noticed their existence. Whether it was tantamount to hypocrisy or not, was my personal opinion.

The gardener/watchman was polishing the Jaguar, mirrors gleamed in the sunlight and the car sparkled, like it was just out of the showroom.

We motored down the sea wall road, towards the railway station, where there was a huge crowd, from all over the East Coast and from Berbice. We turned left, into Main Street and a few yards further on was the Governor's mansion. The guard at the entrance saluted and let us in. I was sitting in front with Peter and felt very important. At the back Ben, Margaret and her father sat with awe struck faces.

We sat in a reception room and waited for the Governor. We did not have to wait long. He greeted us warmly and offered some much needed malt. I had never entered these premises before and I could not wait to tell my editor.

The 'March Past' was indeed a spectacle to behold. The children from different schools wore their unique uniforms all neat and tidy and the boys were ever so smart as they gave the salute. There were two sturdy young men carrying the Union Jacks, one in front and another at the back. The Governor looked every part the King's representative, as he took the salute. Peter and the chief of police watched with solemnity written all over their faces. I really felt I was wrong, to interpret the occasion as a ceremony of sheer colonial imperialism. We then entered the Cathedral and the Bishop of the West Indies and Guiana welcomed the dignitaries. The edifice was full to capacity and there, I could see important men from every walk of life, sat looking pious, waiting for proceedings to begin. Never before had I seen a congregation, where seventy five per cent were Europeans. I imagined this was the time to show loyalty to the crown.

The Bishop opened proceedings as usual, with a very long prayer and set about reminding us of our duty to the crown. The Governor thanked everyone for their presence and spoke at great lengths of the responsibilities of the Empire and the graciousness of His Majesty to hold his Empire in unity.

When the others spoke their volumes, it was time for the Hindu and Muslim representative to speak. Pandit Jai Ram spoke eloquently and praised the Governor for his leadership, in harmonising unity among the races. The Muslim Imam looked ruffled and sweating profusely, went up and offered a short prayer in Arabic and then all hell broke loose.

First he condemned this affair as imperialistic and a betrayal of the people of this colony that gave their sweat to Scottish sugar kings, who lived stylish and affluent lives. "It is time we are handed our own destiny." He was not allowed to continue. The Chief of Police ordered two of his men to take him outside. He managed to free himself and approached the Governor apologising vehemently, saying he was blackmailed into saying those words. I was intrigued with his last statement and told Peter I would meet him later at his house. As a Journalist, I was committed to investigate intriguing matters, especially if it had a connection with the government.

Peter invited the Governor to his residence for a social get-together which was accepted, enthusiastically. I, on the other hand, had my work to do. On my way out, I met my editor. The first thing he said to me "Go and get that story from that man and see me in my office in the morning."

I told him that was why I was staying behind and he nodded in agreement, as I tried to make my way out.

The Imam was standing by the door, looking contrite and with apology written all over his face He was hoping to see the Governor, who had slipped out from the side entrance at the Bishop's request. I went up and introduced myself and told him I would like to hear his side of the story. He promised to tell me everything, on condition that I print his apology to the Governor. This I agreed and then he unfolded one of the most bizarre stories I'd ever heard.

He told me that the politician, Ali Anwar, was engaged to be married to his daughter. Everything was set, the date and place. Then, when he heard I was coming to this event, he told me what to say and threatened to call off the wedding if I did not comply. He further stated that he would have been shunned from the community that have a great respect and regards for him, if this wedding was cancelled. My community would never be able to understand why. They are poorly educated and a thing like that to happen, will only increase speculation that something was amiss, with my daughter. The shame would have been unbearable. I had to do as he asked, if only to preserve my daughter's good name. You do understand. Don't you?"

I felt sympathy for the poor man. I could see the dilemma he was facing and I was determined to drag that hypocritical bastard down from his political platform. I must think carefully and with my editor's cooperation, I'd see to it, that he was on the downhill slide.

Back at Peter's residence, we waited for the Governor and his Lady to arrive. It was not long before he was ushered in the drawing room. Peter had never met the Governor's wife before. On introducing him, the Governor told her that he was the Commissioner for the hinterland and that his wife was away in England, visiting relatives.

Peter made a slight gesture of bowing and shook her hand and quite out of character, he told her "Lady Cavendish, The newspaper did you no justice. You are a remarkably beautiful lady."

"Why Mr. Commissioner, your wife is away and you are flirting?" she said smiling, not meaning anything darker.

"And in my presence" the Governor added.

"It would be hard for any man not to be hypnotised by such elegance, my lady. Now, how rude of me not to offer you a seat."

There were smiles all around. As we sat down, Joseph and Isabel served drinks all around. I took the opportunity to introduce Margaret to the guests without making any mention of who Joseph was.

I discussed, among other things, the Imam predicament and he was sympathetic. I also told him of my mission, to see that he was exposed. I asked permission to call my editor. The Governor suggested that I invite him round. Adding that he would like to know just how he was doing it, he further added. "These young upstarts need to be shown their places."

"I know my editor would jump at it and would even forego going to his mother's funeral, just to be here." I replied.

"I know the rascal well" referring to my editor. "He has caused me some embarrassment in the past but I am prepared to forget it, if only he can help bring this upstart to his knees." the Governor lamented.

The evening was one of the most pleasurable, not because of Lady Cavendish's presence, but mostly because I saw with great amusement, my editor subservient attitude all evening, until when the champagne must have touched a sensitive part of his brain that he shed his inhibitions. He was more relaxed and spoke as freely as I'd ever seen him speak. Lady Cavendish was impressed with the format he intended to print about Ali. As the evening drew to a close, His Excellency told us that he had reserved tables for us at the Club. My editor, hearing this, became excited and as the layered social ladder was the key in every man's life, this was an important evening. My editor was no different. This was indeed, a boost to his social standing, if seen with officials from the highest echelon.

Here again, protocol was observed fully and we were given the best and most secluded room in the club. I may have sounded hypocritical, when I criticised my editor but in that room, I felt as if I didn't belong, simply from the fact that I thought I should be somewhere more humble.

The following morning, I felt as if I were in dreamland the night before. It was only when my editor rang to ask me to come to his office immediately that reality returned.

I thought of Matthew's return which was not far away and knowing that the plane bringing the party from Georgetown would not be even half full, I suggested to my editor that I would seek permission to invite him to Supenaam.

"Would you do that Andy my boy?" he asked.

"I am doing it so you can see for yourself why I am taking so long to complete my work there." I told him.

"You may take as long as you like. Just send me the occasional snips of what is happening." he replied.

Back at Peter's residence, I was given permission to invite my editor. This I did immediately, before retiring.

CHAPTER 14

AN ANGRY MATTHEW

The party arriving at Supenaam, included Toolan, my editor, Matthew, Christine, Diego and Bell, and of course myself and the two pilots. Supenaam came alive as soon as they entered 'Tudor Grange'.

Matthew was standing at the entrance of the drawing room, looking irritable and angry. Suddenly he shouted to Ben "I have been here for more than ten minutes and you haven't brought me a drink. Whatever is the matter with you? Can't you see I am tired, thirsty and angry?"

Ben was astonished at Matthew's behaviour. We all were. Ben's countenance changed and he replied in an angry tone "Now you steady on Matthew Longhorn. I am not your butler. So why the hell are you ordering me to fetch you a drink?"

"Because you are the one always doing the pouring" Matthew replied, his voice friendlier.

Peter trying to bring some sanity back, suggested "Oh hell, I'll get the drink."

Ben got up and objected to Peter's suggestion "No I'll get the darn drink."

Peter, who was having no nonsense about serving the drink, told him "Shut up! You have ordered me about for several years and I made no objections because you did what was right. Now I am giving the orders. I will get the bloody drinks."

Margaret and Isabel came in and quietly told us to sit and relax and they would serve us. Their presence brought a semblance of normality. After a couple of drinks, Ben asked, "Matthew I've known you for a very long time, longer than most people I care to name. Why were you so angry?"

"I will tell you why. We were waiting for our plane to bring us back home from Trinidad. Four hours we were there waiting.

The heat was unbearable and nowhere to get a cool drink. My poor niece and Elizabeth was at the point of fainting, before we were offered some refreshment. What made me really angry was that our plane was on the tarmac, sitting there and going nowhere.

"I went up to one of the airline's staff and told him I needed some answers why we are held up. His reply is that he could not give me an answer. I then straightened myself and in my official tone, I told him that I was the Commissioner of the hinterland in British Guiana and I demanded to see his manager. This was a black man, very polite. I am ashamed to tell you, he turned white and rushed off to get the manager. In less than half a minute, I was speaking to him and instantly he announced that all women and children board the aircraft.

Now I beg the question. What on earth were they doing, keeping us holed up in that darn furnace when the plane was ready to go? It's enough to make a saint commit murder."

The explanation had a soothing effect on Matthew and that explained his outburst.

After a delicious dinner prepared by Bell and the ladies, we sat down to give an account of what transpired during their absence. I began by telling Matthew about the Dutch ruins we had found not far from Bartica; Matthew was very surprised to hear this and questioned us about its exact location.

We decided to summon Warachara and Obeyo. They would probably be able to give a more accurate account of its location.

Diego and his son came in and told us that the chiefs were outside waiting. Matthew was quickly on his feet and we all, except the ladies, went out in the long house to meet them.

Warachara told Matthew that they had known that place for a very long time. As a matter of fact, they said it had always been there and it was sacred to all the tribes nearby.

Matthew asked if they ever entered the ruins. Warachara's reply was that the building was sacred and no one ever entered them. "The spirits that lived there are very powerful. At night, they come out of the ground from a hole near the water falls and dance around it until the morning, then they disappear."

"How often have you been there and how many times did you see the spirits dancing? Matthew asked.

"I been there many times, only watched dancing one time." the chief replied.

He dismissed them and we went back indoors. Matthew was in deep contemplation. He sat there rubbing his chin and occasionally looking at Peter. He then blurted out "Peter you will have to come and see these ruins and make a decision on its future. I will have to organise a party, including the chiefs and any other persons, having any knowledge of it. I must think and help you out."

"Who do you have in mind for this party?" Peter asked.

"Diego. He knows more about this area than most. I will have to take Ben in case we get ourselves stuck and of course you and me and the chiefs." Matthew told him.

"What about me" I asked.

"You city gent will not understand." Matthew replied.

"Now listen to me Matthew Longhorn," my editor interrupted "I may not know anything about life in the jungle, but that does not make me an outsider. I have a duty to the public and so does Andrew. I am going with or without your approval," Matthew had no choice but to accept his decision.

"Toolan, do you want to come? Or stay and keep the ladies entertained?" Peter asked.

"This is the first time I have been in the jungle and you want to leave me out of this historic piece of adventure." Toolan quickly replied.

So with the exception of the two pilots, our party was complete. Then, as suddenly as it takes to wink, Peter asked "How far would you say it is from a river, stream or lake?"

I told him the falls were about a hundred yards from the ruins. He thought for a moment and suggested that instead of us travelling for two days on the tractor, it would be easier if the amphibian were to take us there and back. It would cut travelling time to just a day or two. So it was settled. We would fly there.

Obeyo had his first flight and he was very calm. Enjoying the vegetation below and pointing out some places of interest to Warachara.

We landed further than expected from the edge of the falls. The water was running at a leisurely pace, due to the dry season.

Matthew looked at the ruins and walked around it, several times, before exclaiming the obvious "This is a Dutch ruin."

Everyone laughed at his observation, even the chiefs had a giggle. He decided to go down with Peter and myself, to have a closer look inside. Something was seriously wrong. The boxes for a start, were not where we saw them, when we first visited. The Dutch guilders was strewn on the floor and papers appeared, as if they were rummaged through. Ben had discreetly hiddedn the strong box with the uncut diamonds under some rubble. I hastened to the spot and was relieved to find it still there. I explained this to Peter and he looked at Matthew and asked the obvious question "Do you think someone knew of it and came looking?"

Matthew gestured uncertainty. It was decided that Matthew would alert his trained rangers to keep a watch on the site, for several weeks and to report any visits. They were also instructed to arrest anyone suspicious of illegal entry in the area. I saw Toolan making notes and sketching the ruins. My editor was waiting anxiously, for me to tell him something. I was not allowed to say anything, before consulting either Peter or Matthew. The only sensible thing to do, was to get back home.

A great debate was going on between Commissioner and former Commissioner. My editor was getting impatient and insisted he be told something. I urged him not to try and force their hands, as this could be a very tricky situation. That calmed him down. I asked Isabel to pour us all a drink, Christine and Bell joined us. It was Diego who suggested that the site be declared sacred officially and that would give us the authority to see it remained that way. Ben advised us not to do it. as there was a vast amount of gold in the cave he fell in. "GOLD! Did you say vast amount of GOLD?" My editor joined in.

"I didn't see the gold itself, but I could tell from the walls, that someone was digging there, to get something out. I assume it must be gold." Ben told us, not sounding convincing,

"Gentlemen and if you pardon me, Ladies, we will have to go back and look at this cave and see exactly what Ben is talking about. We cannot declare the site sacred until we have all the facts." Diego suggested.

"You're darn right. We must go back. As you all know, I am not interested in wealth, only to preserve this place for the indigenous population. I must therefore ask the inevitable question. What if we do find a vast amount of gold as Ben said, what do we do?" Matthew reasoned.

"We will have to think hard on this. Tricky, don't you think Matthew? Peter asked.

"Trickier than landing a plane in a storm" was my answer.

"I'll think of something by morning. I shall meditate and find an answer." Matthew eventually concluded.

There was nothing more to be said, until the morning. What else to do but to entertain our guests and we knew how to do this perfectly.

Toolan was still busy with his sketches and seemed oblivious of what was said. He came to awareness, when Ben planted a glass in his hands and poured him a very large drink. Matthew refused to have any, saying that if he is to meditate, he needs a clear head and strong will power. The ladies did not mind us enjoying ourselves. They seemed to enjoy drinking as much as we did. I could not help watching Margaret pouring several for herself. This disturbed me for a while, but I soon put it down to the atmosphere of camaraderie.

In the morning, Matthew was up early and rather than showering at home, he went down the river for a swim. It was unusual for him to do this. I assumed it had something to do with the ritual they practiced in India, on the banks of the Ganges. He had told me so much about his experiences that I was finding myself believing it. My editor was not impressed. He always thought the Indians were a gutless race," or we never would have been able to subdue the sub-continent." I have a feeling he is a racist. There were many instances where his remarks had a powerful under tone of racism. I noticed the way he looked at Ben and Toolan. Never looked at Diego the same way. I assumed he thought he had more rights to be there. Toolan on the other hand, was unlike Ben, sophisticated and clever and exuded confidence.

At breakfast, Matthew unfolded his plan. We were all ears. Before he spoke, Peter interrupted, by saying that any plan Matthew came up with, he would agree to, as he could not think of a solution that would protect and safe guard that place and whatever else there was to be found.

Matthew started by saying, as we all agreed previously, to return and investigate the mine and assess what was there and go from there.

"What happens if there is a lot of gold or diamonds to be found? Who will be the owner and what repercussions will it have on the indigenous nation? Have you thought about that?" Toolan asked.

"We can only have an answer when an assessment is made and a decision of ownership will have to be decided not by us, but the Governor" Matthew pointed out.

"I am not risking my life, flying out there again, if a decision has to come from the Governor. You know what will happen, they will sell leases to foreigners, who will raze the place to the ground with heavy machines, making it look like a construction site. They will ignore any plea from the indigenous nation and where will you stand Mr. Commissioner? You will have a full scale uprising on your hands and you Brits will send in your army and wipe the lot out." an angry Sebastian pointed out.

"That is not an over statement" Matthew conceded. "However, we have to think on the legalities. If we were to be involved in any clandestine activities, it would have far reaching consequences, not only for Peter, but for all of us. May I remind you that unless we have a full assessment of what is there, only then, can we even think of making a decision. There is another issue. The uncut diamonds Ben managed to hide. What are we to do with that if no other treasures are found? The implications are too considerable to handle without careful planning." Matthew finally said.

"I have a solution. I am disappointed you lot did not think of it. Commissioner, you have the authority to grant licenses for gold diggers and diamond seekers? Why not use that power to issue licenses, let's say to Andrew, Toolan and anyone else, interested including myself of course, and you would have your problem solved." My editor proposed.

"But is it that easy?" Toolan asked.

"I do not want any part of it, no matter how much gold or diamonds you find." Diego told them.

Ben joined in by agreeing with Diego. Matthew was out anyway, and so was Peter. He could not issue himself with a license, allowing him the legal rights to explore for minerals in territory he controls, Toolan was half certain. He had to be convinced that it would be the right thing to do, without upsetting anyone.

Peter broke his silence once again. "Gentlemen, this stinks of a conspiracy. We could all be charged with sedition, I am the law of this territory, I say to all of you DO NOT; I repeat DO NOT get yourself into deep waters. I have sworn loyalty to the crown and I am expected to execute my duties accordingly. You do it my way or not at all, that is my final decision."

"I was wondering when you would come to your senses my darling husband." Christine added.

The decision to revisit the ruins was in place, the outcome was uncertain. A disappointed editor and Sebastian consoled themselves with more drinks. Toolan appeared unconcerned.

Matthew dispatched his 'troops' to the site with orders to shoot anyone trying to enter any of the buildings. One of Obeyo's men was to accompany them to show the way.

It was time for some serious debate. Several propositions were suggested and not one of them seemed to have a true legalistic solution. The best so far was to take the uncut diamonds, sell them and divide the cash among those that felt they deserved a reward. That was dismissed as stealing.

Eventually, Peter and Matthew after some deliberation, decided that the plan they had in mind was the only way out. "This is it. Matthew spoke first. "I have a very good understanding with the Governor. I will first explain the situation to him as if it was hypothetical and see his reaction. If it is agreeable then I will unfold the whole truth. Q.E.D"

Peter's suggestion was that we could still exploit whatever was there and share the benefits with the Indigenous Nation, after deducting expenses for equipment and man power. The only question was, what these people really needed, that they did not have already.

It was question time and I took the first opportunity by asking "How do you propose to put your hypotheses to the Governor? That question is for Matthew."

"That is something between that Governor and myself and trust me, it will all be above board." Matthew assured us.

My next question to Peter was "You said these people have everything they need from the forest. That I can understand. Are there no other things useful for their survival that we can give, to make their lives happier? Things that money from the treasures can provide?"

"There are a lot of things we can provide for them to make a better way of life but then, we will then be destroying their culture and the natural rhythm of their lives." Peter replied.

Toolan came up with the best solution. He started. "I have a feeling that there is much to be said for Matthew's suggestion. After all, if given the Governor gives his blessing to go ahead and do what is necessary, then that in itself, makes it legal and no one can question it. I have yet to hear what my dear friend Peter would suggest, if we were to improve the lives of these people here. Let's forget for a moment, the destruction of their culture and rhythm of life. Let's look at the practicality of his suggestion."

Peter started out by saying. "My proposals would be to build a small hospital and pay a doctor to come here once a month to check if not the adults, then the children. I personally, have a dental surgery and I pay a technician from my pocket to run it.

The forest does not really have all the necessary herbal medicines to cure all ailments, least of all the ones we introduced. Installing a cooling house at cold stream for them to store the catches, they do not need immediately. Everyone knows the water there can cool large carcasses for weeks on end and keep it free from infection. These are not luxuries that will redefine their way of life. It will help in a natural way".

"Ladies and gentlemen," my editor stood up and said "I have listened to all the proposals aired here and I personally think that Matthew's case has flaws. There are grey areas in his suggestion. I will go for the Commissioner's suggestion. Just think of the freedom you will have, to spend on this project. The diamonds there in the ruins is to my humble estimate, enough to build several hospitals and pay a full time doctor to help care for the people. Then there is the added bonus, if any one of you were to fall ill, you do not have to rush to St. Joseph for medical help. I am so convinced about Peter's suggestion that I will ask those that agree with me, do so by a show of hands."

Every hand went up, except Toolan. He explained that he was only a visitor and would be returning to America very soon. I was surprised Matthew's hand went up in support. This was one almighty debate. I felt exhausted, too tired to have any dinner.

The next morning I felt as if I had eaten for a week. Isabel quickly did some breakfast and I rushed off to see my editor and Toolan, off to the city.

Diego arrived with his family, to arrange for the trip to the ruins. I thought my presence may not be helpful. I was prepared to follow whatever course of action they decided on. I was happy I'd prepared my snip for my editor. I was sure he would make a huge story of this place and the people here.

The meeting seemed to have dragged on for ages and I was becoming impatient. So I strolled into the office, as they were about to conclude their discussions. It happened that Diego, Matthew, Ben and myself would accompany the chiefs and a handful of their people to revisit the ruins. Sebastian would take us there. We were all set to board the plane, when Joseph came running in to say that Margaret and Christine would accompany us. Matthew shook his head in disbelief.

The ladies squeezed themselves next to the pilot, to get a good view of where they were going and all the time, Matthew looked at them, shaking his head. If only I could read his mind.

It was a smooth landing, considering the narrow space of the river. Matthew's 'soldiers' came to attention and greeted their commander. They told him no one had come near the ruins since they were there. Matthew then ordered them to build two tents for us, before dismissing them back to their posts

We entered the ruins. Ben was the first to get to the diamonds and Matthew confirmed that they are real diamonds. A count began, and we found there were sixty eight large ones, nearly as big as a walnut and dozens of smaller ones. These were taken to the plane in a sack and we earnestly started to examine everything in the building.

There were some broken chairs and a huge table, made of solid greenheart, a small door led to a very large room. It was locked and the key was still in place. Unfortunately, it was so rusted that we were unable to open it normally. Ben was called to deal with it and looked in horror at the many skeletons, lying on the floor. The air as one would expect, was the foulest I'd ever came across.

There was a small cupboard with tunics. Hanging inside the pocket of one of them, was a small note book and the owner's name was written on the inside of the front cover. The notes scribbled in it were unreadable, as no one spoke Dutch. The very last pages looked like maps drawn, pointing to several locations. Diego had a look and nodded his head. That was a good sign. He was not prepared to reveal anything until he had a good look around the surrounding areas.

He first visited the opening of the mine, where Ben fell in and two of the soldiers cleared all around. One of them went down, using the vine rope Warachara had made previously and the other followed. They were there some time. Eventually they called out to Matthew and he was helped down the mine. We all followed, except the ladies, they were busy with the help of one of the soldiers, looking at the vegetation and screaming excitement when they discovered a new species of flower.

Matthew, being an old hand in the jungle had a torch which lit up the tunnel. They started examining the grooves made in the walls and could see no clue to their existence. We went further down, around a bend and heard the sound of running water. It took us nearly an hour to reach the underground river. Where it was fed from, we were unable to determine.

Diego went in and found it was shallow and the water was cold very cold, as cold stream. He surmised that there was probably a link to our cold stream and if that is so, then perhaps there might be nuggets on its bed. One of the 'soldiers' went in and dug for about an hour, without any success. Another went in and the result was the same. The water was too cold for us to follow the river. It was decided that a small raft would have to be made and we would follow the river, to wherever it took us.

The 'soldiers' went back to get the timbers for the raft while we continued our inspection. We must have missed an opening not far from the river, so this became our next area for inspection. Half way down the second tunnel we saw what this mine was all about.

Matthew examined the geology of the walls and was convinced it was a diamond mine. We hurried back to the river to examine the 'pebbles' the 'soldiers' brought out of the river. A feverish atmosphere took hold of us, not of greed, but what it may do for Peter's project. Disappointment swept through all of us, not a single stone proved to be a diamond. After that, we went back to the surface and told the ladies of our disappointments.

The ruins, however, intrigued me more than ever. I was determined to explore the ruins meticulously and to take away all the documents I could find, be it diaries, journals or records of who these people were, I did not have long to search. With Ben's help, I discovered a huge amount of papers. There were dates of 1790 and on another the year 1798 was underlined. I knew these were important dates, establishing events when this place was built and why.

The only question was, why was it abandoned? If I could only find the answer to that question, I would be half way through the mystery. At the moment, there was not a thing I could do, until I got back to Georgetown and looked through the historic files. I also must get someone to translate the Dutch. Here I would have to be careful. For instance, if there were confidentialities, be it governmental or secrets of hidden treasures, the implications could be devastating, whichever way I looked at it. Matthew would be the obvious choice for this undertaking.

After much discussion he suggested that his brother was not only a geologist but could speak both German and Dutch fluently. He had to learn these languages for his work during the war. The only problem was, he was in England and was rather busy at the estate. He promised to telephone him and explain the situation.

Christine overheard our discussion and promised she would speak to her father and tell him the importance of coming over.

My work here was not finished. I could still take time and go to Georgetown and rummage through the historical files to see what I could uncover. At the moment everything appeared to be at a standstill.

Christine and Margaret wanted to go down the mine, so with Ben's assistance, they were able to get down. I was beginning to be fearful for their safety. Ben could be reckless at times. My concern soon disappeared, when I heard their voices.

Christine told me that it was not a diamond mine, she sometimes heard her father speaking of the formation of diamonds from different areas and they all have the same finger print. "This is not diamond bearing territory." she insisted. "There are minerals there. What it is can only be determined by an expert." she continued.

I thought of all the possibilities and the more I thought about it, the cloudier everything got. I would have to wait until Matthew got some answers from his brother.

CHAPTER 15

THE MYSTERY IS SOLVED

Peter had to go and see the Governor. A journey he made every month. I took the opportunity to fly out with him and pursue my investigation.

My editor was down hearted when he heard the news. I told him the only diamonds we'd found were the ones left behind, by the people that built the ruins. He soon cheered himself up by saying he would accompany me to the registrar of history, to check those dates.

But, before we could do that, we had to find a notary, to give us the permission to scrutinise those documents. This was easier said than done. There were so many formalities, I felt disheartened and trotted off to see my parents.

In the evening, I caught up with Peter at his residence. I explained the situation to him and he promised to bring the matter up with the Governor, when he sees him in the morning. This cheered me up no end.

I decided I would start producing the children's column I'd promised Junior and this was an opportunity to fulfill that promise. My editor was not too keen about it at first, but he soon relented when I told him that I would have to tell the youngster that he was the one blocking its creation.

Things were looking up. That evening, Peter had a telephone call from Matthew, saying his brother was only too willing to come to the colony and help out. He also indicated his interest, when he first visited cold stream on his short visit to Supenaam and how he and Catherine missed their grandchild. Peter was overjoyed, at this bit of news and we celebrated just the two of us. As usual, since there were no ladies to prepare dinner, we went to the club for supper.

Toolan had returned to the USA, so Peter suggested we call an old friend to join us, if only to make conversation. This old friend was the lawyer that saved Ben from the gallows.

At dinner, Peter explained what the registrar told me. He became angry and said "That son of a no good so and so, needs to have his powers curbed. Come to my office in the morning and I will give you all the clearance you need. The trouble with these locals, when they are given certain administrative posts, they think they can make their own rules. I will put him in his place. The fact that he is only the acting registrar has gone to his head. Why do you think the British Government only allow their people to head responsible positions? We call it discrimination. I agree with Britain, until we learn to cope with responsibilities, we will forever be held one step down the ladder."

"Calm down Aubre, you are making Marina nervous." Peter told him. Marina shrugged her shoulders and replied "Aubre is right, until we can prove we are able to administer our responsibilities fairly, only then can we be seen to be right for the job."

We discussed the ruins with them and they showed very little interest so we finished our meal and left.

True to his words, Aubre gave us the necessary papers that would give us access to the records. My editor joined me, as arranged and we sat down looking for the date 1780 and 1798. All we can find was, that those dates corresponded with the time Britain eventually took possession of Fort Kyke-Over-All and 1798 was the year the last Dutch settler was allowed to leave. Disappointed as it seemed, I was happy that at least, I had found some relevance to those dates. The only question now was why 1798 was underlined.

It was time to return to Supenaam and Peter was eager to be reunited with his family. Matthew and the others gathered in the office to hear what I had to say about the documents. I could understand their disappointment, when they learned that nothing significant emerged. Matthew later, told me that those documents held some clues, surrounding those unfortunate Dutch men. His brother would reveal all, very soon.

I met Lord and Lady Longhorn, for the first time. Catherine looked nearly as young as her daughter. Jonathan on the other hand, was so unlike Matthew. He was taller and leaner and had the bearing of an aristocrat. His manner was well disciplined and he chose his words very carefully. I could not press upon him to look at the documents right away. Formalities would have to be observed. It was time I left them and join Ben and Diego.

In the morning, I was able to show Jonathan the documents. It was several dozen pages and I imagined, it would take several days to read through, before letting me know of its contents. I was still amazed that this man could leave England, to come here in the wilderness, to help his brother. I had a feeling he was encouraged by both Catherine and Christine. Right now I was only too happy to have him here.

Diego told me that there was a tribe, about a day's walking away, west of the ruins, and that they were hostile to other tribes or anyone else found on their territory. They were the Kukubis, a fierce warrior tribe, unlike Warachara's people. It was possible, that they may have been responsible for the demise of the inhabitants of the ruins. I asked if we were in their territory when we visited the ruins and he said we were. He could not explain why we were not attacked. His only thoughts were that, because Matthew and his 'soldiers' were with us, they refrained from any attacks. "I can tell you this for certain." Diego said. "Matthew is no longer the Commissioner, but I wonder if they knew that. They are afraid of him and his 'soldiers'. I wonder if Peter knew this and stayed behind and let Matthew get on with the investigation." He concluded by saying "It won't be long before we know the truth."

Ben listened, as we talked and suggested that it was he who scared the Kubukis. This was the kind of humour to soothe away the seriousness of our confusion.

I found Catherine a very warm and intelligent lady and above all, I must remember to address her as Lady Longhorn. There were no informalities here. Only Matthew and Peter were allowed that privilege. I was going to find it a bit difficult remembering.

Diego on the other hand, was well taken in with the protocol, unlike Ben, who chose to address them as sir and ma'am, which under the circumstance, was permissible. Although in a more sophisticated circle, one had to stick with protocol.

I could not think of anything else to distract me from my obsession with the ruins. That evening was a blessing. As we sat down to a formal welcoming of the couple, Catherine came and sat next to me and Margaret. Her interest in what I was doing was flattering. Not so much about the ruins, but of the biography of both her son-in-law and brother-in-law. She even indicated that if I was getting married before they return, they would have been delighted to attend the wedding, if an invitation was forthcoming. This, I assured her, and also suggested that I could arrange for the wedding to be brought forward. She lifted her eyebrows and asked "Would you do it just for us? I told her it would only take a couple of weeks to do it, as I had my suit made and a best man chosen. My parents would be delighted.

Matthew told us that their first visit was only for two weeks and one weekend was spent here. There was no opportunity for him to invite them to Berbice, because at the time of their visit, he had never been to Berbice. Peter gently admonished him for preempting his proposal, to which Matthew humbly apologised. So it was set to travel to Berbice, to give their Lord and Ladyships a taste of Berbician hospitality. Peter wasted no time in informing his parents and Christine got so excited about it, that she planned to take her entire entourage of friends in Georgetown, as well. Peter did not look so pleased. It was only when she mentioned the fact that Aubrey and Marina would be in good company, especially with his parents that he reluctantly agreed.

The feting in Berbice did not change, not even when the villagers gave them a taste of their cuisine and traditional singing and dancing. I was surprised Catherine took time to speak to them and asked about their welfare. She was impressed at the way they cope with their everyday lives. The regular tour was organised, visiting Oreala and Skeldon and meeting Isme and my name sake Andrew.

On the way back to New Amsterdam, we went by cars, to see the 'Lady Caroline Clinic' which the famous four had contributed to construct and was now run by the government. There was a plaque above the front which read,

THIS BUILDING WAS ERECTED BY CONTRIBUTIONS FROM

Matthew Longhorn, Peter D'Abrue, Diego Ciprani

And Benjamin Carson

On returning home, Catherine jokingly asked Matthew "Are you going to build something to remind you of me?"

"I am sure your son-in-law and I will think of something."

"I will contribute also dear Lady. So will Diego." Ben added.

"Please, I was only joking. I do not need a monument to be remembered by." she seriously told them.

"I agree with that my darling." his lordship added. Then, uncharacteristically he said "I have not had a drink for some time. Peter, dear boy, let's have a drink to end this magnificent evening. Aubrey tapped on his glass and announced that he wanted to say something. Everyone went quiet, he started out by saying "It has been a long time since someone of noble birth crossed the threshold of this house. A home I respect as my own, ever since I was six years old. It is fitting that such noble persons should bless it with their visit. Peter, my dear friend and Christine and you, Mr. and Mrs. D'Abrue, you deserve this honour."

I looked around me and saw the same old faces. It appeared to me, that the community at Supenaam was an entity that moved around in groups, like a swarm of bees moving from one place to another, sharing the same thoughts and expectations. I was sorry I could not live like that and I hoped Margaret, with her connections to the family, would want me to act in the same manner. This communal movement, I can take only a little at a time. I had to admit though, it was great fun being a member of this family, be it only an adopted one."

I was surprised to see his Lordship in the study poring over the documents. I never dreamt he'd bring them. I went in and asked how far he had gone. He told me later that day, he would give me a full translation. Things were looking up. Ben, Diego, Margaret and I drove to the town centre. We visited a printing firm and asked that invitations for our wedding be made available before we return to Supenaam. "When are you returning?" The gentleman asked. I told him tomorrow. "Mmm tomorrow, you want me to print one hundred invitations for tomorrow? I don't know if that is possible."

"Forget it, I will have it done in Georgetown." I told him.

"I did not say it cannot be done. You will have your invitations at noon tomorrow. Is that satisfactory to you my lord?"

"Perfectly." I told him, gave him the money and we left.

Back at the house, his Lordship was continuing to pore over the documents. After a while, he told me he was ready to give the gist of what was written. I did not want to receive this information all by myself so I sent Isabel to summon the others.

They all settled down and listened to what his Lordship had to say. He began "There is not much to tell about what is written here. This document is no more than a diary. It begins "To whoever finds my diary. Then he explained of the British overpowering them at the fort and seized their guns and treasures. They were treated well for the first few months and later when supplies were getting short, they were forced to cultivate ground provisions and to go hunting for meat. Eventually as things got worse they gathered their valuables and stole a boat, intending to cross the Essequibo and head east, where their countrymen had fled. They were ambushed by a fierce warrior tribe and it was only their firing power that gave them the upper hand.

They managed to capture a dozen of them and used them as labourers to help build their 'fort'. He soon realized that it was vulnerable from further attacks, so he made the prisoners dig a very large pit, to conceal themselves in such eventualities. The labourers misunderstood his instructions and instead of going in a steady decline, they went downwards.

When he discovered what they had done, he ordered them to dig along a straight line going west. Eventually, they came to an underground river so they thought this must lead them far away from here in case they were attacked. The river seemed not to be going anywhere that would serve his purpose so he abandoned the idea and dug another tunnel where they hid most of their valuables except the diamonds they brought with them.

They are not stolen gems but earned honestly by trading with the natives. One day the Kukubis gathered all around, bows fitted with poisoned arrows and demanded that they leave. They took the labourers and locked them in a room."

I stopped his lordship for a moment to reflect. Then, I remembered the room which was impossible to open and I told them that the skeletons in that room must be those of the labourers. Everyone agreed to this deduction and the translation continued.

"It was easy for the labourers to attack us while their friends were negotiating our surrender. He refused to accept their terms and they started shooting their arrows at them before they could load their muskets. Several of his men were fatally wounded. The three of them remaining went in the 'fort' and locked the door". His lordship stopped for a minute then went on to say "They should have gone down the tunnel. It was too late for that. The warriors set the building alight. He took the diamonds and hid it where it would survive the fire and all his documents it would take more than a fire to burn through these greenheart logs. The building was filling up rapidly with smoke. In one last attempt, they ran through the gauntlet of warriors and tried to make it to the tunnel. We were all shot with poisoned arrows and it was then he realised all was lost" It is signed Jan DeGroot Captain General Fort Kyke-Over-all "So there you have it ladies and gentlemen, your enigma solved. There are no diamonds or gold mines no treasures other than, what you found. I would like to visit this place, if only to see the preparations made in the event of an attack. Surely this man, a Captain General would have a better strategy than the one he described?"

There go our dreams of finding great fortunes and using it for the betterment of a community.

On our way home, instead of stopping at Supenaam, we decided to fly straight to the ruins, so his Lordship could satisfy his curiosity.

Catherine was intrigued with this account. She asked "Why did we, The British, I mean, treat our fellow Europeans so desperately. I realise it was war and acquiring territories was on every European agenda. No! I am sorry I cannot accept human beings can be so cruel, least of all we Brits."

"If you will pardon me, my Lady" I said, defending our actions in those years long ago. "We did not have the Geneva Convection at that time. It was a brutal world. We just have to accept it was the way things were. Today we look at the barbarity of Genghis Khan and thought he must a heartless barbarian. We must look at the times. The norm where cruelty was the only way to show you were the conqueror. It was the same with us; we were only following the rules at that time in history. I meant no offence my Lady. I can understand your feelings and I share them."

The debate in human attitude continued. I left and followed Diego up the incline to where the falls are. It was supremely quiet and peaceful. The slow trickle of water over the edge of the falls was like soothing music. I wondered how a place like this, with its serenity and musical atmosphere, could have witnessed indescribable horror and still maintained its grace and harmony.

Diego must have had these very thoughts. He looked at me and asked "Can you imagine a place more worthy to live than here?"

I could not give him an answer. I was too emotionally moved by my surroundings that any attempt to say something, would have choked me and brought tears to my eyes. I could not think of the last time I was so emotionally moved. The power of nature has its own magic.

The party was ready to move on. I wanted to ask his Lordship what he had discovered. I would have to wait until I regain my composure and allow normality to trickle back.

We arrived at Supenaam just before dusk and there were a lot of Warachara people, waiting by the office. Peter became concerned and dashed off with Matthew close on his heels. The chief was very agitated and accused Peter of allowing the Monatos to occupy land which was theirs, "Calm down chief." he told him. "I told the Monatos they can have some of the land Diego has given up, to grow their tobacco. I never gave him permission to take the lot. I will send Jango to settle the matter on my behalf." The chief bowed and looking at Catherine he asked Peter "Where goddess come from?"

Peter smiled and replied "She is no goddess, she, mother of my wife."

"I want to make her our goddess. She come and spend many days in village and she will be our goddess." he told Peter.

Before Peter could give an answer, Catherine told him in a soft tone. "I appreciate your honour. I am happy to be just a mortal, Thank you just the same."

Lord Longhorn had the broadest smile on his face when he told her "You have only been here a week and already the locals want to immortalise you." She gently pushed him and walked away.

Jango returned an hour later, in company with a beautiful young lady. His lordship asked "Why do they not make her their goddess? She is amazingly beautiful."

"I am glad you think so my brother. She is my daughter." He propelled her forward and announced "This Amelia the only real child I have. If I did not have enough to funds to see her have a happy life, I would have asked you to return my half of the estate." Matthew told him jokingly and with a roguish smile on his face.

"Surely you do not mean this young lady is a legitimate daughter? Dear brother.

"As legitimate as you and I, I was bonded to her mother but she left me when she was heavily pregnant and went back to her own village. I never knew the reason, my daughter only came to find me after her step father threw her out. She had a picture of me taken by that scoundrel, Oliver the priest."

Catherine came closer and looked intently at her features and accepted it was Matthew's daughter. "Look, she said to her husband. The features are the same, the same straight nose and the cheeks. If we were to remove some of the flab under Matthew's chin and smooth the skin under his eyes, you would have a replica of her." She demonstrated.

"When you say you were bonded to her mother, what exactly is bonding?" his brother asked

"It is a sacred ritual, where a man and a woman are joined together, according to tribal rites and in their eyes, you are legitimately married. It may not be recognised in English law, but so what." Matthew explained.

"Don't make an excuse old boy. If you say she is legitimately your daughter. Who on earth will dispute that?" his brother finally told him; then placing an arm around her, he escorted her into the house.

Jango returned with Obeyo and the chief of the Monatos . It appeared there was a genuine misunderstanding. Peter was quick to resolve the situation and everyone was happy.

His Lord and Lady wanted to reacquaint themselves with what they briefly saw on their initial visit. I had seen it many times. I did not accompany them. Ben felt the same. Diego and Bell, did it out of duty towards Peter.

The following morning, Catherine asked Margaret if she had chosen her bridesmaid. When she told her she had not, it was suggested that Amelia and Elizabeth could fill that role.

I must have been an idiot. With events happening so fast, I forgot to instruct my parents to inform the Priest and to send out the invitations. There was only ten days left before our visitors would leave and they were keen to attend the wedding. Matthew and Peter were quick to help out and soon my mind was set to rest.

They did a wonderful job, everything went like clockwork. I was surprised my parents did not reproach me for being such a laggard. We had three days honeymooning at the Tower hotel.

On my return to Supenaam, I became very upset when they announced they were returning to England, even though I knew of their departure. I enjoyed their company very much and found Catherine very witty. Elizabeth would not leave their side for a minute and wanted to go with them.

On the eve of their departure, Catherine thanked everyone for their kindness and she presented Amelia with a jeweled necklace. Graciously, Amelia curtsied and thanked her, receiving an applause from everyone.

It was a tearful farewell for the Commissioner and his family. Matthew tried to hide his emotion, when saying goodbye. He looked at Christine's tummy and rubbed it saying "It won't be long before this one comes on the scene. What are you hoping for my dear, a boy or a girl?"

"It does not matter what gender it is, so long as it is healthy and normal." She confided.

After the visitors left, everyone seemed to have lost their appetite for conversation. Even Ben failed to cheer up Matthew with his wild calypsos and occasionally trying to amuse him, with an imitation of the Indian songs and dances.

Several days later, when the melancholy had disappeared, Matthew consulted the others on how to go about sorting out the essential needs of the indigenous nation. Diego quite rightly, told him that the first step was to sell the diamonds and see what amount of cash was available.

"It would be totally impossible to sell them to Mr. Humphries. He would not have that kind of money to pay for them." Peter pointed out.

Matthew intervened and suggested. "We will have to go to Surinam and see Mr. Alberga. Now that the war is over, the stones can be sent to Holland, to be cut and polished, ready to be sold"

"That's too risky I will not want to send that amount of diamonds, without one of us personally in attendance at all times. Let's see Mr. Alberga and see what he has to offer." Peter advised. Then adding, "It is much more convenient for Matthew and Ben to go there and strike a deal with the gentleman. We can allow Sebastian to fly you out and once your business is complete, he can bring you home."

"Aren't you forgetting something Peter?" Diego asked. "We will need a certificate of ownership and a special permit for Sebastian to enter the country. The Governor will also have to verify that the diamonds are the property of the four of us."

"Why a special permit?" I asked.

"Sebastian is an American, his passport was seized and he had been given citizenship of the colony. A permit can be obtained from the immigration people, in his case he would have to obtain special dispensation from the Governor to travel abroad." Peter told me. He then went on to say. "The Governor has left for London yesterday and I am not sure if the O.A.G can oblige."

"Who the devil is the O.A.G?" Ben asked.

"He is the Officer Administrating the Government." Peter enlightened him.

The conversation shifted to the proposals from the four on how to set about improving the indigenous nation's welfare. First, it was decided to ask Doctor Pimento if he would be able to undertake the task. Now he is retired and bored with life, maybe we can inject some form of new life in him. He was always talking of how people can do much more to help each other. So gentlemen, let's put him to the test.

Peter made the necessary telephone calls and eventually got his consent to come and see for himself, before making a decision.

Peter has to go to Georgetown very soon and he will be able to do two errands at the same time. Getting the dispensation Sebastian needed for his permit and bring the retired gentleman here.

When Peter did come back, his face was beaming with delight. He marched in the house with the doctor and we all sat down and refreshed ourselves. He congratulated Peter on his fine choice of malt. Matthew quickly pointed out they were his choice.

Doctor Pimento had a quick look around and proposed that the hospital be built away from all the houses here and a small house would have to be built for him to stay. He did not intend to share residence with any other persons. Peter told him a new dental surgery would be included in the new building, with up to date equipment and an X-ray machine. This was accepted without hesitation. He also suggested that he would have two nurses and a porter on hand. The nurses he will bring from Georgetown and the porter can be one of the locals. He also made up a list of expenses to be paid to him each month. Matthew and Peter quickly looked at it and agreed.

The next question was how to sell the diamonds, if and when, all formalities were concluded. Before they could do that, Matthew wanted to put his idea to the test. Consultation with the others was out of the question. He wanted it to be his idea.

He started out saying. "You all heard what doctor Pimento said about his idea of the hospital and the staff he needs. I think we can live with that. I must add that, although it is supposed to be a charitable project, I can't help but respect the good doctor's decision. The important task is to put together the plan I envisaged. The hospital size will be determined by both Peter and the doctor. The size of the house will be my undertaking. Now what are the other plans I have you may ask. First and more importantly, is to build a sturdy and accessible cold storage structure at cold stream for these people. I have already spoken to both Warachara and Obeyo and they were bowled over with joy. I could ask Peter and the rest of you to finance these constructions, while we dispose of the diamonds. I will come to that later, but right now, it is up to the three of you, to accept responsibility, to go ahead with the constructions and at a later date, we can decide about the fate of the diamonds. I will adjourn here, while my idea is considered."

Diego looked at Peter and Ben to see if he could read any objections to Matthew's proposals. I saw Peter gave him the nod and so did Ben. He looked at me and my countenance remained neutral. I thought it was best not to intervene in such a delicate matter.

At lunch time, they gave Matthew the nod and all that was left for them to do, was to delegate who would undertake the task of selling the diamonds. Sebastian got the clearance he needed to travel. It was now up to the four of them to select who would be negotiator. Again, Matthew took the lead and told them it would be better if he and Ben go to Surinam. I have never been abroad before and this was a good opportunity for me to have an experience of what life in other countries is like.

My parents came to the colony, when I was four years old and always promised that when they had enough funds, they would send me to England, to see my grandparents. I never had that opportunity and now that my grandparents are dead, the chance of that ever happening seemed remote. I expressed my desire to travel with them. Since it would not incur any further expenses, it was agreed.

It was a beautiful Saturday morning when we took off from the Demerara and headed east. The Demerara was transformed into a little stream and soon we were over the Berbice river. It was much wider and longer than the Demerara. Within minutes, we were in sight of the Corentyne River. From the air, it was a real raging beauty. The expanse at its estuary was enormous. They say the Essequibo River is more than twice its size and there is an Island at the estuary of the Essequibo that has an island the size of Barbados. My thoughts were now concentrated on what lay ahead, now we were entering foreign territory past Nickerie, a town on the border of the two colonies and heading for the Paramaribo river.

A feeling of elation gripped me and as we splashed down into the river, a motor boat came to fetch us ashore. This was the immigration people. They quickly looked at our documents and looked at Matthew, who wanted to impress them, so wore his former Commissioner's uniform and helmet. From that moment we were treated as VIPs. I imagined it was exactly what Matthew had wanted. He called this ploy his red tape buster and it worked.

A taxi came and took us to Mr. Alberga's office. As he anticipated our arrival and came out with hands outstretched and warmly welcomed us. Coffee was offered and then he took us to his work shop. There were about a dozen men some sitting behind large grinders and polishing motors others were standing watching as the work progressed.

He introduced to his chief cutter as Hans and his chief polisher whose name was Schultz. They wiped their hands on their aprons and shook ours. Mr. Alberga showed us one of the diamonds they had just finished. It was a very large one, not as big as some of those we had in our bag. I was curious of the men standing watching and asked "Mr. Alberga, who are those men standing and watching work being done? Are they the owners of the stones you're working on?"

"No, no," he quickly replied. "they are apprentices. It is their first day and they are having what you would call, a feel of the trade. Now gentlemen if you will kindly follow me to my office I would like to see what you have for me."

Ben gave him the large bag of stones. He smiled as he tested the weight and emptied the lot onto his huge desk.

"Before I examine these beauties, can I see your documents of ownership?" His request was very polite. Matthew obliged and again, he smiled and started peering at the diamonds, one at a time and smiled every time he picked up another. Eventually, he looked up at Matthew and said "I need not look at all of them now. It is a lengthy business and I am sure you chaps would like a proper meal and somewhere you can rest." We nodded in approval.

He sent one of his apprentices to fetch a taxi and took us to a pension in Water Melon Straat, on the waterfront. The meal was superb, but the accommodation was a bit sub-standard, in comparison to the Palm Courts or hotels of that calibre. Nevertheless, we were content to remain there.

We spent the weekend looking at the city and again, Georgetown was a much more beautiful capital, well laid out with its beautiful botanical gardens and seafront. Later that day, we were taken to a sugar plantation of the same name as the capital of Berbice. New Amsterdam was a popular name, with the Dutch. I did not want to be critical at all times, but it was a small plantation, compared with the one Andrew McIntosh managed in Skeldon.

Monday morning, at about eleven o'clock, a taxi came and took us to his office. Apparently, he had checked all the diamonds, as they were laid out, according to their size. He swiveled around to face us and with that smile that I would always remember him by, he began to explain what was involved.

Before he could finish Matthew said "Mr. Alberga we only wanted you to give us an estimate of the value of these stones. Our intention is to send them to Holland for auction."

"Send them to Holland?" he shouted. There were no smiles on his face this time. "Do you know what will happen if you send them to Holland? Many possibilities, you will be quoted a ridiculous price or worse, they will probably say that some of the stones were stolen, before they reached their destination. I have dealt honestly with you before, Mr. Longhorn.

I admit, the war was on and the situation was not favourable to sell your diamonds there. But the war is now over and the situation has changed. The problem is there are so many dealers there, it is impossible to say who are honest and who are not."

"What would you suggest?" Matthew asked.

"I will be honest with you Mister Longhorn." he started out. I will quote you the best price you will get here or in Holland. I will save you a long journey into an unknown world. I will of course take a five percent of the total as my commission." He paused for a moment, then continued, "Is it not funny. I said my commission and you are a Commissioner." He laughed at his own joke and Matthew joined in, as a matter of courtesy.

"I must consult with my colleagues before I can come to any decision. You were kind to buy us lunch yesterday. Allow us to reciprocate." Matthew told him, which he agreed.

I was beginning to feel somewhat bored and wished to get back to my Margaret. In the end, Matthew agreed to his offer and a bankers draft for eleven million, six hundred and thirty nine British Guianese dollars. It was an unbelievable sum, far in excess of what we anticipated. Matthew kissed the cheque and handed it to Ben, who imitated Matthews's action, before putting it away.

We arrived in Supenaam later that day, to discover there were more problems at the border. This was getting out of hand. Peter had sent Jango to summon Matthews 'soldiers' and have them ready for our return. Matthew was pleased with this action and complimented Peter. We were too exhausted and Matthew ordered Diego to deal with the crisis, as he saw fit.

Before Diego set out on his mission, he asked Matthew. "Are you going to tell us what you did about the diamonds?"

"Matthew smiled at him and jokingly asked "Diamonds, what diamonds?"

"Stop playing games, Matthew Longhorn. What deal have you done?" Diego really wanted to know.

"I will tell you. I have done a fantastic deal and you would not believe how much we got." When Matthew told him, his jaws dropped. Diego was at a loss for words. He mumbled something that was unintelligible and marched off.

I have never seen Matthew in such a childish mood. I had a feeling he had not recovered from the shock of his deal, with that very polite and honest gentleman.

CHAPTER 16
THE KUKUBIS ULTIMATUM

Two warriors from the Kukubi tribe came with a message for Matthew. Since he was sleeping, Diego asked if he could help. They insisted that they speak with Matthew. Diego got angry and told them that Matthew was no longer the Commissioner and if they wished to say something concerning their people, they should speak to Peter. "Peter, new Commissioner now. You speak with him." Diego told them.

They were adamant to speak to Matthew. I decided to stop this impasse and went and woke Matthew, who came out still half asleep. His eyes popped out when he saw who the two men were. Come to the long house." He invited them to sit down and then tried to be friendly, by offering them some refreshments. This, they rudely rejected. Matthew then sent for both Peter and Diego. We sat down and listened to their demands. Firstly, they wanted Susheila to come with them, to be the wife of their chief's son. Secondly, they insisted that no one must visit the ruins again. They also insisted that all the things we removed from there, to be returned and he was to give two bulls to be sacrificed. This was to take place at the site, to cleanse it from the white man's curse. I could see Matthew getting angrier and angrier, as their demands unfolded. Peter placed a hand on him to calm him down. He nodded to Peter in acknowledgement.

Peter tried to prolong his decision. He told them that such conditions would have to be consulted with people more important than himself and that can take many days. They jumped to their feet and rejected any delay. "White man think chief silly? You make decision now or we make bad trouble for all." one of them told us.

Matthew sent Ben to tell Jango to summon his 'soldiers from across the river, while he continued to negotiate their demands. When the 'soldiers' appeared, looking smart and guns slung over their shoulders, they became agitated and threatened to leave. In the meantime, Peter had gone to the house and came back in full Commissioner's uniform. They had never seen a Commissioner in full military attire before and were lost for words.

Peter ordered them to sit down and listened "I shall say this only one time. You tell your chief that Susheila is not our problem, if she wants to be bonded with his son. She will be our problem if she is abducted and taken against her free will. It will then be up to me and my men to step in and protect her. The artifacts we removed from the ruins belong to the government and under no circumstances, will I allow a sacrifice of two fine animals for whatever reason, be it to remove the white man's curse, as you say, or for your own gratification."

"You tell your chief that I, Commissioner of her Majesty's colony, send this message. You must also tell your chief that we would like to have him as a friend, like Warachara or Obeyo. Even the Monatos have reconciled to live peacefully with the rest of the tribes. All other tribes from Triangle to Akaburi, all the tribes are peaceful." Peter was staring them in the eyes, as he spoke.

Then quietly, he held one of them by the hand and beckoned them to follow him, He took them to the site that was marked out for the hospital and the doctor's residence and told them what was going to happen and that they could benefit from it. I did not believe they understood what Peter was telling them. Diego stepped in and spoke in their language. Clearly they understood what Diego told them, but seemed unimpressed.

Matthew tried one last ploy. He called his 'soldiers' to attention and they obeyed immediately and a few more orders from him were instantly obeyed and with precision. They looked impressed alright. Without saying a word, they ran off into the wilderness. Matthew laughed loudly and said "It never fails to impress the enemy."

Peter came up to him and asked "You don't think our impressive display had any effect on them. Do you?"

"No! I never once thought it did. No harm in trying." he replied.

I asked feeling really scared, "We have to prepare for a fight with those rebels. Christine and Bell are heavily pregnant, so we will have to send them to Georgetown, along with Margaret and Amelia. Isabel will have to remain, to look after our meals. I can get a few more of the ladies from the village to help her out." Ben insisted that he would be more than pleased to help her.

"We all know your motive Ben." we said in unison.

With a sheepish look on his face, he defended his decision by saying "I love cooking and okay, I love being with her."

Christine was very concerned about leaving Peter and being all by herself. The thought of Bell and Margaret as company, allayed her fears.

The chiefs Warachara and Obeyo were summoned and told of the crisis. They promised to help if the Kukubis tried to attack. In the meantime, Susheila was summoned to ask of her intentions to be bonded with their chief's son. She was unaware of any of it and calmly said, "If he has all his teeth, she may consider it. It appears that our interest in her affairs is best left for her to decide".

Days passed and nothing happened. To Matthew this was a disappointment. He would rather have it out with the Kukubis now, than later. The uncertainty was a great worry for the man and for all of us.

The ladies were out of the way and that was a step forward. Precautions were under way to protect the workers building the hospital, in case they decided to set it alight. I wonder what Dr Pimento would have thought of all this. Perhaps he might have changed his mind. He did not look like the person who would fight battles for himself or for anyone else.

We were sitting under the old silk cotton tree, enjoying a little sippy, when Jango came running and shouting "The Kukubis are coming and there are hundreds of them. We threw our glasses on the ground and dashed off to get all the guns from

Peter's office. Warachara and his men were coming to join us, so was Obeyo and his men. Our party looked strong and invincible. We were ready to do battle. I say we, I was not a fighting man but I would defend myself if I had to.

There were some old logs near where the men were building the hospital. Matthew told Ben to get some of Warachara's men and build a barricade. He had to do it quick, as they could be heard, not far away. Ben was just about to finish, when they emerged and stopped short of an all-out attack.

Matthew ordered his 'soldiers' to prepare to fire, but only on his command. These men were brilliantly trained and Matthew knew he could rely on them. Peter took about a dozen of Obeyo's men and stood parallel to the 'soldiers' It was an invincible line up. The Kukubis chief came forward and made the same demands, his 'envoys' made earlier. Peter told him he would not change his mind and he was prepared to fight to the end. He did not get an answer from the Governor about ownership of the artifacts from the ruins, so he was unable to give an answer. As for Susheila, he said she could chose whatever direction she wanted to take but that under no circumstances, must she be forced to go with them.

The chief put his bow on the ground and came forward and asked "This woman come, if I ask her.?"

"She will come if you ask." Peter told him. The chief ordered his men to return to their village, with the exception of his son and eight of his warriors. Matthew went and picked up the bow and arrows and presented them to him, as an act of goodwill. The chief looked impressed and told Matthew to negotiate the bonding of his son and Susheila.

She came when Matthew summoned her, all smiles. The son had all his teeth, not brilliant, but they were all there. As a tribute to Warachara and Obeyo, they observed their custom, by putting their left hands under their chin and raising their right hands. This was not their way of saluting, but they adopted the opposition way, as a sign of respect. This was unusual among the tribes.

It was a stressful afternoon. I saw Isabel hiding behind Ben and she ran away when she noticed me.

As usual, we collected our discarded glasses and went about sipping, as if nothing had happened.

Matthew knew this was not the end. We would have to wait for their next move.

A few days later, Peter received a telephone call from Margaret, to say both Christine and Bell were admitted in Saint Joseph's hospital and it would not be long before something wonderful happened.

Peter was overjoyed and planned on leaving, except there was no Sebastian to take him there.

Matthew suggested he send a message, to urge him to return instantly. It was two days before Sebastian turned up, apologising all the way to the office. Matthew scolded him for his tardiness and he became more apologetic. It was too late to travel. The water was a bit low and you needed good light to avoid some of the rocks in the river.

By the time Peter arrived at the hospital, Christine had given birth to a baby boy. Peter was overjoyed. Now he could really say that the D'Abrue name would go on to the next generation.

Peter had arranged for his parents to come to Georgetown and look after Christine and the baby. Margaret was there to help, but Peter wanted his wife to be cared for properly and his mother was the best choice now that he has an heir.

On his return, there was more trouble brewing. In his office were two America military policemen.

Peter found this rather strange. Foreign military personnel were not permitted in uniform, in the colony. Outraged from what he saw, he hurriedly walked up to them and asked angrily, "What the hell do you think you are doing in my office dressed like that?"

"Steady on bud. We had permission from your people in London to come and arrest one of our citizens." The senior MP told him.

"There are no American citizens here, as far as I know." Peter told him.

He took out a photograph and showed it to Peter. A quick glance told him it was Sebastian's. "He is not American, but a citizen of this country." Peter went on to explain how Sebastian became a citizen. The officers did not accept his explanation and demanded he be handed over.

Matthew arrived and took control. "This gentleman is a citizen of this country. He was given that status by the Governor himself. If he has committed an offence in America, then I will advise you to take the legal steps necessary. You cannot invite yourself in a sovereign country and do as you please. I am sure you've heard of extradition?"

"No time for that buddy. I am taking him, with or without your permission." The other MP said, and at the same time, drew his gun and pointed it at Matthew. Peter was powerless to do anything. As they were about to arrest Sebastian, both Diego and Ben came from behind, with their rifles, pointing directly at the two Americans.

"You may arrest him, but you will not be able to take him anywhere. My friend and I are pointing two single loading rifles at you and we do not make unnecessary threats. I would suggest you put your toys away and step away from my friend." Diego's voice was authoritative enough for them to lower their guns and Matthew was quick to retrieve them.

They were escorted to Peter's office and a long dialogue ensued of their legal rights to arrest an American deserter.

"Look buddy, I have been authorised by our people at the embassy in London, to take the son of a bitch back to the States to answer charges of theft and desertion. What more do you want?" The older of the two explained.

"First, allow me to tell you, I am not your buddy, not now, or ever. My name is Mr. Matthew Longhorn, Commissioner retired. You said you were authorised by your people in London. Now can I see any documentation giving you that authority from our people in London?

He took out some papers and showed it to Matthew. It took some minutes for him to read it. He then handed the papers back and said. "I am afraid these papers only authorise to arrest Sebastian. It does not say you can arrest him in this colony. I'm afraid you have no other recourse than to go through the legal channels and obtain the extradition papers. Alternatively, the Governor can revoke his citizenship and even then, you still have a legal battle on your hands. You say he is wanted for theft and desertion. Can you explain?"

"First, he was sent to the virgin islands to catch up with his unit. They were to proceed to Egypt and join other forces there. Unfortunately, Private Sebastian Alverdo stole one of the planes and headed here. That in itself carries a prison sentence of twenty to sixty years. As for desertion, depending on his reason, he can be shot."

"He explained his reason for deserting. He is a pacifist. Is that not enough reason for a man not to go to war? I am not here to defend him. The matter is completely out of my hands. What is not, is that you came here without any proper papers to arrest a British Guianese citizen. That, my man, I will not allow. I am the Commissioner and it is my duty to protect anyone in my jurisdiction. I suggest you return from whence you came and return when you have all the necessary papers to execute your duty." Peter was firm and they knew they had lost their chance.

"We came back by track and nearly lost our lives getting there. I see you have a plane in the river. Any chance of taking us to the city? We will find our way home from there." The spokesman asked.

"I can take you to Georgetown. Unfortunately, it will take a few days. If you give me your solemn word that you will behave as civilized gentlemen, I can let you stay here until we are ready to go. Peter told them in a friendlier way.

"They put their hands on their chests and promised. Peter accepted their pledge and asked Ben to see that they were comfortable.

"Where did you find this giant?" One of them asked.

"I did not find him. He found me." Peter amicably replied.

Ben was told to stay with them, until their departure. I have a strong feeling Peter did not trust them altogether, even though they have given a solemn pledge.

I was therefore left all alone. A feeling of loss took hold of me, as I entered the house. I looked at 'Tudor Grange and felt it more inviting. Unfortunately the two doctors were in residence and I started thinking of my Maggie. Why had Christine taken her away from me? Why could she not survive with her mother there to help? And why could Peter not take me to see her? She is my wife. I think I have all the reasons to object to the way I have been treated. So many questions and no answer in sight.

I went and took one of Ben's bottles of malt and poured myself a very large drink. I was sure he wouldn't be offended.

Doctor Louise tapped on the door and entered. She saw me drinking and asked for Ben. I told her why he wasn't there. She was very surprised to hear what had happened earlier. I offered her a drink, which she accepted. Her hair was still a bit wet from her shower and she was passing her fingers through to help it dry faster. After a while, she managed to get them dry and as she fluffed her hair, to give her a semblance of order. I could not help noticing how lovely she was. I lacked the nerve to pay her a compliment. She looked quizzically at me, as if she was reading my thoughts. Then she asked "Thinking of Margaret are you?"

"Not exactly." I replied and then it was as if she opened the door for me to be brave. I continued. "I am looking at you and I am reminded of the hibiscus tree we have in our garden. In the morning, when the flowers unfurled their petals, they looked so soft and delicate, I sometimes kissed them very gently. Your lips reminded me of those flowers. I would have liked to kiss them just to remind me of those precious moments."

She smiled sweetly at me and walked slowly towards me in a coquettish manner. I was not sure if she would slap me or just be teasing me. Surprisingly she told me "Here is your chance to re-live your precious moments and draw so near to me, our bodies touch." I leaned forward to gently kiss her lips. She clasped me tightly with the grip of a python and until our embrace reached a feverish entwinement, her body oscillating in a sexual manner. A feeling I experienced many times with Margaret. I could not believe I was lying on top of this beautiful lady doctor. She was moaning beautiful sounds of ecstasy. I was enjoying my moment of conquest. She must have drained every ounce of my energy, before releasing me to breathe normally again. It took a very long time before she got up, showered and dressed. I was still lying on my bed. She bent down and gently kissed me and in a very businesslike voice said, "This did not happen. Do you understand me? This did not happen! My husband may not pay much attention to me or my needs in that department, that does not mean he do not love me. He is a very jealous man. If this was to get to his hearing, both of us would die. I am not saying this to scare you. It is a fact." She again smiled and left.

I was in bewilderment. I could not imagine what would happen to me if Margaret found out. What would happen to my marriage? My life, my whole world would fall apart. More than that, what would my parents think of me. A son they brought up to honour the commandments. A son they struggled to send to Queen's College, at great cost, so I could be somebody. It was too much to think about. I wished Ben was with me. He always had a suitable answer for all my problems.

In the morning things were beginning to look a bit brighter. I told myself the best way forward was to tell Margaret the truth and suffer the consequences, like a man. I told Peter that I would accompany him to Georgetown as I had some important business that could not wait.

Matthew was left in charge, while we set off. I felt a bit nervous and Peter could see I was not very composed. He tried to question me about my state of nervousness. All I told him, was that it would all be sorted out once I reached to city. He was not convinced I was telling him everything.

I saw Peter's son for the first time and he was indeed, a very beautiful baby. Everyone thinks their baby is the most beautiful in the world. This was not my baby but, if I was to have one, I wish it would be as beautiful as this little child before me. I took hold of Margaret's hand and led her to our apartment. She looked worried and tried desperately to find the reason for my unsettled behaviour.

I told her the truth, without any excuses for my infidelity. It was natural to see her in a state of shock. She drew away from me and started to cry. I knew I should have waited a few days before saying anything to her. My impetuosity got the better of me.

She would not allow me to console her, no matter how hard I tried. Eventually I asked. "Do you want me to leave this apartment? Just say the word and I will be gone. For Christ's sake say something. I have suffered enough for being so disloyal to you, to our marriage. I will accept anything you suggest."

"I will give you my answer in the morning. In the mean time you can spend the night at your parents."

I had to find an excuse for leaving. It would seem odd that we had been parted for nearly a month and I was leaving her to go to my parents. As I said before, both Christine and Peter are no fools. The excuse I gave was sufficient to convince them that it was imperative I leave.

I deliberately stayed away for a few days and would have stayed away longer if Peter's gardener did not come to tell me that Margaret wanted to see me.

She was sitting on the veranda when I arrived, looking very angry. I thought if she'd sent for me why was she looking so angry? I too became angry and shouted at her. "Are you playing some game with me? I know I did wrong. You must understand that you are partly to blame."

"How did you come to that conclusion?" She shouted back at me.

"If you did not leave me alone for so long, this may not have happened. Pardon me this would not have happened."

"So it is my fault you flirted and made love to that woman." she screamed at me.

"Maybe not, you know that place, there is something I cannot explain. It brings out hidden emotions that you are not aware of until it hits you. It's the savagery of the place, the atmosphere of nature playing tricks on the reproduction organs. Intoxicating as it may be, it is irresistible to the weak and even the strong find it a battle to overcome."

"So what are you saying? Nature led you astray?" she asked sarcastically.

"Let's stop this argument. The family may come to know something is amiss and what do we tell them? I don't expect you to forgive me straight away. Let us at least for the family's sake, behave normally."

She nodded and went off to see the family. I, scared as ever, took a large drink and returned to the veranda. Peter came and joined me. "What's this?" he said. "Drinking alone, you should have called me. I am sure my father would like a drink also. Would you invite him?"

Peter is a clever man. He knew something was amiss, but pretended not to be interested. I wanted to tell him the truth. But I was thinking of Louise and the far reaching repercussions it would have on that lovely couple. Perhaps she might have been experiencing the same magical spell. I wasn't not trying to make excuses for my actions. I merely wanted to know the truth. She knew Ben was keeping the Americans 'company'. She knew I was alone.

Did she come to see me for just what happened? As a journalist, my inquisitive mind was trying to get a realistic answer. The more I tried to get a plausible answer the more complicated it got. Someday, perhaps, I may find the true reason.

So I went and invited his dad. He seemed ever so pleased that I craved his company. As we sat there, taking in the cool Atlantic breeze, Miriam and Margaret joined us. Peter's mother was telling us how happy she was, I eventually got married. To my utter surprise, Margaret told her. "I thought he would never ask." she looked at me and smiled. Whether it was politeness just to make it seem all was well, was beyond me.

CHAPTER 17
THE CONSPIRACY

Ben was left in charge of the two Americans and Matthew was holding the fort while Peter was away. We all thought, when we returned, we would find everything normal. To our amazement, Ben told us that he had taken the Americans to see Warachara and Obeyo's villages, as they were getting bored. Warachara thought they were there to investigate the ruins and went to great lengths to tell them about it. The Americans thought there was a fortune hidden there, especially when they were told of the mine that led to a river.

That evening, they tied up Ben and took the two rifles and all the ammunitions and fled. This happened just a day after we left for the city. Peter thought it was better that they escaped and that in itself solved a lot of problems. Matthew reminded him that they were in our custody and therefore were responsible for their actions while on the run. Peter asked what he would suggest. Matthew asked he be given some time to think about it.

We went about our business as normal, waiting for Matthew to guide us. In the meantime, two of Matthew's soldiers arrived with even more bad news. They told Matthew that the Monatos had joined forces with the Kukubis and were preparing to attack Warachara and Obeyo's villages. Diego was continuing his vigil at Bell's bedside; she had several complications giving birth and was considered seriously ill. He was getting all the support he needed from all of us. Her priest was in daily, giving reassurance of a successful recovery. Diego junior was staying at Peter's residence and would visit his mother with Margaret.

The situation with the Kukubis was having a toll on Matthew's concentration. It had become so critical that everything else, must be set aside, to deal with this emergency.

Matthew and Peter called a meeting with the chiefs. They all wished Diego was there; his input in these situations would have been invaluable.

For reasons unknown to me, Ben and I were not invited to that meeting. I did not consider it a snub. If Ben did, then I could understand. That meeting lasted nearly the whole day, with very little breaks. The longer it took, the more worried I became.

Eventually, when they emerged from their meeting, Matthew looked more troubled than when he went. Peter looked down right despondent.

"It is my first crisis and the darn Governor is enjoying himself in London. His deputy is not equipped with a mandate to send in the volunteers, unless he is authorised to do so. I need to look elsewhere for help. Perhaps Diego's family and friends at Triangle would be willing to help". Peter was telling Ben. He in turn asked Matthew's opinion. "You know something, I never thought of those people. What a marvelous idea, Peter." His face lit up and he told Peter there was no time to be wasted. Sebastian and Joseph were both summoned. Both planes were needed, if help was forthcoming from Triangle.

The journey lasted for about three hours and when we landed, hundreds of tribal people converged by the lake, to bring us ashore. The first question the leader asked was "Where is Diego?" Peter told him about Bell and why Diego had to stay in Georgetown. We were made welcome, with very little fuss. After a long discussion, they agreed to help. The two planes took as much as it could and we set off for Supenaam.

They were housed in Matthew's barracks while his 'soldiers' were able to assemble from various parts of the forest. In the interim, Diego's people were busy preparing hundreds of arrows and short spears for the task ahead. This took several days to complete.

Matthew and Peter were joint commanders. Their army was divided into two with Warachara and Obeyo's men under the command of Peter, while the other half was under Matthew's command. Overall, it was Matthew who came up with a strategy he said worked wonders, when he had to fight the rebels in the North West frontiers. It goes without saying I was extremely fearful of my life. My work was not finished and I had yet to make peace with Margaret. Despite my fears, I went along, hoping for the best.

Some of Monatos men did not like him joining the Kukubis and they stayed behind with their chief's permission. Matthew was aware of this and sent two of his 'soldiers' to summon them.

They were instructed to go to the Kukubis camp and tell their chief, that Peter and his men were advancing North West towards Fort Kyke-Over-all. This position would be about half a day's walk from their village and it would give Matthew a chance to attack from the rear. It sounded great but would it work. Only time would tell. The men were given provisions and an assurance that no one would ever know of their betrayal. To ensure they carried out their task, Matthew showed them a bottle of malt and promised to give it to them, when they returned. It was astonishing to see how their eyes lit up at the prospect.

Matthew's real plan was for Peter to take his men South West, while Matthew followed a North Western route. This will give them an advantage of a near encirclement, when they eventually caught up with the rebels.

They must have miscalculated their directions and instead of meeting at a predetermined location, they found themselves far from their intended target. There was no panic, Matthew calmly told Peter that this position was better than the one they had planned. The rebels were encircled and it was only going to be a matter of time when they were spotted.

We made camp in a clearing and set about preparing something for the men to eat. We dared not light a fire, as this could prove disastrous. The Kukubis, on the other hand, did not expect us to be where we were, so they lit their fires and we were able to establish their positions and distance. Matthew was ever so pleased with himself.

In the morning, we kept track of them, careful not to give away our positions. At one time, we could hear them talking. This was too close for comfort, so we delayed our progress. Matthew looked at his compass and calculated that they were indeed, heading for Fort-Kyke-Overall. We do not know who was commanding them. We only assumed that the Americans were. If that was so, then Matthew calculated that they were not intent on attacking us in Supenaam, but instead were looking for a way of escape.

Our commitment to capture the Americans over shadowed all other considerations. We could not allow them to reach the fort. Matthew ordered the ring to be tightened and to advance at a steady pace, until we were within striking distance. They must have become aware that we were nearby. A volley of arrows went in the air and fell short feet from us. Obeyo's men, quickly gathered the arrows and added them to their bundle.

Matthew ordered his 'soldiers' to the front and told them to wait for his orders to shoot. Another volley of arrows was seen in the air. This gave Matthew a precise location of where they were. He ordered his 'soldiers' to fire, a few seconds later, there were cries from their camp and we were sure we shot, at least a few of them. The soldiers continued firing at Matthew's command and more cries were heard. They thought it best to face us directly and a great rumbling noise was heard in the undergrowth. In an instant, they were only a few yards from us. Rapid volley of fire from the soldiers sent dozens of them falling dead on the ground.

Peter's men continued the onslaught with their poisoned arrows. They were beginning to fall on top of each other. I was shocked when I saw Warachara's son fall, an arrow in the middle of his chest. Some of Obeyo's men were also killed. The killing made me sick and when I saw Warachara lift his son with tears in his eyes, I was completely moved. The Americans were nowhere in sight. The Kukubis surrendered and they were rounded up and taken to their village, by Obeyo and his men.

The rest of us were in full pursuit of the Americans. Matthew was determined to capture them, at all cost. Their flight suggested just as Matthew thought; they were heading for the fort. Matthew smiled and told Peter that they were doing exactly what he'd hoped they would do. "They would have to cross the Essequibo to get to the fort and I don't believe they prearranged boats to meet them for the crossing."

We continued tracking them, until we came to the bank of the Essequibo. Matthew was flabbergasted. The party of about thirty had prearranged transport across the river. By the time we were within gunshot, they were half way across, heading for Bartica. Several shots were fired at their boats without any success. Matthew was enraged with himself. He'd misjudged their capabilities. Peter took a look through his telescope and discovered that, on the banks where the three rivers met, were a lot of men dressed in military uniforms. They bared no resemblance to those of the Americans and they certainly, were not our men.

Matthew took a look and shouted, "I'll be dammed. Those are Venezuelan soldiers. What the hell are they doing so deep in this country? Did our rangers not know of this? What about my soldiers? Surely, they patrolled these areas constantly. Why were they not discovered before now?"

Those questions remained unanswered, for now. The next course of action had to be decided very soon. It was suggested to follow them but there were no boats at their disposal and it would be suicidal to try and swim where three currents converge. The only solution was to send a runner to ask Sebastian or Joseph, to collect us at the lake, south of here. We decided we would signal our position with smoke and hope for the best.

We hoped that by the time we reached the lake, where the plane would be able to land, one of the pilots would not be too far away. We waited for several hours before the noise of an engine was heard overhead. It landed before we could make the signal and thankfully, we boarded and headed for the fort.

It was all quiet; there was no sign of the Americans or the Venezuelan soldiers. Matthew used all his skills, as a tracker, to look for signs of movement in the forest. The only sign he saw, was the inhabitants of the trees and on the ground, it remained quiet. It was a complete mystery where and how they had disappeared.

Sebastian told Matthew that he had spent a long time in this area helping his fellow Americans as a non-combatant. That is how he was able to get the other two planes for them. He suggested they follow the river leading from the fort and head west towards the Venezuelan border. There is a small outpost that trade with the pork knockers and he was certain that was where they were heading. Since there was no other alternative, than to take Sebastian's advice, we headed west. From the air, the jungle looked as if no human being ever set foot in there. No tracks to indicate human presence, not even animal tracks. It was a despairing sight and my heart sank. Horrible ideas came to my mind. What if we have engine problems and are forced to land here? Who will ever dare come to our rescue? We will all perish and I have not made my peace with my Margaret. I should not have been so ambitious to want to come to Supenaam for this interview, with the famous four.

My thoughts were still churning out desperate ideas, when Sebastian shouted "There it is, the outpost I told you about." He was pointing at a little clearing down below. I could barely recognise what appeared to be some small buildings. He started looking for somewhere near where he could land. We had to get down as soon as possible. The longer we were in the air the more chances we had of giving the Americans our position. Fortunately we found somewhere and as we swam ashore, soaked but refreshed from the lake's cold water, it did not take long for clothing to dry out; and soon we were heading towards to outpost.

We questioned some of the pork knockers and they were as ignorant of any Americans, as the local people we met on our way there. We decided to wait and set about posting guards at strategic points, in case they did come here.

A whole day passed without any sign of them. It was generally agreed that we move on and start looking somewhere else. At that very moment, one of the guards signaled that they were spotted, a half a mile away.

We set up an ambush and waited for what seemed like an eternity. They were in an exuberant mood, as they entered the liquor shop. Some pork knockers were drinking from a bottle of rum and they made room for the intruders. We were outnumbered by the many guns they had. The one that looked like the most senior of the Venezuelan soldiers took a few bottles of rum without paying for it and started drinking, celebrating the fact, that they had outwitted us. We waited until they had drunk a lot. One of the Venezuelan soldiers went to the bar and ordered for some food to be served and somewhere to sleep for the night. This was good news for us. We retraced our steps back in the forest and hid ourselves waiting for it to get dark.

Two huge blacks stumbled on us and were amazed to see us. Peter spoke to them, in Guianese dialect and told them who he was and that he would reward them handsomely, if they were to help us.

"What kinda reward you gyne give we if we help out man. You gat gole or dimand in you pocket?"

"No we do not have gold or diamonds, but we can tell you where to find lots of it." Peter told them.

"Den why you not take it and go way?" The toothless one asked.

"Because we have enough. We want to get those Americans and the Venezuelan soldiers who are plotting to take over the entire Essequibo." Matthew took out a map and showed them the size of the county, nearly two thirds the entire size of the colony. He also showed them, proof that since eighteen hundred they were plotting to seize control. It was only the war that stopped them from invading and taking control.

"So dem buggers want to thief me country. You wait here boss man. I go fetch me friends." The same toothless one said.

Half an hour later, he returned with about fifteen blacks armed with machetes. He called out to one of his friends. "Hey dugglah show dem white men wah you can do wid your weapon." In an instant he threw his machete straight in the middle of a tree trunk. "Dah moe fast than deh bullets. No?"

The demonstration was impressive enough to make Matthew lift an eyebrow. Matthew's plans were for the blacks to go back to the liquor store and create a diversion, by making a lot of noise, as if they were drunk. This will bring some of them, at least to investigate. If only a few came down, then the blacks were given instructions of what to do.

Half an hour later, they brought out three soldiers and the two Americans. Fortunately for us, one of the soldiers was the most senior of the lot. With a machete pressed against their throats, they had little else but to listen to Matthew.

"You don't need me to tell you the predicament you're in. You will be considered invaders, the same as being spies, and that carries the death penalty. Britain will never allow interlopers to make her look foolish, in the eyes of the world. Venezuela is nothing more than a third rate country. If this sort thing continues to occur, then his Majesty's government will have no alternative, but to lay claim on your territory. You and the Brazilians have already claimed a great swathe of land in the Roraima region. That was meant as an appeasement for peaceful co-existence with our neighbours."

"Senor, what land you will claim from our country?"

"Apparently, you are not familiar with the natural boundaries of the Guianas. It extends from the Amazon in the East and to the Orinoco in the West, and also, right up to the Guiana Highlands in the South. So you see, we have a legitimate right to occupy these territories."

"Then what is stopping you Senor?" their spokesman asked.

"For the sake of peace. That's why." Matthew barked at him.

"So what are you going to do with us Senor? I will tell you, this has nothing to do with our government. These Americans told us to help them and the United States government will reward us handsomely, and even allow us to go and live there."

"I will have to think about that. My friend here, is the Commissioner of the hinterlands and it will be his decision, of your fate."

Sebastian helped tie up the soldiers and the blacks stood guard over them all night. The two Americans were taken a great distance away and tied to a tree.

During the night, Matthew and Peter were trying to find a solution to this problem. It would be too much to take all of them in the plane and we could not keep them tied up indefinitely. The blacks were prepared to sever their heads and solve the problem.

Matthew came up with a more humane and practical solution. He suggested that we allow the soldiers to escape and take the two Americans back to Supenaam. These soldiers were mercenaries and yet somehow, I had some sympathy for them.

In the morning, the blacks were told of the plan and they appeared to agree. Then, one of them asked about the reward. Peter took a piece of paper and wrote something on it. He looked at the paper and said he was unable to read what was written there. Matthew took the paper and read aloud its contents. "I, Peter D'Abrue, his majesty's Commissioner of the hinterlands promise to reward these gentlemen, handsomely, with uncut diamonds when this document is presented."

"You no give dimand now?" was the question presented to Peter.

"I cannot give them to you now, as I do not have them on me. They are in Supenaam."

"Supenaam? Look boss, if we walk to Supenaam, we die before we get there." Their spokesman said.

"I cannot take all of you to Supenaam in the plane. Why not chose two or three of you to come with us and we will give you the gems." Peter replied.

"Okay, we send Jumbie and this man. All two a dem gat sons hey and if deh don't come back we kill them sons."

"Look Peter!" Matthew reasoned. "Let's take them to Supenaam and Joseph can bring them back here. I know it is costly but remember, these gentlemen risked their lives to help us. At least let's show some gratitude."

"You are absolutely right." Peter agreed.

"Where are we going to get these diamonds to reward these men?" I asked. "For all the good my memory serves me, I remember we sold those diamonds to Mr. Alberga didn't we?"

"We only sold the very large ones. The smaller ones we kept in my office." Peter answered.

The men were thankful that we honoured our promise. Curiosity got the better of them and one of them asked, "Whey you gat all them dimands? You show we?"

"We found them by accident." Peter told him.

"Man! Me like accident like dat, happen to me every day." he replied and let out a hearty laugh, before heading for the plane. He suddenly turned around and asked, "Wah you do wid dem Americans?"

Peter told him the law would deal appropriately with them.

CHAPTER 18

DIEGO'S RETURN

Matthew telephoned Diego to tell him of our escapades and that the Americans would be sent to be incarcerated in the city's jail, until the Governor returned from London. He learnt that Bell was well on the road to recovery and they would be coming to Supenaam soon. From Matthew's countenance, I could tell that Diego was rather excited to meet his friends.

Peter, was escorting the Americans, along with half a dozen of the soldiers. I did not ask to go along. Peter suggested I did. I thought about it for a minute and then it occurred to me, that it would serve a purpose, as I could confront Margaret about our future.

The Commissioner of police told us that he would not accept the Americans as prisoners. This would contravene an existing arrangement with London and Washington. He told us that since the Governor was abroad, it would be better for Peter to contact the Home Office for instructions. That developed into a serious row, between the two and Peter was adamant that the prisoners be incarcerated in the city's jail. After much deliberation, it was agreed that the prisoners would be kept confined in the prison.

I could not wait to see Margaret. Peter's mother started crying when she saw me and I thought something dreadful had happened. She told me that Margaret went to see Bell at the hospital four days ago and did not return home. She was sick with worry and fearful of telephoning me of events.

I was shattered. A wave of thoughts flooded my mind until I was unable to concentrate. I spoke to Christine and she was ignorant of her whereabouts. Then, I thought of the young man she was interested in, long before I met her. Christine was unable to shed any light on the matter. The only person who would know, would be Isabel and she was in Supenaam. I did not want to speak to her on the telephone. Her indiscretion would only exacerbate the situation. I had to be tactful, to get the right answer. I simply have to wait until I return to Supenaam. I decided to remain calm and go about my other undertakings normally. How could anyone remain normal when their other half had gone missing? I thought of placing her in the missing person's column. That would have only opened me to ridicule and what on earth would my friends will have thought.

Peter knew of my dilemma but refused to discuss, it unless I brought it up. Miriam saw the distress in me and suggested that I go with her to church and ask God for solace. I am not a Catholic but I agreed.

Good news for Peter. The Governor had returned and it was imperative for Peter to meet him and discuss the ongoing problem with the Americans. Also he needed to tell him of the crises we faced, with the Venezuelan soldiers and the Kukubis. He asked me to accompany him, which I did.

"Good morning Peter." A cheerful Governor greeted him. I heard you had some huge problems. Sit down and have some coffee and who is this newcomer I see you have here?"

"This is Andrew Bowry. He is with the Chronicle. He is at Supenaam at the moment, doing some interview, for a biography of Matthew and myself along with two others who you know very well." Peter told him.

"Mmmm, I never had anyone asking to do my biography." he remarked.

"Perhaps, when I am finished with your Commissioner, I will do yours." I told him, feeling very important.

"Perhaps. We'll see" he concluded.

Peter told him, all there was to tell and my involvement in the episode. He was rather impressed and suggested he go to Supenaam to personally congratulate the chiefs and their men, for helping the Crown,

Peter agreed as this would really seal the bond of cooperation. Lady Veronica came in the room and kissed Peter on the cheek. She told him that she had a message for Christine and a little gift for Elizabeth. Peter assured her, that Christine would make some sort of arrangements to collect them.

His Excellency changed his mind of going to Supenaam. Instead, he suggested that the ceremony took place on the lawns of the mansion.

"What a good idea." Peter told him.

"I am planning a march through the town, from Eve Leary to Main Street. We can discuss the details later." he added.

As far as I was concerned, these were unimportant issues and my legs were itching to move on. Peter sensed my impatience and bade farewell.

Diego and Bell were already at Peter's residence, when we got there. Beda, his mother's maid, were assisting her and cradling the baby gently in her arms. I do like babies, but this was not an opportune time for me to start tickling the child's cheek and making faces at it. It may sound heartless but at that moment, I could not be bothered about other people's happiness.

I was all set for Sunday service. I wondered how the Catholic went about their service. I had to follow Miriam and see what she did. It is the same God after all, that we all worshipped.

I took my seat with everybody else and waited for the priest to commence. A long line of Sister Nuns streamed through a small door and occupied the two pews at the front. My eyes were playing tricks. I looked again and it was Margaret in their midst. A powerful urge tried to drive me to go and confront her. Here, in the sanctity of God's house, I dare not. It was like a giant hand pressing me down.

Miriam, must have seen her, as she held my hand, looked at me and shook her head. I have at least knowledge of her whereabouts. I doubt if she saw me. She knew Miriam would be there, so obviously she must know that her whereabouts were exposed.

Outside the church, Miriam told me to act normally and she would sort out my problem. It was several days later when we went to the convent and told the Mother Superior of the situation. Margaret was summoned and she was clearly shocked when she saw me. We were left alone, to discuss the problem at hand. She told me she came here to join the nunnery. Unfortunately, she was told she was not suitable, but could stay on, until she rediscovered her peace of mind. Not able to become a nun? I wonder what you have to be to shut away the pleasures of life, to become a nun. My immediate concern was to find out exactly what her intentions were and I was not getting anywhere near a solution.

She told me to give her a week more and she would telephone me of her decision. I had no alternative but to do as she asked.

Miriam was patiently waiting in the car and the driver was pacing around like a caged animal. I knew he wanted to get to the rum shop, to join his friends. He looked at me and quickly hopped in the vehicle and before I was properly seated, he started driving off.

At Peter's residence, I saw the Governor's car parked in the drive way. Miriam went ahead of me to check. She came back and told me it was Lady Veronica alone, visiting and she was in the drawing room with Christine. I entered and greeted them with a smile. Lady Veronica appeared in a care free mood. Christine asked if I could serve them some sherry. "I am sorry to hear of your dilemma Mr. Bowry," she began, "I know exactly how you feel." I did not reply, instead I went ahead, being the butler and immediately left the room. I had a few telephone calls to make, so I went in Peter's study to do that.

One of the telephone calls was to my editor. He summoned me to his office, for an important task.

I was really pleased. He asked me to sit down, something he'd never done before then and he called one of the junior type setters. I'd had many conversations with him in the past and he seemed in an amicable mood and displayed a good sense of humour.

"You know Mohammed?" he asked causally.

"Of course I do." I replied just as causally.

"He has a problem and he thinks you may be able to help him. I will leave you in my office to sort it out. I'll see you after lunch." he told me before disappearing.

"Well Mohammed, what can I do for you?" I asked.

"Well sir, I don't know how to tell you this, but I have no real friends, I can rely on for this important business." he started out. "I have to tell you everything, from the beginning. For you, being an Englishman, you would not understand. Someone asked my father for me to marry his daughter and I've been invited to go and see what she looks like on Sunday. I can take some friends and the man will prepare lovely food."

I stopped him and asked, "Why do you want me to accompany you? I do not know this man." I told him, feeling a bit awkward.

"You see sir, if you accompany me, the man will know I am not just anybody. He will think I am an important person. If I like the girl and agree to marry her, he will be pleased." he explained.

"This is a ridiculous story. Are you telling me you have not seen this girl before and you are prepared to marry her, if she is pretty?" I asked, trying to understand all the facts. I had heard of these things going on, but I thought it was only gossip. Who on earth would want to commit their entire life to someone, dependent on that person being good looking.

"It is how things happen with the East Indians. It has always been like that. East Indian girls cannot be seen flirting with a man, like the blacks do. People will call her all sorts of names and she will find it impossible to get a decent man to marry her. Will you help me?"

The look in his eyes spoke volumes. Yet I was not prepared to commit myself to such an undertaking, until I sought advice. This I relayed to him, and he appeared to be satisfied with my reply.

I decided to go to Peter's residence where I knew Diego and his family would be. They were sitting on the veranda. I joined them and discussed the situation with Margaret first. Diego told me that he'd had his suspicions that she had gone to the convent. He couldn't be sure, which is why he hadn't mentioned it. Everyone seemed to know of my problem. It was there and then, that I decided I would let matters take whatever direction it chose and stop worrying.

The other matter on hand was that concerning Mohammed. I explained it to him and he suggested I take Ben with me. He told me Ben was familiar with all the various customs and would be the ideal person. With Margaret's problem set aside, I decided I would help a fellow human being.

I telephoned him and told him of my decision and that I would be coming with another friend. He was ever so happy. I even thought for a minute, if I were anywhere near him he might have kissed me!

I rejoined Diego for a drink and found myself at peace when Peter's parents joined us. The Atlantic breeze was a soothing remedy for tired hearts. I closed my eyes and soon drifted into a deep orbital sleep.

I was happy to be back in Supenaam. Seeing Ben was the tonic I was waiting for. He gave me a bear hug, as if he'd not seen me for years. I knew then, I would finally have some peace of mind, irrespective of whatever decision Margaret may come up with. He was so happy when I told him, what I'd promised Mohammed and could not wait for the day to come.

Diego Junior was like a caged animal set free. He ran down the embankment to familiarise himself with the surroundings, then raced up, running through the rooms at Tudor Grange. It was not until Bell shouted at him to be calmer, that he settled down on the veranda, teasing the squirrel monkeys. I was more than pleased to see someone so happy.

We have some more problems. Matthew told Peter he was taking Ben and me to see Warachara. He did not mention the reason and Peter did not ask.

Warachara told Matthew that some of Monatos' men, who helped us arrest the Americans, were seeking shelter in his village and that it could cause enormous problems with their chief. The Monatos wanted them to return to their village. Matthew was unable to find a rational answer to this delicate problem. In the end, he decided to go to their village and confront their leader who was called Suluwe.

It was the first time I had seen him in person. He appeared to have an amicable disposition. Matthew explained to him the circumstances, under which his men were forced to do as he ordered. He insisted that the men were unaware at the time that they were in actual fact, betraying their leader. If the chief did not punish them, Matthew promised goodwill and friendship forever.

Suluwe agreed, on condition that he be given a bottle of malt, the same as was given to the men. Matthew did not hesitate and agreed, even though this was against the rules.

At about nine o'clock the following morning, I went down to the office to telephone my editor, that I would be bringing some important news and that I'd decided to go with Mohammed, along with a friend.

Matthew over heard my conversation and felt somewhat let down that I hadn't asked him to go to this extraordinary meeting. He told me he was well acquainted with these sorts of procedures and had participated in many of them, when he was in India. I had to ring Mohammed again and tell him of the situation. "The more the merrier." he shouted over the telephone. Matthew was like a school boy, when I told him he would be welcomed.

I wore my wedding suit for the occasion. Matthew looked very smart in his safari suit and Ben, as usual, wore his shirt over his trousers.

We were warmly welcomed by the family and offered comfortable chairs in the living room. I had never experienced this sort of thing before and looked to Matthew and Ben for guidance. The young lady's father served us a cool drink each and started asking Mohammed a lot of questions, of his work and his past time. I told the gentleman that I'd known his prospective son-in-law for many years and that he was a decent and honest person. He was nodding with a smile as I spoke.

The girl's mother escorted the young lady in and presented her to Mohammed first and then to us. She smiled and showed a set of gleaming white teeth. She was quite pretty. Her older sister, even prettier, followed and sat next to her. After exchanging views on religion and various aspects of life, he finally asked. "Now young man, what do you think, will my daughter be suitable to be your wife?"

I was astonished at the question. Matthew looked at me and indicated not to say a word. It was then Mohammed started speaking. "If I can have a word with my friends first, I will be able to say what my intentions are."

The party left the room and he began to ask us questions. "Well what do you think? Is she pretty enough to be my wife?"

My head was swirling in confusion. This bizarre situation had come to me as a complete surprise. Matthew suggested that he arrange to speak to the girl alone. Then he remembered that it would not be possible without a chaperon. It was agreed on condition that the elder sister be present also.

The four of us went down the small garden and sat on a bench. While they were talking I was looking at her sister and wondered if she was married. She turned to Matthew and asked, "You said you do a lot of meditation, Mr. Longhorn, was it in India or in the jungle?"

Matthew went to great lengths to explain that part of his life. She then asked the strangest of question. "Do you believe in telepathy?" Matthew said he did, but never practiced it.

She stretched her right hand out and told me to grab it at the wrist and to close my eyes. This, I did and then she opened her eyes and looked at me in a strange manner. She then said, "Mr. Bowry, you are a troubled man. I can read your thoughts and you are trying desperately to resolve what is troubling you. You have a strong will, and that in itself, will see you through"

Matthew winced at her comments. Matthew stretched his hand out and asked that she tell him his thoughts. After a minute she said, "You are wondering if my father will serve you any whisky. I can assure you, although we are Muslims, the men do have the occasional drink. I will inform father."

"Before you go young lady, what do you do?"

"I am a teacher and yes I know you are wondering if I am married and the answer is no. I have far more important things in life to do than cooking for a husband, who only looks at me as the provider of his children." She was bold in replying. I couldn't help admiring her. I don't mean her beauty, but her attitude to life. This is the kind of person I would have loved to meet.

"Can I ask you a question, what is your name?"

"I am sorry, my sister is called Agatha. It is a Christian name we all have. Our Muslim names are used only to register at school and for legal purposes. My name is Samantha." she boldly said.

"If I were to ask you out, would you come?" I realised, only too late that I should not have asked that question. Matthew was clearing his throat and looking at me. To my surprise, she said "Of course I will, but with a chaperon." I smiled at her response, while Matthew was shaking his bowed head. It was time for us to join the family.

Ben was sitting, looking rather cheerful with a glass of something in his hand. He raised it and said "Cheers. We were having a ball while you sat in the sun getting thirsty." he said with a cheeky smile.

What happened next was totally out of the blue, it even caught Matthew by surprise. Mohammed, was again asked of his opinion of the young lady and his intentions. "Well sir to be quite honest, Agatha is a very beautiful young lady and if I were to follow tradition I would have given an affirmative answer. As it stands I do know this is against traditions. But to me these are modern times and although I am a Muslim I have to be ready to face the future as I see fit."

The father interrupted and asked, "What are you trying to say?"

"I think that beauty alone is not enough for a successful marriage. I do not know what Agatha's aspirations are. I know only too well that what I will be asking, may not be approved." he started out, before being interrupted.

"What are you asking?" I could see this was all too sudden for him to take in.

Mohammed continued, "We had a chat in the garden and it was a general discussion. The finer points can only be discussed in private."

"In private!" he shouted, and looking at me, he said in a more acceptable tone "You know that is not permissible."

"I know that Sir, but hear me out, then judge me. I would not dare think of being completely alone with her. There should be a chaperon at a discreet distance, so we can speak freely to each other, if only to discover what is involved. If I accept marriage, it will not be for love, only because of traditions. This is the most important question. What happens when the honeymoon is over? What will we have to bind us together?"

Samantha took courage and said, "I think Mohammed has a point Papa."

"You are a woman. This does not concern you. Now go in the kitchen and help your mother." he sternly told her.

Mathew got up and held on to both his lapels. "You know Sir, I spent most of my years in India and lived like a native for a great deal of it. I fully understand your position. What Mohammed said is not unreasonable. I would undertake to be that chaperon and to see everything is done properly. I could go on forever in support of Mohammed's suggestion, because I can see a lot of merit in this brave young man's argument."

To our amazement he agreed and seemed happy with Matthew's suggestion. We left, after an elaborate supper, Kashmir style. I could not help thinking of Samantha and her telepathy. It was more than that to be honest. I was not only struck by her beauty, it was her sharpness of mind and articulate diction.

Some weeks later, Peter was preparing to go to Georgetown to make arrangements for the parade. Matthew and I went with him. I desperately wanted to speak with Margaret, for more than one reason.

The meeting was confrontational. She was adamant that she would not give me a divorce. She promised to return home with me, but only as a show of unity. She swore she would not share a bed with me, or any other man. I told her it was unacceptable and I must find a new partner, whether she divorced me or not. "You are going to live in sin, then?" She asked.

"If I have to." I replied sharply. She turned her back towards me and asked me to leave. Angrily I told her. "You would have been better off taking that job as a hostess, it would have served a better purpose."

I left with a deep feeling of accomplishment. My thoughts immediately turned to Samantha. I wondered if she would enter some sort of arrangement with me. I felt foolish thinking like that. They are decent people and she has her reputation to think about. I desperately wanted to meet her again. I thought of Matthew and wanted go with him, when he would be acting as chaperon, on condition that Samantha would come along. Matthew read my thoughts and agreed.

The jaguar stopped at the entrance of the gardens and we strolled towards the kissing bridge. Mohammed and Agatha were left alone, at a discreet distance and I started speaking with Samantha. Matthew pretended he saw an unusual flower and went in that direction. I held Samantha's hand but she hurriedly withdrew it. I became unsure of proceeding with my intentions. We talked of many things but never got close to what I had in mind. I told myself I had to do this some time or the other and here was the perfect opportunity. "Samantha" I said, a bit choked, "I have a hypothetical proposal for you." I did not finish what I wanted to say. She placed her index finger on my lips and said, "You are thinking of asking my father's permission to marry me. You are already married. I cannot consider such a proposal."

"Hear me out, before you come to any conclusion." I told her. I explained the situation with Margaret and pleaded that she give it some thought. She looked amenable to my suggestion and told me she would have to speak with her father. This was more than I'd hoped.

I relayed our conversation to Matthew, who appeared perplexed. He promised to help me when the time was right. I proposed we do it then, since we had to take them home. He did not look too pleased. Instead he told me he would speak personally, to her father, to see his reaction.

I waited in the car while Matthew and the girls went inside. It was more than an hour when he came through the door and beckoned me in.

I felt as if I was in front of a judge, waiting for my sentence of execution. "So you are asking my permission to marry Samantha? I understand your situation and will consider it, only if my daughter agrees. I will let you know through Mohammed. I am not surprised with all this. I am a father and I know my daughters. I've allowed things to happen that I never dreamt I would do. You will hear from me. I have to speak to the Imam and other members of my family. You do understand this I hope?" he said with a reconciliatory tone in his voice.

CHAPTER 19
PAGEANTRY AND MARRIAGE

The news of the parade spread to all the counties. There were literally tens of thousands of people, standing on the sea wall, hoping to catch a glimpse of this pageant. Not very many things of interest, happen in this God forsaken country. The Governor, with Matthew and Peter, flanking him in the rear seat, led the parade, driving at a very slow pace. The volunteer force was immediately behind, followed by some of Matthew's soldiers.

Then, the two chiefs dressed in their most ornate tribal costume, both walked with dignity, with their men behind. Then it was another lot of Matthew's soldiers, bringing up the rear. The crowd cheered enthusiastically, waving and shouting. Half way along the seawall road, the car stopped and Matthew came running to show the chiefs the Atlantic Ocean. He explained to them that this was larger than all the rivers and lakes he had seen and it was a thousand times larger than his forests. He looked impressed and smiled.

The crowd followed, as far as they were permitted, until we reached Main Street and the Governor's mansion. It was a prolonged ceremony. Eventually, the chiefs were given medals of bravery. Monatos' men were congratulated for their part and were given certificates of valour.

They were then invited to a room in the annex building and served refreshments before leaving.

I thought of telling both Christine and Peter of my situation and also to let them know of my intention towards Samantha. Christine was sympathetic but could not agree with me on the issue of Samantha. Peter's position was neutral. I told them I could no longer accept their offer of occupying the flat and I that was prepared to move on. They agreed and told me I could stay there for as long as I remained unmarried.

Peter told us that he would have to remain in the city, long enough for the man coming from London to refurbish his surgeries with modern equipment. Matthew looked surprised and asked who this mysterious man was. Peter told him his name was Nyman and that he travels the undeveloped world, modernising old antiquated surgeries.

"Not Les Nyman?" Matthew asked in surprise.

"Do you know him?" Peter asked.

"Know him. I know him very well indeed. I remember the first time we met was at an Officer's ball and he was there with one of the most beautiful Indian ladies I'd ever set eyes on. I know her name is Helen. I remembered it only too well. If I am not incorrect I think she was some kind of an actress. Do you know if she is travelling with him?" he asked Peter, who responded by saying he did not know.

We were all committed to remain in Georgetown. There was only the one plane available. I decided to go with Matthew and Ben to see Samantha's father. I was not in a hurry. As it stood, if I could get things started I would feel more at ease when I returned to Supenaam. Matthew and Ben decided to accompany me.

Mr. Omar was very accommodating. He called his wife and Samantha, and he disclosed the news to me.

"I hope you will understand Mr. Bowry" he began. "What I will tell you is not a decision I unilaterally made. I was at the mosque yesterday and consulted with the Imam and a few elders. While they are in agreement with the marriage, they felt it should be a legal contract. Some of them were a bit rude. I do not want to repeat what they said. Although I do not agree with all that was discussed, I have to abide with the majority's decision."

"I would like you to tell me all that was said and only then will I be able to act." I told him, feeling a bit nervous.

"I agree with the legal side of it. That is for a legal wedding." He started to explain. "What I don't agree with, is the fact that they think the white man laws are for the white man. What they are saying, is that the Muslim wedding will not be legal in their eyes and if for some reason or the other, you may decide to ditch my Samantha, I have no legal rights to hold you accountable," "Then what are you saying?" I asked, for the sake of confirming what he had told me.

"If it would not be a legal wedding, then my family agrees with me to refuse your request." He was most apologetic in his reply.

I was about to say something when Matthew stood and in his authoritative posture, told him. "Mr. Omar. I respect your decision. Any decent father thinking of the welfare of his child would arrive at the same conclusion."

Samantha bowed her head in disappointment. I told her not to give up and that I would do all I could, to see we got married. She smiled, as she raised her head and thanked me for my words of consolation. Matthew then gave a solemn promise that he would do all in his power to see we were married.

"And you can count on me too!" Ben added.

We borrowed Peter's car and went to the convent. A diminutive nun opened the door and asked our business.

"Please tell the Mother Superior that Matthew Longhorn, a friend of the Commissioner is here to speak with her."

I wondered why he had to say, a friend of the Commissioner. It all became clear when she welcomed us and invited us to her office.

"So you are a friend of the Commissioner?" she asked.

"Yes Mother Superior. I am here on a serious mission of mercy and understanding. I wonder if it is at all possible to see Margaret. This young man is her husband and there is something of great importance that we would like to speak about. I would appreciate it if you would be present, if only to see that what we would ask of her is not unreasonable."

While she was considering what to do. Matthew looked around the church and asked "When are you going to refurbish the interior of this beautiful church?"

The Mother Superior looked puzzled at him and asked. "Did you ask when we are going to refurbish the interior, Mr. Longhorn? Why did you ask that question?"

"It appears to be in some deteriorating state." Matthew told her, with his tongue in his cheek.

The Mother Superior told him, that it was under consideration and it would be only a matter of time when funds would be available for such an undertaking. I could see the game he was playing and was not surprised when the Mother Superior asked him if he knew a quicker way to do the job. She might be a religious person, but she was playing Matthew at his own game.

Matthew responded by telling her that he might be able to persuade some of his colleagues to undertake such a task. "God's house is every man's house" he told her, looking for a positive response.

Margaret appeared holding a rosary in her hands and sat next to the Mother superior. Matthew told her that it was selfish not to agree to a divorce, if she was not willing to live with Andrew, as husband and wife. Mother Superior interrupted by saying that she was fully aware of the treachery, that had caused her to take such drastic action. Matthew argued that circumstances were far beyond my control and that I regretted every minute of it.

"The church does not agree with divorce. If Margaret chooses not to consent to it, then there is nothing I can do." she defended Margaret.

"Yes Mother Superior. You can do a lot to help." Matthew told her.

"How did you come to that decision?" Mr. Longhorn was her question.

"You may not know it, but I am of the Jewish faith, not a practicing one and I do know a lot of other religions. In your Testament, did Christ not say to turn the other cheek when assaulted or words to that effect? And also did he not say forgiveness is the key to eternal life?" Matthew asked, like a lawyer quizzing a defendant. Then adding, whilst tactfully looking at the church wall, he continued. "Whatever decision you arrive at, I will continue to persuade my colleagues about the refurbishment."

The Mother Superior did not react to his last statement. I am sure she heard and pretended it was of no importance. Instead she said, "You have the gist of Christ's teachings. Not accurate, but near enough. I cannot promise you anything. All I can say is, I will try and reason with her when she is in a more accommodating mood" she assured us.

We left with a feeling of hope. I decided to take them to their club for lunch and a bit of sippy, as Ben often said.

Later that evening, we arrived at Peter's residence and found Margaret and the Mother Superior in conversation, with Both Peter's parents. Matthew lifted an eyebrow and looked at me inquiringly. I shrugged my shoulders.

We were all a bit tipsy and tried to act as normal as possible. We greeted them with the usual courtesy and sat down, while they finished their coffee.

"I am not entirely against drinking, Mr. Longhorn. What I am against, is that you, a responsible and mature person should be encouraging this young man to this sort of socializing." The Mother Superior reproached Matthew. Then turning to me, she said. "As for you, young man, you should be ashamed to be in that state. Now, before I can speak to any of you, I would like you to go and freshen up." She reminded me of my mother when my father became disagreeable.

We did as ask and returned in a much sober state. What she told us was unbelievable. "I have spoken to Margaret at great lengths and I think she has something to say.

Margaret did not look up, instead she kept her head low and started to cry. Mother Superior told her to take courage and tell me what she had decided.

She began. "It is only when Mother Superior told me that under certain dispensation, I will be allowed to stay at the convent, for as long as I wanted, that I have come to this decision. It does not mean that I have forgiven you. I shall never forgive you Andrew. I still love you but I cannot be your wife in the true sense of the word. I shall soften my unforgiving stance by allowing you to go ahead and sue for a divorce." she hastily told me, before getting up to leave.

I tried to thank her with a gentle peck on the cheek. Instead she turned away and said goodbye. Matthew went and held the

Mother Superior's hands and thanked her for her kindness and effort. Peter summoned his chauffeur to take them back to the convent. I stood on the veranda and watched them leave, unable to take in what was said. Matthew, waving goodbye, reminded her that he would speak to his friends about the church. She gave him a broad smile and waved.

The next day, we waited for Peter's chauffeur to return from the airport, bringing Matthew's friend. "I want you to listen to me Andrew." he said to me. "What will be said when my friend gets here, will give more historical facts of my life story than you dared to imagine."

I can hardly wait. I knew he had a colourful life but he never spoke at any great lengths about it. Perhaps a little splutter to make comparisons. Les Nyman got out from the car and was greeted by both Peter and Matthew. I could see from the elegant way he strode up the stairs that this man had breeding and a military gait that was unmistakably recognisable.

"I want to welcome you here and to make you as comfortable as possible." Peter told him, then made the necessary introductions. Then turning to Matthew he asked. "Do you recognise this warrior?"

"I do indeed, I really do. I never expected to ever see him again." They gave each other a brotherly embrace and it was my turn to be introduced. Peter told him who I was and why I was there. We eventually sat down and ended the formalities with some champagne. Christine suddenly said. "I seem to recognise you from somewhere. I really cannot think where that might be, but I am sure it will come to me before you leave."

The visitor looked puzzled and replied. "If I had crossed paths with you dear lady, I would have certainly remembered. How can anyone forget such a beautiful face?"

"Is that how you charmed the beautiful Helen into marriage? Matthew teased. Then looking at me he asked, "Are you taking notes Andrew?"

"That is exactly what Ben asked me, when I first went to Supenaam." I replied adding, "I have a good retentive memory.

"That is what he kept saying to me when I asked if he was taking notes." Ben added.

Early the next morning Peter and Matthew took their guest to his surgery in the city. Ben and I went to see Aubrey about the divorce. It turned out to be simpler than I thought. He told me that if both parties agrees, and I were to admit my adultery, it would be a matter of weeks before I would be free. I was so jubilant, I wanted to dance. My dignity got the better of me. This was a real occasion for celebrating. Supenaam has changed me a great deal. Before I went there I hardly drank. Perhaps it was because it was so costly. In Supenaam, they seemed to be making the stuff. The cabinet was constantly filled with the best malt whisky money can buy. It did not take much to encourage Ben. So the rest of the day was spent talking and drinking, not excessively just enough to get us merry. I must remember not to be in a state of drunkenness, when I visit Mr. Omar. Today was not that day.

When we arrived at Peter's house they were all sitting on the rear veranda, taking in the Atlantic breeze and had a glass of something. Even Peter's mother had her glass filled with whatever she drank. Ben and I refused to take any more. Trying not to be embarrassing, we said goodnight and went to bed.

I was up very early, after a quick breakfast I took a taxi and went down to the editorial office to complete an article I wanted in the next day's papers. I would also mention the arrival of Les Nyman and his connections with the former Commissioner.

When I got back they were all out. Except Peter's mother. She told me that they had gone to meet the Governor and to introduce Les to him. I was lost in my loneliness. No Ben or Matthew to talk to, I started thinking of Samantha and how she would accept the good news. I wanted to have a drink, but thought the better of it.

It was hours before they finally stepped out of the car and came rushing upstairs, greeting me as if I were away for ages. Before I could say anything, Matthew interrupted. "I know you wanted us to go with you to see that beautiful Samantha. I tell you what, I am taking Les with us and leave Ben behind."

"You do no such thing. I am coming with or without an invitation" he blurted out.

Inevitably, the four of us set out on that historical journey. Unknown to me, Matthew had telephoned Mr. Omar, to inform him of our time of arrival.

The family were seated in the living room when we arrived. They all had a gloomy look about them. Samantha was the only one brave enough to smile and asked. "Did you get something positive from her?" Before I could say anything, Matthew relayed what had transpired at the convent and the eventual visit. He told them exactly what was said. Samantha was so excited, she sprang to her feet and hugged me. This infuriated her parents and her father shouted. "You have no shame my child behaving like a loose woman before your guests and more importantly before the eyes of your parents?"

She apologised and explained that she was expecting the worst news imaginable. Her father looked with crossed eyes and pointed a warning finger at her. She bowed her head in submission. Les looked in amazement and commented, "This is the sort of behavior that is forbidden in that part of India, where I was stationed. I imagine people here, outside of their native land, are a bit more liberal."

"Absolutely." Matthew added.

"What part of India you were stationed Mr. Les?" Omar asked

"Just call me Les. I was in Bengal on patrol in the Sunderbans. Preventing people from killing too many tigers." Les told him.

"Did you see any tigers?" Omar again asked.

"I saw a few, but they were all killed by people wanting their skins for the tourists and the bones for the Chinese." was the reply.

"What the Chinese want with bones? It is useless." he again asked.

"They used it for their medicines. I cannot see what purpose bones can serve as medicines." Les ruefully replied, then he asked "Has any decision been made of this young man's future?"

"I will have a final consultation with my immediate family and inform you." Mr. Omar told him. I can see he is playing a game and I was in no mood to play silly games. My frustration was removed when his wife told him. "There are no more discussions. Tell the young man what we all agreed. Or Syed Omar, I will do just that. Can't you see they are in love and you're behaving like a prison guard." his wife told him with no hint of a compromise.

"You are right, I did behave unreasonably. I am really very sorry" He turned and looked at me apologetically and said the words I was waiting for. "This family will be pleased to accept you as our son."

I jumped and grabbed him in the strongest hug I ever gave someone. There were hands all around and as usual, in these occasions ended with a delicious Indian feast.

Peter was ready to return to Supenaam and I left Georgetown a very happy man. The sun was just sinking in the horizon displaying a tumultuous array of different shades of red as its rays pierced the openings of the trees. A gentle breeze tossed the branches, as if cradling them to sleep. I heard some parakeets whizzed past and I wondered whether the sinking sun was having a sinking heart in them.

Night is a dangerous time for the non-nocturnal creatures and they are fully aware of this. Precautions were taken to avoid any confrontation with those eager to make a meal of them, whether it was an early dinner, a late supper or a very early breakfast. It does not matter when their demise takes place. The ultimate decision is to keep safe. On the other hand, one must think of the nocturnal creatures, whose duty it is, to provide food for their young and to fill their empty bellies. Nature seems to not have an answer to this imbalance and the only order of survival, is dependent on the cunning of those that know how to survive.

The Indigenous Nation believed that a bird built its nest, north to south, to prevent the sun exposing them to would be predators. I have not had the opportunity to put this theory to the test. Perhaps, one day I would find the time to do exactly that.

As the plane splashed down on the river, my thoughts again, returned to the creatures living there. I asked myself some questions. Are we right to use the river as we pleased? Should we not think of the fish and the caiman, that may be resting and let them have their peace. The same as we get irritated when Diego's cockerels started their early morning crowing and awakening the entire neighbourhood. I imagine we do what is best suited to our needs and to hell with the rest of the world.

There were strange thoughts that entered my head. I never took a second look at the workings of nature before. Here in Supenaam, it is different, you are forced to take heed or perish. I am a survivor.

As I walked towards Tudor Grange, my thoughts turned to the temptation that l may face in there, in the form of Louise. I was not prepared to allow this to happen. As I stood at the entrance contemplating my next action, the door opened and there she was, standing, looking invitingly at me, "Are you not coming in?" she asked. It took a minute for me to answer. "I am sorry Louise, I am not going into that house ever again. Not while you are there." I told her with firmness, she never expected.

"Am I not your hibiscus with the pink soft petals as lips anymore? she again asked.

"Remember the hibiscus, it is a flower that only lasts a day. In the morning when they opened to exhibit their tender beauty, it is time for appreciation. Whether you noticed it or not, it is evening and time for the flower to wither and die and for the wind to blow their dried up petals like ghosts to rot in the earth." I was looking her in the eyes, as I spoke.

"So my lips were dried up and waiting to be floated away. Please come in and we will talk more sensible."

"You are not listening, I want no more trouble from you, now or ever. You are a Jezebel. Don't you ever speak to me again, or I will let this community know what you really are." I told her with confidence.

She slammed the door shut, and as I stood there, marveling at my decision, I heard her husband ask who was at the door. She told him it was me coming to say I would be residing at the Guest house as there was another guest taking his place.

CHAPTER 20

THE CORE OF THE INTERVIEW

At the guest house, I told Ben of my intention and he was pleased to have me as company. I am really beginning to appreciate his quality, as a friend.

Later, we joined the others, who were eagerly awaiting our arrival. I knew it was going to be a long night. I gathered my pencils and papers and sat comfortably in a Berbice chair. It is one of the most comfortable chairs for relaxation. Why it is called a Berbice chair is beyond me. From what I saw of the Berbicians I can only surmise that it is because of their relaxed attitude and easy going demeanour, the chair was given that name.

As they continued delving in the past, an entirely new world began to emerge and I was seriously fascinated. It came to a point where Les was so surprised that Matthew was about to marry the Princess, he heard so much about.

"What prevented you?" Les asked

"Stupidity and honour." Matthew replied

"I don't understand" was his next question.

"Stupidity in asking my commanding officer for his permission. I know what you are going to ask and the answer is yes, I did not need his permission and I could have gone ahead and done it. Unfortunately it was honour, I was bound by tradition, to honour my commander's decision. It was not long after, that she married her husband and I was again sent back to Shimla." Matthew explained.

"I heard you were sent to Dolali that hill station where soldiers with health and mental problems go to recuperate." Les told him.

"After that incident, I went native. I don't regret it for a minute. I sometimes don a dhoti and sat on the banks of the Ganges, meditating with the other holy men and they would go in the river and wash themselves. They would look at me to see if I would follow."

"Did you wash in the river?

"Of course not, even though I considered it, as they do a sacred river, I would not wash myself in it." Matthew told us.

"Why is that, Matthew" Ben asked.

"The river is considered sacred in the Hindu religion. I could not go and bathe in its water, because it was highly polluted with rotten human flesh left over from the many crematoriums. My commander was horrified at my behavior. It was then I was sent to the hill station to regain my 'dignity' I spent a few months meditating and ignoring their plea for me to return to 'normality'. When all seemed lost I was sent home with a pension.

Back at the family's estate I became even more bored with the everyday ritual and the parties for members of various ministries. It was on one occasion that a senior member from the home office suggested, that I take up the post of Commissioner in British Guiana. I'd never heard of the place before. I looked at the map and saw a tiny strip of land on the shoulders of the South American continent. I began reading books about it and stories from other travelers. When I learnt that only a tiny bit along the coast was inhabited, I became increasingly interested and accepted the post."

"Do you really think Ahmed Khan was a real threat to our empire." Peter asked.

"I am yet to come to a clear decision of that man. I was told he came from an aristocratic family and was disillusioned by the fact that he would not succeed his father as heir to their little empire. He considered his elder brother where rumour abounds of his homosexuality as incapable of running the family business. His father refused to name him the heir, so he took up fighting us to get rid of his frustration. I must add, I found him a lovable rebel." Matthew told us.

"How did you come to this conclusion?" I asked.

"It was not only one incident but many, where he could have wiped us off the map and chose not to do so. Instead, he played games with us, not because he was a better soldier but because he had the advantage of knowing the terrain, like the palm of his hand. I will tell you another thing that made me admire him. Once I had the misfortune of being ambushed by his men, they could have slaughtered us mercilessly. Instead, they took us to his command post deep, in the most northerly part of a place, called Peshawar and inside of what looked like a huge tent was a palace under canvas. Once inside, you could be forgiven for thinking you are in a palace." Matthew looked really taken back in time, as he gave us this account. I was not certain of all that he'd said and had some serious questions to ask.

"You said we had total control of the subcontinent. Why then were there rebels trying to get control of some of the domain we ruled?" I was forced to ask

"You could not say we had total control. No conqueror is in total control, not when some of the Maharajas were powerful enough to launch a significant attack and sustain it with prolonged resistance. In order for us to appease them, we devised various plans to avert such actions. For instance, when I was sent to Rajastan, I was no military advisor and the Maharaja knew that. My job was to test his loyalty to the crown and believe me or not, the wily old man knew it. I was told to advise him, that to remain loyal to the crown, we would protect his Princely state from invasion. I told him of a dynasty far greater than his who is planning an invasion, not only to seize his domain but to go further south, far into the Deccan valley and take control of an area so vast, we would not dare challenge him. He of course believed it for a while. You must remember that India was not a colony, but an empire, in its own rights. Matthew appeared to come to the end of his life there. It was Les who told us some interesting historical facts.

"I think we could have held on to India if our approach were more amenable and accommodating to the aristocracy. They held the key for a sustained occupation. Of course, we always thought that imposing our so called superiority was the vital factor to remain in control. It worked for a while, until the cracks started appearing. No empire can survive by sheer force alone. The involvement of the people in all administrative positions would have been vital for a peaceful occupation." Les argued.

I think I have heard enough about your life Matthew. I must turn to Peter and delve into his life, during the real war. I think it is getting late and we all need some rest.

I sat in bed thinking for a long time, about my forthcoming marriage and the way I admonished Louise. It appeared harsh, but that was the only way to put an end to any further involvement with her.

I heard an owl hoot and then my thoughts returned to the one I had prior to our splashing down. Why is that bird hooting in the middle of the night? What signal is it sending and to whom? It was too complicated for me to reason. In the end, tiredness took hold of me and I drifted into a peaceful sleep.

Peter was too busy with his own work. After breakfast, Matthew wanted to show his friend the source of the gold that made them famously rich. I was not eager to go, but Ben and Diego reassured me that they would show me something that would be of great interest.

At cold stream, I was surprised to see that the cold storage unit was not there. He took me down a path about a mile nearer to Warachara's village and showed me what turned out to be a surprise. It was a cold storage building of about three meters by three meters, packed with freshly killed carcasses. There were agoutis, deer, wild hogs, Tapirs, my favourite peccaries and many other animals, unknown to me by name. Also, there were birds hung by their necks, all along the walls. I love the peccaries for their audacious attacks on unsuspecting jaguars, their arch killer and the valiant fight to the death they endured.

As we drove back on the tractor, to cold stream, Warachara and Obeyo were coming towards us, accompanied by a dozen of their men. I imagined that they were visiting the storage unit to collect the meal for the day. Instead of carrying on, they signaled us to stop and asked that we take them to cold stream. Ben thought this was a strange request. He reluctantly obliged.

Diego was surprised we brought the chief here and demanded we give an explanation. He accepted what Ben told him and hastened to add "This river was to be a secret. I know I can trust the chief, but some of his men cannot be trusted to keep it a secret." A worried Diego explained.

After much deliberation, the chief was allowed to explain his visit. He began with what appeared to be a silly excuse, at first. He turned and spoke directly to Matthew. "I want to see a river for myself. My people told me you have gold from here. Is this true?"

"It is true." Matthew replied.

"Why keep secret from Paramount Chief. I am Paramount Chief and you old Commissioner keep secret. Obeyo and I decide we take river for Indigenous nation. You old Commissioner not trusted no more."

It was an unexpected confrontation. I did not realize that when Ben told me there were surprises awaiting, it would be this. Diego stepped in and told him that the only reason it was kept a secret was to protect it from outsiders coming and stealing, what is rightfully theirs. He accused Diego of betrayal and became very angry.

Matthew was also getting fed up with his attitude. He assumed his authoritative posture with his hands holding on to his lapels and said "Now you listen to me Paramount Chief. I have always been honest with you. I have put my life at risk, not once but dozens of occasions. I've been bitten by a Bush Master and nearly died to prevent your people and forest from poachers, loggers and trophy hunters, and always, I did it to preserve your way of life. Not mine, but yours and the people living from Supenaam to Kaburi, in the West and unto the borders of the great towns in the North. Most of the money we got from the gold is spent on your villagers.

"The doctors that came and helped your women and her husband who is trying to get the international community to accept your position to maintain a pristine forest, by collecting specimen of plants and birds to show at the international convention for the preservation of the earth's wild places.

Our flying machines, as you called them, are part of that struggle. We can get to places faster than the interlopers can run. I may not be Commissioner but I still hold a strong hand in what is decided here."

Matthew was exhausted and he looked it. Warachara, calmly placed a hand on Matthew's shoulder and in a soft tone said, "Old Commissioner speaks truth. I will tell my people to make sacrifice to your truth telling. I go now and speak to my friend Obeyo." He then made the most courteous of withdrawal and disappeared among the trees.

Les was listening, with attentive ears of the exchanges and was visibly perplexed. Matthew told him the relevant facts. "It is true that the gold we found here was the foundation for the great fortunes we made. The gold in itself would have been a means of a little more luxury. We exchanged those nuggets for diamonds that were hundreds of times more valuable. That is where the wealth for these friends of mine came. You know Les, I have given my entire share of the estate in Somerset to my brother. I have and I say this with no regrets. My share, worth millions from the sale of the diamonds, I gave to a young man I appreciated as a son. My life is one of peace within myself. The peace and tranquility money cannot buy.

"This place reminds me of Harapa. I had to escort a group of archeologists there. That was another time we made it, because that enigmatic Ahmed Khan allowed us to travel. I deviate, coming back to my point, at Harapa there were dozens of archeologists from Russia, France, Germany, Italy and other countries, looking for clues for a lost civilization. I never lingered long enough to find out if they succeeded or not. What I am trying to say is, the money grabbers are only trying to fill their pockets and leaving desolation behind. I do not want, in fifty years or more, people coming here as they did in Harapa, looking for clues for a lost civilization and the relics of the past. I will stand up to any man, any country, the world if needs be, to defend this land. That is why, I am still here. This is my mission in life."

"Steady on old friend. I think you have said more than you wanted." Les told him, then asked "Did you say you gave your brother your half of the estate? Matthew, I never dreamt you would change so dramatically. I admired your way of life. Whether I can sustain such a life, is debatable. Who is this brother that is so lucky?"

"His name is Jonathan and he is Christine's father. They came here for a weekend adventure and she fell in love with Peter. Unknown to him, she became pregnant and the obstinate person she is, refused to reveal that fact to him. It was not until he went to England that he learnt the truth. I guess it will all be made clear, when Andrew interviews him later this evening." Matthew told him finally.

As Matthew earlier said, it would all be revealed. So it was when we sat down for a sippy after dinner, Peter began relaying to me, events leading to his arrival in England. It was a fascinating story, the way he endured the hardships of life, in the army, albeit as a non-combatant. His marriage to a girl from a Jewish family. Most interesting, was the way he found out he was Jewish, by birth and the way Matthew brought about that revelation. It seemed strange to me, that someone brought up as a strict catholic, would suddenly realise his roots were imbedded in another culture, another religion and to accept, without question was indeed, honourable.

Stranger than ever, is the fact that he was able to endure the abuses from his Commander, just because he was a colonial and that he was able to befriend men of the highest rank, whether it was the Navy, Army or Air force. He tried to excuse his success with his friendship with Christine and her family. Catherine came from an aristocratic family, with powerful connections. Meeting the Rajkumar was the highlight of his life. The very man who eventually married Matthew's Princess.

He told me of the agonising moments he had, making his guest happy and comfortable. The Governor at the time, refused to acknowledge their presence, as an official visit, but was kind enough to entertain them lavishly at the mansion. I was particularly interested in the way he was trained to be a dentist, in a time of war. I imagined that it was a reward for his unceasing efforts, to help in times of dire need, with not only the wounded, but those that had lost loved ones.

"I can only reflect on when I was living there, only six years old and finding my parents struggling to cope with the hardships of life. That was one of the reasons my father accepted the post, as head of the church, at the Mission. I was now committed to marry Samantha and to remain here, in his colony, for the rest of my life. Speaking of marriage," I turned to Les "do you have a specific date for your return home?"

"I have, as a matter of fact. Why do you ask?"

"I would like very much for you to be at the wedding. There are going to be two ceremonies. First, we will have the legal formalities, which will be done by my father, who as you know, is a priest and the traditional ceremony, this will be done with great pomp and celebration by her people." I told him.

"I will not miss that wedding, for all the diamonds in the outback." he replied enthusiastically.

"Then you and Matthew will have to help me plan the whole thing. I was married briefly before and that was hurriedly done. I want this to be easy and relaxed and for all my friends to enjoy the wonderful day with me." I was near to tears as I spoke.

The major part of my interview was complete. All that was left, was for me to tie up the loose ends with Diego and Ben, and my job there would be finished. I began to feel sad and nostalgic and I'd not even left the place.

CHAPTER 21

THE WEDDING

Matthew and Peter came to see me at my lodgings. They told me that they would be going to Georgetown, the following day and would like me to accompany them. I asked why and they told me that they were planning to print some special invitations and it would be nice if our pictures were set on the inside of it. It sounded a marvelous idea. I asked if Ben could come, along as he would be left all alone, with only Isabel to distract him. It was agreed, and the next day we went straight to the photographer, after collecting Samantha. It took just a few minutes and we were asked to return the next day to collect the pictures.

Our next stop was at police headquarters, in Brickdam. Samantha and I were told to wait in the car, while the two went in and came out after about twenty minutes. I did not ask their reason and they did not say. We took Samantha to her dressmaker and left her there with instructions to telephone when she was finished.

Ben and I joined Les on the veranda, where he was chatting with Peter's parents. Christine came and joined us and she was very distressed. She complained that she was finding it impossible to cope without someone like Margaret to help. She told us that Beda, her mother's maid, was efficient, only with the household work. When it came to confidentialities, she was useless. Isabel was more used to her, but unfortunately she had to stay with Peter, in Supenaam. I thought of someone that could help and proposed that she have a chat with her. I could see her eyes light up at my proposal and I arranged to go and see her as soon as Samantha telephoned.

I was never so pleased to see Christine, looking as happy as she did, sat in the front seat, with her husband.

We drove down Middle Street, until we came to Cummings Street, turned left, as my memory served me, into Third Street and there, on the right, was the house as I remembered it. Mrs. Pereira opened the door and I gave my condolences. Her husband had passed away with typhoid, he caught in the bauxite mines, up the Berbice River.

I told her why we were there and she appeared a bit more relaxed. "It's not been easy, since Ralph died. The bauxite company is dragging their feet with paying the compensation. The insurance company is worse. They are asking all sorts of silly questions, which I find difficult to answer." she told us, looking depressed all over again.

"If you give me the name of the insurance company, I will be able to help. The bauxite company can be dealt with legally. I have a friend, who I am sure will help you and you can pay him when it is all over." Peter suggested.

"That's very kind of you Mr. D'Abrue. I will take his address before you leave. In the meantime, I think your wife wants to speak with Deborah. Can I make you some coffee in the meantime?" she ended, asking.

Christine and Deborah went in another room, while we sipped a cup of very strong coffee. Later, they emerged with smiles spread across their faces. It told us everything.

"She is exactly what I am looking for. The only problem I have, is to rearrange your apartment, to make room for a single young woman." she told me.

"That's fine by me. I am sure Samantha would not mind if we moved into the flat below. As a matter of fact, I think it would suit us better." I told her.

The next few days were spent making arrangements for the wedding. I found it tiresome and left Ben to sort out the more mundane parts of it.

Peter, Matthew and Les would disappear for long periods. I was curious of their whereabouts, as this was uncharacteristic behavior. I never tried to get to the bottom of it. I was too busy with the interview I'd collected and most of my time was taken up trying to coordinate all the facts, to make it readable.

My editor was very helpful. He even lent me his secretary, to scribble it in shorthand, which saved a lot of valuable time. Ben would sometimes pop down the editorial office and make everyone laugh, with his home spun philosophy.

The big day eventually arrived and I was very nervous. I could not remember being nervous when Margaret and I were married. The hall where the two ceremonies were to be held, were ornately decorated. Peter had employed the best in town to do the job. My father was to perform the legal Christian part first and then the other would be done by their Imam.

As usual, I stood in front of my father, flanked on my left by Peter and Matthew. Les led Samantha to join us and my father began with the necessary announcement of the marriage. I felt like laughing, when he turned to me and asked "Do you Andrew Timothy take this woman Samantha Bibi as your wife? To cherish and to remain loyal for the rest of your life?" I replied with the obvious answer.

"And do you Samantha Bibi take this man, Andrew Timothy as your husband to cherish and remain loyal for the rest of your life?" She also gave the relevant answer.

I was amused initially, because it was the first time I'd witnessed my father doing a wedding and I noticed that he did not use the words one normally hears at weddings. I imagine it is the Evangelist way. I must admit, I found it simple and to the point. He did not ask me to kiss the bride and neither of us made an attempt. I guess it was because her parents were watching and she wanted to show respect. I was glad I did not make an attempt to do that.

We were later seated on soft cushions in front of an Imam. Her parents were behind and some of her close relatives. Since it was a double Muslim ceremony, her sister and groom were seated next to us. I could not help feeling humble. All eyes were on Samantha, I was briefed of what to say and prompted to say it, at the appropriate time. It all went well and I became nervous again, when I had to make a speech. I did not know exactly what to say, when the people here may not be aware of the things said at a Christian wedding, where we had a Master of Ceremonies and jokes flow in abundance.

This was a very religious event. I took courage and decided to say all the correct things. I started "Ladies and gentlemen, this is the first time I am married under your custom. The dignity exhibit here is overwhelming. I would like to thank everyone for their understanding. I am forced to say, that this in itself, demonstrates what understanding and tolerance, can achieve. If we choose to ignore the colour of a man's skin and accept his culture and religion, we can all be better human beings. If we look at our fellow men and see him as the creation in the image of our Maker, then we would have crossed a major hurdle in human understanding.

My sincere thanks go to my parents for their solidarity in supporting this marriage and to Mr. and Mrs., or should I say my new parents, whose tolerance prevailed to make this event possible. Unashamedly, I declare my deep love for my darling Samantha." There were sounds of oooohs from the congregation, followed by a rapturous applause.

After a brief pause, I continued. "Now I accept her family as mine. I must not forget the friends, without whose support, I would have found this event challenging. I say a huge thank you to Commissioner Peter, Retired Commissioner Matthew. My old friends, Ben and Diego and his family, and most sincerely to the Commissioner's wife, Christine, whose efforts to make our marriage a success is beyond evaluation. Least of all, I must not forget to thank Les Nyman for delaying his return to England, in order to support me."

In conclusion, I clasped both my hands and made a gentle bow to Samantha and the rest of her family. There were no Master of Ceremonies and Matthew took that role. He spoke at great lengths of the love I received from the community in Supenaam and here in the city. Then it was the bride's father's turn to reply. He spoke of his doubts of my intentions and his ploy to deter me. It was his wife who made the final decision for him. He then went on to say how remarkable it was for me to say mankind must be tolerant to each other. Then he reminded his congregation, that for a Christian to say that word, tolerance was a testament to what is written in the Quran, namely, peace, love and tolerance. The three most important aspects in human understanding. We were then offered to wash our hands from bowls of scented water, with petals floating at the top and given a hibiscus to dry our fingers. I looked at the flower and declined the offer. I need not say why.

The rest of the day, was taken up first, with a man bursting onto the stage, singing a love song, followed by a woman joining him, swaying her hips as if they hung on hinges. This was followed by a host of dancers, crowding on the stage, singing and dancing. Others joined in and I was asked to take part. I did not have a clue of this kind of dancing and declined. Matthew, Ben and to my surprise, Les, danced like it was part of their culture. I could only sit up and enjoy the entertainment.

In the end, at about five o'clock, it ended with a lavish feast. Christine took Samantha away and I was told to wait for Matthew. He was still dancing, so I sent someone to call him. He went and fetched my parents and asked them to follow him. I said my goodbyes and left. There were three cars waiting. Christine and Samantha, sat in the back of the jaguar. I sat in the front with Peter, the rest bundled in the other two. We went straight to Peter's residence and two suitcases were placed in the boot and we were speeding towards the airport. Unbeknown to me, they, that is Peter, Matthew, Ben and Diego, had paid for our honeymoon, a week in London and a week in Paris. Samantha and I were in shock. Then, I suddenly remembered, we didn't have passports, or tickets. "Oh yes you do" Christine assured me, she then produced the passports and tickets and hotel reservations.

"How did you manage to do all this without our knowledge?" I asked in total disbelief.

"With a little bit of cunning," Peter began to explain. "When we took you to the photographer, we were getting the passport pictures and if you remember, we went to police headquarters. While you sat in the car, I arranged for the officer to have yours and Samantha's documents ready in time. It took a lot of planning. It was Christine's idea of you honeymooning both in London, the land of your birth, and romantic Paris.

The first day was spent contacting some of my relations and telling them all that had happened. The following two days I could see Samantha was not very happy. For some reason or the other, she refused to discuss it.

On the fourth morning, as we were about to enter the dining room, she turned and went to the desk and demanded to see the manager. Instead of escorting her, he merely pointed where the office was located. She gently knocked on the door and the manager invited us in. He asked us to sit.

Samantha was very angry when she said in a voice I'd never heard before. "You do not know who I am and I just don't have the time to explain." She was not allowed to finish what she was about to say. The manager was apologetic and asked "Lady, if you tell me your problem, I am sure I can remedy it." "I hope you do, or this matter will end in all the headlines of your newspapers." she replied.

She continued, "My husband and I are here on honeymoon, organised by our friends, the Commissioner of the Hinterlands and the retired Commissioner and some of the most influential people in the colony. Here, in the heart of democracy, I am being treated like a second class citizen and it appalls me. We have another week at your sister hotel in Paris and should I encounter such behavior, I shall have no alternative but to cancel the reservation and return home."

This was one side of Samantha I could have never known existed. I have a strong and determined wife and I was proud of her. I was unable to understand how she got the courage to put an end, to what was clearly a tricky situation. The fact that she never mentioned it to me and dealt with it personally, was in itself, testament to her character.

The manager asked if she could point out the person or persons that caused her such humiliation. She answered his question by saying that the people involved could not be held responsible, as she felt it was the management's responsibility to brief their staff.

The manager was visibly angry, not with her, but what he heard. "You leave this to me dear lady. Did you have your breakfast?" I told him we had not. He escorted us to a very cosy corner and personally went and got a menu.

Then, he ordered a waiter to stand at our table and attend to our every demand. He was given strict instructions not to leave the table. I can see other diners looking in our direction, unable to understand what was happening. Samantha's face lit up and smiled at some of them.

After breakfast, the manager came to us and said "I telephoned your hotel in Paris and they will be sending a car to collect you from the airport and a bottle of cool champagne will be in your suite." Again he apologised before departing. I really felt sorry for him.

On our way to the gardens, we were approached by a young couple. The young lady introduced herself and then told us "Edgar and I are also on our honeymoon. Perhaps we can stick together and you can tell us all about South America. They turned out to be very friendly and before long, we were going to various venues together. I told them if they wished to visit British Guiana, they would have the most fabulous holiday of their lives. I gave them addresses and telephone numbers, if they wished to make contact.

Paris was indeed, a romantic city. I will not make comparisons, as both cities had their unique charm. A limousine was waiting for us and indeed, a magnum of champagne with flowers. I was expecting to see caviar. Alas, there was no sign of it. I was not disappointed.

Samantha was opening up to the new life she so suddenly found. She started sipping tiny amounts of champagne at first and when she found it exhilarating, took a second glass of it. I knew she never drank alcohol before and I was a bit terrified she may get tipsy. She looked at me and asked "Are you surprised I am enjoying the champagne? I am a Muslim but I do take the odd glass of wine when at parties. My father knew of it but kept it a secret from my mother, who would have probably died of a heart attack had she found out."

It was time to return home and as the plane taxied out onto the runaway, I felt sad leaving this beautiful city behind. I thought of Diego and Ben and his amenable demeanor and things started to brighten up.

Les was at the airport to catch his plane back to England. I was very happy to say goodbye personally. He gave Samantha a kiss on both cheeks and told us to visit him in Willesden, if ever we decided to go back to London. Peter and Matthew were there to drive us back to the city, where the real life would begin.

The thought of returning to Supenaam sent a sparkle of joy in me. I am not sure what Samantha would make of it. I wondered how Christine and Deborah were getting on.

When we were rested I decided to ask Samantha if she would be able to cope with life in the jungle. She replied by saying. "Andrew if you survived three months there then I think I will."

"You have only recently been married and you are already talking of surviving." Christine queried, as she joined us on the veranda. A favourite area for relaxing, due to the constant cool breeze from the Atlantic. Deborah was close behind and Samantha started talking women's talk. I pretended not to listen. She was saying how lucky she was to find this job here and how enjoyable life had been, since she moved out from her home, because of the persistence of a suitor whom she disliked utterly.

Her mother was encouraging the young man, simply because he had a very well paid job and it would have made life easier, if they were to marry. "I did not hate him. It was his arrogance. He felt he would be an asset to my mother and used that as a ploy to get to see me. I never went anywhere with him. I simply did not trust him. You know what mothers are, they persist until they get their way. I was determined not to let him have his way with me, if you know what I mean." She had a determined look on her face as she spoke. I knew she was exactly of the same character as my Samantha and I was beginning to like her.

Peter came and told us that Les was back. His flight was cancelled due to the airport workers in Trinidad being on strike and he did not know when his next flight would be.

He had the longest face possible. "Dam! Dam!" he half shouted "All that waiting, for nothing. Airlines have no consideration for passengers. Surely they must have known something was afoot. Mind you, I am not disappointed I am stranded here, in this lovely city and among great friends."

After a few days rest, we were ready to return to Supenaam. Samantha went to spend some time with her family. I suggested she remain there, until I'd finished my interview with Diego and Ben. She was not taking my advice. I knew I could not win this argument with her and I was not going to try.

Aubrey, Peter's school friend came visiting with an enormous problem. He was telling Peter and Matthew of his disappointment with the result of a murder trial that was concluded with the most serious question of injustice. "I will tell you all the facts and you decide whether the two of you can help. Before I go further, I must say that I am not asking because of our deep friendship, but in the name of justice. You must have read in the papers of the murder of a man committed by his young son. The jurors quite rightly, found him guilty of the crime.

It was up to the judge to exercise leniency in view of the circumstances. As usual, the judge asked if the defendant had anything to say before passing sentence. I will read verbatim from the transcript I brought with me. The young man told the judge "Yes my lord I am guilty and I do not regret it for a moment. My father was a bully and was habitually inebriated. He was such a bully that when I was six years old, I was forced to become a nanny to the rest of my brothers and sisters and there were quite a few of us. He would beat me while I was asleep if I did not attend to the crying infant. My mother was giving birth year after year and I was the one to care for them. I was a virtual slave. Not only a nanny, a cook, errand boy and housemaid. I had little time left to spent on my studies.

When he discovered I was not doing well in school, he would flog me mercilessly so much so that there were several abscesses in my forearm. I suffered it all quietly. On the day of the incident, he had a serious quarrel with my mother. He was so angry, he poured gasoline on her and the baby she had in her arms. When some of my brothers went and hugged her, pleading with him, he poured gasoline on them and was trying to strike a match. I took a stick and hit him on his head. I did not realise how hard I struck him, but he fell dead on the ground. The neighbours rushed and examined him and confirmed he was dead. I felt relief.

No more beatings and maybe some freedom to live like a normal person, having time to play with my friends, even engage in some school recreational activities. Something I dared not dream about. I am glad he is dead he was a tyrant and a wife beater. If in God's eyes I have committed an unforgivable sin. Then I will ask God to look again, at the creature he made. I am sure God will shake his head in dismay at his creation, that went horribly wrong."

The judge listened intently and before pronouncing sentence said "You have committed an unpardonable sin the act of patricide. I can say this; if you were charged with murder and found guilty, I would not have hesitated to sentence you to death, as the law requires. However, the lesser charge exempts you from that. I have no alternative but to sentence you to the maximum allowed in law. And that is a life imprisonment. It will give you time to purge yourself of this dreadful act and in time, will give you the strength to understand the gravity of your crime. In all religion, it is mandatory to honour and obey your parents no matter what they are."

Even the prosecutor and the other lawyers shook their heads in disbelief. Of course I lodged an appeal. These things take time and I personally feel that this young man should have been treated more leniently. I have drafted a petition that I think, if presented by both of you, to the Governor, it will expedite the process and bring about the early release of that young man. Now Peter, you are the Commissioner and you know the young man's father.

Both you and Matthew are friends and advisors to the Governor who has the mandate to request leniency from the appellant judges. You know how long the normal process takes. It could be years and may even end up before the Privy Council. The Governor's involvement will shorten it to a minimum of months."

Peter then asked. "You said I know the deceased. I cannot remember meeting him."

You remember the time your father nearly shot him, when he tried to terrorise the villagers with a machete?" Aubrey reminded him.

"I remember it quite clearly, now that you have mentioned the incident. I did not know it is the very man." Peter replied.

"We will do all we can, Aubrey. It is a shocking story." Matthew asked "Who was the judge?"

"The Honourable V.R.Singh QC" Aubrey told him.

"That is why he gave such a harsh sentence. Matthew began to explain. "He is a Hindu and they strongly believe in total submission from their children. I heard a story from one of the Gurus in India, who told a story of a young man who got married and it was the custom for the bride to go and live with his parents. In less than a year the mother died and the father who was asthmatic and bed-ridden needed constant attention.

The young man's wife got so fed up with his constant demands, she plotted with her husband to throw him in a well, in the next village. The old man overheard and pretended to be asleep when they carried him. As they prepared to throw him in, he said to his son. "Please do not throw me in this well. It is this very well that I threw my father in, when he became a burden to me and your mother. Take me to another well and there you can do as you wish. The young man hesitated for a while and decided to take his father home and personally look after him."

"So what is the moral of this tale Matthew?" Ben asked.

"If you cannot work it out then I will be wasting my breath telling you." Matthew replied.

At this point Aubrey turned to me and said "You are a journalist. You can take up the story and let the public know of some of the harsh realities some children face with violent parents. There is too much of it in our society. One thing we must remember and that is, if this young man is to remain in prison for a very long time, I would have lost the battle to save him from self destruction."

"My role is limited. The editor has the last word on crusades." I told him. It was then Les began to unfold a new scenario. He started by saying "I am a new member of the Rotary Club of Greenford and until I became a member I did not realise they were such a force in helping the world's needy and displaced people. I think in a case like Aubrey mentioned, there might be scope for some kind of help. It is a pity the community in Supenaam is so small.

You people would have been ideally suited to get a charter for a club. I am thinking if it is not possible for Supenaam, why not get one here in the city. Matthew is President of that famous exclusive club, where all the members are executives and administrators. The venue is perfect and with a little persuasion you can muster enough to establish a club, You can call it the Rotary club of Demerara or Georgetown whatever you like. What do you think Mat?"

"He is always looking for worthy causes to defend. Here is your opportunity to be a god in your own right." Peter added.

"Sounds like a good idea. Let's get Aubrey's appeal off the ground first." Matthew's response sounded positive. Then he added. "You may have seen the herd of cattle across the river in Supenaam. That herd only came about because of donations from a Rotary club in London"

"There you are and another thing in your favour, I will be able to give a talk on Rotary to your prospective members and get the ball rolling." Les added.

I am happy my Samantha is with her parents at the moment, she may think I am involved in too many activities. I think I will have to let her know who the boss is. It is my strong belief that we should have an equal voice in making decisions.

Because of Aubrey's plea, the journey to Supenaam was on hold. Matthew suggested that we take Les to Surinam, to look at the out of date dental equipment the dentists are forced to work with. The war may have brought peace to the world but progress in certain directions was very slow. Les thought it was a brilliant idea. I must let Samantha know. Perhaps she may want to join us. I will only allow it if Christine comes along.

CHAPTER 22
MATTHEW IS ON TRIAL

Our journey to Surinam was very successful. We visited some antiquated surgeries in Nickerie and Paramaribo where several surgeons gave orders for new equipment. Les was overwhelmed with the success. We even had time to visit Matthew's old friend a Mr. Alberga a diamond dealer. When he heard that Samantha and I were only recently married he gave her a small brooch encrusted with tiny diamonds before we flew back to Georgetown.

Since there was no other business we decided to head for Supenaam and leave the Governor to sort out the affair with the young man.

Diego and his family, along with Ben, Sebastian and Joseph were all at the water's edge, waiting for us. They cheered, as Christine and Samantha got out of the plane and there were hugs from all of them. An onlooker would have thought that we'd been away for years.

Some days later, I managed to get both Diego and Ben to sit under the silk cotton tree for a long interview. Before I could begin, Ben pointed out to the recovery of the tree and the lush new branches. I casually looked at it and set about my task. Diego started telling me of his ancestral connections with the conquistadors.

"My ancestors saw a possible genocide and to avert it, they cooperated with the Spaniards and tried to accumulate as much gold as they could find. It is a pity cold stream was not discovered then, it would have saved a lot of lives.

They saw my ancestors were doing their best and allowed them to have free movements in their fortifications. Inevitably. Inter-marriage occurred and a new race of people began to emerge. They were eventually, given a great swathe of land we now call Triangle to settle. For some strange reason, the other tribes did not want any social intercourse with us. Perhaps they thought we were not good enough, to be their brothers or perhaps, they may have thought that we were superior, because of our Spanish ancestry. Whatever the reason is anyone's guess. It turned out to be great. Our tribe expanded and now we are the largest in that area. Because of a cow, I came to Supenaam and it was here that I met and fell in love with Bell, and got married. I travelled extensively to Canada and Europe and learnt many skills from engineering to farming."

He paused for a minute and listened. He then told me that he heard someone scream. I remembered Samantha and Diego Junior, had down to the river for a stroll. I thought she would be safe with him. Even though he was only ten years old, he was a very careful lad mature for his age. Nonetheless, we decided to take a look. We saw the two walking backwards and a huge caiman was walking slowly towards them. Diego told them to stop. As they did what he asked, the caiman stopped also. Diego laughed and told us that the reptile was old and almost blinded with age. It was only its sense of smell that made it follow them. They would have been in serious trouble, if it was a young mature one. Diego took a huge branch and prodded it back into the river and watched it swim up river. Samantha ran and grabbed me, as if her life depended on my reassurance and I was only too happy to oblige.

Again, my interview was interrupted by unforeseen eventualities. I decided to call it off, for the rest of the day and to show Samantha and Les the rest of Supenaam. The farm and the herd they had seen. It was Diego's lodge that was of interest. I remembered when she saw Tudor Grange and the rest house. She could not believe she was in the jungle. Her first impression of Tudor Grange, was the only thing to make her agree to remain here for the rest of my stay. Doctor Louise and her husband were asked to move into the Rest House. Tudor Grange was to become ours and Les's new home. I do not think Louise was very pleased about it and I heard her argue with Peter over it. It was

Christine, who told her that she could either stay there or find alternative lodgings.

Bell invited us in her lodge and gave us strong, freshly ground, milky coffee. Later, Diego offered his regular glass of malt. Samantha asked for a sip and immediately went to the window and spat it out. "How could you drink that stuff?" she asked. "Your stomach is probably made of steel." she ended.

As if to prove a point, Bell took a glass and poured herself a small drink and sipped it comfortably, much to Samantha's amazement. Diego Junior brought a bottle of wine and offered her a glass, which she drank, without any fuss.

Diego then took her to see the Indigenous Nation's village and here again, Samantha was overwhelmed by the sight before her. The chief always knew when visitors came to see them and always displayed themselves in their traditional way. As was customary, they were offered a drink, which was the foulest I'd ever tasted. I wondered what Samantha would think of it. I dared not forewarn her of it. To my great amazement, she drank it, without making any faces. Bell asked her if she was pregnant, to which she said she was not sure. Bell suggested that doctor Louise would be able to give her an examination. That suggestion sent a shockwave through me. I was unable to say anything.

On our way to Tudor Grange, we stopped at the guest house and requested an examination. Doctor Louise invited us in. I could not have refused, as her husband was standing next to her. Samantha was getting dressed after the examination and Doctor Louise came and we started talking.

She told me she was sorry what had happened and that she did not realise I was going to tell Margaret. Now that I have made a new start, she hoped we could be friends and just friends. She sounded so sincere. She told me that her husband's work was nearing its conclusion and that he spends a lot of time with her, attending to her every need "and I mean every need." she repeated. I relented and told her that I was just as much to blame. My impetuosity got the better of me and I invited them to join us at the party, prearranged at Tudor Grange. She confirmed by saying that she was looking forward to it.

The usual crowd was there, chatting and ribbing each other, when we finally came down. Christine was telling us how picturesque it looked outside, with the fire flies darting among the trees. The bull frogs started croaking and Ben reminded us, that the rainy season would soon be upon us. "I hate it when it rains." he told us.

Diego reminded him of the benefits "It is well for you to hate the rain, it is a blessing. For a start, it lowers the temperature considerably and life can be a bit more tolerable. Think about the poor trees and plants, not to mention our own crops."

Matthew told him the downside was, when the snakes and spiders start looking for dry land. Sometimes they make themselves comfortable under the bed. Diego sent a shiver up everyone's spine when he said, "We have a visitor here already. There is a snake on the veranda and its crawling on the hand rails. Don't worry, it is not poisonous, it's only a young boa constrictor."

"I'll deal with it." Ben said causally. In an instant, he went on the veranda and lifted the reptile and threw it outside. He came back with the back of his hand bleeding,

"My God, it's bitten you." Louise exclaimed.

"That's ok, it's is not poisonous and no harm done. I've handled a lot of them before and I was never bitten. Perhaps this one lost its partner to a rival, it may be looking for one." he replied, causally.

"I must treat it, non-poisonous or not. There is still enough bacteria in its mouth to cause serious infection. You follow me." she insisted.

For a moment, I thought she wanted to get Ben alone. I had to perish that thought, when she asked Amelia to accompany her and help.

I was about to put some music on, when I heard Bell shouting at Diego and she seemed rather furious. "I did not mean for you to shut up, the way you took it." Diego was most apologetic.

"It is not the first time. I can never say what I want. You men always dominate conversation at get-togethers. I am not having it Diego Cipriani. I want to go home." she insisted and started crying.

Both Christine and Samantha went and consoled her and eventually, she decided to stay. Christine then took up her argument. "It is true what Bell said women have very little opportunity to express themselves at parties. I am not saying this only in defense of Bell. It was something I noticed a long time ago and only put up with it, for the sake of decency. I accept that this is a male dominated society. All we ask for, is some consideration to express ourselves freely, without waiting for a time slot."

"You are lucky to be with the men at parties" Matthew was heard saying. "In India, the women are kept separately and are not allowed to participate in any conversation."

"Oh shut up Uuncle Matthew!" Christine ordered him. "You are not in bloody India now. This may only be a colony of Britain, but behavior here is a lot more civilized than that." Her tone was less aggressive in the end.

"Matthew, you have to put India behind you and look forward. I am sure India will one day, step into the twentieth century." Les told him

"Les Nyman! You are a traitor to a dear friend." Matthew rebuked with a wink. He then continued to defend himself "People always thought of India as a nation emerging from the stone age." He suddenly stopped and shrugged his shoulders before continuing. "Les is right, I do dwell too much and too often on my past. Do forgive me. Since this is the last time, I will ever bring my past to bore you. Allow me this one last word."

There were some mild protests from the ladies. I took the opportunity and declared that I would like to hear what Matthew wanted to say. He looked at me and smiled. "Perhaps one day, when we are alone I will explain." he assured me.

"This is your moment. Seize it and put an end to it." I was adamant I wanted to hear what he had to say. I then said to those present, "I do not think Matthew or I will consider it rude if you were to find something else to do while he elaborated."

Matthew hesitantly began "Most of my stories, have been retold many times and I agree with my niece, that it is becoming boring. There is one piece of vital information, and if Les is as honest as I always believed he is, he will have the courage to endorse my last words on the matter. Christine made a very derogatory remark about India and that is what I wanted to defend.

The country is not the primitive empire that Britain ruled for centuries. It is as sophisticated as any other European nation. Britain herself, was impressed with its fine architecture and grand palaces. For me, it was the philosophical side that I greatly admired, its vision of life and death. We all see death as the final stage of our existence. far from it. Death is only the beginning. If I were to ask the question of what life and I mean, the energy that propels a person through his existence.

That answer would be difficult to answer, unless of course, you are familiar with the mysteries of life itself. I will explain. The single miniscule molecule that is responsible for our propulsion through life, is what generates the energy for that purpose. To understand its workings, is to communicate with the inner-self and many secrets are unfolded. There is an unfathomable source of knowledge, not only for the individual but for mankind. It could unfold the secrets for immortality. The secret is there, go and find it."

"I am not too happy with what you said, Matthew. This secret of immortality is somewhat bleary and covered in mysticism. I personally, am not too keen on those dark secrets." Ben told him.

"I am not surprised. If you were observant of my life, since you came here, you could have deduced that I am not insane and therefore, since my actions were of a sane person, it would have given you enough grounds to consider why I threw away fortunes, to remain as I am and as happy as any one of you." Matthew was not allowed to finish his reply. Les interrupted by saying "I must add, I was not certain at first, of Matt's intentions in life. I thought at first that he was simply fed up with all the killings that go with insurrections. I was wrong. I could see vividly now, him squatting with these men in saffron robes on the banks of the river, the Hindus call Mother. Hearing his incantations and listening attentively to those men, I considered parasites. Waiting to be fed and given somewhere warm to rest. Here for the first time, I am beginning to realise that there were more to it than meets the eye." Les Nyman's support for his friend was adding a serious note.

Unsure of what to believe, I told them I was not too sure about immortality, because of what I read in a scientific journal, that some leading astrophysicists are claiming that in a few billion years, the sun and all the planets, including earth, will be vaporised by the expansion of a dying sun. I told him his theory of immortality had no legs to stand on. My challenge was met with an explanation I found startling.

Matthew held his lapels, as he normally did, when trying to assert authority. His legs straightened, as if about to salute, before continuing "On the contrary, my clever friend. It is true what you said, but that does not mean that life will not continue. The energy I spoke of, is indestructible and where there is an end, there is a beginning. I believe astrophysicists are beginning to understand the wonders of life and its secrets. Maybe they are keeping it for themselves. I have learnt that these investigators of life's secret, are like men searching for gold or diamonds."

"They know it is there, somewhere under the earth. The only thing to do, is to search until it is found. That is exactly what those men of faith are doing. Until it is found they must keep on searching. To give you a simpler and nearer at home analogy. Let's take cold stream for instance we discovered gold by sheer accident. Lots of it and then the quantity decreased, occasionally after a long time we would find more gold albeit in small quantities. What does that tell us? Anyone with the minimum of intelligence will know that there must be a source where it comes from. To find that source, one must try to find the way to it. That is no easy task, digging through millions of tons of mountain rocks, needs the thoughts and perceptions of a keen and investigative mind to guide you there." he told us and continued "This is what these men are doing, seeking a way to find their dream.

Looking for a dream and not finding it, makes it more intriguing and tantalizing. Not finding it does not mean it is not there. It will take monumental will power and concentration to delve into the deepest recess of the subconscious mind, to achieve that. It may not happen in a single lifetime, because we are not genetically developed, to find this Holy Grail, but after many generations, as we evolve, the goal gets nearer. We are the pioneers of this great adventure. I am happy to be a part of it. I'd like to ask Diego a question. How many men do you know have survived a bush master's bite?"

"I have only known three men and a woman being bitten and they all died within minutes."

"You saw that serpent bit me with the great anger we caused it, by disturbing it. Yet I lived when everyone else gave me up for dead. You Diego, even wrote my obituary and were prepared to bury me minutes before you fired those two shots as a farewell salute to an old soldier. I ask you another question. Were you surprised that I stirred and eventually woke up as if from the dead?"

"I was not the only surprised one there. The vicar held his hands to God and thanked him for the miracle." Diego replied with a look of disbelief on his face. He then continued "I always thought of that incident and decided to agree with the priest that it was a miracle. Later, when you explained that you were in full control within your mind and that it was the paralysis, the muscles suffered through the effects of the venom, that prevented your arms from moving, when given the command from the brain, that I realised, there was more to this miracle than I dared believe."

"Diego has said it all and saved me the ignominy of being a bore. I shall leave you to ponder on what I said. I know Peter understands some of it. He is fearful of stepping into an unknown world and I cannot blame him. Here is where I terminate all talks of my past." Matthew ended. I sensed a sad note in his voice. I could not help thinking the old man was deliberately keeping back some of the things he knew and was hoping that someone someday, someone will force it out of him. I, for my part heard enough to send my mind spiraling into an unknown world.

It was very late when the party and talking was over. Samantha and I led Les to his room and we went to the uppermost part of the tower bedroom . It was cool and a gentle breeze greeted us, as we lay cuddled together.

It was rather late in the morning, when we both surfaced. Matthew's talk was continuing to swirl in my head. I was in no mood to make a fresh challenge. As a matter of fact, if I wanted to maintain my sanity, the sooner I should dispose of those thoughts the better.

I nearly had all the material I came for. It had taken twice as long as anticipated. It was not a total waste. Only one bit of this episode remained to be completed and I was sure I would be able to fill it in, by simply listening. I hoped my editor would be pleased.

Getting up late was not my idea of a good start for a day's work. I was still confused with what Matthew said and more than ever, I was determined to put it all behind me. Today is a new day and I intended to let it start with something new.

Les was having breakfast, when we went down and joined him. Isabel, a maid who has no boundaries for decency said "Too much love making in the night Master. I better give you something to strengthen you." I could see Les was shocked, and Samantha in no uncertain way, told her to shut up, mind her own business and serve us breakfast. She, in her usual manner, simply swung herself and sucked her teeth. This, in itself is considered rude. I made a mental note, to bring this matter up with Christine. Les was still looking at me with a horrified expression on his face.

We all ambled down to the office where, we knew the others would be and found them seated around Peter and Matthew, in a deep discussion.

"Do have a seat." Peter invited us. He then began explaining what was discussed in our absence.

"I received a telephone message from the Governor inviting us to go to Georgetown, to discuss some important issues concerning the young man, whose appeal will be heard very soon.

Matthew and I decided to go in the morning, ahead of the proceedings. We do not really want this to fail. If any of you wish to come along you are welcome. You can indicate with a show of hands."

As usual, everyone's hands went up. It reminded me of a shoal of fish following the leader. I instinctively put my hand up. I could not see the reason. It was, as I said, like a shoal of fish. Samantha and Christine decided to remain with Bell and the children. Sebastian and Joseph were given strict instructions to remain with them, until we returned.

Peter sent for Chief Warachara, to inform him and also to ask that he kept an eye for the protection of the ladies and the children. Peter told me later, that he did not have to ask for the chief's help. Informing him of what is going on is important for good relationships and asking him to keep an eye on our ladies, is a great honour for him.

Sebastian went off to service the plane, while the rest of us went down the river to enjoy some cool breeze and perhaps, get an opportunity to see the monkeys playing cat and mouse with the young caiman. It was their way of entertainment and I must say it was a very dangerous pastime. The mothers of these young ones were still protective of their off spring, which could prove to be a lethal game.

Fortunately, there was no cat and mouse game today. Our only bit of excitement, was to see an eagle swoop and drag its talons on the surface of the water and flew away, with a fish. I hope it is a piranha, as they were getting plentiful in the rainy season.

Across the river, we saw the villagers were busy gathering vegetables for the flight tomorrow. One stood up and held a very large yam in the air for us to see. Ben got tired seeing the same thing over and over again, so he invited us for a drink instead, to break the monotony.

We were overjoyed when the ladies joined us and it became another sippy occasion all over again. We were even surprised when Joseph came in quietly, in company with Amelia and Sugar Bush. I was beginning to wonder if there was anything going on. I knew Sugar Bush was Matthew's bonded wife and no ceremony of breaking that bond occurred while I was there. I'd only heard of it but had never been a witness to one.

I decided to ask Diego what happens on such an occasion and he took the time to explain "It is a simple ceremony." he started out. "The pair normally ask the chief and his elders to be present and if it is the man wanting to break the bond, the woman presents him with an arrow. All he has to do, is to break the arrow and throw it on the ground. In the eyes of the community they are no longer bonded."

"Are Matthew and Sugar Bush still bonded?" I asked.

"Of course they are." Diego responded. "I see them getting together all the time when Amelia is not about."

"Why is that?" again I asked

"You are naïve. Can't you see the age difference? What do you imagine she would think of her father, with a wife younger than herself?" Diego was kind to explain.

It was all beginning to make sense. Les looked at me and raised an eyebrow. Then he whispered waggishly. "Matthew knows where to look for eternal life."

"You know something Les, I think you are just a scoundrel and old Matthew, was he really that of an enigma when you first met him?" I probed.

"Not really, he was always getting in trouble with his commanding officer, through his friendship with that cavalier Cavendish. I never cared for his behavior. He too often used his connections with people in high places, as a cover for his bad sense of discipline and insubordination. I think Matthew was a stabilising force and he leaned heavily on that." Les' picture of Matthew's former life was portraying a different view of what the man is today. "When was the first time you met this Cavendish person?" I asked

"I had my sergeant on a charge of insubordination and I was to give evidence. In came this Cavendish and told me to drop the charge as it was every soldier's right to be insubordinate at some time or the other. It goes to show character. I was of course, appalled at his comment and dismissed him with a warning, to be careful with his own behavior."

"How did he react to your comment?"

"In his usual manner. He flicked his swagger stick in a mock salute and went on his way. That was on the only time our paths crossed. Coming back to Matthew, after getting himself in trouble, through no fault of his own, he was sent to Rajastan. I think that is where he met the love of his life. After his tour of duty was finished, he became a changed man. Learning the local dialects and becoming involved with his present day thinking."

"I must thank you Les. You have really deepened my knowledge of this enigmatic and lovable individual."

CHAPTER 23
THE BIG PROMISE

Our visit to see the Governor turned out to be an informal affair. Instead of sitting behind his huge desk, to address us, he pulled up an armchair and sat next to Matthew.

"Well gentlemen, did it need such a large entourage to come and see me? I am impressed. Now Matt, I have read the letter you and Peter sent and I must admit I can see why you are so concerned.

Yesterday I had a visit from the three appellant judges and they made it quite clear that they will not be influenced by anyone. I must agree with that. Although, I am the Governor, I have no jurisdiction to control judges. They were quite sympathetic with what I had to say. I even mentioned that the Commissioner was deeply disturbed by the disproportionate punishment imposed on the young man. They did however, mention that it would help, if both of you could make yourself available to make a statement on behalf of the accused. This of course, I confirmed and they are expecting to see you in court later. What are you going to do for the rest of the morning? Can I offer you some coffee while I deal with another urgent matter?"

Without waiting for a reply, he ordered his aide to serve us the refreshments. At this stage, the First Lady appeared and kissed Matthew on the cheek and took him and Peter to another room. It was some time before they emerged with smiles all over their faces.

The three Appellant Judges looked rather young. They were all King's Councilors. Their magnificent wigs, adding grace to their status. They were poring over some papers, before asking the defense council to put forward his argument. I thought Aubrey made a persuasive appeal on behalf of his client.

It was time for Matthew to address the judges, and then Peter. It turned out to be longer than I anticipated. Several hours later, they eventually nodded to each other and the most senior of them spoke.

"This court listened to the many pleas from several people of repute. I must add, in the years that I became an appellant judge, I never listened to more pleas for mercy and having listened, we are in agreement that the sentence handed down was indeed severe. It is our ruling therefore, having considered all the evidence and circumstances and the time the defendant spent in custody, that he be released immediately. There is one important factor we would like to clarify. It is a known fact that men who are charged with patricide find it impossible to live normally and peacefully in the community they once lived. Since this young man is under age, he will need counselling and for someone to take him under their wings. Are there such provisions made by any of those pleading on his behalf? If not, then I will have to release him in the care of the proper authorities, until such time, he comes of age."

In an instant, Matthew, without consulting any of the others, stood up thanked the judges and pledged to care for the young man. The judges were in an agreement to release him into Matthew's care. It was then, I heard his name for the first time, as Kadar Sharma.

Paltoo ran and hugged Aubrey, then Matthew. He was too emotionally moved to speak but his actions were enough to convey what he felt.

He was taken to Booker stores for some decent clothing and shoes and eventually, we all ended up at Peter's residence. There were some odd moments, as the young man was not accustomed to such sophisticated dwellings and although I'm sure he was grateful, he did not appear happy. That was soon dispelled though, when Ben introduced himself and said a few words that made him laugh.

It took a while for him to settle down in his new environment and very soon, he made friends with Beda, the maid of Peter's parents. She seemed to know what to say and to give him to eat. Now that he was settled we could safely leave him in Beda's care.

Peter's mother knew these people very well and soon she was speaking to him as if she was one of them. I could hear laughter coming from the kitchen and I knew all was well.

The rest of us went on the veranda, with the proverbial drink in hand, to discuss the young man's future. Matthew, quite rightly, thought it was his priority to explain what he had in mind. "I know all of you thought my undertaking was impetuous I will disagree. I had an idea that the outcome will be exactly as it turned out so in my mind. I formulated a plan which I think everyone will be in agreement. For a start, we all know, without being prejudiced, that this young man will never be able to fit in our community, or our lifestyle. I have therefore, made arrangements with Sebastian that he keeps him in his cottage and I will double his salary. As you know, Sebastian has a small house that is, in constant need of clearing and his meals are something to be desired. He will have all the help he needs, even helping out with the planes when they needed servicing and cleaning. In actual fact, Sebastian would benefit more from the services of this young man, and who knows, may even teach him to fly. That is my plan. I hope it works."

"It's a brilliant plan Matt." Les told him and shook his hand. We all drank a toast to Matthew. This was interrupted with the arrival of Peter's father. "Starting already!" were his first words to us, looking at our glasses. "I might as well join you. I am feeling bored here, not my style. I missed my weekend trips in the river. With so much hunting and fishing left undone, it's not natural. I will tell you something for free, don't ever retire. I noticed you were still the Commissioner, maybe not in name but you are clever and thank God Peter is not jealous of the way you try to run things for him. He allowed you to do this, because he understands what it is to have authority removed from you."

"I don't think you understand Joseph. I am the one that removed that authority and gave it to your son. I wanted to break the mould. Your son was the right candidate. The inhabitants of this country have just as much right to share power with us. In case you forgot, it is I who promoted your son to the second most important job in the land. It is through me that he became the …"

Matthew stopped, as if someone had placed their hand down his throat. "What is it you wanted to say my old friend?" Joseph asked, looking a bit concerned.

"As you say, I am an old man, not much older than you. I have said enough. I had to stop where I did, or I would have regretted it to my last days." Matthew had that rueful look on his face. The two friends embraced each other and whispered in each other's ears, something I did not hear.

"Why don't you come up with us to Supenaam, There are an abundant of fish for you to catch. As for wildlife, you may have some problems there. I am under severe pressure from my conscience to protect them. Only a limited amount can be taken out for food. You do understand my problem Joseph." Matthew told him in the most sympathetic way

"Then I can perhaps hunt their food requirements and have some fun at the same time. What sort of game fish do you have up there?" Joseph asked.

It was Ben that replied. "Oh, I say, we have quite an assortment of game fish. The Hymara for instance, will give you one hell of a time to net it, then there are these enormous catfish. The size is unbelievable and don't forget the legendary arapaima, taller than you and weighing several hundred pounds."

"Why is it fishermen have this habitual way of exaggeration. I am a British Guianese not some dam foreigner." Joseph told him.

He turned to Matthew for support and when that was given, Joseph was still unconvinced. It was Peter who convinced him. "It is true dad. When I was there, as a very young man, I was taken on a fishing expedition for that very fish. Unfortunately, it was a small one weighing about two hundred pounds." That appeared to have convinced him. Without hesitation, he decided to come with us.

He then asked "What about the young man? He appeared to be at home with Beda and Miriam. Let him stay for a while and get used to people of a different culture. Then you can take him when you bring me back here." Joseph suggested.

I hoped this was the last time I'd be going up and down to Supenaam. I didn't mind the plane ride. It was more the disruption in my work. I must telephone Samantha to let her know I would be coming a day later. To add more woes to my troubles, Sebastian came and told Peter that the plane buoys needed water proofing and that could take several days.

I'd had enough, I decided I was going to spend the days with my parents and see my editor, to give him the bad news

"You know something Andrew," my editor started to say, "I really don't know if you are deliberately delaying your return to the city. Are you enjoying your work? No, No don't answer that. You will only give me some extraordinary excuse why you are held up. Is that Matthew Longhorn has anything to do with this delay?"

"Not exactly. He had been reluctant to discuss some aspects of his life. Then unwittingly he disclosed some of his most inner secrets. Something I would never have been able to extract from him." I replied.

"Now I want you to go back and tell him that I want a seat on that plane, whenever he is ready."

"Is that wise. Matthew is not one to take orders. Especially when it is not connected with Supenaam." I pointed out.

"Dam you man. Then ask him if there will be a seat for me." He paused for a minute and then told me "Forget it, I will telephone him. Those two behave like two women whose hormones were late in developing." At this point, he picked up the telephone to make his call. I took the opportunity to make a quick exit.

The rain was still falling, when we returned and Joseph was beginning to regret his decision. I must heed the warning from my editor. The reason he was here was not clear to me. The only way to impress him, was for me to be engaged in a serious conversation with Peter. I think my editor must have spoken to him and he was willing to come and sit while I try to glean the last bit of vital information from him. I must first get to understand the duties of a Commissioner. We all heard of his enormous power over the Indigenous Nation but unable to grasp what that entails. My first question to him "Peter can you relate to me your duties as a Commissioner?"

"It is not that simple." he began to explain. "First, let me remind you that there are only colonies that have such a system. The other is British Honduras, a creation of the colonial administration. Here in British Guiana, it changed a bit, to give more authority to the Commissioner of the hinterlands. The reason being, that ninety percent of the colony is pristine forests and the Indigenous inhabitants are very protective of it. We have unscrupulous loggers and gold and diamond seekers, polluting the rivers which became unsustainable for the inhabitants. A mandate was given to the Commissioner, to have full powers to arrest, charge and even hang, those that persistently ignore the law."

"Have you or Matthew ever executed anyone for any of those offences?" I asked.

"Matthew did, on one occasion, when I first arrived and that was a rare occasion. The man blatantly violated the terms for exploration and killed one of the rangers. He had documented the events and sent it for the records to the Governor. I have never been so unfortunate." Peter told me.

"Why you say unfortunate?"

"I don't know if I would have been able to carry out an execution. I would have probably sent the culprit to the capital for trial and punishment." Peter replied.

"Do you feel there are any issues concerning your administration that needs addressing?

"I certainly feel that way. For instance, we are now the guardians for border controls. You were here when we had that abortive attempt to seize a great portion of the colony by Venezuelan mercenaries. It was Matthew's quick thinking that led to the formation of a patrol to guard our borders. There have been suggestions of splitting up the region into more manageable sections, with each having a District Commissioner with the same powers as I have."

"Do you think it is a good idea?"

"Absolutely. I have my surgeries here in the city, as well as New Amsterdam. It will give me not only time to look after my patients, but also to spend much needed time with my family. Rabbi Solomon is a bit concerned that Elizabeth is about to become a teenager and she sees very little of me. Even Christine gets in some strange moods when I am away for long periods."

"What do you think will happen to the Indigenous Nation if the sectioning of the remote regions were to be implemented?

"I think it will be a good thing. For a start, the chiefs will be empowered to say who visit their land. The same as we have in Oreala where a permit is required for visitors for a certain period only."

"I think we will call it a day and continue this another time. I must see what my editor is doing." I thanked Peter for his informative and cooperative manner. We parted company temporarily.

I found my editor chatting with Ben and Diego. Peter's father joined them and I heard some of their plans for the Arapaima fishing. Ben was telling him, that the last one was a bit of a shamble, due to the fact that it was a very long journey and they lacked the facilities to make a proper raft. Diego pointed out that the journey could be made with the tractor as far as the Idle river, and from there by foot, where they will have enough time to build a proper raft if the timbers were loaded on the trailer.

Ben interrupted, by asking where they would sit. Diego shook his head and looking towards the heavens for patience, told him they could all sit on the timbers.

I told them that I would join in the hunt and they agreed, on condition that I do my bit with the preparation. I not only undertook to do my part, but to do that of my editor, who did not have the slightest clue or the ability to do what was required. I hoped this little ploy would release me from the constant pressure he'd been placing on me.

Diego was to lead the expedition. A tractor with the trailer was soon ploughing its way along the dirt track, made by the Indigenous Nation for their hunting. We were not allowed to make any other track, unless agreed by Warachara and he was there to see us obey the law of the land. The temperature had risen to about ninety degrees. Unusually hot for this time of the year. I imagined that the rainy season was over, which was much cooler, had caused us to feel the sun's rays more intensely. My editor was perspiring profusely and kept asking how much further more we had to travel. Ben in his waggish manner, told him it would be another two hours. He looked at Ben and said something under his breath. I am sure it was not something complimentary.

When we reached Idle River, everyone except Diego, went straight to it and dipped their feet in the cool water for relief. Diego looked on, shaking his head. The raft took us an hour to build and the four paddles we brought, saved us a lot of time.

It was time for the real test. Joseph and my editor sat at the front, trying to paddle. Ben noticed they were not helping, so he took the paddles and gave me one. About a mile downstream, some smaller fish were leaping in the air, perhaps to escape the jaws of the arapaima. Whatever signal that sent to Diego, we will never know. He told us to keep on rowing, until we came to a point where another stream emptied its water into the Idle River. A few yards further up, Diego told us to stop rowing. He slipped in and trawled the water with his hands. Then, to make it look like an accident, he pulled my editor in the river. No one suspected he could not swim and it took a few hands to pull him back on the raft. He was still coughing when he eventually settled down on his seat.

To our great surprise, Peter's dad slipped in the water and started doing exactly as Diego was, trawling the water with his hands. He must have felt something huge, as there was an almighty splash and for a brief second, we saw a giant tail flick the surface, before disappearing. This was the moment Diego was waiting for. He turned to Joseph and congratulated him for his efforts. It was his turn to be tossed like a toy. He spewed the water from his mouth, took a deep breath and went under.

The water started bubbling and Joseph again, to our amazement dived in the direction of Diego. Warachara was looking in bewilderment. Suddenly, he uttered something and took his headdress off and went in to join the duo. A great battle ensued and I had an irresistible urge to join them. To me, it looked like fun. In a second I was in the water and landed on the back of the largest fresh water fish in the world. I heard Diego telling me to stay on top. I tried to get some grip to stay on. Eventually, I got hold of its large lateral fin and held on to it for dear life. This creature was stronger than I could have ever dreamed of. Warachara came to my rescue and took hold of the fin, until the mighty Ben was able to tire the monster down. It took the five of us nearly an hour. Eventually, Warachara stuck both his hands on either side of its gill. That subdued the fish. We thought the struggle was over, as we tried to drag it ashore. The fight was not over, the fish was only resting for the next fight. It tossed the five of us as little toys. Warachara who must be an expert for this kind of fishing, kept his hand in the gills. This apparently, prevented the beast from breathing properly and eventually, the fight was over.

Using the span of his hand, Diego told us the fish was sixty two inches long and probably weighed around three hundred pounds. My editor asked Diego "Is this real or did I dream it?"

"Since you are not asleep then you are not dreaming. It is real." Diego told him.

He came up to me put an arm around my shoulder and said "They will never believe me, when I tell them I took part in catching the largest fresh water fish in the world. This is an adventure the city dwellers will never experience. There is one more intriguing piece of a puzzle I must solve before I leave."

He did not say what it was and I did not ask. It all became clear, rwhen he approached Matthew and asked "Did you give this river its name or was it the Indigenous Nation?"

Matthew gave him a roguish smile and told him when he first arrived, there was no name for the river. "The indigenous nation only referred to it as Peyachoca, which is the region in which it runs. I decided to give it a name, which is reminiscent of a famous river where I found my salvation."

The fish was gutted and covered with palm leaves and we all sat around it on the trailer, homeward bound.

It was my editor, who asked Diego what food this great fish ate to give it such a size. Diego told him, that as far as he is concerned, no one ever tried to investigate its eating habits.

"All we cared about, was catching and eating it."

"That's a shame. We could have discovered that if only I had thought of it sooner." He said ruefully.

"How could we have known that? Someone asked.

"We could have examined the contents of its stomach, before we ditched it. Perhaps the next time you catch one, you can do exactly that and forward the results to me." my editor told Diego.

It is surprising how fast news travelled. The tractor did not come to a halt when about a dozen or more of villagers came to meet us and without saying a word, took a major part of the fish and disappeared with it. "This is common practice." Diego told my editor, before he started enquiring of their actions. I too was a bit puzzled. I am an observer and learn from it, better than asking questions.

Later that evening, as we sat down to celebrate our successful fishing, I was able to extract the last remaining details of Peter's colourful life.

CHAPTER 24
PAGEANTRY AND GOODBYE DEMERARA

We arrived rather late that afternoon. Everyone was extremely tired. After a quick wash and change of clothing we assembled in Tudor Grange. I felt sad looking around me, seeing the smiling faces I'd come to know and love, and knowing full well that it would only be a matter of days when I would have to leave and perhaps, never to return. Samantha must have felt something also, as she came and sat next to me, holding my hand as she sipped her drink.

Christine was supervising Isabel with the dinner, when she came out screaming for Ben to come and help. Ben, being a very good cook, walked slowly towards the kitchen and we heard him emitting his thunderous laughter. It turned out, that Isabel was unable to take the skin off, from the peccary and in frustration, cut it up, skin and all and put it to cook. Dinner was spoilt, so we decided to cook something else on the spit outside.

It turned out to be a jolly affair. The moon was out in all its glory and a huge bon fire was made a distance away. This was to keep the insects and any other irritating creatures away.

I began to feel even sadder. Afraid that I might spoil the party, I told Samantha I was going to bed.

In the morning, my final task lay ahead. I somehow did not want to finish my work. I thought if I went slowly, I would be able to extend my stay for a few days more, which would give me time to adjust my emotions about leaving.

I was extremely happy when Peter announced that he had to take his family and my editor back to Georgetown. At the same time, he intended to bring the young man, Kadar Sharma to Supenaam, to get him settled in.

I would be fascinated to see how Kadar will adjust his life here, in the heart of the wilderness. I personally felt that both

Matthew and Peter, were taking on too much. Matthew was already planning with Ben, to take him under his wings, the same as he did when Peter first arrived.

The days passed and no sign of Peter or his protégé. When they did eventually arrive, Kadar looked a bit disorientated. He began looking under the trees for something, whatever it was, would be difficult to ascertain. However, Ben took hold of him and led him to his lodgings. Matthew and I sat under the silk cotton tree, waiting for them to emerge. We could hear laughter from where they were. The suspense was too much for Matthew. He took me by the hand and led me to where they were. Apparently, Ben was telling him how the young girls in the villages go about without any clothing on their upper bodies and also, some other naughty things I dared not mention. Matthew scolded Ben for being immature.

There was nothing we could do, until Peter was available to discuss what he had in mind. Personally, I thought too much importance was attached to this young man's welfare. It was not until Peter decided to ask our opinion, that I had a full grasp of the situation.

"First of all, it is up to us to make sure there is some stability and sense of purpose for Kadar to establish himself as an individual carving a new life. We must remember, he is still a teenager and I am totally annoyed with Ben for his frivolous behaviour and giving the young man the wrong impression of life here. I know I owe Ben a lot, but at the same time, I was hoping he'd thrown away his boyish behavior and grown up. It was at this point, that Ben stood up and banged his hand on the table and spoke in a louder than normal voice. "Now you listen to me, Matthew Longhorn, I have been a babysitter all my life and maybe that is why I behave like a baby. I have no family I can call my own. You at least, have a daughter. Don't you think my life would be empty if I did not put some sort of spice in it? What could be more spicy than some sexy conversation. Go on, throw me overboard, if that makes you happy. I know my obligation to Kadar. I was only trying to cheer him up. Tomorrow, you will see what I mean, when I introduce him to Warachara. Then you can say if my services for caring and protection is infantile."

I had never heard Ben speak so angrily, especially to Matthew, the doyen of the community. I think even Peter was petrified by his behavior.

To bring some semblance of normality, Diego went and brought a bottle and placed it before me and said "You are always a bystander in these odd moments. Pour everyone a drink and make sure you give that big man in the corner some also." He was smiling as he spoke and that did the trick. Ben grabbed the bottle and poured the drinks instead.

Whatever transpired between Ben and Warachara, was a total secret. The two of them that is, Matthew and Ben came out with huge smiles on their faces.

Samantha and I decided to visit the caimans' nesting grounds. It was our way of saying goodbye to everything that was part of Supenaam. Diego insisted on accompanying us. He quite rightly told us that a caiman could outrun any man on land and in the water they are absolute masters.

He was right. There, on the wrong side of the bank, were four huge monsters regenerating themselves with the sun's rays. They may look huge and immobile and that was soon demonstrated when one lunged towards us, at a speed that defied the imagination. Diego knew how to handle the situation. He told us to run up the steep embankment and remain there. Strangely, I felt no fear at all. Samantha appeared calm. Maybe it was Diego's calmness and confidence that gave us that assurance. Diego took a branch that was lying nearby and gently prodded the reptile in the face. It started hissing with rage, constantly prodding, to seek an opening to attack. Diego's persistence in keeping him away, paid off. Eventually, it calmed down and turned around to join his friends.

The calm and confident mood in Diego suddenly disappeared. He looked at me with rage in his eyes and scolded "Don't ever underestimate to intelligence of these creatures. I knew you were heading for trouble. I did not try to stop as I wanted to teach you a lesson. You must remember, if ever you decide to return here in the future." I could only acquiesce to his angry remarks.

Samantha started crying, which seemed to quell his anger and a comforting arm around her shoulder did the trick.

On the eve of our departure, huge bon fires were lit in a mile radius around the square. The long house was decorated with the usual palm leaves and wild flowers, some so rare and exotic, it would cost a fortune to buy in the city. I was totally unaware of what it signified. Drinks and glasses were placed on the long table, reminiscent of tribal meeting with their Commissioner.

By seven o'clock, the chiefs, Warachara and Obeyo were joined by some other chiefs. I knew they were the head of their tribe, because of the head dresses they wore. The elders and villagers from the tribes, gathered in a crescent on their right. An opening was made and the young men streamed in from behind, to join the group. There were about thirty, most of them all teenagers and they formed another crescent on the left of the chiefs.

Haunting music started playing, from flutes made of bamboo and the most choreographed dancing I'd ever seen began first, slowly and then into a full rhythmical swaying of heads and hips. This was increased with stomping with one foot and kicking with the other. No one had time for a drink. We were all mesmerized with the spectacle. This went on for half an hour and then it suddenly stopped. The youths started singing and clapping slowly and then the chiefs made a large opening between them and a group of young girls came streaming through. They were topless with brightly coloured skirts. They came out with their backs towards us, until they formed a circle, then they split into two groups, facing each other and as before, started dancing to the same haunting melody we heard before and as before, the swaying of the hips were gentle and in tune. Unsuspectingly, they went in a semi-circle formation and started what looked like, the most erotic dancing I ever saw. The energy it took, to keep them going was phenomenal. This went on for an hour with various variations of their dancing.

I took a peek at young Kadar and saw him almost mesmerised by it all. I could not help feeling a bit lustful myself. It was enough to make any red bloodied virile man feel that way. My thoughts were still with me, when the young Kadar leapt out and joined the girls, doing his own kind of dancing. The chiefs and their attendants were amazed at this behavior. For some reason, they allowed him to carry on. Matthew made an attempt to rescue him, but when he saw the chiefs were smiling at Kadar's dancing, he eventually sat down.

The girls appeared to welcome him and soon, they were trying to dance like him. Eventually, it became a mixture of East Indian and indigenous dancing. We were happy at the cooperation showed by our entertainers.

All the time, while this was going on, Samantha was looking at me from the corner of her eye. Then she looked at me, full in the face and asked "Do you need a glass of water darling?"

"Why do you ask?" I questioned.

"Oh, you look so hot and dry. I thought of giving you something to cool that volcanic explosion in you." she replied and at the same time, nudged me with her hip.

I placed my arm on her shoulder and stroked it gently. It was my way of reassuring her of my love.

During this brief interruption, I lost contact with the celebration. The next time I looked, young Kadar was enjoying himself with one particular young lady and the chiefs appeared amused by it. All, even Matthew and Diego were smiling.

The music suddenly stopped and the girls and young men disappeared. All the chiefs came forward and bowed and spoke in a common language to Peter through Diego.

He told us that this pageant was to show their appreciation towards Andrew, for writing to let the outside world know what a paradise the forest could be, if left alone.

I was lost for words. I never in my wildest dreams, expected such an accolade. I told Diego to tell them it was a privilege to let the outside world know and understand their desires to keep their homeland free from loggers and other unscrupulous interlopers.

Two of the young ladies brought a basket filled with rare exotic flowers and presented it to Samantha. It was explained to her that they can grow in the city but needed much care and attention.

Diego thanked the young ladies on our behalf, and then he told me it was my turn to thank the chiefs. I asked him how and he told me to place both my hands' palms down, under my chin and make a gentle bow. First to my right and then my left, and to walk a few steps backwards. "The chiefs have paid you the highest honour and you in turn must thank them in the same manner."

I then asked what was going to happen to Kadar when this was all over. "What Kadar may not know, is he has chosen a future bride for himself. The young lady he 'proposed' to, accepted his offer and he is bound by tradition to honour it." he explained.

"What happens if he changes his mind or pleads ignorance?" I asked.

"In your law ignorance is no excuse. It is the same here. Anyone entering the Indigenous Nation's homeland must learn its customs, what is acceptable and what is not. I think young Kadar has done well. The girl he 'chose' is the daughter of a high ranking chief." Diego told me, with confidence.

It was getting late and I'd promised Samantha I would help her pack. She was standing next to Ben and I explained my delay, which was useful information. I suggested we leave the packing until the morning. Ben offered to help, which was great news for me.

Another morning and another day in Supenaam. Diego had come to tell Kadar what he had unintentionally done. He did not realise that Matthew had already told the young man and that he'd accepted the situation, without the slightest protest.

Ben was helping with the packing, so Diego and I strolled down the river chatting. There was a sudden swoop and a squeak. Diego looked in the direction from where it came and pointed out a harpy eagle, with a squirrel monkey hooked on its talons. I have never seen a harpy eagle before, let alone one with its meal hooked on its talons. Diego told me it was taking it back to a nest that probably had a chick in it. He told me that if there were no chicks, then it may have eaten the monkey on the ground. He suggested, that since he had never seen a young harpy, this was a good opportunity to look at one. I let myself be dragged into another adventure! Half a mile away, he noticed a fig tree, laden with fruits and suggested we look carefully, among the highest and strongest branches.

Diego, is a man of the forest and sure enough, there in the upper reaches of the fig tree, was a nest. The harpy was of a dark grey on the back with white feathers on the head and underside. Its yellow beak, tearing away at the flesh and the mother gently feeding its off spring with it. We could barely see the whole chick but what we did see, was white feathers on the head and below. So many things happening on my very last day. It suddenly occurred to me why there were no birds or monkeys about when there were such an abundance of fruits. He explained that no sensible bird or monkey would dare go near that tree, where a harpy eagle is nesting.

Samantha was very angry I didn't invite her. It took me a long time to convince her, that the encounter was unexpected.

I gathered my papers and made a bundle, tying them with palm fibers. The suit cases were packed.

Ben took hold of both of them and tucked the bundle of papers under an arm and trundled off, like an over fed duck, towards the embankment.

Everyone was there. Matthew, Peter, Diego's family, Warachara and the other chief, whose daughter Kadar danced with. I asked Peter what was going to happen to the young man. He causally replied that he was going to let his technician teach him the trade and he could then go and work in his surgery, in Georgetown and as for his future with his bride, with the help of Diego, he would sort it out.

On my way to the river, I saw the villagers on the other side, gathering their vegetables and fruits, to be loaded into the airplane, to be sold in Georgetown. We had to wait for the loading to complete.

I turned my gaze towards the buildings, and especially Tudor Grange. Its two tall towers, spiraling majestically skywards, a real diamond in the jungle, with luxuries that would put most homes in the city to shame. Next to it, is the old lady. The Rest House built by Matthew, some twenty five years ago with all the comforts of a normal home. Admittedly, it did not have the luxury of running water, as in Tudor Grange, but the overhead oil drum converted as water reservoirs served the same purpose. There was Joseph, who I still address as father-in-law, strolling slowly towards us, to say his goodbye.

I'd been here just over eighteen months and I'd been married twice and divorced once. I thought of my folly with Doctor Louise. I could not help feeling sorry for Margaret and her self-imposed life of solitude. A life I helped create. But I had a new life with Samantha, someone I loved dearly and I vowed never to let anything or anyone destroy the happiness I share with her.

Joseph by now, reached us and with an outstretched hand, bade goodbye and wished us both a long and happy life.

The moment had arrived and as everyone boarded the airplane I turned and waved at Warachara and his villagers and blew them kisses as I walked for the last time, down the banks of the Demarara.

THE END

novum PUBLISHER FOR NEW AUTHORS

Rate this book on our website!

www.novum-publishing.co.uk

The author

Alford Khan, is the eldest of twelve children was born in Adelphi Village in Berbice, Guyana. He studied at the Berbice High School, after which he worked with his father who was a dentist and tailor. On completion of his tutelage and dentistry, he left for the UK and found employment as a civilian with the Royal Army Dental Corps. In 1968 he established his own dental business in London and is still active in that field.

Alford Khan enjoys life with his wife and four children (three daughters and one son).

He loves adventurous travel and socialising with his Rotarian friends. He is the founder of a registered charity, a past President and honorary member of the Rotary Club of Greenford.

At the age of eighty two, he has discovered a new talent and has become a prolific writer. Demerara Adventures is his debut novel.

novum PUBLISHER FOR NEW AUTHORS

The publisher

> *He who stops being better stops being good.*

This is the motto of novum publishing, and our focus is on finding new manuscripts, publishing them and offering long-term support to the authors.
Our publishing house was founded in 1997, and since then it has become THE expert for new authors and has won numerous awards.

Our editorial team will peruse each manuscript within a few weeks free of charge and without obligation.

You will find more information about
novum publishing and our books on the internet:

www.novum-publishing.co.uk

Alford Khan

Up the Demerara River

ISBN 978-3-99048-300-8
378 pages

An intriguing story about an aspiring dentist Peter, moved to a place called Sappanam and got acquainted with good friends. The environment and his good relationship with wise people changed his life pattern from a disciplined dentist to a Commissioner. Watch out for this interesting story with fascinating characters and the subplot within that involve romance, adventure and unquestionable success.